Praise for
RALPH PETERS
and
TRAITOR

"A MASTER STORYTELLER."
Washington Times

"DEEPLY SATISFYING . . .
a sleek, well-muscled thriller . . . Peters balances
all this action and intrigue on a cast just big
enough to keep the double-crosses spinning."
Kirkus Reviews

"PETERS CREATES STRONG CHARACTERS
AND PUTS THEM IN
BELIEVABLE SITUATIONS."
San Francisco Examiner

"RAPID-FIRE . . .
a constantly unfolding plot . . . a slam-bang
conclusion . . . Peters deserves credit for not
following a formula path."
Booklist

"PETERS IS FAST REACHING
TOM CLANCY STATUS AS A
WRITER OF POWDERKEG
STRATEGIC-MILITARY NOVELS."
Newport News Press

RALPH PETERS

TRAITOR

AVON BOOKS  NEW YORK

AVON BOOKS, INC.
1350 Avenue of the Americas
New York, New York 10019

Copyright © 1999 by Ralph Peters
Inside cover author photo by Kat Peters
Library of Congress Catalog Card Number: 98-46862
ISBN: 0-380-79738-0
www.avonbooks.com

First Avon Books Paperback Printing: January 2000
First Avon Books Hardcover Printing: April 1999

AVON TRADEMARK REG. U.S. PAT. OFF. AND IN OTHER COUNTRIES, MARCA REGISTRADA, HECHO EN U.S.A.

Printed in the U.S.A.

WCD   10 9 8 7 6 5 4 3 2 1

▲

To my brother,
Bruce Robert Peters,
who always knew Holmes had a dark side;
and to Henry Nowak,
"Mr. Noir."

▼

In the Gospel of Luke, soldiers approached John the Baptist, asking: "And we, what shall we do?" And he said to them, "Rob no one by violence or by false accusation, and be content with your wages."

Money changes everything.

—Populist philosopher Cyndi Lauper,
amplifying Tom Gray's reinterpretation of
the works of Karl Marx

CHAPTER 1

I MARCHED BACK UP TO THE GRAVE AFTER THE CROWD faded. Washington in July. Uniform clawing at my skin.

Arlington is efficient. A mini-excavator had already arrived to fill in the hole. A workman with graying hair and weight-lifter biceps stooped near the folding chairs, picking up the casings from the salute. He sensed me and straightened his back.

"Done come back for another look, Colonel?"

I nodded. A poor-man's colonel, with silver oak leaves.

"Who this gentleman be, don't mind my axing?" His face gleamed.

"General Farnsworth. Mickey Farnsworth."

"Good man?"

"The best."

The laborer showed a broken line of teeth. "We going to take good care of him for you. Don't you worry, now."

"You can keep on working. I don't mind." But I would have minded. The metal box lay still at the bottom of the hole, kissed with dirt.

"No, sir. We don't do like that. We don't never start till everybody gone. It the rule."

A black bird settled on a green branch, sun oiling its feathers.

"You just takes your time," the workman went on. "I always be glad when somebody come back. People don't come back no more. See what I'm saying? I mean, your wives, maybe. Maybe they does. For a while. But everybody get forgot about equal."

Mary Farnsworth at the graveside, struggling to maintain a dignity worthy of her husband. She stood up straight, and the ceremony was long, and I was afraid she might faint in the heat. I started in her direction when it was all over, but the generals who had lost a rival for promotion flocked around her, cooing sympathy. I could not get past their aides.

"He was a great man," I told the workman. "A hero. Nobody expected him to go like this."

"Heart trouble?"

I almost laughed. "His heart would've been the last thing to go." Farnsworth had been in better shape than a lieutenant fresh out of Ranger School. And it had been a big heart, too. I disciplined my voice. "Hit-and-run. He was jogging." I looked up and the sun narrowed my eyes. We had all thought Farnsworth would be the next Colin Powell, and now he was senselessly dead.

The workman smeared the sweat over his forehead

and sighed. Looking down through the trees, across the river. Into the marble city. "We all dust in the eyes of the Lord." He gestured with a big arm, sweeping over the white lines of markers, the dead in their thousands. "This place here just like Heaven, Colonel. Everybody equal. No man's stone bigger than his brother's. Every man get fair treatment. See what I'm saying?" He looked at me again. "But people don't come back. Everybody just be forgot. That's the way of the world."

"I'll come back."

The workman smiled. "I be happy to see it."

I smiled, too, for a moment. "You don't believe me."

He shrugged. "No offense, now. I mean, maybe you come back here for a while. Then you forgets. That how it supposed to be. It all right. He still be your friend up in Heaven. Hear every word you say. Hear you right now."

"We shall not see his like again."

The workman nodded slowly. With immeasurable gentleness. "Now, that's pretty." He turned and the sun gripped him. One of his eyes looked as though milk had been poured over it. It was the sort of thing you notice right away. If you're awake.

Suddenly, I felt disgusted. With myself and with the world. I felt I was missing big things all around me. But I had no idea what those things might be. I felt stupid and angry.

"Listen here now, Colonel, sir. You ever needs

anything round here, you just axe for old Rickie York. Anything at all. Hear?''

"Thanks."

"You just takes your time now." He shuffled toward the shade. "And God bless you."

There was no more time. I had to go back to work. Then pick up Tish's present before the shop closed. And waste time meeting an old friend who was not a friend anymore, because I did not have what it took to say, "Fuck off, Em. You never even return my phone calls. I'm going home to wish my girl a happy birthday."

I felt I should do something else for General Farnsworth. But the human repertoire is limited.

The heat was terrible and my eyes had begun to ache. I looked down into the grave and said, "I'll come back."

The Ivy Club is two blocks from the White House and the suits that go in and out fit perfectly at the shoulders but not at the waist. Instead of a doorman, the club has a human catcher's mitt. He looked at my uniform as though I had wandered over from the delivery entrance.

"I'm here to meet Emerson Carroll."

"Of course, sir. Mr. Carroll expects you in our bar. Do you know your way around the club, sir? The bar is on the second level."

Worn-down Persians on the floor. Museum wood-work. Smell of steamed vegetables and wax.

It was Tuesday evening and the club was nearly

empty. Em sat alone in the bar, smoking a cigar over whiskey. He had been a terrible sight at the burial ceremony, and even in this softer light, his face looked ruined. I don't know whether I had been more surprised by the speed of his physical decline or by the fact that he had bothered to turn up at Farnsworth's graveside. Emerson Carroll was a second-tier player edging toward first-tier status. He was big stuff in this town. Dead generals were of no use to anybody.

"You look like Cornelius Vanderbilt," I said.

Em did not get up. He smiled without showing his teeth, and I could smell the whiskey. One of the fundamental rules of social biology is that hard liquor is especially tough on golden boys. He swept his fingers back over his ashen hair, briefly tightening the skin on his forehead. He did not offer me his hand.

"John, I do not believe for a moment that you have the slightest idea how Cornelius Vanderbilt actually looked. Sit down." He had a legacy accent from a New England China-trade family. As a lieutenant, he had been daring and fun, full of wicked stories about the Kennedy kids. He had joined the Army to piss off his father, but the novelty had faded after a single tour of duty. For all that, he had possessed a gift for soldiering, for leading. And he tossed it.

At first, we kept in touch. But the comms broke down over the years. I saw his name in the papers. Sometimes in the political gossip, otherwise in the business columns. By the time I was assigned to

Washington, Emerson Carroll was Grand Poobah for Government Relations at Macon-Bolt Industries, the largest defense contractor in the world. He was also a player on every defense panel and foreign relations committee on the Potomac. He invited me to one party. The men talked to the Congressmen they were buying and the women whispered about the Congressmen who were buying them. I failed to measure up.

Now here we were. A shaken fat man at a funeral, Em had begged me to come. He seemed to have regained his composure in the meantime. Maybe it was the booze.

"I thought you had to be dead to join this place."

Em shrugged. "It helps. But it's not a requirement." He noticed me looking at the cigar. "Like one?"

"I still don't smoke."

"Cigars don't count."

"It all counts."

His mouth was as narrow as a knife scar. "Ever the puritan. Although not in all things, as I recall. You'd do fine in this administration, actually. The President has marvelous negative capability." He stubbed the cigar into the ashtray. "Montecristo. Never the same if you relight them. Drink?"

I ordered a beer. Em tapped his glass for another whiskey.

He settled back in his chair and stared at me. "Well," he said finally, "you're looking well, John. All that clean living. Still run every day?"

"What's on your mind, Em? Or do burials just make you nostalgic?"

"Don't be a shit," Em said finally. "I *still* consider you a friend, John. If a neglected one. Town does that to people, you know. Get all caught up in this government business. Incredibly inefficient, the way we run this country. Never enough time for the important things." He considered his ruined cigar.

"Got it. So what do you want?" I had a special grudge against Em these days. I was one of the legion of staff officers sweating blood to keep an underfunded Army alive, while Em's corporation was about to sell the Department of Defense an airplane that even the official estimates said would cost us two hundred billion over the next ten years—which meant three hundred billion, minimum.

The Next-Generation Fighter-Bomber was going to do everything perfectly. It would be the most capable, survivable, and lethal aircraft in history. Except for the fact that we did not need it and could not afford it, the NGFB looked like a great deal for America. Corporate welfare as an art form.

We had soldiers and their familes on food stamps, living in pits. We didn't have training dollars and our medical care had collapsed to the Spanish-American War level. The threats on the international horizon were thugs with old Kalashnikovs and mass murderers with Elvis haircuts and peekaboo terrorists. There was no mission in sight for Em's three-hundred-billion-dollar airplane. If one popped up unexpectedly, we already had enough techno-junk to do the job. We were short of the dull stuff that mattered. Like infantrymen and trucks. The NGFB was going to break the defense budget. But Congress was going to fund it. Bugger the troops. You could feel the vote coming.

Just in case Senator Schweinefleisch got nervous, Macon-Bolt Industries was running full-page ads in the big dailies telling the country what a bargain the NGFB would be for the national defense and for mankind. It was going to keep America's sons and daughters alive. The Army and Marines would not even need to deploy. The NGFB would bomb the global village with voodoo precision. The "public service" ads were a business expense that would be charged back to the taxpayers by way of the NGFB's funding. It was the ultimate self-licking ice-cream cone.

Macon-Bolt also happened to be the nation's biggest campaign contributor. To both parties. And to every PAC with a downtown address. For insurance, the corporation's CEO, Bob Nechestny, had loaded his boardroom with retired generals and admirals who showed up once a year to earn their half a mil. They slimed through the Pentagon in not-quite-right suits, just dropping by to say hi to their former subordinates. The Mexicans had their style of corruption, we had ours.

Em shifted in his chair. "All right. Look. I'm sorry. I've been a bastard. The original thankless friend. But I do have some questions I'd like to ask you, John. Things . . . I can't ask just anybody."

He looked at me with an intensity that brought back memories of better times. "I'm asking for your help. At least for the loan of an ear. I'm asking in an unaccustomed spirit of humility. You may be the only person left I can trust."

I knew Em was a con and I put my guard right back up. I wondered how many questions he had. I kept flashing on Tish and the birthday present in the trunk of my car and on sex. A snort of mortality always makes me want sex.

"I can't do an all-night bullshit session, Em. I've got something scheduled."

Em waved that away. "Won't take long. Give me half an hour." He shifted and straightened his tie. Suddenly, he looked like he was having a bad time on the witness stand. "John . . . do you know any-thing about the blast at that French aircraft research site yesterday?"

"The bombing?"

"Was it a bombing?"

I shrugged and drank. The beer tasted good, but I could get a beer anywhere. "So the newspapers seem to think."

"I'm not interested in what the newspapers think. Don't give me that." Voice cold now. Impatient. Very much the corporate muckety-muck. Em was not steady on course tonight.

"Come on, Em. You want classified information? From me? I don't owe you anything, and I don't break the rules."

"I'm cleared. For Christ's sake, John. I have clearances for programs you don't even know exist. Defense industry has—''

"No way, pal. Call one of your four-star butt boys. Anyway, France isn't my turf. I don't work current intel anymore. I'm just trying to make sure we've still got an Army left when you're done grabbing the money.''

"Just tell me what people are saying around the Building. What's the scuttlebutt?''

Then I got it. Or thought I did. "That's cold, Em. Pretty goddamned grim. That lab was your competition, right? The French aircraft industry.'' I laughed. "You blow it up yourselves? Or just have a streak of good luck?''

Em didn't rise to it. He leaned closer with his wrecked face. I imagined a different sort of life for him then, not all successes and corporate perks.

"*Please*, John. I need you to come through for me on this. It's more important than you can imagine. Very sensitive stuff. Can't you give me *any* insight?''

The answer was no. I had seen the footage on CNN, read the *Post* in the morning, and scanned the Early Bird. A high-security aircraft research facility outside Toulouse had been flattened by a bomb. Midmorning, for maximum employee attendance. Hundreds dead, including some high rollers. Oklahoma City, with red wine for lunch. But I had not read any intel traffic on it.

"All I've got is the POAC stuff,'' I told him. "Wisdom from the locker room. Same line you're hearing from the media. Algerians. FIS crowd.

Bombs for Allah. The frogs have their hands full. 'The Empire Strikes Back.' "

Em finished his whiskey and briefly held up a finger in the direction of the bar. "Want another?"

I shook my head. I was not going to play happy hour at the O-Club with him.

"Keep me posted on this one. Anything you hear. Will you do that, John? It's more important than I can tell you right now."

"I didn't think the French were serious competition for you boys."

"They're not. Can't even build the designs they steal. Country's nothing but a museum."

"So why the interest?"

"It's not about competition."

"What *is* it about?"

"I can't tell you." A bitter look passed over Em's face. "And you don't want to know." He reached for his wallet. The effort popped sweat onto his forehead. "Here." He handed me a card. "This number's unlisted. Use it."

"Em, you've just moved from treating an old friend like shit to treating him like a dumb shit. Why should I help you out on this? Or on anything? So Macon-Bolt can extort an extra twenty or thirty billion from the taxpayer? I don't do Washington intrigue. And I don't trust you."

The bartender hovered again. Em smiled. "It really is good to see you," he told me. "Like old times. You always had that charming crusader streak."

Which is why, he seemed to say, you're still only a lieutenant colonel in the Army.

"Okay," I said. "My turn. Just to satisfy my curiosity. What brought you to the Farnsworth show? I figured a major general would be flying way below your radar coverage."

"For Christ's sake, John. Farnsworth and I go way back." His eyes switched to the direct-fire mode. "All three of us do. You and I both owed the guy. Any other battalion XO in the Army would've court-martialed our asses. You would've never even made captain and the DIS boys would've yanked my clearance forever."

"You don't exactly ooze gratitude these days."

Em looked genuinely surprised. "John . . . Farnsworth and I were *friends*. Well . . . maybe not what *you*'d call friends. We didn't take the blood oath of the Templars. But I've seen quite a lot of him these past months."

That answer did not track. I had not worked directly for Farnsworth in the Pentagon, but our projects overlapped and we saw each other often. He and Mary regularly invited me to their home for dinner. At least until Tish entered the picture. Mary did not approve of Tish. But the general had never said a word about seeing Em again. Em's corporation was the Dark Side, out to reduce the Army to a ceremonial battalion so the Department of Defense could buy more solid gold toys with wings.

"He never told me that he'd seen you."

Em did not meet my eyes. "Special-project sort of thing. You weren't read on."

"Don't give me that secret-handshake crap."

He raised his face. Drawing himself up from a well of thought. "Look, I don't know why he didn't say anything. Don't let it hurt your feelings. I know he thought the world of you. He was proud of you. But the project stuff was for real. In fact, that's already more than I should've told you."

"It doesn't track." I looked away from him and stared into the windows of the building across the street. The last office workers were stuffing their briefcases.

"John?" Em said after a pause. "Please. Just close that particular folder. There's something else I need to ask you. It's . . . something even more important."

He looked ten years older than he should have. Maybe fifteen. He played with his empty glass.

"John . . . do you believe in redemption?"

"What?"

"Redemption."

"As in God and repentance and forgiveness?"

"Not exactly. I mean, yes. But in the here and now. Do you think we can atone for the things we've done wrong?"

"What kind of things?"

"Bad things."

His hands were shaking. When he saw me looking, he folded them together. But the flesh still trembled.

"Jesus Christ, Em."

I thought he was going to break down on the spot.

But the air changed again. He sat up. And smiled. A smile carved into the face of a corpse. He nodded toward the entrance to the bar.

A young woman in a blue dress had stopped at the head of the stairs. Framing herself in the doorway so we could admire her. The dress was slight—a breeze would have dissolved it—and her legs looked as long as a politician's list of excuses. She carried a wispy briefcase. Her features were the precise sort that make you suspect old families of selectively killing their infants to improve the breed. Hair blond, worn short. No jewelry. Not the kind of girl whose labels stick up at the back of her neck.

She extended her pose for a few seconds before starting toward us. Theater, with plausible denial.

Em stood up. I followed his example. Without losing his smile, he whispered, "She's getting ready to leave me. You get to know the signs."

All I could think was: That girl doesn't need Em.

"Corry, I'd like you to meet John Reynolds, my old Army buddy. John, Corry Nevers."

She turned out to be shorter than the impression she created. She gave me her hand. It was dry and cool. "Emerson's told me ever so much about you."

"Corry's on Senator Faust's staff. She's absolutely in charge of defense policy on the Hill."

I glanced at my watch. Thinking of Tish. More anxious than ever to leave.

"Why don't you two just sit down and get acquainted," Em said. "You always appreciated good wine, John. Corry's a wine drinker, too. I'll go search out something a bit better than the bar blend.''

And he left me with her. As soon as he cleared the doorway, she leaned in, breath vanilla, and said, ''You don't look old enough to be Emerson's Army buddy.''

It was one of those times when you want to say something clever and fail to say anything at all.

She leaned closer. ''I suppose he's going on about his redemption thing again.'' She showed perfect white teeth the way another woman might have flashed thigh. ''He's turning into such a bore.''

One of the best things in life is a lover who is genuinely glad to see you walk in. Tish gave me a real kiss and the zipper line on her jeans plowed into my crotch.

''Happy birthday to me,'' she said.

''Happy birthday, Tish.''

''I was afraid you wouldn't get home before I had to go.''

I could smell the dinner she had made to celebrate her own birthday. ''Sorry. I had to stop by and see a friend. Serious stuff.''

We had not been together long enough for things to be spoiled.

''Oh? Who?'' Asked with that innocence she had preserved through some miracle. Despite her choice of occupations and the tattoo on her shoulder. She hugged me again. ''Sometimes I just want to squeeze you.''

shape of the case. But she was still going to get a
surprise when she lifted the lid.

"*John,*" she said. Her eyes went hyper-alive.

"Well, check it out. And happy birthday."

She undid the latches like a kid tearing off wrap-
ping paper. Then she knelt before the opened guitar
coffin, a Buddhist in front of an altar. She did not
even touch the instrument.

"John . . . is that . . . ?"

"An original. For the most original woman I
know."

She touched it then. Stroking the neck. Ebony fin-
gerboard, mother-of-pearl insets. It was an old Les
Paul Gibson, the rocker's equivalent of a Stradivar-
ius. Finally, she lifted it out of the case. A Les Paul
is awkward to hold unless you've got it strapped over
your shoulder. Tish just clutched it against her ribs
and breasts. Without even trying to shape a chord.
Then she began to cry.

"Nobody's ever been so good to me," she said.
"Not in all my life. Nobody."

We lay in bed with the dinner downstairs waiting.
Whatever might have been incomprehensible to others about the John and Tish Show, there were plenty
of good things on the program. The twilight came in
the window and her white flesh shone.

"I wish I didn't have to play tonight," she said.

"Me, too."

"I've got to get going."

"Right."

She rolled closer and I held her. My nose touching the little line of earrings.

"Thank you," she said.

"Taking it with you tonight?"

"I didn't mean about the guitar. Thanks for being you. But thanks for the guitar, too. It's wonderful. You're from Fairy Tale City."

"I'm anxious to hear you play it."

She roiled her skin against me. Cool, a little wet. The ear retreated and hair rushed my mouth.

"I'll play it for you first. I'm not going to take it tonight. I have to get used to it." She flipped onto her back and dropped her head into the pillow. "It's scary, you know that?"

"What's scary?"

"The guitar. It probably cost more than my car."

It had cost a lot more than her car, which had more rust than paint. Tish raised the issue in a voice that had no greed in it, only wonder. She had lived a musician's vow-of-poverty life for a decade. Credit cards maxed out until they were voided. She was not much of a cook, but she meant well and she was a mistress of kitchen economies. Her Telecaster and amp had been her primary possessions. When I met her, she lived in one clean room.

"If you're thinking about your car," I told her, "it means it's broken down again."

I could feel her blushing.

"Can I borrow your car? Just one more time? To make the gig. I'll be careful."

"You know you can borrow the car." I rose onto

an elbow, admiring the dark lines and palenesses, not wanting her to go anywhere. "You have time to eat something before you go?"

She rolled toward me and shadows moved against shadows. "I'll get a sandwich at the club. It's free for the band. There's another way I'd rather spend my time."

There were plenty of things that did not match up in our relationship. At the Pentagon, I worked the kind of hours that unions had fought against at the turn of the century. Tish played evenings, or did late shows like tonight. Her friends, who had missed the integrity of the sixties but not the prejudices, wondered what Tish saw in a fascist baby-killer. My friends were convinced they knew exactly what I went for in Tish. We blew them all off and stole every moment we could between the end of my workday and the beginning of hers. We lived for the weekend afternoons.

We met in one of those Georgetown book-and-music stores where the clerks dress in black and spend their lives waiting for a break in their "real" occupation. It was after work and I was in uniform, picking up my fourth copy of Marianne Faithfull's *Broken English*. It was The Recording Nobody Ever Returned.

I noticed Tish. Couldn't miss her. Picking through the discs with that red hair and a cast-off undertaker's suit that was the thrift shop's answer to Armani. But it took me only a few seconds to file her under What-do-you-do-with-the-body-in-the-morning?

She was the one who got things started.

"Excuse me," she said. "You might not like that one."

I looked at her as though she had slapped me.

"I mean," she said, "like . . . you don't look . . . I mean, have you ever *heard* that? It's uh . . . colorful. I mean, I just wanted to be . . ."

A Gen X girl scout, helping me across the musical street.

"I bought my first copy of it on LP," I said. "In Germany. In 1979."

"I'm sorry. I wasn't trying to be rude. I mean . . ."

With an emotional sunburn on her face, Tish pushed a flame of hair behind her ear and stared at me. Waiting for punishment. When I got her full face and read the eyes, there was a vulnerability to her that made me soften my voice.

"You a Marianne Faithfull fan?" I asked her.

"Are you kidding? She's a *god*. That's her all-time greatest. It's one of the best albums ever. If I could just make one recording like that . . ."

We had coffee where they knew her and she asked me to come hear her band. The music was good enough, but not great. Tish played with passion that veered into frustration, as if she could not move the music from her soul to her fingers without losing the best of it. I told her I had enjoyed myself. And it was true. I had enjoyed watching her. She had the look, if not the gift. I pegged her as one of those minor talents damned to appreciate greatness without possessing it.

I liked the feel of the air around her. I admired her earnestness and loved the mick hair. In the beginning, I also got off on spiting her friends. Who imagined me grinding innocents between my jaws. She, in her patchy naivete, wore a *little* black dress that showed the blue guitar tattoo on her shoulder to Mary Farnsworth's dinner guests. Then she compounded her sin with a heartfelt comment about Newt Gingrich. Nobody bothered to learn that she also did volunteer work with inner-city kids and loved nineteenth-century English novels, accepting each word with the avidity of a child. We taped every BBC miniseries so we could watch them together. At night she held me as if I were the only man in the world.

"Got to go," my birthday girl said at last, kissing me once and rising.

"Wake me when you get home."

She showered and went out with her hair wet.

I listened to her footsteps on the pavement, then I listened to the city sounds. Bus grunting to a stop on the corner, dropout moms laughing with each other as they strolled home to Indian country. The urban surf of cars. Sirens. A boom box proclaiming doomed identity. The air-conditioning unit kicked back in. Capitol Hill, America's ground zero.

I pulled on my shorts in the darkness and went downstairs. Tish had made vegetarian lasagna for her birthday dinner and I fetched my plate from the setting she had arranged on the kitchen table.

There was a note under the plate. It said:

This isn't my real birthday anymore.
My life started over the day I met you.

It struck me that I should have gone to hear her play on her birthday. But my mornings started early, and we had worked out our patterns. I went to the important Saturday-night gigs. And Tish understood. But I sat there over her make-this-last-until-payday lasagna and felt as though I had failed her.

I put my food down the garbage disposal so she would think I had eaten it, and went back to bed.

More city sounds. A domestic scene in the yard of a house two doors down that had been turned into rental units. An automobile alarm. Faint jazz from a neighbor.

I could not stop thinking about Farnsworth. And about Em. I could smell Tish on the sheets, and missed the feel of her. The best nights of my life were those when she was not working. Yet I could not imagine a long-term future with her.

I lay there awake, sensing great things moving beyond my range of vision. Except for the hour with Tish, it had been a very bad day.

When I did crash, I crashed hard. I have no idea how long the doorbell had been ringing before it registered on me. I jerked up. Tish had a habit of forgetting her keys. Or her wallet. Or the be-on-time watch I had given her at Christmas. I found my shorts again and pounded downstairs, yelling, *"Coming."*

I yanked open the door and found myself an arm's length from Em's girl. She stood in the cast of the hall light, still perfect, wearing the same tease-the-peasants blue dress. But her eyes had changed.

"Em's dead," she said. "They killed him. Help me."

CHAPTER 2

Hysteria comes in almost as many varieties as love. I had seen it in men lightly wounded, and in refugees with dead families and burning houses behind them, in mobs and in mosques. Hysteria was part of the scenery in the post-Cold War Army. In Corry Nevers, hysteria took one of its quieter forms. She trembled, inhumanly taut, and could not answer a question until the third time it had been asked. Then she cascaded words.

She and Em had gone over to Lespinasse for dinner. For high rollers only, the restaurant was just off Sixteenth Street, well within the downtown safety zone centered on the White House. But as they walked back to Em's car, two men stepped out of a doorway. They had guns and said they wanted wallets. They shot Em several times and ran, empty-handed, leaving Corry screaming on the sidewalk. In another triumph for the mayor's

24

imperial guard, the cops took her in and yelled at her for a couple of hours just in case she was the killer.

She was so spooked that she begged me to let her come upstairs while I got dressed. Whenever I made an unexpected move, she quivered like a hammered board. I sat her down in the kitchen and made tea, which she did not drink.

I wished I had been a bit nicer to Em the evening before.

Corry did not meet my eyes. The tightness in her threatened an explosion.

"I can't believe it," she muttered again. "I still can't believe it. I should've—"

"Nothing you could've done. Listen . . . just tell me something, okay? Why did you come to me?"

"What?"

"How did you even know where I live?"

She stirred the tea she had not drunk. Gripping the spoon so hard her fingers mottled.

"What brought you to me, Corry?"

Surprise molded her face. "Em trusted you. He talked about you. A great deal. More and more often. He told me . . . he said I could count on you. If there were any problems." Her facial muscles hit trouble. "I thought he was crazy." Tears. It occurred to me that these were the first I had seen. "I mean, he couldn't have known what was going to happen." Her wet eyes searched. "Could he?"

One bad day was spilling into another. I had been hard on Em and I did not like myself very much.

And I did not much like Corry Nevers. Maybe it was jealousy. Even now, she had a classic feel Tish would never possess. Tish turned heads. Corry Nevers changed lives.

"I'm afraid to go home," she said. "I know it's wrong. But I feel like they'll be waiting for me. That they might know where I live. I'm the only witness."

Random-victim thugs did not work like that. Dully, I asked her, "Were they wearing masks or anything? You get a good look at them?" The words did not penetrate. I was ready to ask again when I heard familiar footsteps on the sidewalk.

Tish let herself in and hurried into the kitchen. With all the lights on, she must have assumed I had stayed up to greet her. When she saw Corry, she really saw her.

"And who," Tish asked, "is this?"

"*I*'ll drive her home," Tish said. "You need to sleep."

I had gone upstairs to get my wallet with my driver's license. Tish followed me, in a heavy metal mood.

"Tish . . . she's scared. She'd probably feel safer if I took her."

Tish rolled her eyes operatically, but settled them back on me. "Scared? I guarantee you, that girl hasn't been scared since the day she was born. God, you're so blind sometimes."

I smiled. "Keep your voice down, okay?"

Tish leaned over the bed. "I know what she's up to."

"For Christ's sake, Tish. Her boyfriend just got gunned down in the street. She watched the man die. She might be just a little spooked."

Tish punched her fists into her hips. "Yeah? Well, how come the first thing she does is take a taxi to the house of some guy she just met? I mean, she's efficient. I'll say that for her."

"She explained that."

"I'll bet she did."

"If you want to come along for the ride . . ."

"Why can't *I* drive her home? Just what would be so terrible about that?" Tish shook her head. "I swear to God, John. Maybe you've been all around the world, but sometimes you don't understand a thing."

"Got to go."

Tish changed the climate. "Wait. *Please*. Yeah, okay. I'm jealous. Who wouldn't be?" Celtic eyes programmed for suffering. "I mean . . . I can't wait to get home. I'm just thinking about it all night, you know? And I walk in. And there's my guy all snuggly with Miss Ritz-Carlton . . ."

"Tish, I have no interest . . ."

"John, you don't *know* what you have an interest in. That first night . . . you didn't think you were interested in me, either."

"Tish . . . it's almost four in the morning."

She crossed her arms. "Exactly. If you went to bed right now, you could sleep for a little over an hour. And I guarantee you, she and your buddy were shacked up in far Northwest. Five bucks says there's a river view. You'd never get back in time.''

The truth was that I ached to sleep. Too much had happened too quickly. I could not quite grasp the world around me. And Tish was dead on: Em's place was way up in Northwest. Long drive from Capitol Hill, even in off hours.

''Don't just drop her off. Go in with her, make sure she feels safe. She really is scared.''

''I'll hold her little hand,'' Tish said.

All my career, I had been trained to pay attention to my instincts. Now, when it counted, I ignored them. All I said was, ''Call me if anything seems out of whack, okay?''

Tish gave me a pitying look. ''John, I swear. You really do need somebody to protect you from the big bad world.''

Corry Nevers accepted the change in chauffeurs without comment, but I sensed that she did not like it much. She had used the time Tish and I spent arguing to reconstruct herself into the kind of woman who walks out of a K Street elevator and looks right through any man who doesn't make a couple of hundred thousand a year.

On the way out the door, she took me by the hand. The eyes that had been indigo an hour before had faded back to ice-water blue.

''Thank you,'' she said. ''You've been wonderfully understanding. Em was right about you.''

She held on to my hand just long enough to really piss Tish off.

By the time I got back into bed, I had less than an hour before it was time to hit the shower and pull on a uniform again. I flopped on my belly and went out hard.

I thought it was the alarm clock. But it was the phone. By the time I figured it out, I had knocked the clock onto the floor and nearly took out a lamp.

"Hello?"

It was Tish. Her tone woke me the rest of the way. Then I registered the screaming in the background.

"*John*," Tish said. "You've got to get over here. *Hurry*."

"Where are you? What's the matter?"

Tish was shouting now, but not into the phone. "What's the goddamned address? Tell me the goddamned address."

"Tish. It's all right. I've got Em's address. Calm down. What happened?"

Tish sobered her voice. But I got the deep fear in it. "John, just *hurry*. You need to see this."

"What is it? You called the police? What—"

"I *can't* call the police," Tish said, but the words did not sink in. All I registered was her panic. "I *need* you."

"Tish, you've got my car."

"Call a cab. Anything. *Please*."

"Buddy," the detective told me, "you're trying my patience." He had badged me and introduced himself as Detective Lieutenant Dickey. His name almost made me like him for a fraction of a sliver of a millisecond.

"I can almost buy the blondie running to you for career counseling after her boyfriend gets popped." He wiped the back of his hand across his chin. "People do stupid things under stress. And I can figure out how the downstairs neighbor hears more than he needs to and stumbles in on this and winds up giving blood." He looked around the bedroom where he had isolated me for questioning. Like all of the rooms in Em's apartment, it had been destroyed. Walls knocked in, hardwood floors torn up. Quite a job for one night. "I can even understand," the detective continued, "why your old lady drives blondie home. Oh, I got that, all right." He pulled his chair closer to mine. "But what I still don't get is why she calls *you* before she calls the police." He made a seen-it-all face. "In this town, mister, you call the cops when you got a problem. You don't call the Army. So how about inviting me into the information age and telling me where you fit in here?"

I would have told him where I fit in, if I had known. I thought I was sitting in a chair. Just as I had thought I was just having a drink with an old friend the night before. In the reality I had not yet figured out, I was tumbling down one flight of stairs after another. As for calling the D.C. cops, the detective had a weak grip on reality. The locals were as scared of the police as they were of the criminals.

"I've told you everything I can think of," I said.

"You said yourself people under stress make bad judgment calls. Tish probably figured I'd know what to do."

The detective looked at me as though he had caught me with a gun in my hand and I was trying to convince him it was a flower.

"Buddy," he said, "your girlfriend does not strike me as the helpless type."

Em's lost world lay all around me. Antiques smashed, pillows slashed. Drawers emptied onto the floor. I did not see anything that might have belonged to Corry. They could not have been together long.

Another plainclothesman half knocked and came in. Carrying papers. Dickey looked at him, and the plainclothesman smiled.

"Interesting crew, Lieutenant. Check out the red-head's record."

Tish never said anything to me about a police record.

The detective took the papers and made a performance out of looking at them. He clucked and shook his head, smiling a little smile that made me want to knock him out of his chair. I wanted to know about Tish, and he knew it.

"Well, Colonel. Looks like you're a model citizen. Not even a speeding ticket. So how'd you get mixed up with Miss O'Malley? I take it . . . you do know about Miss O'Malley's record?"

"I know all I need to know about her," I lied.

"And you don't care that she pleaded guilty to cocaine possession? That she hasn't been off probation a year? Tell you the truth, she should've done time, considering the amount.'' He smiled again. ''But she's a looker, I guess. If you go for that long, lean type. Figure she knew what she had to do. Got a 'Suspicion Of Receiving Stolen Goods' in there, too. But you would've known all about that.''

Tish had buzzed me in the front door. When I came in, she was sitting in a broken chair, staring at the body. Corry Nevers had bunched herself in the corner. All screamed out, sobbing and shaking. I called the cops immediately, too thick to wonder why the intruders had left the phone working.

Tish dropped her tough-girl act and I held her until the police arrived. She kept her back turned to the body and trembled.

There was nothing I could do for Corry. I let her sob.

I've seen corpses. Not as many as some other soldiers with a couple of decades of paper in their 201 files, but more than most Cold War commandos. I can recognize a strong hand and a clean kill. One slash across the throat had nearly taken the old man's head off.

Lot of blood in a human being.

The cops straightened out Corry long enough to learn that the dead man was the downstairs neighbor. Poor bugger probably heard noises he could not explain, and he was from a generation that did not ignore a neighbor's troubles.

I looked at the detective and said, ''If you need

to keep me here, I'd like to call in to work and let them know I'm not AWOL."

Dickey put his hands on his knees. As if to rise. But he did not get up.

"Buddy," he said, "you got a connection to two murders. And you got a girlfriend with a sheet. But I don't want you to worry about that. I want you to just go and put on a nice clean uniform and protect us all from the Russians or the Serbians or the fucking Canadians or whoever's coming this week." He shoved a hand back over scraps of hair. "You can go."

"What about Ms. O'Malley? She hasn't done anything."

The detective laughed. "How about interfering with the scene of a crime? Maybe even an obstruction of justice count, if I write it up smart. We even got a 'Failure To Notify' ordinance here in the District." He waved a hand. Swatting a fly. "Get her out of here. And keep her off the powder, okay?"

"And Ms. Nevers? What happens to her?"

The detective judged me again. "Thinking about trading up?"

"She's all alone."

He grinned. "A woman like that's only alone if she wants to be."

I moved to leave. But Detective Dickey was not done saying goodbye.

"Hey, soldier boy. You probably think I'm the shits. Useless fucking D.C. cop, right? Well, how about *you* try to keep this town clean with no budget and nobody gives a damn.'' He gave me a smile of hatred. ''You guys with your million-dollar toilet seats.''

They were holding Tish in the entranceway. As I walked out, two fat men in white were loading a body bag onto a stretcher while a cop ate an Egg McMuffin.

''You never told me you had a police record,'' I said. The morning traffic crept along Massachusetts.

Tish put her face down into her hands. ''Please. Could we talk about it later?''

The Volvo idling in front of me had a bumper sticker that said, ''My child is an honor student at Barksdale Pre-School.''

''Yeah,'' I said, shifting up into second. ''Later.''

Tish was crying. ''You want me to get out?''

We hit another light.

''I don't know what I want,'' I told her honestly.

She touched my forearm, then quickly removed her hand. As if she had scorched it. I kept my eyes on the traffic. But I got the peripheral of her lowered head. Hung by the seat belt.

''It wasn't my coke,'' she said. ''And the stereo stuff. I was seeing a guy who turned out to be a bastard. He was using my place as a stash. I didn't know about the dope. Or that his gear was stolen. I swear to God. I didn't know, John. He kept the coke in a locked suitcase. He was dealing out of my place when I was at gigs. I didn't know, I didn't *know*.''

Her body shook. "I'm so stupid. He screwed me over so bad."

Her hand stirred, lifted, retreated. Horns blared when a car did not respond instantaneously to a changed light.

"You lied to me," I said.

"I *didn't* lie."

"Silence is lying."

She wept bitterly. "I didn't want to lose you. I was afraid. Can't you under*stand?*"

It was my turn to be silent.

"Didn't you . . . didn't you ever fall for the wrong person?" Tish asked. "Didn't you ever make a mistake? Not even once?"

A smacked-in Dodge cut me off and I hit the brakes.

"Maybe I did," I told her.

When I got into work, the guys were gathered around the television in our conference room.

"How can that motherfucker *say* that?" Scottie had just come back from Bosnia, where he had lost two soldiers to a land mine because the Army could not afford decent mine detectors.

The SecDef was on C-SPAN, testifying before the Senate Armed Services Committee. Except for Scottie's outburst, the room was morbidly quiet.

". . . no doubt in the minds of the experts, Senator. Our military needs that aircraft. And by maintaining the projected purchase quantity, we can maximize per-unit affordability. It's going to cost us, but the services are prepared to sacrifice. In terms of the American lives it's going to save on tomorrow's battlefields, the Next-Generation Fighter-Bomber is a bargain.''

Colonel Maurey switched off the set. The boss, a full colonel, silver eagles and a brush cut. ''All right. Back to work. Let's just try to keep the world together until the wonder-plane comes on line.''

It was heartbreaking to hear the SecDef tell such a big lie. Every one of us knew we did not need that airplane and that it would break the defense budget. When you got them alone, even the Air Force and Navy pilots would admit it. But they wanted it anyway, enraptured by the technology. Invisible to radar, intercontinental reach, max payload, protective suite right out of Star Wars. The Navy would get a carrier variant. The generals and admirals were like middle-aged guys who buy Porsches when they really need family vans.

I followed Colonel Maurey into his office and gave him the highlights of the past twenty-four hours. He was the kind of man who could have had good suits and a corner office. Instead, he wore a polyester uniform and manned a battered desk in a windowless cubbyhole.

He leaned back in his chair and said, ''How much time do you need?''

''Sir, I'd like to take leave through the end of the week. Go to my buddy's funeral. Visit Mary Farnsworth, see if there's anything I can do. Think a little.''

''What's on your work calendar?''

"We're clean on the suspenses. Future Conflict NIE's on track. Nick can cover the attaché reception for me. I was going to catch the shuttle down to TRADOC on Friday, but that was just for hand-holding."

"E-mail me the leave form." He put his hands behind his head. "Sounds like you're having some run of bad luck, John. Be a little careful, okay?"

"Yes, sir."

"So how was Farnsworth's ceremony? I got held up in the Watch."

I shrugged. "Chief came, Secretary didn't. Standard mix of regret and crocodile tears. Less than he deserved."

"Farnsworth . . . will be missed," Maurey said. From his mouth, those four words carried more punch than a full-page obit in the *Post*. "Call me if you need anything."

"If you need anything at all," I told Mary Farnsworth, "just call me. Please."

She looked at me gently. As though I were the one in need of comfort. Mary was a member of what Southerners call "The Other Aristocracy," and she had a fineness that would have shamed a queen. She was the only person I knew who poured coffee from silver for every visitor.

"I appreciate your thoughtfulness, John. But there's nothing, I'm afraid."

At that point, anyone else would have fallen back into tears. Not Mary. She sat erectly and spoke with the same precision with which she transferred a lump of sugar to her cup. Maintaining the calm that had always been such a contrast to the hurricane she married.

I sipped my coffee and scanned the room, half expecting to find things changed. But everything was exactly as I remembered it. Antiques from Mary's family, their wood so dark it was almost black. And Farnsworth's "Buffalo Soldiers" print above the fireplace, bad art well meant, tolerated by Mary. Farnsworth had been born in 1947 in a shack not twenty miles from the mansion Mary's family had built during Reconstruction, when corruption briefly crossed the color line. His father had worked a mule, while her mother rode Arabians. Farnsworth had been a big man, a West Point defensive lineman, and Mary had a deceptive look of fragility. Their married life had been a long smile, yet they had no children. Only the younger officers whose careers Farnsworth had guided.

Mary laughed. "John, you have always been so transparent, even to Mickey. He knew you thought that old print of his was just awful up there. I believe he thought you and I were in league." Before I could respond, she said, "And how is Tish?"

From Mary, this was an olive branch the size of a redwood.

"She's fine."

"I have been unkind to her. My behavior has been small and unforgivable." Her eyes convinced me that brown was the color of mercy. "I suppose Mickey and I have been living in a fool's paradise, surrounded all our adult lives by the military. I suppose we lost touch a bit." She sighed. "Young people these days just seem to approach life so differently." Warm, immaculate Mary. "Do you think Tish will ever forgive me?"

"She means well."

"Don't apologize. I haven't even made an effort to get to know her. And she's your girl. Our John's girl."

"She's different. It's only that . . ." The truth was that I did not want to talk about Tish just now.

"Oh, John." And now she came close to tears. "It's just that . . . Mickey and I . . . we were trying to plan your life, too. I thought I knew exactly what kind of girl you needed to marry. Just like Mickey planning your career. I wanted you to marry the perfect wife. And I set myself up as the arbiter of perfection." She touched one eye with a milk-coffee finger. "We meant well, John."

"I'm not married yet."

Mary mastered herself, correcting her posture ever so slightly. She changed the subject with her typical grace. "You must be the tenth caller today. And I dread to think of the evening. But you are the only one whom I believe *want*ed to come. I thank you for that, John."

I almost said that her husband had been a second father to me. Instead, I just asked:

"Made any plans? Or is it too soon?"

Mary turned her head to the side. She was still a

beautiful woman and I can only imagine the impression she had made on a young lieutenant home for his first leave. A stopover in Baton Rouge, en route to Vietnam.

"I don't know. It's all so sudden, it's . . ." She disciplined herself again. "More coffee, John? I think I might like to teach again. In the city. Mickey would admire that."

"Mary, I have to ask you something. Did Em Carroll ever come over to the house? Recently, I mean."

Mary's face was open. "Oh, yes. More and more often. I was so glad he and Mickey had gotten over those hard feelings."

"They were friends again?"

"Thick as thieves. And those boys were up to something, let me tell you. They'd just go off into Mickey's study for hours. It started last winter. We hadn't seen Emerson for ages." I sensed her doing her social navigating. "I asked Mickey to invite him to one of our dinners. When you would've been there. For old time's sake. But Mickey said no. Some sort of little boys' secret. Their little club. I did wonder why you weren't included. You all used to be so close."

"Mary . . . do you have any idea what they were up to? It could be important."

I could see by her expression that she did not know. "They seemed to have some sort of project they were working on together. But Mickey never talked about it to me. We rarely talked business."

"Do you know which one of them got in touch with the other first?"

Mary thought for a moment. "I truly couldn't say. Not with certainty. I have this feeling that it was Em. That Em was the one who called Mickey. But I can't be sure."

"Did Em . . . seem happy to you?"

"Em has never seemed happy to me. He's not that sort of man."

"But how did he seem? The same? Changed?"

Mary gave me her eyes straight on. "You mean the drinking? Of course, you can tell that just looking at him. But he didn't drink excessively when he came by. Mickey would not have tolerated it."

"Did he say anything about work? Did he seem unhappy—"

"John, whatever is this about?"

I did not know what it was about. I was searching. With one of those hangovers you get from lack of sleep. I almost told her about Em, but could not shoot the words at her yet. I had my finger on the trigger, though.

Mary broke the silence. "Is something wrong? Is Em in some kind of trouble? That boy was always in one tub of hot water or another. Why, I remember when you—"

"Mary, Em's dead. He was shot down in the street last night. It was in the morning paper."

"That can't be," Mary said. "It's—"

"Mary, I'm sorry. I should've waited to tell you."

"I can't believe it."

"I'm sorry."

"Right after . . ."

I ached to talk about it. To say, Yeah, hell of a coincidence. The stink was already spreading. Even I could smell it, and I'm slow.

The doorbell rang. Mary closed her eyes for a moment before rising.

It was their minister. I excused myself, absorbed in my own riddles, even though I could tell that Mary did not want me to go.

"Call me," she said. "Let me know about Em's funeral."

I did not have the sense to tell her to be careful.

I called Rob Burns—Robert Mayhew Burns—and made an appointment to talk. He was gracious, if baffled by my impatience. He could not see me until six. So I drove to kill time. I did not want to go home. Not even to change. I was not ready to face Tish.

Rain swept up from the Chesapeake. Summer in the District. Rain comes down, steam goes up. I had to turn on the air full blast to keep the windows clear. Finally, I pulled into one of those scenic-view lots along the Virginia side of the river and sat. Even in the rain, there were joggers out from the Pentagon. I let the windows cloud.

Rob Burns belonged to one of those dug-in D.C. families whose members never run for office. They take law degrees, or maybe a Poli-Sci doctorate, and enter government under the wing of a mentor. The family had produced four cabinet members in a hundred years. Rob was a few years younger than I was and had already done two years as an Assistant Secretary of Defense before the administration changed. I had dated his sister—no, his sister had dated me—for a couple of months. Until I realized she was just checking a block, sleeping with a soldier the way some people sleep with a person of another race, just to find out what it's like. She rode in the hunts out in western Loudon and Fauquier counties and did not regard me as her intellectual or social equal. She was probably right on both counts, but she could not make me like it. I hit it off with Rob, though. Now he was sitting in a think tank on Eighteenth Street, waiting for the electorate to turn again.

I drove back into town against traffic. With the suburban set brutal in the outbound lanes. My uniform soaked with sweat. When I cranked up the air, it just got uglier.

Radio on. Dow up. A jetliner down. First Lady on the edge of indictment. A terminal liberal deplored the SecDef's Hill appearance, asking if all the money we were spending on weapons systems would not be better spent on education and jobs training. He whined, but made sense.

I was beginning to feel like a traitor to my kind.

I went up Fourteenth and cut left. Secretaries dashed through the rain. The homeless milled, oblivious. Men in suits held briefcases over their heads or clashed umbrellas. A taxi had broken down in the middle of Connecticut.

Nine bucks to park the car. The Army still had a no-umbrellas regulation we would not change until the Marines blinked first, so I jogged through the downpour. By the time I reached the lobby of Rob's building, my uniform was clinging to me like an old-fashioned bathing suit.

When the elevator door opened on Rob's floor, the defense attaché from the French embassy was standing there waiting to go down. We had met at a couple of the town's countless receptions, but he gave no sign of recognizing me. Maybe it was my drowned-rat look. Or maybe not. We pushed past each other.

The receptionist was heading out, but she let me pass. Rob's personal secretary laid down her papers and pretended I was worth knowing. Rob waved me in. He sat behind his desk, on the phone, surrounded by signed photos of everybody who had mattered over the past fifteen years. He motioned for me to have a seat.

I stood. Dripping.

"Yeah, Trent," he told the receiver, "I know. But he's got you outmaneuvered on this. Look at the polls. I think you should cut your losses. Right. That's absolutely right. Sorry I can't be more encouraging. Right. See you Friday."

Rob slapped the phone down and looked up. "Hard to make the Hill understand that a majority doesn't mean what it used to. It's like herding cats." He leaned toward the door. "Joanne, I won't need you anymore today, thanks. Leave the coffee on."

Sitting back again, he said, "For Christ's sake, have a seat."

"I'm soaking."

"Chairs are replaceable. Friends aren't."

"Thanks for seeing me."

"Any time, any time. Even if I didn't like you, John, I'd make it a point to be seen with you just to piss off my sister."

"How's she doing?"

"Vicky always reminds me of Bob McNamara. Walking proof of the banality of evil. What's on your mind?"

"Saw de La Vere on his way out."

Rob's family ties were to London, not Paris. His private attitude toward the French was very American, and he was always glad to share it with friends:

"Poor buggers have been in a funk ever since Pamela Harriman died. 'Nobody understands them.' De La Vere's on the warpath about the fate of the Eurofighter and the possibility that Macon-Bolt's going to corner the expanded-NATO aircraft market. Bob Nechestny's turning into the king of the world while Dassault and Aerospatiale go down the crapper. You see that picture of Nechestny doing the handshake thing with Havel, by the way? When NATO's new girls get dressed, they're going to wear Macon-Bolt exclusively. Expansion's serious dollars, and the frogs can't compete. And that bombing at their research lab seems to have been quite a blow. Shook de La Vere, you could really tell. Poor sap wanted to know who *I* thought might have done it. Their intel ops must be on the skids, too. Pathetic. Don't deserve their actresses, that what's-her-name. . . ."

"Rob . . . I'd like to ask you something. Just between you and me."

"Ask. You want some coffee? It's probably stale."

I shook my head. "You knew Emerson Carroll, right?"

He frowned. "All too well. Terrible business. Hard on the family. Only son." He ran his fingers down the back side of his tie, freeing it from the tuck at his waist. "Knew Em for ages. Since Sidwell Friends. When Em's father was down here. Early Nixon period. Looking back, I'm not sure my father didn't have an excessive interest in poor Em's mother." His eyes looked at memories. "You know how it goes. Dinner parties, tennis, the usual suspects. Em's father resigned rather suddenly, if you recall. Took the family home to the north pole. Or Harvard, anyway."

"Give me your frank assessment. Of Em. Please."

Rob calculated. "You knew him?"

"Long time ago. We were lieutenants together."

He sat back. "Christ, I never even knew he'd been in the Army. Hard to picture." He cocked his head as if lining up a shot at billiards. "You want the for-real? Okay. But it stays in this office, John." He looked at my wet shirt. "I suppose I didn't share the conventional view of Em. He was supposed to be a comer, but I saw him as already on the way out. Time was when a man could be a drinker in this town, but not anymore. And Em could be surprisingly clumsy. Heavy-handed, just when he thought he was being clever. The way he cornered Senator Faust into hiring his girlfriend, for instance. You can't pull that kind of shit anymore. At least not often. People remember, the bills come due." He smiled. "Girl looks the part, though. I'll say that for her. Freezer blonde, carved legs. Ever meet her?"

I felt so bad I was ready to get up and go. But somebody turned on the batteries in my brain. "Rob, you know everybody and everything in this city . . ."

"You sound like a Congressman who wants something."

"Tell me about Macon-Bolt Industries. What's the view from inside the Beltway?"

He swiveled in his chair. The rain changed direction and smacked his window. I could smell my uniform drying.

"No secrets there. Bob Nechestny's turning into the *éminence grise* of his generation. Think those Indonesians had access? Bob walks into the White House whenever he wants. Or into any office on the Hill. That is one CEO who really brings home the bacon for the shareholders. For which he is recompensed. And, not coincidentally, Macon-Bolt happens to be the biggest campaign contributor in this country. Hard money, soft money. Bob Nechestny could fix anything short of a Supreme Court decision—and I'm not at all sure he couldn't do that, if he really wanted to." Rob smiled. "So . . . you and the rest of the United States Army just pissed about that airplane deal? Or is this personal?''

"Maybe both.''

He shook his head. "Well, my advice is to accept the inevitable. You can't beat Bob Nechestny and Macon-Bolt. No point in even trying.''

"The NGFB is going to gut the Army budget.''

Rob laughed. "And everybody else's budget, too. Somebody whispered in my ear that even the Air Force brass are having second thoughts. Allowing for cost overruns, they're looking at an Air Force that'll consist of that airplane and not much else a decade from now.''

"Think they'll do anything about it? Is there—''

"Not in your lifetime. Come on, John. You know how it works. The generals and admirals support Nechestny, and when they retire, Macon-Bolt hires them. Biggest scam in the country.'' He glanced at his watch. "John, it really is good to see you. But I have *got* to go. Breaking bread with a few senators from the other camp tonight. I think we're going to get a tax cut this year after all.''

I stood up. "Thanks.'' I think I felt even worse than I looked.

"Pull the outer door shut behind you, would you?'' Rob said. "Problem with street people crapping in the foyer. And, John? Do yourself a favor. Don't fool around with Macon-Bolt. It's a losing proposition.''

"See you at Em's funeral?''

He made a "yes'' face. "I'll probably fly up. The

mother really is a sweetie. But, John . . . you're going to be surprised how few people show. If you go. It'll be an education for you. This is a hard town."

Outside the building, a man with a storm of dirty hair sat under a blanket, singing hymns and cursing. The rain had faded to swamp air. I guess thinking slowed me down, because Rob caught up to me in less than a block.

"Forgot to ask you," he said, falling into formation at my side. "Who's going to replace Farnsworth on the Futures panel?"

"No idea."

"Well, give me a ring if you hear anything, all right? You're my inside line. And, John . . . the views I expressed upstairs? Just between us, right?"

I stopped and faced him.

"No disrespect," he said. "It's just that . . . I was being extremely frank. Damn it, John, there's just something about you that makes you seem trustworthy. But in this town . . ."

"It's my lack of imagination," I told him. "Don't worry about it."

He stood there looking at me. "Of course not. I'm sorry," he said. "But let me give you some advice. From one friend to another." He expressed everything with the lower half of his face, nothing with his eyes. He, too, would be a cabinet member one day. "Don't trust anybody."

▲
CHAPTER 3
▼

I STILL DID NOT TRUST MYSELF TO GO HOME AND DEAL
with Tish. I got a takeout burger and ate in the PX
parking lot at Fort Myer. The rain came in the passenger's window, but I did not bother to close it.

I had two problems: Tish, and then all the other
business. Farnsworth and Em. I thought about Tish
first. And last. And in between. I knew I should hand
her walking papers. But I was not sure I could give
her up.

I had a problem with trust. A problem the size of
Texas. Maybe it comes with my line of work. Betrayal is humanity's number two pastime, and I had
spent a couple of decades watching foreign murderers
dressed in ragtag uniforms go at it. I could think of
plenty of reasons why Tish would not have wanted
to tell me about the cop business in her past. No
matter what the real story might be. But she should
have told me. My work depended on my security

clearance. She knew the rules. Not even a joint allowed in my house. A cocaine bust rated a mention.

If she had been quiet about her police record, there were plenty of other things she might have kept to herself. I did not want to think about those things. But I did.

Through it all, I could not stop thinking about making love to her. And being with her. The rain struck and steamed.

I forced myself to focus on Farnsworth and Em. And Em's airplane. These days, conspiracy theories were everywhere. In the streets, the press, the water supply. You started out wondering if the mechanics at the garage were cheating you and ended up convinced that JFK had been murdered by Elvis.

Yet, in my career, I had not seen one scrap of evidence of a conspiracy. Not in our government. Not anywhere around it. Unless it was a conspiracy of mediocrity. And I could not imagine why anyone tied in with Macon-Bolt Industries would need to conspire. The NGFB was as good as sold. Initial funding had already been approved and the big money would start with the next defense budget. Nothing was going to change it, and cloak-and-dagger nonsense could only hurt.

There had been some bad coincidences. But, in the Army, you saw those all the time. Fate waited until you were down to kick you hard. Maybe there was some big death-dealing conspiracy out there. With Buck Rogers aircraft and hundreds of billions of dol-

lars in the kitty. Or maybe my buddies had hit a run
of bad luck.

The truth was that Em's death still was not real to
me. Maybe Farnsworth's death wasn't real to me,
either. Maybe I was just going through the motions.
The old bugger on that apartment floor had been
cardboard.

All my thoughts led back to Tish. She was real.
And I hated it.

I waited until I knew she had left for her gig, then
went home. The place was drenched with her. The
droopy curtains, the smell of the kitchen. Every
shadow. A decomposing copy of *Far from the Mad-
ding Crowd* ambushed me by the phone. Walking in
that door was like getting punched.

There was a message on the answering machine
from Corry Nevers. I erased it and went upstairs. The
Les Paul lay centered on the bed in its little coffin
of a case. With a note:

"Please take it back for a refund. I don't deserve
it. Tish."

I didn't know what anybody deserved anymore.

I was not ready to have a rational discussion with
Tish, but I had to see her. Her band was playing a
gay club off Dupont Circle. Straights were allowed
in if they paid a cover.

The military was in the middle of a witch hunt
about sex. No court-martial panel would believe an
officer went to a gay bar unless he was looking for
a blow job, so I went upstairs, where it was dark and

I could see the stage without being seen. The balcony action was grim. A kid who looked like Audrey Hepburn with facial hair asked if he could sit down, but he went away when I shook my head.

Tish never got it quite right. She had a little talent. She was good in repose, on the quiet numbers. She was meant to be a cabaret singer. But she wanted to flail and wail. She played her scarred guitar as if choking an enemy. Red hair whipped and clung to her cheeks, and her sweat flew like breaking glass. She had her leather pants on, despite the heat, and she looked like trouble. Unless you looked hard. Then she looked afraid. To me, she looked beautiful. I felt sick down in my guts watching her. Wondering what she was really all about. And if it was over.

I was afraid I could not trust her to tell me the price of a quart of milk. I had been around enough to know that such feelings can pass. Faith comes back. Mouthful of kisses, and people sucker themselves. I was not sure I wanted that. I was afraid of her in a way I had never feared fists or guns.

I left as the set ended. I did not want to meet her in the club, did not want anybody in the band to spot me and report to her. I walked the streets for a while. With Connecticut Avenue full of people who had been unpopular in high school and who had found one another in the city. Drivers hunting parking spots clogged the back streets. Lamps lit townhouse windows. Back on the circle, a heavy girl sobbed in front of an espresso bar.

I went home. There was a message from my boss,

asking if I was okay. I left a return message at his work number: all quiet on the western front. CNN told me we had just renewed China's most-favored-nation status, and a White House spokesman told the country that a big-haired woman was lying about the President. The spokesman did his job wonderfully, without actually using the word "lying." Somebody from another planet might have believed him.

I moved the Les Paul off the bed and trashed the note from Tish. I lay down in my clothes. Just for a minute. And conked out.

Tish woke me with her body. We didn't talk. We made love as if we wanted to hurt each other. Then we held one another with arms like shackles. I smelled her hair and wished the world were a different place.

I woke up again in darkness. Sensing something wrong. Tish was not in the bed. I listened, and I heard her.

She was sitting on the edge of the bathtub, crying. The raw way children cry. A night-light lit her like a candle. She knew I was standing there, but she did not look at me. She covered her face with her hands. She was naked and shivering in the heat. Finally, she said:

"I just want to die. I love you so much. I just want to die."

"It's all right," I said. On time delay. Lying.

She shook her head and wept. "It's never going to be all right. I've ruined everything. You'll never believe me. I wreck every fucking thing I touch."

I put my hand on her shoulder and she quivered. As if I had hit her. Then she jumped up and clung to me.

"Oh, God, I love you," she said. "You're the best thing that ever happened to me. Please don't make me go."

"Tish . . ."

"I love you so much." The words broke up. A bad radio transmission.

"I love you, too," I said. I hope I meant it. I think I meant it. In that moment.

She cried on. "You don't understand. I love you all the way. I love you like everything there is in love. All of it. I love you. I want to have babies and everything."

I tried to pick her up. But somehow I wasn't strong enough. Underfed Tish. She weighed more than a continent now.

"And I can't," she said. "I'll never have babies. I've done stupid things. Stupid, stupid things. I'm so fucking stupid. Oh, God. Forgive me. Please. Forgive me."

In the books we read now, people do not ask forgiveness. Everything is permitted except that. If the actions of another wound us, it is we who are inadequate. Freedom is all. Maybe it would be better if life really were like those books, if I had not felt what I had felt toward Tish. Sitting in my car in the rain, I had imagined a scene like this. Wanting it.

I could not find any more words for her. There

was so much fear in me, and it was all twisted up with love and desire.

Tish clutched me until I gathered the strength to pick her up and carry her to bed. I turned my back and she laced me in her arms.

In the morning, Corry Nevers called while Tish was in the shower. She asked me if we could get together to talk. I told her I wished her luck, but did not see what we had in common to talk about.

"I'm afraid," she said.

"Don't be."

She began to sob. "It's horrible."

"You'll get through it."

"You don't understand. It's something else. They won't let me go to the funeral . . ."

"What?"

"Em's parents. They closed the funeral. 'Only immediate family.' Nobody else can attend. I called and asked. They won't let me come. His mother never liked me."

I had regarded the funeral as an unwelcome duty and I was ashamed at the way Corry's news made me feel. Pathetic, the things that relieve us. Getting off the hook is one of the basic human pleasures. I sucked a few more details out of her and eased her off the phone by promising she could call me if she ran into real trouble.

Tish came out damp and smiling. We did not talk, but treated each other with exaggerated consideration.

I was not going back to work. I had the leave days
to burn. And the sun was out again.

Tish and I walked over to Eastern Market for
breakfast, then headed down to the Mall in the morning's last coolness. It was our private holiday. Hill
staffers hurried past us in suits that stood off from
their shirt collars. The women marched in solid colors and running shoes. We held hands.

I had decided that my fantasy about some great
conspiracy involving Em and Farnsworth and Macon-
Bolt was just that. I was not going to make any calls
or poke any more anthills. Let the dead sleep in their
graves. Maybe Tish and I wouldn't last forever. But
we were going to make the most of the time we had.
To hell with the rest of the universe. Below the Capitol, charter buses bled tourists in souvenir T-shirts.
The tourists managed to be noisy and reverent at the
same time. Most of them were overweight.

"I want an ice cream," Tish said.

"You just had breakfast." But I got her a Dove
Bar. Walking along in her cutoffs, she had a grace
that she never managed onstage. Runway legs. The
freckles she hated were coming out under her eyes.

"I want you to keep the guitar," I said.

She didn't answer.

"It's a separate thing," I told her. "I want you to
have it."

She stopped and kissed me. Wet. In front of two
Japanese tourists.

It was a good day. We walked to all the monuments and did not see anybody we knew. We grazed

through a new exhibition at the Freer and ate poisonous hot dogs from a vendor. We went home in the heat and drank beer and made love.

Tish had a rehearsal scheduled for late afternoon, and she had to go. She took another shower. And threw herself back down on the bed beside me.

"I feel like such a shit," she said.

"You are a shit."

"No. I mean . . . it's something else."

My insides tightened.

"My car still isn't fixed. Can I please just borrow your car one more time? I'll get mine to the garage tomorrow morning. I promise."

"Take it," I said. "I'm not going anywhere. I figure I'll just stroll over to the market, buy some salmon steaks, and make dinner for anybody who's interested."

Tish rolled over and made noises to which I would have responded differently with another half hour's recuperation.

"I love you for your cooking," she said. "I'll be home early."

"Drive carefully, huh?"

I watched her dress, afraid I could never give her up. She asked where I had parked the car and I told her down the block. I listened to her leaving and tried as hard as I could to postpone thought. I ached to build a fortress for two. Where nothing or nobody would ever be able to touch us.

When the car blew up, the windows shook but did not shatter.

* * *

"Give me a break, huh?" Lieutenant Dickey said. "I don't buy the crybaby shit, soldier boy."

Explosives have their eccentricities. The blast had blown my car into the middle of the street, tossing the doors into nearby yards. Yet when I got to it, the black mummy that had been Tish was still visible in the flames. Seat belts work.

The cops had been chewing on me for a long time. I don't know how long exactly, but it was already dark beyond the windows of the police station. Dickey was the only one who had not given up.

"Come on," he said. "Make it easy on everybody. You tell the truth, you might not even do any time. You can go to court in your soldier suit with all your medals and tell everybody how sorry you are. Now tell me the truth. It's all a drug thing. Right? You and your little redheaded coke freak. You been moving dope. Wholesaling it to the dumb brothers out in the hood. Right?" He made a "Gotcha" face. "So what is it? You didn't pay the man on time? Or we got a turf battle on our hands? Maybe we got a whole bunch of soldier boys in on this? Setting up their retirement jobs. Showing the gangstas how to run a real operation. Military precision and all that crap. *Plan*ning. Mind if I smoke, soldier boy?" He lit a cigarette with a plastic lighter. "You give me the names, dates. I'll do everything I can for you."

I looked at him. There was no rage in me, and no fear. Just emptiness.

Dickey filled the little room with smoke. "Come

on, pal. Let's make a deal, huh? Or do we want a lawyer after all?''

"I don't need a lawyer," I said. "I haven't done anything wrong."

The detective got up and patrolled the dirty linoleum. It might have been an interrogation room in Syria instead of Washington. Everything was crude and half broken. I heard voices of disorder beyond the closed door.

"Listen up, hero. I don't know what kind of game you think you're playing. But you're tied to three murders now."

"Four," I said.

He looked at me. Mouth open like an asthmatic flounder.

"Last weekend," I said. "A general named Farnsworth was hit by a car. Over in Virginia."

"I don't do Virginia," the detective said. "Talk to me about the District."

"Everybody thought it was an accident. I think it was murder."

"Just get back to the business we got in front of us."

"I'm not sure what the tie-in is," I said. "But I—" Suddenly, I did not want to tell this man anything. He wasn't the Law. Just a bully dying of cholesterol. "Charge me, or release me," I said. "Isn't that how it goes?"

He snorted. "What? You been watching cop shows or something?" He spread his arms and planted his fists on the table. Leaning toward me.

"You better step out of your dream world and start thinking hard. That was your car that went up. Now . . . maybe whoever did the wiring job had some inside information that your girlfriend was going to take it for a drive, but two and two says they were after you, soldier boy. If you're not nice to me, I just might release you. And it's starting to look like a cold, cruel world out there. What are you going to do if I boot your ass out of here? Where you going to go?" He smiled. But I was miles ahead of him. "I figure whoever did the car job isn't done. The good news is that they are in a position to save the government the cost of your trial and subsequent incarceration. Now . . . who tried to blow you up? Tell me about the drugs. Start at the beginning."

"No drugs."

"Then *what*?"

"I don't know."

"Who did it?"

"I don't know."

He folded his arms and stood above me. Every time I was ready to shoot back, Tish came to haunt me. I saw her now. Split screen. Tish beside me, red hair on the white pillow. And the black thing in the flames.

My eyes let me down again.

"What?" the detective said. "I'm supposed to pity your ass or something? Did we lose our lover girl? The great love of our life?" He tossed his cigarette butt on the floor. "Give me a fucking break. Hey . . .

maybe you'd like me to call you a public defender. Then you'll do time for sure.''

"Charge me. Or release me.''

He leaned over the table again. "Pal. Buddy. Soldier boy. You don't seem to get it. Serious crime, serious time. I could toss you in the can for seventy-two hours just for your attitude. Hey, but maybe you'd like that? What's that fairy-tale bar you said you went to?'' He made a disgusted face. "You like your bread buttered on both sides, maybe? What's the goddamned Army coming to, huh? 'Don't ask, don't tell,' right?''

I looked up at him. "You're wrong about everything,'' I said calmly. "You couldn't be more wrong. If I knew who set the bomb, I would have told you the minute I saw you.''

"Because you love me personally? Or because you love cops in general?''

"Because I loved Tish O'Malley.''

He laughed. "Nobody loved Tish O'Malley. Her own family didn't love her. Or maybe her stepfather loved her a little too much, if you can believe the sheriff out there. She was a hard case, buddy. White trash with stars in her eyes. And coke up her nose. Hey, you know what's good? Know what she studied out at Cornhole Community College? Pharmacy. Ain't that something? A girl with a plan. Maybe franchise her own chain of meth labs.''

"I didn't know she'd been to college.'' I was instantly sorry I had said it.

"It wasn't a lasting relationship. Your sweetheart

didn't have lasting relationships. Hey, you two didn't talk much, did you? What else you want to know about her?''

"I know all I want to know," I lied.

His smile knotted. "I got another idea. Maybe she double-crossed you. Yeah. Wouldn't that be just like her? Her and her retro-scene smack-pack friends. She double-crossed you on the dope, and you found out. And you took her out.'' He brought his face down close to mine. It was not a pleasant view. "So what happens now? You planning to move in with that little blondie? What's her name? Caddy Mercedes?'' He backed away. "Well, let me give you some advice. Man to man. It won't last. She's going to marry one of those rich fucks from Great Falls. You're the kind of food she leaves on the plate.''

"Think you'll ever get around to working on the murder of Tish O'Malley?'' I asked.

He pinched my cheek as if I were a baby. "Gotta love those soldier boys. They're cool customers. I guess you kind of sense that I don't like you. And you're wondering why. Well, let me tell you. I don't like you smart-ass fucks who come into this city and shit all over it and then go crying that the jigaboos can't govern themselves. You think you're above the law.'' He reached for another cigarette and lit it with the rhythm of old habit. "This city doesn't have a fucking chance. And I love this city, you know that? I was born and raised here. And I hate people like you who come around fucking with it.''

"You're still wrong."

"Oh, yeah? About what this time?"

"Everything. You've got a perfect score."

He drank smoke and said, "That so? Well, you're either an innocent man and so naive it hurts me to think about it. Or you are one vicious shit who deserves an Academy Award. Either way, you're a fucking loser." He smoked and stared through me. Then he said, "Know what? I'm going to turn your ass loose. Because I want to see what happens out there."

I made it two blocks from the police station, then sat down on the stoop of an old house that had been turned into offices. And I cried.

After a while, I sensed somebody standing in front of me. Layers of clothing, despite the heat, and a Santa Claus sack over his shoulder. A knitted cap over cascades of hair. His beard made his head enormous. With the darkness and filth, I could not tell his race.

"She leave you, man? She make you go? Women so hard sometimes."

I didn't have any money, so he moved on. I walked. A police cruiser slowed beside me. I thought they had come to take me in again. But it was only that after-midnight curiosity.

Trying to think about Tish was like staring at the sun. I could only think around her. And I kept thinking about that goddamned guitar. She had taken her Telecaster to the rehearsal that never happened, and the left-behind Les Paul had become a sort of orphan in my very unclear mind.

Quirky Tish. I had given her a James Salter novel I reread every couple of years. Yapping at her about how it captured the complexity of the human heart and the interplay of male-female relationships. She read half of it. Then she gave it back. Telling me, "I don't want to read about how people *are*, John. I *know* how people are."

I really did love her now. Now that it was safe.

I wanted to know who killed her. While trying to kill me. I wanted to know who it was and I wanted them to suffer tortures I had not yet invented.

You could read Tish two ways. As a hustler with a little talent for music and a lot of talent for sex. Or as somebody who had played her best game with a bad hand. When she played music, for better or worse, Tish gave it all she could. And I was determined to believe that she had given me all she could in the love department. The positive spin, in Washington talk. The detective had done that for me.

If Farnsworth's death or Em's had been unreal to me, then the loss of Tish was unimaginable. I could not believe I would never feel her beside me again.

A block short of my house, a car nosed in beside me. A white guy leaned out to ask directions. Born slow, I bent to help. And darkness got me.

CHAPTER 4

TOUGH GUYS, WITH THAT LEANNESS YOU SEE IN OFFI-cers from the *paras*. They weren't big. But they were hard. The kid didn't speak English worth a damn, but the fortyish guy spoke it without the least sign of brain-strain. I had not paid attention in high school, so when the boys talked frog, the only words I could make out were *merde* and *mort*.

The kid had bar fighter's hands. Jerry Lewis with Gold's Gym biceps. His inability to ask questions directly pissed him off. The older one had the narrow face and close graying hair of the men who lose their wives to bad-asses in French films. But this character was a bad-ass himself. Reptile in a polo shirt. He bent down toward the chair and knuckle-punched me in the stomach again.

"Why kill them?" he asked again. "You made fools of us. Wasn't that enough? Why did you have to kill them?"

I gasped for air. As soon as I could stitch words together, I said, "Why'd you kill Tish? Fuck you." Hoping I sounded angry and not too afraid.

We had been through the Q&A before. Twice.

Cuckold backed off, disgusted. More French. The only word I understood was *amateur*.

Cuckold folded his arms and looked down at me. In the bare white room. The only furniture was the heavy wooden chair in which I sat strapped. The chair was a specialty number. And there was a big aluminum suitcase. Sometimes Jerry sat on it and stared at me while he smoked a cigarette. The French smoke all the time because it's their last competitive skill.

"My partner," Cuckold said, "does not believe you are very receptive to education."

I tried to shrug, but the leather straps held me tight. The chair had a wooden seat and two big slats up the back. It was not ergonomically correct.

More French. *Merde* again. Existentialism making a comeback. Cuckold said, "My partner is convinced your American educational system is made of shit. Have you studied logic? Or dialectics? Is the university so inadequate? Or is my assessment correct? Do you think we are so stupid you can lie to us?"

For punctuation, he nailed me in the stomach again. He was very good. I felt it right up against my spine.

By punching me in the gut over and over again, they had given away one important thing. They did not want to mark me. I figured that meant they were not going to kill me, either. I was still looking at the world as a black or white, either-or proposition.

Cuckold walked away and sat down on the floor with his back against the wall. The guy had watched a lot of Belmondo in his formative years.

Back on the street, they had not given me time to throw a single punch. I woke up in a car trunk with a hood over my head. I did not have a clue where I was when they yanked me out and walked me over gravel. Then I banged against a doorway and bounced along a corridor. They slammed me down in the guest chair. A door shut. Straps went on and the hood came off.

Jerry tossed Cuckold a cigarette. Followed by his lighter.

"Let's review. First of all, your lover. Our regrets. We had nothing to do with this . . . event. We had no interest in her. Allow me to say that she looked like an amiable woman." He smoked and his eyes narrowed in his narrow face. "Whether you *are* stupid or just playing the fool, you must see that whoever set the car bomb was after *you*. Not Mademoiselle O'Malley." He made a gesture with his fingers. As though rubbing snot away from the tips. "You must see that your own people have decided to kill you. You know too much. Fortunately, you are also disposable. Like your whole fucking culture."

I almost told him one more time that I had no idea what he was rambling on about, but it seemed pointless. The French had been jerking off like this for most of the twentieth century. Reality did not impress them.

"So what do we have?" Cuckold went on. "We have an American lieutenant colonel condemned to death. For doing his country's dirty work." He flipped his butt and it bounced off the tip of my shoe. "John Reynolds, you are being a fool. We are your only friends. No. Allow me to say it with more honesty. We *could* be your friends, if you helped us. You would have the gratitude of the government of France—which still counts for something, you know. And you would be performing an act of justice." He rolled into a crouch. Balancing on the balls of his feet. "What are you going to do? You know they're going to kill you."

"I don't even know who 'they' are, for God's sake." I had developed a wheezing speech pattern. As if my stomach had crowded up into my lungs to hide. "You've got this all wrong."

My hosts spoke French again. The younger one got angry. Whole lot of *non*. One thing that did not track was the relationship between authority and age. Jerry was still at the body-piercing age. But he was perfectly willing to give Cuckold a hard time. Different organizations, I figured.

Cuckold turned back to me. "Okay. We will simplify things. 'Lay the cards on the table,' as your people like to say. Of course we spy on you. And you spy on us. Everybody spies on everybody. But there are rules. Sometimes we fuck with you. Just like you fuck with us. But no French agent has killed an American agent. Or even an American citizen, I don't think.'' He made a pout and waved his hands. ''Maybe we've had little problems in Africa, maybe sometimes things got out of hand down there. But that comes from dealing with the *noires*, right? You Americans should understand that, I think.'' He held out an upturned palm and bounced an invisible ball. ''But here? No. In France? No. Everybody understands the rules.''

He strode over to me and broke one of his own rules. He cupped my chin in his hand, pressing his fingers and thumb into my cheeks. It was the first time either of them had touched my head since I got thumped cold on the street. Unless you count lifting the sack off my head upon arrival at Club Med. He brought his face close to mine, a human hatchet, and his eyes managed to be angry and dead at the same time. He stank of smoke. ''You bastards broke the rules. And I want you to tell me why.'' He let me go and stepped away, a boxer between rounds.

Jerry said something brief and sharp, but this time Cuckold ignored him. He came to me again. Smoke close. Hate close.

''Wasn't it enough? That you have made fools of us, 'the stupid French'? Why blow up the laboratory? Are you that fucking insecure? Or that vicious?'' His face shook in front of me. ''You *won*. And you still had to kill everybody . . .''

I'm slow. If there was a mental PT test, I'd wind up in remedial training. I still did not realize all that he was telling me. Of course, he didn't realize it, either. All that would come later.

Jerry stood up and pissed against the far wall. It offended Cuckold. He probably figured it matched the American stereotype of the French male a bit too well.

"There was no justification for killing all those people," Cuckold went on. Backing off. His voice had quieted. "None. You had your laugh. You cost us plenty." He nodded toward Jerry. "Now . . . my partner and his people believe you set the whole thing up, that you fed us the plans with the end already in mind. Knowing we'd still have to gather the best technicians in France to work the thing out. So you could kill them in one neat strike." Single-syllable laugh. "And blame it on the Algerians." He looked down into darkness, ready to drag me in after him. "I shouldn't tell you this. It's a breach of discipline. But I think you need to develop a . . . a perspective on your situation. My partner's wife, she was in that building." He looked down at me. "So far, they have identified one of her feet."

None of this made sense to me. But I did realize that, for the first time, I really did know too much. Thanks to Cuckold himself.

"Personally, I *still* don't think American intelligence is that good," he continued. "I respect your industry. And your technical intelligence means, of course. But your agents are children." His chin dimpled as he judged me again. "I think my colleagues are wrong. I do not believe you planned all this to wipe out our top people. I think it started out as something of a schoolboy prank. But then you saw an opportunity. And you moved.'' He put his hands on his hips. It made him look thinner, smaller. ''Colonel Reynolds—John—I believe you know exactly who placed that bomb. You know the Americans who did it. And you know the filthy fucking collaborators in France. You know who, and how, and why. Hey—wake up.''

He delivered the hardest punch yet.

''Oh, God,'' I said. Although I'm not sure my speech was clear enough for even God to understand.

''Come on, fuckface,'' Cuckold said. ''Talk to me.''

My muscles quivered. All the way up to my neck.

''*Listen*,'' I said. ''*Please*. Just . . . listen for a minute. I swear to God I don't know what this is all about. I don't know anything about bombs, or plans, or anybody laughing. All I know . . . is that three people I knew are dead. And one stranger. Maybe two of them knew something about an airplane. One did for sure. But *I* had nothing to do with this. Tish had nothing to do with this. I don't know anything about the laboratory bombing. Just what was on the news. You've got the wrong person.''

He surprised me. The control vanished. He went into a fury and punched me so hard he lost his aim and started working on my ribs. He nearly knocked the chair over. Jerry had to come over and pull him away.

My eyes opened in flickers and tears broke down

my cheeks. Nothing to do about it. I hurt. I would have killed them both if I could have.

Jerry had his arms around Cuckold, who was sobbing. Unreal. I tasted acid and blood at the back of my throat.

Finally, Jerry came over to me. Shift change, I figured. But he just put his hands on my shoulders and stared at me.

"I understand . . . how he say to you. He tell you . . ." He spoke slowly, with the words coming painfully. "He tell you my wife, she is . . . she *morte, non*?" He gave me a Charles-Manson-goes-to-Paris smile and tapped his forehead. "A lie. Not my wife. *Non*. The wife from him. *Très jeune, très belle. Comprenez*? Maybe he kills you."

Cuckold would not turn and look at me. I wondered if he had killed Tish. In miscalculated personal revenge.

Jerry sauntered back to the suitcase. Instead of sitting down on it, he undid the latches. Inside, small mechanical devices lay embedded in gray foam. He lifted out a device that looked like a power drill with a suction cup on the end, then fitted it against an object the size of a pack of cigarettes. Satisfied, he separated the items again and brought the drill toward me.

He snapped out something in French and Cuckold looked back over his shoulder. Face ravaged. "Last chance," Cuckold said. "Tell us what you know."

I was afraid now. I had been afraid all night, but that had been only a little fear compared to this. I

did not like the look of the tool in Jerry's paw. The
new fear came big and pulsing.

"Honest to Christ, I don't know what's going on.
You know more than I do."

Cuckold stood in profile, slender, showing me his
cleaver of a face. Sweating tears. "My colleague's
machine leaves no marks. It's very good. But it was
not designed by the best people. They were not like
the people you killed. So sometimes there is nerve
damage. Maybe you will be lucky."

Jerry moved behind the chair and I found out why
the slats parted in the middle. He pressed the device
against my spine.

The world exploded. I've been hurt a good bit—
sports injuries, Army mistakes—but I had never en-
countered pain like this. I had never even imagined
that such pain could exist. Time stopped. I could not
see. I flipped like a fish in the chair and screamed.
Maybe seconds, maybe minutes later, I realized that
the device was not touching me anymore. And the
big pain was gone. But the shock was like the worst
hangover on earth.

"Please . . ." I said. "Please . . ."

Just to underscore the point, Jerry dosed me again.
This time, the whole world screamed. My muscles
raged against the straps. I would have given anything
in the world to make that pain stop, done anything.

When my vision came back, Cuckold was squatting in front of me.

"Talk," he said.

I tried to talk and gagged. It took me a long time

to form thoughts, words. "Em . . . Emerson Carroll knew something. I don't know what. He asked me about the bombing, if I'd seen any reports." I gulped air. "Nothing. I didn't see anything. Hear anything. Locker-room gossip. Everybody thought the Algerians . . ."

"Shithead," Cuckold said. Jerry taught me about pain again. I do not know for certain what my body did. Maybe I only thought I was fighting the straps. Maybe I held perfectly still. I don't know. There was only the pain and it was endless.

Years later, Cuckold asked me, "Are you ready to talk now?"

"Farnsworth. Major General Farnsworth. Futures guy. Some connection to Em. To Emerson Carroll. Old friends. All knew each other. But they didn't include me. Em was troubled, upset. I don't know." Suddenly, I found the strength to shout. *"I don't know, I don't know, I don't know . . ."*

They gave me the pain again. For years and years and years. Nothing I could do would make it stop.

"Tish," I cried.

I remember that. Because the pain had already stopped, but my body had not realized it. There was just enough unfried brain left to listen to myself.

"Don't be a hero," Cuckold said. "Talk."

Only the leather straps held me together now. I did not know anything else. I could not even make up lies. I could only gasp, far short of speech.

The machine touched me again. For an eternity of

pain. I believed I was dying. Because I could not imagine such pain without death at the end of it.

I blacked out. I think it was only for a matter of seconds, but I'll never know for sure. When I opened my eyes again, Cuckold was examining me up close. He looked bewildered.

"Shit," he said when he saw the life in my eyes, "you really don't know."

"You can get up." Cuckold's voice. He reached back over the seat of the car and helped me right myself. Then he pulled off the hood. During the pain game, I had soiled myself. Dignity was a memory. They had to be tough just to stay in the car with me.

Heading up 395. Sparse traffic. Predawn. Ahead, lights outlined the roofs of the high-rises on Skyline. I knew exactly where I was. But it was unreal, too.

"Listen to me," Cuckold said. "Try to understand. The people who blew up our laboratory. These are the same people who killed your lover. Who tried to kill you. They killed your friends." His face shone in the highway light. "No matter what you think . . . no matter what you want . . . we are on the same side now."

He was asking for too much brainpower. I did not think my nervous system would ever work again.

"They will try to kill you. They will not give up. Perhaps we can help you, I don't know. Frankly, you are not so important now. But I would help you if I could. If I can. All this killing . . ." He turned away and looked at the highway. ". . . this is madness."

"Will I be all right?"

He looked at me quizzically.

"The thing you used. Is it permanent? The . . . way I feel?"

He shrugged. "I think you will be okay. Probably. Sleep it off."

"It doesn't . . . I can't make sense . . ."

"Sleep. Think about it tomorrow. If you are still alive."

As we crossed into the District, he gave me a spiel about working together. For some vague common good. He promised he would be in touch, but did not offer me any means to contact him. He apologized for what they had done to me, sounding almost sincere.

"We have to drop you here," he said. Jerry had pulled in along a sidewalk in Indian country. But it was quiet now. Even dopers go to sleep eventually. "We cannot take the chance. They may be waiting for you. And, by the way . . . do not attempt to run to your counterintelligence people. You have no marks on your body. No traces. There is no evidence for what you would say. And they will only kill you for your knowledge." He leaned farther back over the seat. "And we would not be friends anymore. We are the only friends you have left, John."

It was all a dream. I was just floating through it. Remembering the pain. Tish, all the rest, had disappeared. Numb, dumb me.

"Get out," Cuckold said. "You need help?"

I got myself out. Most of the way. Then he

grabbed my wrist, holding me partway inside the car.
I saw the lower half of his face as the lips moved.

"Bonne chance."

Yellow tape crisscrossed the front yard. "Police
Line—Do Not Cross." It had sagged toward the
ground and I stepped over it. Lifting my leg hurt.
Then I turned again and reached down. Bending hurt.
I ripped the tape free and balled it up. I figured
Dickey had left it there just to screw with me.

At least the cops had locked up after themselves.
I let myself in. You could feel the dawn coming up.
The day was getting off to a good start. With sirens
in the distance.

I ached to sleep.

The cops had trashed the place. Looking for evidence. Or maybe Dickey was just making a point. I
took a plastic garbage bag up to the bathroom,
stripped, and put my clothes in it. Then I got under
the shower. I could not straighten my back. I
crouched there until the water turned cold. I had not
begun to soap myself. I hate cold water, but I could
not move. Finally, I cleaned myself. Shaking. After
I dried off, I pissed blood. That gets your attention.
I stumbled toward the bed.

Odd, how the brain works. When it works. Despite
the bad-party wreckage of the bedroom, I realized
something was missing.

Someone had ripped off the Les Paul I bought
Tish.

D.C. cops.

I curled up like an infant and smelled Tish on the sheets.

It was full daylight when the banging on the front door woke me. Obviously, the doorbell had not been man enough to do the job. The banging kept up, real *Don Giovanni* stuff. Body aching, I clumsied around the floor until I found a pair of jeans the cops had flipped out of the closet. A coffin of heavy air moved with me.

I blundered downstairs, shirtless and barefoot. Stiff, fragile, and beat. I had to hunt through the kitchen until I found the key where I had left it on a shelf.

My visitor pounded away.

I also picked up the largest knife I could find.

I did not believe anybody was going to try to kill me like this. Not by daylight. Banging on my front door. But a reasonable amount of caution seemed to be in order.

When I looked through the peephole, I saw Corry Nevers.

She was about to hammer the door again when I opened it. Stronger than she appeared. Health-club type.

After looking me up and down, she cat-smiled and said, ''Aren't you ever dressed?'' Then she pointed that little marble nose toward the knife in my hand. ''I'm not *that* dangerous.''

''What do you want?''

''Don't be hard.'' A parting of the lips, a widening

of the smile. Enough to make brokers and bankers swoon. "Please."

I am not a rude man by nature. But when your girlfriend has just been killed and it looks like somebody is out to kill you, when you've just been tortured, you're pissing blood, and the cops recently held a frat party in your home, your social skills deteriorate.

"What time is it?" I said. I felt like I had slept about fifteen minutes.

She glanced at her watch. Cartier tank job. "Quarter after twelve. Did I wake you or something?"

"Late night."

"The police?"

That got my attention.

"It was in the *Post*," she said. "About your girlfriend. I just wanted to say I'm sorry. She seemed . . . nice."

"She wasn't nice. She was glorious. But not nice."

She stood there in the heat. Perspiration by Tiffany's.

"That's a lovely thing to say about a woman. 'Glorious.' " Her smile withered. "I don't think anybody would say anything that nice about me. If I died."

I let her come in. Mr. Wisdom. She barely got inside the door when the trashing registered.

"Courtesy of the D.C. Police Department," I told her. "They're convinced I'm some kind of narco."

Uncertainty in that silver voice now. "Can they . . . are they allowed to do that?"

"This isn't Chevy Chase, sweetheart. Now, what do you want?"

I had misjudged her. The way I had misjudged everything else in my short-term memory account.

She began to cry. "I'm *alone*. Can't you understand? I'm scared. I don't know what to do. I tried to go back to work. I thought it would help. But I'm a basket case. I keep thinking . . ." She hid her eyes with her hand. A fly that had followed her inside circled her blond hair. She waved it away and I saw smears under her lashes. "What do *you* want? All I wanted was to talk to somebody." Sobbing now. "I read the paper. I read about your girl . . . about your car . . . I thought we were the same now."

Even crying, she looked like an ad in a five-buck fashion mag. Misery chic. I stood there in my jeans, dumb-handed, with my guts hurting so bad I just wanted to go back to bed and curl up.

I almost touched her. The comfort thing. But something stopped me. I had an inexplicable sense that she and Tish were enemies, that betrayal followed Corry Nevers like a shadow.

When I thought of Tish, I remembered something else. I had not done one of the fundamental things a human being in my position was obliged to do.

"Go in the kitchen. Find a chair. Sit down. Wait for me."

I did not exactly bound up the stairs, which gave me plenty of time to wonder whether the cops had taken Tish's papers. What few she had. I needed her address book. An item the investigators certainly should have taken, if they really believed Tish was involved in criminal activity.

The police had ripped through Tish's things. Guitar picks prickled underfoot. Dickens lay on top of Charlotte Brontë. But the cops seemed to have been interested mostly in her underpants, which covered the floor like little signal flags.

They had grabbed her guitar, but they had not bothered about the address book. It was a ragged little thing. I had always resisted the urge to page through it. Now I had an excuse.

I knew her mother's current name was Bennet and that she had moved to Michigan. Tish had not volunteered anything more, and I had not asked. You did not have to know her long to realize she had not left a lot behind when she got on the bus out of town.

I dialed the number. Hoping nobody would answer. Hoping her mother would be at work in the middle of the day. I knew I had to do this, but I did not want to.

Someone picked up on the fourth ring.

"Yeah?" TV in the background.

"Mrs. Bennet?"

"Yeah."

"Ma'am, are you the mother of Patricia O'Malley?"

"You a cop or something? That little tramp in trouble again?"

"No, ma'am. I'm . . . Tish and I were . . ."

"You one of her boyfriends? Listen, buddy, I don't know where she is. I got no idea. She don't tell me."

I could smell alcohol through the phone line.

"Hey, you," her mother went on. "When you catch up with her. You tell her something for me, all right? You tell her she's an ungrateful little bitch, all right? Tell her just what I said. Hundred dollars a goddamned month. You call that gratitude? After all I done for her? She thinks she's a goddamned Catholic saint for sending her mother a hundred bucks a goddamned month. I'll tell—"

A male voice took over the line.

"Fuck off, buddy," he said.

When I went back downstairs, Corry was cleaning up. The blessing of coffee filled the air.

"Did you know you have seven messages on your answering machine?" she asked.

No, I didn't know. And I was not ready to listen to them. I sat in a chair she had righted. It even hurt to sit down.

"Can I make you something to eat?"

"Sit down," I told her. I did not think I would ever be able to eat again. "So you went back to work?" Maybe it was the Victorian novels in my bedroom, but I felt like the girl should be in mourning for Em.

She did not sit down. She raised the halves of a broken plate, as if in wonder. "I thought it would take my mind off things. But I'm not worth much."

"You really like your job?"

She did not understand the question. "It's great. Senator Faust is terrific to work for. I'm learning a tremendous amount. And you meet people." Abruptly, she put down the broken china and leaned against the dishwasher. "But today I just couldn't . . . I don't know. It was a dumb idea. Going in. It didn't work. I guess it was even disrespectful. In a way. To Em." A wistful smile. Maybe real, maybe practiced in front of a mirror. "Does that sound old-fashioned?"

I wondered if she was sleeping with the senator and almost asked. He was tall, still had his hair, and played well on the talk shows. Big money, lot of power. This girl's kind of guy. Em was just a rung on a ladder, and Corry was born to take the elevator.

"Corry, would you please just sit down? Don't put anything else away. Just sit down and tell me what this is all about. Please." I touched my stomach muscles and found them unfriendly. "If you'll pardon the lack of self-esteem, I don't think of myself as your type of guy. You must have friends. Plenty of them. I don't understand why you're here."

She did as she had been told and sat down. A duchess taken prisoner by the workers and peasants.

"I'm afraid," she said.

"You don't look afraid."

She hit me with those killer blue eyes. "I'm afraid to look afraid."

"Bullshit line. What are you afraid of?"

"I don't know. If I knew, maybe I wouldn't be so afraid."

"Has anybody contacted you? Bothered you?"

She shook her head. The beautiful-hair commercial. In slow motion. She was Manhattan, not Washington. "Nobody. The police haven't even called back."

"They're busy. So what are you afraid of?"

"What are *you* afraid of? Don't I have as much reason to be afraid as you?"

"Who says I'm afraid?"

"Do you always answer the door with a butcher's knife?"

"It's a frontier neighborhood."

"I think you're afraid of me. And I can't figure out why."

I tried to meet her eyes with the level of self-confidence to which she had been born. "Handle with care. The girl has a black belt in male psychology. And she does not like answering questions."

"Ask. Ask anything."

"Were you going to leave Em?"

"Em tell you that?"

"That's not an answer."

She looked at the floor, and her voice lost its confidence. "I couldn't wait to leave him."

"Why?"

"He hit me. He was a drunk. He stank. Is that what you want to hear about your old friend?"

"Em wouldn't hit a woman."

"He hit me. When he was afraid. He'd get drunk.

And hit me.'' Her eyes stabbed in my direction. ''I've never known a man who wouldn't hit a woman. When he was desperate.''

''What was he afraid of? Why was he desperate?''

''It was lots of things.''

''Name one.''

''He was afraid I'd leave him.''

''But you didn't.''

''I couldn't afford to.''

''Stocks have a bad year? Uncle run off with the trust fund?''

Her eyebrows climbed. ''Who do you think I am?''

''Who *are* you?''

''I'd like to hear it from you. Is that what the hostility's about? Who do you think I am, John?''

I looked her up and down without embarrassment. ''Cordelia Nevers. Rich girl playing at government. Waiting to marry richer guy. Fund-raiser cocktail-party wife by birthright.''

She laughed. It was unnerving. Her laughter reminded me of the way Tish laughed at me when I deserved it.

''It's Corrine. Not Cordelia. The last name was Neverosky. My grandfather shortened it because Hunkies couldn't get a job outside of the mines. My mother and father had a contest to see who could drink themselves to death first. Dad won. I went to Penn State on a help-the-girls scholarship and worked summers in the last knitting mill in North America. Because I have fast hands. I could make more that way than I could on some internship with an ass-grabber. I came to Washington because I wanted to change things. But mostly I wanted to change myself. I moved in with Em two days after I met him. Because he was charming when he drank just the right amount, and he had all the things I thought I wanted, and on our second date he introduced me to the Secretary of the Treasury. In the back of a restaurant where the tips are bigger than the paychecks back home. He got me my job. And fucked me like a bully, and slapped me when the sex didn't work. Sometimes he'd disappear. Hours, days. But I didn't have much money, and I had my first real leg-up job, and I was afraid of Em and all he could do in this town.'' She looked at me with a fierceness that reminded me of Tish slashing off a guitar solo. But Corry Nevers sat perfectly still. ''Happy now?''

No. I was not happy. I think that, more than anything else, I hated the parallels with Tish's life. And the smarter choices, the comparative success, of Corrine Neverosky.

The phone rang. I was grateful to the caller in advance. Walking the long seven or eight feet across the kitchen, I wondered if I would ever get anything right.

''Hello?''

''*John?* John, is that you?'' I recognized Mary Farnsworth's voice. But I had never heard her voice like this. ''John, can you come over here? Please? Could you come now? Somebody's been in the house . . .''

*   *   *

"I've got to go," I told Corry.

"What's the matter?"

"A friend's got a problem."

"Is it part of—"

"Corry, please. Save it. I'm sorry I've been such a dick. But, one, you're better off knowing less, not more. Two, I don't know much myself. Three, hanging around with me is probably the unsafest act you could commit." I put my paws in the pockets of my jeans and my abdomen went neon with pain.

"I'll come with you."

"Bad idea."

"Maybe I could help."

"No. I told you. I'm not safe to be around."

"I don't care. Maybe we're safer together."

"And maybe we're a bonus target whenever we're within bursting radius of each other."

"What does that mean?"

"You'd better go back to work."

"I don't want to go back to work. I can't concentrate. I can't think about anything except—"

Impulse struck. I picked up the phone.

"Information for what city?"

"Washington, D.C. Police Department. Homicide."

"Please hold for the number."

I redialed and told them I wanted to speak to Detective Dickey. The woman on the desk said he was busy. I told her I was a suspect in a murder case. She said:

"Well, he *still* busy. But I axe him if he want to talk to you."

Dickey came on the phone. "Who is this?"

"America's Army."

"Yeah? What you got, soldier boy? I'm eating lunch."

"Remember I told you about the other murder? The general I think was murdered? Over in Virginia?"

"Out of my jurisdiction. Hey, how come you haven't been returning my calls?"

"His wife just phoned me. Somebody's been in her house. Maybe the same crew that tore up Emerson Carroll's apartment."

"You a detective now? Everybody's a fucking detective. Goddamned television."

"Her name's Mary Farnsworth. She's at five-two-one-one—"

"I told you. Virginia's out of my jurisdiction. What're you trying to do, get me to blow the case on some technicality? Dream on."

"Don't you care about this?"

"You got a lawyer putting you up to all this crap? Hey, why don't you just come over here and write out a confession."

"Just tell me one thing. Just one thing, okay? I understand why your crew tore up my place. Maybe I understand it on a couple of levels. But did you know one of your boys stole a very expensive guitar from my bedroom?"

"Don't call them 'boys.' They're sensitive about

the term. And nobody tore up your little drug den. And I guarantee you, nobody stole no goddamned guitar. And listen. While you're on the phone. Hyacinth needs the name of your insurance company so she can finish up her report on the car. What's more, I told you about claiming the body. You're a non-relative and you'll have to—''

I hung up.

Corry smiled at me as though I were a fool. ''I wish you'd let me help you.''

I turned away. This was just wasting time. I had to get dressed and go. Mary Farnsworth needed me.

I had climbed halfway up the steps to the second floor when I realized I had overlooked an important practical matter. I bent down over the railing and hurt and called, ''Corry?''

In a moment, she was standing at the foot of the stairs.

''Are you all right?'' she asked.

''Did you drive over here?''

She smiled ravishingly. ''Need a lift?''

CHAPTER 5

"THE POLICE DON'T BELIEVE ME," MARY FARNSWORTH said. "They insist I'm merely distraught." She was the only woman I had ever known who could not only use the word "distraught," but sound natural doing it.

We stood in her living room. Nothing broken, nothing even out of place to a visitor's eye. I had tried to leave Corry out in her car, but Mary would not have it. Too hot, she insisted, and too rude. A flawless hostess, even in distress.

It was clear that Em had never brought Corry to the house. She was a stranger to Mary, who was trying to figure out our relationship. Mary had no idea about Tish, must not have read the papers or watched the local news. It was jarring. As though Tish were still alive in a world that excluded me.

"What made you think somebody was in the house?"

Mary looked wronged. "I don't *think*, John. I *know*." Then she softened. "I've always been able to tell a thing like that. It runs in my family. We . . . have a sense for presences."

"Were there any signs? Anything missing?"

She shook her head. Slowly. "Nothing stolen. But they were in Mickey's study. I *know* it, John. Things were ever so slightly out of place. As though the cleaning woman had gone through it. I believe they went through the rest of the house as well. But I'm certain about the study. Mickey's desk chair had been moved. You know how precise Mickey was about things. So dress-right-dress. That chair was moved. And then there was the call from the Pentagon."

"What call?"

She looked weary. Her hair was only ninety-nine percent perfect. If my own life had not upended over the past few days, I would have been on the side of the police. I still was not convinced. The crew who had been searching homes had not been quite this neat elsewhere.

"Somebody wanted me out of this house. A major called. He *said* he was a major. Brady. Terribly officious. I swear, I wanted to slap him right over the phone. He told me I needed to come by to sign for the personal effects they had cleared out of Mickey's office. He said I had to identify each item." She grazed two fingertips along her temple. "It did seem a bit brutal. But the Army has changed so much over the years, and I supposed that was how they do business now. So I drove in. But the room number he gave me belonged to some sort of Air Force recreational services staff. Nobody knew anything about a Major Brady. So I went upstairs to Mickey's office. They were *not* expecting me.'' She smiled at a remembrance. ''The survival assistance officer had gathered Mickey's things himself. He was going to bring them to me. There was no need to sign anything.''

''You told all this to the police?''

''They wouldn't listen. As soon as I said that nothing seemed to be missing, they lost interest.'' She glanced at Corry, then turned back to me. ''I'm so sorry. I haven't even prepared coffee. Would you like to sit down for a bit?''

''Mary, for God's sake, we don't need coffee.''

''I'd love a cup,'' Corry said.

Mary applied a smile that her mother had taught her and said, ''Do please sit down. Your family name was Nevers? I believe there are quite a few Nevers downriver in New Orleans. Old stock, terribly proud of the French connection. They never recovered from being sold to the Americans.''

''My family's from the north,'' Corry said.

''I could tell,'' Mary said. She smiled beautifully.

I wished Corry would just disappear. I had selfish designs on Mary. I wanted to talk to her. About Tish. To tell her what had happened. I needed to talk to somebody, and Mary was the only clean soul within range.

Mary went out to the kitchen. Corry would not meet my eyes. She studied the room as if appraising

the furniture for auction. After a minute, I followed
Mary.

Mary jumped when I came in. She stood at the
counter, measuring coffee, and I had made her spill
a loaded spoon.

I did not have a chance to speak. She turned on
me, whispering in anger.

"John, I don't *like* that girl. And I'm ashamed of
you. If you and Tish are having a little spat, I want
you to apologize to her. You just stop on the way
home and buy your Tish flowers. A *lot* of flowers.
And I expect the two of you for dinner next Friday.
At seven-thirty."

"Mary, I have to tell you something."

She put her hands on her hips, which was something I had never seen Mary Farnsworth do. It was
a gesture from her ancestors, from the slave shacks,
a mustering of strength for a fight. Her nostrils
pulsed. "I swear, John, men just make me *so* mad.
And you, of all people! I thought you were a gentleman. And I had *always* judged you to have a faithful
heart. Why, if you were just the tiniest bit smaller,
I'd put you over my knee and spank you."

I helped her with the coffee and said nothing of
consequence.

Coffee steamed from Mary's silver. But Mary
served it over invisible ice. She had gone as rigidly
formal as if we were line dancing at the court of
Louis XIV. Corry either was oblivious to Mary's attitude or didn't care.

Talk died. We drank.

Finally, Corry said, "You have such lovely antiques. It must be your hobby, Mrs. Farnsworth."

"They're family pieces," Mary told her. "John, be a dear and pour Miss Nevers more coffee."

I did exactly as I had been told, then said, "Mary . . . you said you thought whoever was in the house moved a chair? By the general's desk?"

"Yes, John."

"Could I have a look? Would you show me?"

"Certainly." She stood up. "Do stay here and relax, Miss Nevers."

I followed Mary across the hall and into the room General Farnsworth had used as his office, library, counseling chamber, and poker den. A sea captain's desk took up nearly half the room. It had been built without pillars of drawers so it could double as a table. A PC occupied half of the desktop. Military history books sandbagged the walls and floor. The souvenirs of long service—plaques and plates and banners, diplomas and signed photographs of heroes, a cadet saber and shako—made a private museum. Mary had permitted a certain immaculate clutter in this one room of her house. The general had acquired habits that looked like discipline, but Mary was the family drill sergeant. The room appeared to be just as Farnsworth had left it, but there was such a density to it that I would not have been able to tell if anything had been moved.

Mary shut the French doors behind us. "She is insufferable, John."

"Mary, there's nothing between us. She just—"

Mary Farnsworth looked at me with frozen brown eyes. "Maybe *you* don't think there's anything going on. But that's not what that girl thinks."

I looked at the desk chair. Corry had a peculiar magic. I had never known anyone who inspired such instant dislike.

At any rate, I wanted Mary to knock it off. Her talk about Tish had dumped me in an emotional slaughterhouse. I needed to tell her what had happened, but I did not have the spirit for it.

Instead, I asked, "How was the chair moved?"

Mary grew businesslike. "Whenever he finished using the computer, Mickey would tuck his chair back under the writing part of his desk. He just liked it that way. It was how he ordered his world."

The chair was centered under the computer.

"Okay if I turn it on? Just kind of check things out?"

"Go right ahead." She drew closer to me. "What do you think . . ."

But I was not listening now. I punched the button to turn on the monitor, then reached down to flip on the brains. Wondering if I needed a password.

A password would not have helped. The power lights came on. But the screen never filled. I poked keys, but nothing happened.

"Where did he keep his disks?"

"Right there on the shelf. By the—"

No disks. Empty space.

"Oh, my God," Mary said.

It was real again.

I got down on my knees. "I'm going to have a look inside this sucker. Okay?"

"Anything . . ."

"I might break it."

"Go on. It doesn't matter."

I switched off the machine, then yanked the plug. The computer was an older model, boxy, but lighter than it looked. I laid it flat on the carpet.

No tools required. The screws fell away and the top flipped off. The hard drive was gone.

"Is something wrong?" Mary asked. "Should I call the police again?"

I stared at the gutted machine, all questions and no answers. Then I snapped the cover back down and put the box back in its place.

"Mary, listen to me. I don't think you should call the police. I think you should forget we ever touched the computer. Forget the missing disks. Something's going on, and you need to stay out of it."

She cast those brown eyes down at me. "And Mickey was involved? In whatever you're talking about?"

"Please. Just forget about everything." I could read her mind: *If my husband was in it, and if it cost him his life, I'm damned well going to get into it.* "Mary, could you just go visit your family? Or some friends? Any place far away from here?"

"I'm not about to—"

"Listen to me. This is dangerous. And you can't help. Your husband didn't want you in on this. He didn't even want me in. But I'm in, and you're not, and I'm *begg*ing you in his name to get on a plane and go."

Mary didn't like it. She did not like it one bit.

"Mickey never had time for cowards," she said.

"This isn't about cowardice. It's about survival. You'd hurt, not help."

She thought that over. Wanting more information. "Who else knows about this, John?"

I looked up at her. Just beyond the line of her skirt, I saw Corry. Standing at the French doors.

Mary finally promised me she would get on a plane that evening. Corry and I left. I expected a storm of questions, but Corry just drove.

"You can drop me at one of the rent-a-car lots down on Jeff Davis."

She looked at me from behind her sunglasses. The superbabe. She belonged in a German convertible. Or a white Jag. But she drove a little Jap number. The kind of car a woman on the make could excuse as practical for an urban lifestyle. Corry had made a series of smart choices in her life. Just as Tish had made a long line of dumb ones. Corry Nevers would not have gotten a tattoo in a thousand years. And one earring hanging on each ear was plenty.

I still liked Tish better.

"You can borrow my car," Corry said.

"Thanks. I was born to rent."

She glanced over at me. Little Miss Ray Bans.

You imagined wind in her hair even with the windows shut and the air on.

"Mrs. Farnsworth didn't like me very much."

"She's upset."

"I felt like she *hated* me." She locked her face toward the highway. Jewelry-ad profile. "She didn't know about your girlfriend, about what happened? Did she?"

"No. She's a media dropout."

"And she thought you were two-timing?"

I smiled, despite myself. "That's an old-fashioned expression."

"Time stood still where I grew up."

"Yeah. That's what she thought."

"And that woman *liked* your girlfriend? I mean, no offense, but I can't imagine—"

"Fuck off, Corry."

"I didn't mean it like it sounded."

"Bullshit."

"Well, I'm sorry."

I still wanted to cry like a kid when I thought about Tish. I had really humiliated her about the blue-guitar tattoo. In mean, little ways. The shit we lay on people. And live to regret.

"Truce?" Corry said. Soft-voiced.

"Whatever."

"Want me to turn on the radio?"

"Suit yourself."

She switched on NPR low. "So . . . I don't get it," she said.

"You don't get what?"

"Her place wasn't all torn up. The way Em's was."

"They knew where to look. They knew what they wanted."

Corry shook her head. "Maybe. But you know what I think? I think it could be two separate players. Looking for the same thing. Maybe they're in competition."

"And what exactly are they looking for?"

She tipped her sunglasses higher on her nose. "Whatever it is, you can enter it into a computer."

"What if . . ." I said, ". . . what if it's all the same bunch? Only they've been getting too much attention. A burst of killings. The press. The cops. Everything spinning out of control. Maybe whoever's behind them told them to put on their table manners."

"So what do *you* think they're after?" Corry asked.

"Haven't a clue," I lied. The pain in my belly and back had long since convinced me it had something to do with Em's airplane. "How about you?"

"I don't know . . . but it must have been something Em had access to. And this general guy. I just can't figure out where you fit in."

"Same as you," I said. "Guilt by association."

A cop car blasted by us on the berm. Up ahead, traffic had slowed.

"Take the next exit," I said. "There's a back way to get onto Jeff Davis."

"You really could just borrow my car."

"Listen." I reached over to crank up the radio. Martha Raddatz, voice sober-sexy, reporting from the Pentagon. There had been a massive explosion at an aircraft research facility outside Atlanta. Fires still burning. One hundred and fourteen bodies had been recovered, but over a hundred more workers remained unaccounted for. The casualties included civilian scientists as well as military advisers from the United States Air Force and Navy. The lab was rumored to have been a prime site for work on the classified avionics for the Next-Generation Fighter-Bomber.

"Goddamned frogs," I said.

"What's going on?" Corry said, all the cool out of her voice. I suppose my reaction was contagious. "Does this have something to do with us?"

"Bastards," I said.

She turned onto the exit ramp. *"Please* tell me what's going on."

I looked at that gorgeous face. Easy to admire, hard to like. I wondered how much longer she would be alive. Hoping only that things had escalated to a point where we didn't matter anymore, that we might be forgotten.

"It's a shooting war now," I told her.

Maybe Mary Farnsworth didn't like her, and maybe I couldn't let myself like her, either. But the realization had begun to penetrate even my bunker of a skull that Corry Nevers had genuine fears of her own. When she dropped me off at rent-a-car alley, she acted afraid of the dark. At five on a summer afternoon. Just before she drove off, I agreed she could come over later.

She had a way of getting what she wanted.

The economy was booming. I had to march to three rental outfits before I found one that had a car available. I got a Ford that was falling apart. At a crummy day rate.

Merging into the after-work crawl over the bridge, I searched the radio for additional details on the bombing. At the bottom of the hour, the death toll had risen by twelve. I stopped at a market to buy food I did not want and walked the aisles like a prisoner in the exercise yard. After that, I could not avoid going home any longer.

Home was Tish. And Tish was dead. Everything she had ever touched in the house was an emotional atomic bomb. I boiled water for pasta and played the recordings on my answering machine.

Several calls from reporters. I did not copy down the names and numbers.

One call from my boss. Another from Army legal affairs. It was Friday evening and I figured there was no point trying to return the calls. I could see them in person Monday morning.

A call from Dickey that had been overtaken by events.

A message from a member of Tish's band, asking her if she was dead or if it was somebody else in the papers.

And a creamy voice suggesting I change my long-distance company.

I dumped in the pasta and got out the phone book. "F" for funeral homes. I ate first and had a glass of wine from an opened bottle, then called the number on the ad that seemed the most gringo.

When I described what had happened to Tish, the voice on the other end cautioned me that it would be hard to make her look exactly the way I remembered her.

"Maybe I didn't make myself clear," I told him. "She's cinders. No open casket. No viewing. No wake. I just want to bury her."

"Have you consulted the rest of the family on that?"

"I'm all the family she's got. I want a cemetery south of the river. Someplace clean. And pretty."

"And you'll be wanting spaces for how many, sir?"

I thought about that longer than I really needed to.

"One."

"You might want to consider the savings—"

"*One*. Listen, do they still make wooden caskets? Not cheap ones. Nice ones."

"Oh, indeed they do, sir. We have an absolutely gorgeous eternal bed in mahogany. And a top-of-the-line imported rosewood model."

"Can I have a look at them?"

"Why, of course. Certainly, sir. That's what we're here for. And you *did* specify an interment the day after tomorrow?"

I wanted to scream at him, "Just fucking bury her, all right?" Instead, I said, "Yes. And I'd be grateful if you could find a Catholic priest. The deceased wasn't a member of a local congregation."

"And flowers?"

I thought again, hating the need to think about any of this. "Roses. A lot of them. Yellow roses."

I had given Tish roses several times. But it was only the first bouquet, the yellow ones, that had made her cry.

I went upstairs and worked through Tish's address book. There were not as many names as I had expected. Mostly clubs and other musicians. Little drawings of faces by the entries. With smiles or scowls. I rated a big smile. The sight wrecked me for half an hour.

I phoned the names I recognized first. Each call was like lashing myself with a whip. Some of her friends wanted practical details I did not yet have, or needed consolation I could not give. Others, clumsily polite, just wanted to get off the phone. One bastard told me, sympathetically, that with Tish it had been only a matter of time.

"I never bought that straight act of hers," he said. "You could feel the hunger, you know?"

When I was done, I just sat with my head in my hands. Until the phone rang.

The caller identified himself as Karl Aalstrom. Big voice. Selling something.

"I'll bet you don't remember me," he said. "The

basic course. Out at Huachuca. Remember old Aley Aalstrom? We had some times, Johnny boy.''

We had not had times, but I did remember him now. Second Lieutenant Karl Aalstrom. He and a ring of other students had been caught cheating. The intel school should have booted them, but they were just lieutenants and the chain of command was trying to keep the attrition rate down. So they slapped their wrists and gave them extra training. Later on, I heard that Aalstrom was caught falsifying TDY vouchers and did not even make captain.

"Yeah. I remember. What's up?''

"Oh, just checking in. Old times and all. Think maybe we could get together for some chow? Or a beer, anyway? On me, Johnny boy. Life is good. I'm living large.''

"It's a bad time.''

"Just a few minutes.''

"I'll have to take a raincheck.''

He breathed like an asthmatic. Or a sex caller. "John? I'm afraid I can't take 'No' for an answer. You see, I work for some people who need to communicate with you. They brought me in from the West Coast so we could sit down and talk. They called me because they found out you and I go a long way back.''

"We don't go a long way back. What's this all about?''

"John, we don't really want to talk about this over the phone, all right? Why don't we just meet somewhere—''

"I don't have time. And I'm not interested." I didn't hang up, though. And it was a good thing, in the end.

"Johnny boy. Listen to me. One old friend to another. You *want* to make this meeting."

"Give me one good reason."

"I understand you like guitars," he said. "How about a mint-condition Les Paul Gibson?"

Corry showed up at the door just as I was leaving. She didn't care where I was going. She wanted to come along.

"No. I'm meeting a ghost from the past. Wait here, if you want."

She could not think of an argument fast enough. Or maybe she read the determination in my voice and figured the fight would not be worth the ammunition. She accepted my offer. I told her to stay upstairs and not to answer the door or the phone. She nodded. Eyes gone elsewhere.

It was dusk. I got down on my knees to check the car's underbelly. Then I checked under the hood. Nothing that I could see. The neighbor kids thought I was a hoot. The adults crossed the street to avoid me.

The traffic had faded. I sailed south with the windows down. Checking the rearview mirror. If anybody was following me, I couldn't spot them. All quiet on the Potomac.

I pulled off at Shirlington. Aalstrom knew the D.C. area. He had specified a linkup in a microbrewery cafe that was loud and anonymous. GS-7s through

-11s, with their ties loosened. Young women in their first business suits. Waitresses with jogger's legs and too much education to be efficient. I wondered if I would recognize Aalstrom. It didn't really matter, since he was obviously going to recognize me.

I beat him to the powwow tent. I took over a stool that gave me an intermittent view of the door and disappointed the bartender by ordering a Diet Coke. A few of the women looked at me as if I were in the running but not leading the pack.

Aalstrom strutted in, big and blond, with too little hair worn too long. The dark shirt and linen sport coat were upscale Tijuana. He carried a good-looking briefcase, though. New York shuttle meets Brentwood. The hostess intercepted him. He pushed up too close to her.

He saw me, waved, and took the girl with the menus hostage until he had me in a booth in a corner. He handled the briefcase with care.

"Jesus Christ," he said, slapping his hands together, "it's good to see you, Johnny boy. God Almighty, I wish I still had your physique. Army keeps you hopping, I guess. Me, I got to get back on an exercise program." He tapped the swell of his stomach. "Got to get rid of the old heart-attack sack. Jeez, though, you hardly look a day older than you did out at Fort We-got-ya."

He looked beat and old. Em's car-lot cousin. I tried to remember if Em had been any closer to him than I had been. I didn't think so. But Em had always had his secrets.

"So what's up, Aley? What's this Les Paul Gibson crap?"

He looked genuinely disappointed. "Don't you want to order first? You're my guest, Johnny boy. Live large."

"Talk to me."

"They do killer burgers here—you know that? I stop by every time I'm in town. Can't get a decent burger in L.A. anymore. Fucking broccoli patties. Tofu hot dogs. Where's it going to end?" He dropped his smile and his menu. "So what're you fucking around with all this for, Johnny? It's not your brief. Why bring down all this pain on yourself?"

"I'm an unreconstructed Protestant. We like pain. Why don't we start at the beginning?"

Aalstrom rolled his eyes and gave me the polarbear salute. Palms held high. "Beginning? Who knows how it all began? The here and now is what matters, Johnny boy. And the future. You should think about your future."

The waitress slapped down a basket of soft pretzels and mustard dip.

"Get you guys something to drink?"

"Black-and-tan, angel," Aalstrom said. He appraised the girl as she scribbled. "I bet you're really a model. You a model?"

"I'm an economist," the waitress told him. I ordered a draft and she moved on.

"So let's talk," Aley said. "Just like old times. Now, I represent some people. Business interests. Serious players, Johnny boy. Now . . . the people I represent are the only rational actors in this whole circus. They want to put a stop to all this violence. They're disgusted by it. And they're prepared to pay.''

"They want to pay *me* to stop the violence?"

His face said I was letting him down big-time. "Johnny boy, do not give me unnecessary grief, all right? I'm trying to reach out to you. You *know* what I'm saying."

"I don't have any idea what you're saying."

The waitress put down our drinks. There was too much foam on the beers. "Take your dinner orders, guys?"

"Later," Aalstrom told her. "My friend isn't hungry." When she moved on, he said, "Hey, I'll bet she's been fucked so many times her brains are fried. College does it to them, you know?" He shared his eyes with me again. Leaning in so that the edge of the table creased his gut. "How much money will it take? Lay your cards on the table."

"Money for what?"

"Get real. Talk to me."

"I don't know what you're talking about, Aley."

Another big shake of the head. "You really are the dumbest joker on earth if you don't take this money and run. So okay. I'll open the bidding. How about five million? That's still a nice piece of change. Deposited offshore—no Freddy Fuck-Around stuff. You like the Caymans? Bermuda? How about Panama? Name the bank. Shit, we can even put it in Canada for you. Make it look like you inherited half of Ontario. Treasury boys'll never find it. Hosers can't run financial institutions. Nothing but Mexicans with college degrees. Chinese are going to own the place in a couple of years. Hey, we'll even create an investment history for you. How about it? Five mil sound good? Beats Army pay.''

''Five million sounds great. What do I have to do for it?''

''Johnny, would you stop this? You are alienating a true friend.''

My turn to lean across the table. So close I could see the veins webbing his nose. ''Just tell me straight out what you want.''

To his credit, Aalstrom did not turn away. Suddenly, he looked a lot harder.

''Johnny,'' he said, ''I see you've never been in a courtroom. Or you are playing it very fucking dumb when you should be playing it cool.'' He backed his big head away. As if drawing a deep breath. Then he moved in again.

''They want the disks. Every fucking one of them. Every copy you might have made trying to be clever. No more bullshit.''

''I don't have any disks.''

He wanted to grab me. To hit me. Maybe this was his shot at the big time. ''Fuck you, Johnny. Just fuck you. Everybody knows you got the disks. Who else is going to have them? You tell me, huh?'' He could barely hold himself on his side of the table. Big hands clenched and unclenched just inches from me. ''They're all fucking dead, Johnny boy. All the little shits who thought they were players. Dead, dead, *dead*.'' He brought his eyes closer. Life had not been good to him. ''Dead is forever, pal. Stay alive. And help an old friend out while you're at it.''

''I don't have any disks. I don't know what I'm involved in. If I am, in fact, involved in something. Which is starting to seem like a safe bet.'' I surprised him. I leaned closer and grabbed his wrists and forced them down on the table before he knew what was happening. I got the tips of my thumbs right on the nerves and went deep. ''But let me tell you something, Mr. Les Paul Gibson telephone bullshit. If you . . . or any of the scum who sent you here . . . if you had anything . . . *any*thing to do with the death of Tish O'Malley, I guarantee you I will live long enough to make you pay for it.''

I hit his nerves hard, right where you can grind them against the wrist joint. It's a good skill. Em had taught it to me a long time before. Laughing down in Mexico. His father had hired a private martial arts instructor for him when he was a kid.

Aalstrom nearly lost it. Doing a sit-down jig. Trying not to shout. Tears crowded in his eyes.

I let him go, took out a five, and dropped it on the table.

''Should cover the beer.''

''*Please*,'' he said, working his wrists. ''Don't go yet. I have something for you.''

''I'm waiting.''

He looked at me. A big wounded bear. ''John . . .

I'm *beg*ging you. Deal with me. Let me have the disks. It'd be good for both of us.''

I tried to make my voice level and real. ''Aley, I'm telling you the truth. I don't have any disks. Except for the ones that go with my PC. You can have those, if you want. They're not very exciting.'' I puffed beer-stained air. ''I just seem to have stumbled into all this. And I wish I could stumble back out.'' I turned my head slowly from side to side, not quite looking at him. The sight of him was painful. How people lose in life. ''But I do not have these disks you're talking about. And I've already been hurt about as bad as anybody could do it. So tell your crowd to look somewhere else.''

Aalstrom wasn't living large anymore. He looked smashed in. ''John,'' he said at last, ''I wouldn't tell anybody else what you just said. About not having the disks. Especially if it's true. Right about now, the possibility that you're holding those disks is all that's keeping you alive.''

''Shit.''

''What's that supposed to mean?''

''Just what it says. Goddamn it. You kill my girl, try to bribe me, and threaten to kill me, too. And you want to make nice.''

''Maybe . . . you should *try* to find those disks.''

''Aley, you're big on old-times-sake. How about doing me a favor? Just tell me what this is all about. What's on these magic disks that I don't have?''

He lowered his face. Looking at the spoiled menu.

"Can't do it, pal. Got to keep on the right side of Jesus."

"Shit."

Aalstrom sighed. "You're a great disappointment to me, Johnny. But I guess you figured that out." He roused himself and reached for his briefcase. "Tell you what. Let me lay down my last card." He took out a manila envelope with a bulge. "Got something for you. You like movies?"

"Drama? Or comedy?"

"You're going to like this one. Little video. Just for you. It's an exclusive." He extended the envelope. "Somebody'll be in touch."

"What is it?"

"Just watch it. Go home and watch it. It'll put things in perspective."

I took the envelope. And got up to go.

Aalstrom smiled again. "Bet you a fifty I screw that waitress tonight."

I was sorry I wasn't a betting man.

CHAPTER 6

I DID THE SECURITY THING AND PARKED A COUPLE OF
blocks away, then took an indirect route home. The
darkness had weight. Heat grabbed skin and would not
let go. In the park, the brothers were drinking and getting Friday-night loud. Most folks out on the street after
dark just have to keep an eye out for muggers. I was
waiting to get shot. Or kidnapped again. Or to turn
onto my block and find my house blown up.

Corry had turned up the air and the cold smacked
me when I stepped in the front door. Stereo cranked.
Marianne Faithfull. *Broken English.*

Changed into cutoffs and an old Key West T-shirt,
she still looked Ralph Lauren. Smiling to greet me.
She had not stayed upstairs as agreed.

"Turn that down," I said. "No. Turn it off. Or
put something else on."

She pouted and bent over my stereo. Lean tanned
legs. Her shirt climbed her back.

The music stopped. She straightened.

"Was that your girlfriend's? I'm sorry . . ."

"Why Marianne Faithfull?" My voice sounded paranoid even to me.

She looked baffled. "No special reason. I just hadn't heard it in a while. It used to be one of my favorites. In college." She held the disc case in her hand. Judging the cool-unto-death look of the cover. "To tell you the truth, I was a little disappointed. She seems so . . . obvious. I guess my tastes are maturing. Did I do something wrong?"

"Forget it."

She smiled again. "So how was your visit with your friend? Can I make you some coffee? Oh, the phone kept ringing. Four times, I think. I let the answering machine get it. The way you said."

I walked into the kitchen. Realizing belatedly that Corry had put my place back together. With remarkable skill and speed. As if she had known where everything belonged. When I left, the wires had been ripped off the back of the stereo and the CD player had been on the floor. I was glad it still worked.

I put the envelope with the video down on the counter and played the messages. My boss, voice hot. *Call me, John.* I looked at my watch and decided to wait. There were a couple of grunts from Dickey. *Get with me, soldier boy. We need to talk.* The funeral director had two cemetery plots he wanted me to look at. And a persistent reporter named Ricks from *The Wall Street Journal* had left his number again.

Corry put on Chet Baker. She sat on the floor with her back against a small suitcase, legs dolled out. Looking up at me as though our relationship was deeper than it was ever going to get. I just said:

"Thanks for the cleanup work."

"I appreciate you letting me stay here. I mean . . . for letting me sleep here. It makes me feel a lot safer."

I did not remember agreeing to anything of the kind. And there had not been a suitcase in her hand when she hit the door earlier. But I was too beat to argue. She could stay if she wanted. My sofa had carried heavier bones. I wanted to be alone. But I didn't, either.

I offered to get her some linens, but she had already found what she needed. The upstairs was still a wreck. But she had done a good deed on the first floor.

The video would have to wait. That was private business.

What were they going to show me? Test flights of the NGFB? Sweeping fake bad guys from the sky? Were they going to appeal to my patriotism? Or demonstrate some imaginative instruments of torture?

It could wait until morning.

"I'm turning in," I said.

"Is the music too loud?"

I shrugged. "It's fine."

"I just love Chet Baker," she said as I climbed the stairs. "Why do musicians always get mixed up with drugs?"

The sheets still smelled like Tish. Like Tish and me. But the scent was getting fainter. I wondered how long I could go without washing them. Then the wondering stopped, sudden as a head-on collision.

I woke to warmth and slow movement and night. I had been way down and it took me a while to swim back to the surface. I did not come up swinging. That was either a good thing or a bad one, depending on your perspective.

Corry Nevers hugged me from behind. Still wearing her T-shirt. But nothing else.

"I was afraid," she whispered. "I'm afraid all the time now."

I pulled away. The bright city darkness worked in through the blinds and I saw her.

"This isn't part of the package," I said. "Get out of here."

She wasn't ready for that and started to cry. I sat up on the edge of the bed, thinking that I needed to start wearing pajamas. My body was a scum traitor pig.

Corry trailed her fingertips down my back. I jerked away again. Then I stood up. Embarrassed. Even in the dark.

"You and me live on different planets," I told her. "Tish hasn't been dead forty-eight hours." My anger was not quite sane. Certainly not proportional. "Poor old Em didn't have any idea, did he?"

She was really crying now. "I thought we . . . I thought we could just . . . comfort each other. That—"

"Fucking stuff it. Knock it off, Corry. I don't know what you're up to, but leave me out of it." I wanted to throw something. Break things. Of course I wanted her. And there she was. On sheets still scented with Tish. As if Corry were trying to erase my memories, to bury the scent with her own.

For a truly mean instant, I considered getting back into bed. What did it matter, at this point?

Corry got up. I thought she was going to retreat downstairs. Instead, she fastened herself to me. With my body proving the feminists right: Men are swine.

I broke her hold and grasped her by the upper arms. Forcing distance between us.

She was beautiful in the darkness. Wickedness adorned her.

"You want me," she said. "I know you do. Please. I'm so lonely."

"No."

She was gone when I got up, but she had left her suitcase. And half a pot of coffee. Hard woman to shake. At any other time in my life, I would not have tried.

I brought in the paper and worked through the front-pager about the lab bombing down in Georgia, slamming myself with caffeine. Big trouble down in the Peach State. The United States had gone to war over less.

I knew too much, and I did not really seem to know anything, and I did not know where to go. This was way off the Army's reservation. The cops were no help. I was not going to go to the French, that was for damned sure. And anybody who would hire Aley Aalstrom to make their tough sales for them did not have much market appeal.

The coffee charged through me. I was still pissing blood. But it did not look quite so bad. I decided that the smartest thing I could do would be to check in at Walter Reed and let the docs earn their specialty pay. Knowing that I would not do it. I could not even steel myself to return the phone calls from the night before.

I remembered the video. I could not recall where I had put it and did not find it immediately. I panicked, cursing Corry, imagining she had stolen it.

The envelope was sitting in plain view. Where I had left it.

The cops seemed to have had a thing about wires. They had pulled them all out. Corry had not gotten around to reconnecting the VCR. I worked as fast as I could, back stiff and unforgiving. I was just capable enough to match red with red, white with white, and yellow with yellow. Then I had to find the remote. Finally, I got the video in and eased down on the carpet in front of the tube.

Nothing. I could hear the tape running. But there was no picture. Or sound.

I checked the connections. Then I tested the television. It worked fine by itself. I dug out the instruction booklet. In the end, I shook the VCR hard and did everything but smash my foot down on it. It hissed.

And gave a few little grunts. But it refused to show the video.

Life was not smooth.

I got dressed, body a catalog of aches. I tried to think of friends who might be home, then decided that the last thing I needed to do was to get another non-player involved. Taking the tape with me, I locked up and headed for the rental car.

No bombs in evidence. A fat kid tried to sell me melted chocolate. I could understand only half of what she said. "Help keep youth off the streets," I think. Another D.C. hustle. I told her maybe next time. And got in the car.

Talk radio loved the Georgia bombing. The right blamed the left and the left blamed the right. A White House spokesman declared that the FBI was investigating a possible Iranian connection, but added that the President cautioned all Americans to respect the contributions of our citizens of Iranian descent. Given the guy's recent difficulties, "contributions" was a poor choice of words. The bottom line was that none of the talking heads had a clue.

I went to a discount appliance store in the near burbs. Where things are cheaper than at the PX. A young man with a ring through his lower lip asked if he could help me.

"I need a VCR. Plain vanilla. And I want to use my own tape to test it."

"Right." He judged me. "You want to go Korean, man. The Jap stuff is money for nothing. Four heads?"

"I just want it to work."

"Right." Walking me down the aisles. All the TVs were showing *The Godfather, Part II*. Only in Hollywood could Al Pacino pass for a tough guy. "Trust me. This right here is, like, the best deal in the store. And it just happens to be on special. This must be your lucky—"

"It hooked up?"

"I was just going to switch it over." He bent toward a junction box. "Slip in your vid, man. You're going to love this machine."

I did as he told me. I could not wait. A born fool.

Tish appeared on twenty or thirty screens. No sound. But she was sitting in a room raw as a barracks, hunched over the Les Paul Gibson I had given her for her birthday. Holding the guitar like a martyr clutching a cross. And wearing the same clothes she had worn the last time she walked out of my door. Our door. Oblivious to the hidden camera, she looked worn and cried-out and utterly beautiful.

"Serious babe," the clerk said. "She your daughter or something?"

I bought the VCR. I would have bought ten of them. All I wanted to do was to go home and watch the clip of Tish over and over again.

But I did not go home. I needed to take inventory. I went to Arlington Cemetery.

I parked in the visitor lot and marched up through the crowds. Tourists in shorts on their way to see JFK's grave. Then snap the poor troopie sweating his rocks off in front of the Tomb of the Unknown Soldier. I cut left and climbed through the heat. The grass crunched.

Farnsworth lay on the high ground. In winter, you would be able to see all of the city's monuments across the river, but leaves blocked part of the view now. The flowers had been removed and the grave sodded. I wanted to be alone, but I had hoped faintly that the gravedigger—or whatever the politically correct term is for a boneyard worker these days—would be around. I had liked him. A lot better than I liked myself at the moment. But the only life in evidence was a bird picking at the grass.

I sat under a tree. Probably violating six different rules. And watched the general's grave as if I expected him to speak first. A jet wrenched the sky, coming down into National.

"Christ, sir," I said, "you should've brought me in. If you could trust Em, you could've trusted me. Now here I am, in the middle of all this shit, dumb as a rock. And somebody's got my girl."

The bird hopped and poked. A fly probed my defenses.

"So who's zooming who?" I asked him. "Where do I start? Give me a hint, huh?"

I felt as though a smarter man would have pieced the story together days before.

The French were scum. But that did not fall into the surprise category. By their own admission, they had stolen the plans for the NGFB. It looked like we had bombed them in retaliation, whoever "we" were. It shocked me. Because I believed it was true. And it was a massive, terrible thing. I could not conceive of any industrial secrets that were worth it. I did not want to believe my kind were capable of such an action. I suppose Tish was right—I really didn't have any idea how the world worked.

So we bombed the French. Then the French bombed us back. The French had to have done the Georgia number. Still, that surprised me, too. I would not have believed they had it in them anymore. Sinking a Greenpeace rowboat was one thing. But whacking a couple of hundred American scientists leavened with military officers was something else. There was obviously a lot more to the NGFB than the full-page ads and the Senate testimony let on. Some black program within a black program.

Something about the French—about my own personal Jules and Jim—clawed at me. They had not said a word about any disks. Even though everybody else on this side of the Atlantic seemed to be after them. But there was another thing, too. Cuckold had yipped and yapped about us making fools of them. Even before the bombing. I wondered what that was all about.

A tourist couple poked down a lower row of graves. Lost. Or hunting for a relative. The woman bobbed along the headstones as if keeping count. The man looked at the grass, then at the sky. He wore a white sun hat with the brim down and I could feel him sweat from a hundred meters away.

I brushed off my pet fly.

Em's guilt trip. I figured he knew a lot more about us bombing the frogs than he had been willing to tell me. And he knew the big secret about that airplane that was worth killing for. Em could be cynical, but, to his credit, this time around it had been too much. That triggered his redemption thing.

And it meant that Macon-Bolt had a connection to the bombing of the French lab. At least enough of a tie for Em to find out about it. And repent. It was a new level of cutthroat capitalism.

Em turned to Farnsworth because the general was the only man left he could trust who had any clout at all. The two of them probably figured they could do a good deed, for God and country. Expose the criminals. But the criminals had better intel. And an operational capability the Hardy Boys had underestimated.

Who, exactly, were the killers? Why were they playing with bombs? They certainly weren't amateurs. This was a heavyweight bout.

What was on the disks I had never seen that made them worth killing for? My mind kept flipping the channel back to black capabilities. Maybe there was some phenomenal wonder-weapon component to the NGFB. Something so revolutionary we did not want its existence known. Even by an ally. To the extent the frogs were allies.

Why kill the general and Em, but settle for just grabbing Tish and muscling me? Why rip up the floorboards in one place, but not in another?

At least I could sketch the chain of logic that put

me in the game. They would have been watching Em. And he was dumb enough to ask me to share a drink, and I was dumb enough to take him up on it. They ran my ID wide and deep and hit on my old ties to Em and Farnsworth. They tore up Em's apartment, but left the phone working because they had it tapped. Tish called me. I went over. So they figured Em had done a battle handoff of the disks to me. Or that I knew where they were and grabbed them before the cops came. Now I was in the cesspool, with Tish a hostage, and no idea how to get her back.

If Tish was alive, who had gone charcoal in my car?

And where did Corry Nevers fit in?

Corry was a size-six moment of truth. If I had met her back when my relationship with Tish had been on cruise control, I probably would have taken the detour and got away without paying the toll. Pathetic, what you realize about yourself. It was easier being faithful to Tish when I thought she was dead, or now that she was a prisoner of the video lifestyle, than it would have been on any old day when we were happy.

I had never really taken Tish seriously. I always kept some distance between us. Yet I had never loved anybody the way I loved her. I did not know exactly what that meant, but I was afraid it was not good news. Tish seemed born for trouble. Which is probably a good third of why I fell for her. I had always thought of myself as a big, bold risk-taker. But I was a coward when it counted.

It's rot to say that anything good comes out of a mess like this. But it's useful to get a clear look at yourself. Buying somebody an expensive guitar is easy. The truth is that whenever I felt Tish drawing me too close, an invisible bitch from the Officers' Wives Club whispered in my ear that she was damaged goods.

Now all I wanted to do was to go home, hook up the new VCR, and watch the film of her over and over again. She was alive. And if I ever got her back, I was not going to blow it.

The only good piece of advice I had gotten from anybody had come from Aley Aalstrom. When he told me that even if I did not have the disks, I had better act as though I did. That was as plain as the business end of a gun now.

I seemed to own that one solid fact: The disks were my shot at getting Tish back alive. And at staying alive myself.

Who had them? Where were they? Where did I start looking?

I stood up, miserable with sweat.

"I never learned anything," I told Farnsworth. "I wish you were here to help me. A lot of people are dead now."

I scribbled a mental note to call Mary and make sure she had gotten on the plane as promised. Then I headed back into the city.

*   *   *

As soon as I put the VCR box down by the television, the doorbell rang.

It was the Cuckold of Paris.

He did not get one word out. I grabbed him by the shirt collar and yanked him inside, kicking the door shut behind us. I hit him so fast he could not get his arms up to block.

He went down right there in the hallway. But he was tough. Instead of going out or running up the white flag, he scissored me with his legs. So hard he almost broke my ankle.

We grappled on an old throw rug. Too close to hit hard enough to make a difference. I was bigger, but he had a mean streak and more martial arts behind him. He used his legs and feet. The scumbag smelled like he did not use deodorant.

"Goddamned Eurotrash," I said. Or grunted. I broke free just long enough to hit him in the gut with all my weight behind it. Recalling the way he had hit me.

He was thin. My fist almost made it to the floor. It stressed him long enough for me to give him a jab to the snout, then deliver a big one with my knuckles going in between his jawbone and cheekbone. I could count teeth under the meat.

"You . . . fuck . . ." I was not at my most articulate. But I threw in plenty about vengeance for Georgia and what I was going to do to him if he had Tish. Not a lot of clarity of thought or complete sentences. But this was the first time I had gotten to blow off steam. When you've been everybody's punching bag for a while, it's great to get a turn in the gloves.

"Didn't . . . do . . . it . . ." he said. "We . . . no . . ."

Then he kicked me hard. Just missing the combat zone. It threw me off balance. Before I knew it, the little bastard was on top of me. Pounding away. Trying to get at my face. I rolled both of us backward. Cuckold flailed like a hostage in a trunk.

"We . . . didn't . . . do . . . it . . ." he said.

We were trying to hurt each other. Hitting hard. But it was funny. Neither of us wanted to do irreversible damage. Nobody went for the eyes, which is where you head if you're serious. We both knew how to kill somebody. This was just guy stuff.

I threw him. He crashed against the stereo stand. Which pissed me off again. I went in swinging, but I was still on my knees. You can't get leverage that way.

He threw a handful of CDs into my face. Then he punched me low in the belly.

It hurt.

He jumped to his feet and aimed a kick at my face. I moved just in time, more luck than skill, and got my hands on his thigh. Then the little shit was on his back again, and it was my turn to kick.

Even banged up, he was fast. He rolled and threw a blind kick backward that caught my hip. In the couple of seconds I spent reeling, he scrambled back to his feet.

I grabbed him again. Before he could get his footing. And threw him against a chair. He tumbled into the upholstery. This time I landed on his guts with one of my knees. It felt indescribably satisfying. It's amazing that grown men don't do this more frequently.

The fight went out of him. But I wasn't done.

"Why'd you do it?" I yelled. "Why the hell did you do it?"

He was a rag. His hands did not even close into fists anymore. His head rolled. I put one in between his eyes so hard it hurt my hand. The bridge of his nose collapsed like chicken bones in a dog's jaws. The sonofabitch shot blood onto my chair.

Somebody had been pounding on the door for a while. Maybe his partner. I didn't know. Hardly cared. I was deep into the fight, which had been going on for maybe a minute. I intended to finish Cuckold before dealing with anything else. The rest of the world could bugger off.

I heard Dickey's growl:

"Open up. Police."

"So who's this?" Dickey asked. "Your drug partner? What do we got? Falling-out among thieves?" He turned to one of the uniforms. "Keep them separated, all right?" Pointing a thick finger at Cuckold. "Get that piece of shit out of here. Now. Take him down to the station."

Cuckold had struggled to his feet. Fighting to make sense of the world. His eyes would not settle. But he stepped away from the approaching cop.

"I'm a diplomat," he said. "I have immunity. I am from the Embassy of France."

Dickey put his thumbs in his belt loops. "Yeah? You paid all your parking tickets?"

"You cannot arrest me. I have diplomatic immunity."

"Got an ID, Mr. Ambassador? Wayne, check Pierre's pockets, huh?" Dickey swiveled his big head back toward me. "Okay. My Saturday's fucked and my patience is gone. Who is he?"

"He's French. He's a spy. And a thug. He's tied in with that bombing down in Georgia. The research lab that went up."

Dickey snorted. "Not my jurisdiction. What was he doing on my beat?"

Actually, I wasn't sure. I had no idea why Cuckold had shown up at my door.

This was all too slow for Dickey. "Billy, take Pierre La Fuckface down to the station. Check if he's got dip. Make nice until we find out. But take prints. And he doesn't walk until we find out if anybody else wants him." He spit out something invisible and gave me The Face. "You're pretty good at beating up little guys, soldier boy. Ever do any debt collecting for your old lady's drug crowd? Looks like Lucky Pierre landed at least one, though. Make that two."

"This guy was involved in a terrorist act against the United States. Diplomatic immunity doesn't count in a situation like this. You need to contact the FBI."

''Right. Would you like me to call J. Edgar directly, or should I go through Efrem Zimbalist, Jr.? We'll find out if he's Yassir Arafat or not. In the meantime, you and me got some talking to do. Oh, by the way, you're under arrest. Wipe the goddamned blood off your lip while I read you your rights.''

''What's the charge?''

Dickey ignored me. Doing his spiel.

As the cops led the Frenchman out, he whispered, ''Do not tell them anything.''

I don't know whether he meant it or just said it in front of Dickey to screw me.

Then Dickey and I were alone. The detective finished his recitation.

''What's the charge?'' I asked him.

He smirked. ''What do you think?''

''Come on. If you were any kind of cop you'd know I haven't done anything. Unless pounding that little shit's face in counts.''

Dickey looked up at me. I could tell he did not like the physical arrangement. He much preferred me sitting down.

'' 'Conspiracy to traffic in illegal drugs.' ''

''That's bullshit. You know it's bullshit. You *have* to know.''

He smiled. ''Yeah? Well, I guess we'll see. Conspiracy's a great statute, you know that? Separates your *Habeas* right from your *Corpus*. I think of it as the superpunk provision.'' He smiled. ''I just want to hear what you have to say after a weekend in the slammer with your fellow residents of the District of Columbia.''

I closed my eyes. Held up my hand. "Wait. Look. Just tell me what you really want from me. Give it to me straight.''

Dickey turned toward a side wall. Shaking his head. Exaggerating it. "What *I* want from *you*? Maybe I just want to have lunch, huh? My fucking treat. I want you to *talk* to me, pal. Tell me something I don't know. Help me clear up two murders, maybe three. Or what's your latest count?''

"Tell you what. I'll do better than talk. I'm going to *show* you something.''

You-can't-con-me eyes. "Show me what?''

"I just need two minutes to hook up the video.''

Dickey laughed. It sounded like falling bricks hitting the sidewalk. "What you got? Hot tapes of your girlfriend or something?''

I looked at him. "That's exactly what I've got.''

His mouth opened. But before he spoke, the doorbell rang again.

"You're a popular guy," Dickey said. "Open it. Invite them in." He drew his gun from beneath his jacket with a smoothness I would not have expected. He stepped back, just an inch out of the line of fire from the door.

It was Corry. Dressed for success. With a bouquet of flowers.

"I'm so sorry about last night," she said quickly. "I was a selfish bitch." Then her eyes moved off me and widened. I did not have to turn around to know that Dickey had moved into the open. With his gun.

I forgot that Corry and Dickey had already crossed paths in the wreckage of Em's apartment. I was forgetting a lot of things. I just said:

"It's all right. He's a cop."

Corry stood in a wash of sunlight, just enough sweat on her forehead to make her human.

Her eyes were not good. She looked ready to run for it.

"Come right in, Ms. Nevers," Dickey said. "You're just in time for the matinee. Isn't that right, soldier boy?"

When I turned around, Dickey gave me a look of absolute disgust.

Showing Corry the video had not been part of the plan. But my plans did not seem to count for much at the moment. Dickey put his gun away, Corry laid down the flowers and her purse, and I hooked up the new VCR.

We stood in front of the television.

Seeing the image of Tish again hit me in the stomach harder than the Frenchman had ever done. The clip was not long, not over a minute. But I had time to replay a lot of memories.

When the screen went black, Dickey turned to me and said, "So? What's the revelation?"

I hit the rewind button. I wanted to see it again.

"It means she's alive," I said.

Dickey lifted an eyebrow. "That a fact? Buddy,

all I see is a tape that for all I know is a year old.
You got to show me some leg."

"It wasn't Tish in that car." I felt like a child
who cannot make his parents see the obvious. "Can't
you . . . do DNA testing or something? On the
body?"

Dickey barked out a laugh. "He wants DNA testing! Soldier boy, we don't even have spare tires for
our cruisers. I copy my fucking reports at Kinko's.
And the mayor ain't the one picking up the tab." He
gave another, lesser bark. Yet for all his barstool
bullshit, I could sense just the slightest change in
him. "So tell me about this tape of yours."

"The guitar she's playing—let me run it again."
I hit Play. "Look at the guitar. I just gave it to her.
For her birthday. I just picked it up last Tuesday. I
have a dated receipt." I looked up from the image,
desperate to see a change in Dickey's expression. "I
never made any videos of her with it. I don't even
own a video camera. She never took it out of this
house, either. And the clothes. That's what she had
on when she walked out of here the last time." I felt
I should be able to convince him through the sheer
intensity of the truth. "Remember when I called and
bitched about your guys stealing the guitar? That's
the one. Whoever grabbed her came back here for
the guitar. They knew everything. Everything about
us. Every detail. They knew the guitar would convince me that they had her, that she's still alive."

"You're talking trash. I don't see proof of
anything."

"*Please*. Listen to me. *She's not dead*. Tish is alive. I can't explain the car. I don't know what happened. I don't know who was in it. I don't have any idea who's got her. But she's *alive*." I wanted to grab him. "Don't you want to find her?"

I wondered what Dickey's game might be. Even a D.C. cop could not be this stupid, this unwilling to consider the evidence. I stared at him, crazy for some way to convince him. Or, as a minimum, to buy time. I could not afford to go to jail, with Tish out there waiting for me to unscrew things.

Dickey did not say anything right away. I took that as a good sign at last. But something else occurred to me while I waited for him to decide Tish's fate and mine. There was a third person in the room with us. And Corry Nevers had not said a word.

"All right," Dickey said. "Give me the tape."

"What?"

"I said give me the goddamned tape." He shook his head. "I must be nuts."

"What are you talking about?"

He looked at me as though he found me inexpressibly stupid. "I'm not going to bust you. Not yet. But I got paper on you. And I can drop it anytime I want. Remember that. Now give me the tape."

"Why do you need the tape?"

My intelligence dropped another rung in his eyes. "It's evidence, for Christ's sake."

"Can I at least make a copy?"

"Uh-huh. Sure. And then we go to court and some

fuck in a thousand-dollar suit gets up and says, 'Your Honor, this evidence has been tampered with.' Right. Sure, I'm going to let you make a copy.''

''Please. It means a lot to me.''

Dickey chugged the snot back in his nose. ''The tape? Or the slammer? This is not a trick question.''

I gave him the tape. I felt like I was handing over Tish herself.

He wiped his forehead. Sweating in the air-conditioned room.

''Now,'' he said. ''Speak slowly and clearly, and tell me how this tape came into your possession.''

On the backbeat, I told him, ''It was in an envelope. On the doorstep. This morning.''

He thought for a moment. Then snorted again. ''Trusting souls. Must be out-of-towners. So . . . you're telling me this French bozo has something to do with it?''

''I don't know. Maybe. I don't know who has her. I want to know.'' Then I remembered. ''But I'd bet a month's pay he's tied into that laboratory bombing.''

''Not my jurisdiction. So what did you mean, he's a spy?''

''He's got a partner. The other night—''

A fist whacked the front door and a cop voice called for Dickey. The detective answered and he and a patrolman mumbled cop codes and street numbers to each other. After a moment, Dickey strode back to me. He had a repertoire of disgusted faces that should have been cataloged by the Smithsonian.

''You and me are going to have to talk. But right

now I got a twenty-year-old some hero used for extended target practice plus her six-year-old daughter with a bullet through her neck. Life in a wheelchair. If the kid's lucky. And you're probably wondering why I got such bad manners. Accompany me to the door, Colonel, sir.''

In the doorframe, he grabbed me by the upper arm and yanked me outside. He was much stronger than I would have guessed.

''You fuck me,'' he said, ''and you're going to jail till you look like Santa Claus.'' He turned his wrecked eyes up to meet mine. ''And just for the record, I liked your old girlfriend better. Dumb fucking cop that I am.''

Corry stood by the television. Posed. Perfect. I remembered the exact feel of her rubbing against me in the night.

She pushed her hair back over her ears. One side, then the other. Chin held low. Lips opening like a wound.

''You lied to him,'' she said. ''You had that tape last night.''

''So turn me in.''

She smiled. The lip maneuvers were much too complex for a woman her age.

''No way,'' she said. ''We're in this together. We're partners.'' She glanced around the room. ''You can't seem to keep things tidy. By the way, I don't remember seeing a vase for flowers.''

"There's one down in the basement. If I were you, I'd be out of here at a run."

"I don't see how either one of us can go back," she said blithely. "I *am* glad your girlfriend's all right. Who do you think has her?"

"I wish I knew."

"Does your eye hurt?"

"Is it black?"

"It looks like it's going to be. A little. What was the fight about?"

"It was a cultural thing."

She stood there in her summer suit. Proper. Real Senate Caucus stuff. No matter how I tried, I could not stop remembering. Her flesh luminous in the darkness. And the feel of her curls against my thigh.

Corry walked to the front door, opened it, looked out, and came back.

"They're gone," she said. She glanced at her watch. "I have to get back to the office. The senator wants me to take notes for him at a hearing. Can you believe Congress is working right through the weekend? In July?" Her eyes were harder than her voice. "This is not what I want to do for the rest of my life."

"I thought you loved your work."

"I've had worse jobs. Sometimes it's good. But I can imagine a better life, too."

"Corry . . . we're getting this all wrong."

She smiled, refusing my doubts. "I think we make a good team. Even if you still don't like me."

"I thought you were scared."

"I am."

"Then why—"

"You know why. And I'm not ashamed of what I feel. So don't be a pig about it."

"I'm in love with Tish."

"I'll take that chance."

"I'm going to get her back."

"I'll help you."

"You don't believe I love her."

Corry looked away. "I don't believe you'll love her forever."

"I don't trust you."

She smiled. "Don't worry. I won't embarrass you again. I'll wait."

I shook my head.

"You don't know me, John. You don't know me at all." She picked up her purse and stepped close to me. "Do you have a gun?"

"This is D.C. Only the criminals have guns."

She reached into her bag and lifted out an old *film noir* thirty-eight.

"Here," she said. "Take it. I don't want you to get hurt."

Corry walked out. I just stood there in my living room, gun in hand, a statue memorializing village idiots everywhere. The phone rang.

I figured it was my boss. I got ready for the anger. Wondering where I should start the explanation.

It was Aley Aalstrom.

"Johnny, how you doing? Is this weather, or what?"

"What is it?"

"Hey, you alone?"

I looked down at the pistol. "Yeah. I'm alone."

"Good. Great. We can talk. You seen any good videos lately?"

"Maybe."

Aley chuckled. "Want to tell me about it?"

"What do I have to do?"

"Johnny boy . . . you *know* what you have to do. There was never any question about it. Get Republican. Respect property rights. Return those disks to their rightful owners."

"I need time."

I could picture Aley on the other end. Big jaw with the bag of fat under it. Shifting from side to side.

"Hey, John. Buddy. The good fairy just handed me a note for you. Want me to read it?"

I did not answer.

" 'Dear John'—hey, is that classic, or what?— 'Dear John. Miss you. I desperately need you to prove your love. Or I'm going away forever. Signed . . .' What about that? No signature. Guess she ran out of time. Bet she's one sweet piece of horseflesh, Johnny boy. Bet you wouldn't want to lose her." I heard the weight of his breath against the mouthpiece. "So what do you think?"

"Fuck you, Aley."

"That's right. Shoot the messenger. You know, you're a goddamned inspiration to me. Some people think you've already moved on. That you're jumping that little blondie who keeps landing on your branch. But I been sticking up for you. I tell them, 'No way. Our John's the last of the big-time romantics. Faithful to the end. She could rub it right over his lips and all he'd do is recite the Lord's Prayer. Lead me not into temptation,' huh?" He chuckled. "You're *great*, Johnny boy. You know that? You got star potential. Gary fucking Cooper. People be*lieve* in you. Hey, you think your redhead's ever been gang-fucked?"

He hung up. I held the phone against my ear until the line went shrill, then held it a while longer. The gun in my hand felt like fate.

CHAPTER 7

MAIL SMACKED THE HALLWAY FLOOR. AN INSTANT later, the flap clapped shut. I put the revolver in the drawer with the tea towels. My *Atlantic*, Tish's *Rolling Stone*. A missing-children flyer. The phone bill, counterbalanced by a promise that Publisher's Clearinghouse was going to give me a trillion dollars. No death threats or ransom notes.

The phone rang again.

I thought it might be Aalstrom calling back and answered accordingly.

"Switch off the attack mode," Colonel Maurey told me. "Go into receive."

"Yes, sir."

"When I tell you to call me back, you call me back. Got that?"

"Yes, sir."

"I want to know just what in the hell you're up

to, John. But that's going to have to wait. General Gabrielli wants to talk to you. We've been trying to get through to you since yesterday morning.''

"Sir, I'll march upstairs first thing Monday morning. Sackcloth and ashes.''

"Monday morning won't cut it. Write this down.'' He gave me a phone number. "That's his aide's pager. Call immediately. The guy's hot.''

"Know what it's about?''

"Colonels don't ask three-stars for explanations.''

"Yes, sir.''

I had briefed Gabrielli a few times. The Army's procurement czar, General Buy-it. He was typical for his rank. Laminated with humility, vain to the bone. His staffers claimed to like him but spoke disloyally after the second sentence. He had led a brigade in the desert under a slow, careful corps commander and had managed to keep his tanks perfectly on line. Pentagon gossip said he was plugged in across the river.

I feared the coming conversation.

I dialed the aide's pager and got a swift callback from a cell phone. The aide introduced himself as Major Ripley, the tone of his voice making it clear that, due to his position, he outranked all but a few lieutenant colonels. Yet he did not fail to say "sir.''

"I understand General Gabrielli wants to see me.''

The aide responded in a muffled voice. "Sir, the general's putting right now. Can you hold?''

"Isn't it a little hot for golf?''

"Golf is the general's passion.''

"He winning or losing today?"

"General Gabrielli never loses."

"Is General Ripley your father, by any chance?"

"Yes, sir."

It figured. You saw a lot of generals' kids go through the Pentagon as senior captains and junior majors. Punching that ticket. The system was so closed and smooth it made the Mafia look sloppy.

"Colonel Reynolds," the aide said. "Hold for just a moment, sir." I listened to voices, indistinct words, white noise.

Ripley came back on the link. "Sir, the general will be at his home on Fort McNair at eighteen hundred. He'll be expecting you. You are not required to be in uniform."

The uniform business, at least, was a blessing. Given the weather. The world's finest Army clothed its officers in polyester, the miracle fiber. Hot in the summer, cold in the winter. Probably because, back during the first confusions of the sexual revolution, a Chief of Staff's wife told him she wasn't pressing any more of his goddamned trousers.

I straightened a bit of the mess Cuckold and I had made, then took another shower. The water stung my lip. Which was swollen, with a nice crack in it. Lilac mark just off my left eye. On the positive side, my urine had faded to pink.

I stood in front of the full-length mirror on the back of the door. My body was black-and-blue and bent. When life was normal, I worked out hard. Staying in good shape was one of the things of which I was proud, a fundamental duty. Now I looked like Grandpa after he wrestled the bear. I pulled on a polo shirt and khakis. On the way out, I rang the funeral home and told the answering machine that the customer had risen from the dead.

I popped onto the freeway at the Sixth Street ramp, blending with the lazybones Saturday traffic. Heat blurred over the city. I got off before the bridges and followed a tourist bus down toward the waterfront restaurants. At McNair, the MP on the gate checked my ID.

Fort McNair sits on the best piece of real estate in the District, a sanctuary thrusting out where the Anacostia River empties into the Potomac. At the tip of the little peninsula, the National War College occupies a magnificent, wasteful building that goes back to the days of Teddy Roosevelt. But the fort's serious occupants are the generals in the row of old brick homes that look out on the river. The view is a developer's dream.

Gabrielli's nameplate had been fixed on a two-story that would have passed as a mansion a generation before. Now most of the single family homes in suburbia were as big or bigger. But the Route 7 crowd did not have a water view.

The aide let me in and guided me through a couple of rooms furnished with the frilly crap bored wives buy on bus trips to factory outlets. The air-conditioning gave the place a basement smell. Gabrielli waited in a study that caught some of the river light, still in his golf clothes. Orange polo shirt with a V of salt

stains on the chest. Green-and-white plaid slacks.
General officers should never be allowed to dress
themselves off duty.

Gabrielli was a big man. Taller than I was. His
greeting sounded as though he was clearing his
throat. His hand was wet, with strong fingers but a
pulpy palm.

"Sit down, sit down. Want a Coke? Dan, get Lieutenant Colonel Reynolds a Coke, would you? And
call the Army and Navy Club. Leave a message for
Punchy Hunt. Tell him Gail and I might be a few
minutes late."

Gabrielli sat with his back to the westering sun. It
dropped shadows on his face. He did an appraisal.

"Lieutenant Colonel John Reynolds. I appreciate
you taking the time out of your weekend. You appear
to be a very busy man. Your boss couldn't track you
down for love or money." He smiled just a little.
"Poor Maurey was really jumping."

"Sir, I was on leave."

He waved that away. "Water under the bridge.
Now, John, you've always struck me as a talented
soldier. Good briefer. Self-assured. Knowledgeable.
Had a battalion command yet?"

"No, sir. I'm a FAO. I'm not on the command
track."

"Well, you never know. Things happen. Understand you have a pretty good record?"

I made the mush face required in response. The
aide put down a glass with ice and a can of Coke,
and left again. I let the drink stand.

"You strike me as the sort of officer who really loves the Army. Who really found a home in it. Not just passing through."

"The Army's been good to me, sir."

"Love your country, too, I'll bet. Not just words. Real commitment."

I shrugged, and nodded. The truth was that my country seemed far away at the moment.

His jaw lifted like a dozer blade. "It's a great country. Greatest in human history. And the Army . . . well, the Army's been good to all of us. Damned good." He canted his head and a shadow slipped over his face like a veil. "Have to be realistic, though. In times like these. An officer can have a spectacular record—spec*tac*ular—and still find himself passed over for promotion. It's gotten unpredictable. I've seen it with my West Point classmates. Even on my own staff. Army's getting smaller. Not everybody survives the cuts. I'm sure you've seen plenty of your friends and colleagues go down." He sighed. It sounded like a snore. "We just can't hold the line anymore. Hill doesn't understand us. White House hates us. Except when it's time for a photo op. And the American people are ungrateful. They've already forgotten how different the world looked just a few years ago. We did our part—and we're still doing it. But . . . a career . . . well, it's just not the secure thing it once was. A man has to have Plan B." He leaned forward, as if to straighten a badge or ribbon on my invisible uniform. "What's *your* Plan B, John?"

I had semi-formed thoughts. Possibilities. But they had receded over the past few days. My concerns had been more immediate.

Gabrielli sat back again. "You remember General Hunt? Punchy Hunt?"

I had never met Roscoe "Punchy" Hunt. But I had heard plenty about him. Snake-eater. Jungle junkie. No spot too hopeless. As a young officer, he had supposedly bitten away the throat of a North Vietnamese captain who tried to jump him. While shooting down the man's comrades with his forty-five. Sometimes you heard six dead Vietnamese, sometimes seven. Another story had him strangling a CIA man he pegged as a sellout in El Sal. He was the kind of soldier who had a classified personnel file that leaked legends. A few years back, he had retired, abruptly, as a three-star, with honors piled up in front of him and whispers behind his back.

"I've heard about him, sir. But our paths never crossed."

"Know what he's up to in his retirement?" He gave me a little space in which I was not expected to fit an answer. "Punchy put his own team together. Drawn from the best of the best. Officers recently retired. A few NCOs he knew personally. Some talented special ops boys who decided to hang up their uniforms a little early. Just to work for Punchy. He calls them 'The Hunt Club.' Oh, there's some incorporated name. All alphabet soup. But 'The Hunt Club' is the draw. Now, I don't want to start talking business and naming names, but old Punchy's got himself a charter from one of our largest defense corporations—real patriots—to do the sort of things active-duty officers are unable to do these days. Special foreign liaison missions. Investigative scouting. Negotiations at the sub-media level. Media management, for that matter. His people are doing a tremendous amount of good for this country—and you never hear a word about it. And, I might add, they are very well compensated financially. Old Punchy always took care of his subordinates. Really good care." He smiled without showing teeth. "Think of it as payback for all those cold nights on the German border or wrestling rattlers out of your fartsack down at Hood. Might be something that would interest you. If you were looking for a job."

He bent his torso forward, passing into a deeper shadow thrown by a rolltop desk. "You see, John . . . the country might forget us. The people out there don't care about anything but money and transient pleasures. No values, no sense of honor. I mean, just look at them." He gestured toward the city's heart. "No pride in the important things. Slovenly, unscrupulous, selfish little people." He brushed his nose with a knuckle. "But we still have friends. Friends we can count on. In defense industry. They need us. Just as we need them. We won the Cold War together. Crushed the Russian economy. We could have fought the bastards, had it been necessary to do so. Now we need to do everything we can to keep our guard up. With the Chinese on the horizon." He raised a heavy eyebrow in the darkness of his face.

"Russians, too. You never know. They could come back. They are a people drenched in evil."

"Sir . . . the Russians are going to be flat on their backs for half a century. And the Chinese—"

He held up a big hand. Directing the conversational traffic.

"John, I don't want us to get bogged down in a philosophical discussion. I have other commitments. Although I would be delighted to discuss these issues with you in depth at a later date." He slanted his head at a boxer's angle. The late sun burned his skin and lit the stubble along his jaw. "Now . . . this business in the newspapers. Plus all the innuendo. Not good for the Army, John. Not good at all. Officer's car bombed. Police involved. A woman dead. A woman of . . . questionable compatability with the Army family. And I've heard rumors—nothing definite, let me be clear about that—that you've gotten yourself mixed up in matters even more . . . troubling." His big head swayed like a cobra rising from a basket. "Serious stuff, John. Sort of business that could ruin a promising career. Or worse. The Uniform Code of Military Justice can be ferocious."

"Sir—"

"Don't interrupt me. I'm trying to help you." He shifted in his chair and brown shadows climbed toward his eyes. "I made a decision to keep the lawyers off your back. In light of your past record. I intervened personally on your behalf. The Army doesn't need another scandal, John. Can't afford it right now." I saw his eyes. Glowing in amber, the only part of his face not in darkness. "Do you want to hurt the Army? When we're fighting for our lives on this goddamned budget thing? Do you want to crap on your friends and comrades and everything you've ever stood for?"

"Sir . . . what . . ."

"I'm not asking you to do anything contrary to your conscience. Do not misunderstand me. I just want you to do the right thing. Support this country's defense." He grunted. "Don't goddamned betray it."

"Sir, what is it you want me to do?"

He looked at me and straightened himself in his chair. Torso rising into the light. I thought of the cobra again. But there was anger now, too. A lot of it. His expression, even his posture, conveyed passion. Well beyond the normal range. John Brown dressed for eighteen holes.

"You know what you have to do," he said. "That's all I have to say, Colonel Reynolds. The choice is yours. Take care of your country—and your own future—or take us down the road to ruin."

"Sir, if this is about those disks, I've got to—"

He leapt out of his chair. As if a phantom Frenchman had hit him with the tool they used on me. "I don't know what you're talking about. I don't know any of the details. This was just a counseling session. For your own good. We're concerned about you. Now, if you'll excuse me . . ."

He banged out of the room. In seconds, the aide reappeared to take out the trash. He looked at me pityingly.

"Christ," he said. "Whatever he wanted, you should've just done it."

I didn't look at him. I stole one last view of the river from a general's mansion. The sun had turned the brown water into gold fields strewn with diamonds.

"General Gabrielli always wins," the aide reminded me.

Man does not live by fear alone. I drove back to the Hill and turned onto Pennsylvania Avenue Southeast. There was a little Greek place where Tish and I had acquired a regular table. Although I knew it was foolish, I intended to have more than one glass of wine with dinner. Had I been on the *Titanic,* the divers would have found my skeleton in the champagne cellar.

Gabrielli had shaken me badly. The door had shut on my last refuge. At the back of my mind, I had always counted on the Army being there for me. But Gabrielli *was* the Army. And he was going to make sure he was someplace else when I shot the red star cluster.

I grabbed a parking spot down from the restaurant. The evening simmered. The few human beings on the sidewalks looked like they had no place else to go. I locked the car and took a deep breath of city.

As I turned, I saw the Peugeot. Brown, rat-bitten job, it sounded like a garbage disposal. The car pulled in at an angle, corralling me between its passenger side and my own car. Cuckold jumped out of the backseat. With a gob of white gauze and tape over his nose. And a 9mm pistol held low.

"Get in," he said. His voice sounded as though he had pinched his nostrils shut. "Or we will kill you here."

He made way for me to get into the backseat and nudged me once with the gun barrel. Jerry was behind the wheel, drumming his thumbs and checking the mirrors. Cigarette organic to his lower lip. Cuckold jumped in beside me. Jerry put the pedal to the floor and the car gargled down Pennsylvania Avenue. Heading away from civilization.

"You really do have diplomatic immunity," I said. "So . . . do you work for de La Vere, or does he work for you?"

Cuckold parked his 9mm against his leg. "That was stupid. Very stupid. What you have done today. You are a fool. And your police are shit. I wanted to help you."

"Everybody wants to help me."

Jerry turned up by the combat Safeway, then cut right again. Working the back streets. In a couple of minutes we were in a part of town you did not want to be in after dark. Jerry was either trying to lose a tail or making wrong turns. We pulled in across the street from a cemetery. I knew the area from my early-morning runs. When the gangbangers were getting their beauty sleep.

"Get out," Cuckold told me. "Look happy. Walk between us into the cemetery."

"Sounds happy to me."

When we got out, the folks cooling off on their porches stared at us as if we had arrived from Mars. A little girl in cornrows let her jumping rope go slack. An old man shook his head. Cuckold had his pistol in his pocket, but he wasn't fooling anybody on this street.

"I hope you both brought weapons," I said.

"Shut up. Go inside. Follow the path."

Cuckold had called me an amateur the night we met. But I was not even playing. Cuckold and Jerry, on the other hand, were supposed to be pros. And they had gotten it hopelessly wrong. I pegged the cemetery as a dead drop they used with agents. When everybody else was doing it over the Internet.

The headstones were old and vandalized. A noseless, stub-winged angel presided over a litter of malt-liquor bottles and a pink condom. Jerry led the way behind a mausoleum and we tripped over a pair of terminal dopers sprawled against the granite. They did not even lift their eyes when our shoes struck them.

We turned away to find another spot.

A service building stood at the end of a line of graves. Cuckold said, "Over there. Sit down."

I sat down on a low stone bench. With Cuckold standing over me and Jerry squatting as though he had grown up in Indochina. I had questions for *les frères* myself. But I wanted to hear what they had to say first.

"Listen now," Cuckold told me. "France did not

do this thing. We did not put the bomb in your laboratory.''

"Right.''

"It is the truth. You must listen. We cannot fight. There is no time.'' He held his hands out in front of him, palms up, fingers clutching air. ''We are not the bombers. It was a great surprise to us. We would not be so obvious. It would not be so soon.'' He looked at the dying sky. ''We want to . . . stop the people who hurt us. Not just to make a body count. That's the American way. Not ours.''

"And I'm just another gringo dumbdick.''

"No. Oh, perhaps you are a fool. But you can still help us. And help yourself. How can I make you understand that we have not done this bombing?''

"If you didn't, who did?''

On a low ridge, a line of figures in baggy shorts blacked against the sunset in a medieval dance of death.

Cuckold looked at me with that earnestness that makes the French so comical. ''We do not know. We do not understand it. My partner believes it was the same people who made the bombing in our facility. Perhaps it's true. I am uncertain.''

"Just for the sake of cafe conversation, who would these people be? *Who* did both of the bombings?''

Sirens in the background. Maybe one of the locals had called the cops when they marked the big bulge too far to the side in Cuckold's slacks. But I doubted it.

"We don't know,'' Cuckold said. ''It is a great

mystery. We don't know why your people attacked us. And now you have made an attack against your own laboratory.''

"You believe Americans did both jobs? That we blew up our own people? Come on.''

He looked dumbfounded by my naïveté. "Who else? Nothing else makes sense. Only we do not know which Americans.''

"I thought Europeans always blamed the CIA.''

The bandages on his nose rumpled. "The CIA is not so brave now. Too much bureaucracy. Everyone watches them. And we are French, not Europeans.''

A shot popped in the distance, followed by two more. Cuckold jumped. But Jerry did not.

"Listen to me,'' Cuckold said, stepping closer. The air had thickened with shadows and he wanted to see my face. They had picked a truly dumb spot for the meeting, unless they planned to leave me here. But that did not feel like the case. These boys were desperate, but they wanted results, not more trouble.

I still believed they had bombed our lab.

A piercing voice from the background cried, "Shit, bitch. Do it now.''

Jerry and Cuckold conferred in French. I could not get any of it. Little black flies found us. Cuckold and I swiped at them. Jerry ignored the bites.

Maybe Gabrielli had done me a favor. By giving me a reality check. I had long regarded the Army as the last refuge of virtue, but at least one shining three-star had shit on his shoes. Lot of thinking to do later.

I certainly did not like these cowboys. But I had reduced my life to one clear goal now: Get Tish back alive.

I knew two things. First, for all their dramatics and pistol-waving, Balzac and Dumas were not interested in hurting me. At least for the moment. Second, they really needed my help.

Cuckold stepped back toward me, wiping out an old crack vial. More efficient packaging had made the vials all but disappear. A couple of years back, they had been all over the sidewalks during my morning jogs. They crunched like roaches.

"My partner," Cuckold began again, "he says he does not know how you can think of yourself as a man. He says it is obvious. The people who have made the bombings are also the ones who have killed your lover. But you do not care. You let them kill her and see no requirement for vengeance. He would not want you near his sister."

"Does she shave her legs?"

It's easy to be flip once you realize you don't have to be afraid. I was far more spooked by the neighborhood than by Belmondo and Delon.

"Do you feel nothing for her?" Cuckold asked. "Nothing for the loss of such an amiable woman? Have you already accepted this blond woman as the replacement? And Americans call the French cynical."

I made a decision.

"You're reading yesterday's papers, pal."

"What does that mean?"

"You haven't heard the news. She's alive. You're not in the loop. You need to hire a good consultant."

Cuckold looked at Jerry. And oozed out some French. Then he snapped back to me.

"*Who* is alive?"

"Tish O'Malley. My girl."

They really were not in the loop. Depardieu could not have done surprise so convincingly. Cuckold fired off more French. Jerry caught the surprise epidemic and moved closer to me. Aching to speak for himself.

"You should have paid more attention in school," I told him.

"How do you know this?" Cuckold demanded. "What are you saying? Everyone knows she has died. It is in the newspapers."

"You trust the media?" I shook my head exaggeratedly. "Come over here. Take notes, if you want. She's alive. I've got a videotape. Or had one. She was unmistakably alive on that tape, and the tape was unmistakably made after the car bomb jacked up my insurance rates." I looked at him. "A man named Aalstrom handed it to me in a burger joint last night. Karl Aalstrom. A-a-l-s-t-r-o-m. Claims he's out of L.A., but I don't really know where he's bunking these days. He's been running errands for some tough hombres. Maybe the people who bombed your lab. So why don't you go find out? Now let's get on our horses and ride out of here before the scalping party arrives.''

Cuckold looked down at me. With darkness rolling over us, it really was time to go. Pistols or not. Around here, pistols were for the fourteen-and-under crowd. The real bangers carried AKs or better.

''You're lying,'' he said. ''You have created this story to confuse us.''

''Right. But I'm supposed to believe you didn't toss the firecracker down in Georgia? You're begging for information, and here I am giving it to you. And *you* don't believe *me*?''

''Describe this man. This Aalstrom.''

''Medium height. Forty-two waist stuffed into size thirty-eight slacks. Figure it out in metric. Too much sun and too much bad living on his face. Forty, but looks fifty. Thinning blond hair. Dresses like Euro-trash. You'll love it. Probably wears sunglasses to bed. If you've been tapping my phone, you've got his voice.''

''We are not listening to your telephone.''

''Then you missed your shot. Somebody is.''

''If you lie, it helps nobody.''

''I couldn't make Aalstrom up. His nickname's Aley, by the way. You can't miss him. He's every European intellectual's image of American manhood.''

''Where do we find him?''

I smiled. We were having a contest for dummy of the year. ''If I knew, I'd put you on his ass this minute. He has it coming. But don't worry. You'll find him, unless you flunked the basic course. He's so stupid he's using his own name.''

"Maybe we will find him.''

"Listen to me . . . and no bullshit. Aalstrom's a small-timer. But he's working for big boys. He's a garbage collector in a fancy neighborhood. If you can roll him up, I suspect he'll be extremely informative.'' I looked at Jerry. "I'm being straight with you guys. All I ask in return is this. Any information on Tish O'Malley, you help me out. I'm not sure how much I really care about what you've done or haven't done, at this point. I just want Tish back. Alive. And undamaged. Deal?''

Cuckold shrugged. "We have no interest in the girl. If we find her, you can have her. If she truly is alive.''

"And any information about her. You share with me, and I'll keep on sharing with you. But no more freebies.''

More French.

The background noise had risen like the water level in a pool. Bad voices and ripples of sounds you did not want to investigate.

"Boys, we really ought to get out of here,'' I said.

Cuckold squatted down a few inches from my face. "All right. We will make the deal. Now, there is something else. There are rumors about computer disks. Perhaps you know about these, too?''

"No idea. What's on them?''

Cuckold's nose patch held an echo of light. But his eyes were black.

"Perhaps the information is important. There are no details." He glanced up at the dark shape of his partner. "But I will make you an offer on trust. If these disks present themselves to you—I think you will know what they are—in such a case, the government of France would help you. In return for the disks. We would provide you with money. So that you and your lover could begin life again. Someplace discreet."

"Sorry. I don't know anything about your disks. But . . . just for the record . . . how much are you offering?"

Cuckold fingered his chin. Reading the braille of his stubble. "Let us say . . . one hundred thousand U.S. dollars? It could provide you with a new beginning . . ."

France really was on the mat.

"Can we go now?" I asked.

We went. The cemetery was an all-purpose community center after dark. Party zone. Love nest. Target range. I walked fast and made Bocuse and Escoffier keep up. Somebody had brought in a boom box. It rapped pure hatred. I figured the owner must be a tough customer if he could bring his electronics in here and not expect to get stripped. Near the gate, I felt sure we were going to face a lineup of gangstas, but the shadows turned out to be kids. They might have taken on one of us, but not three.

"Man, you got a dollar?" one of the smaller kids asked me.

"Shit," an older boy laughed, "he ain't give you no dollar, motherfucker."

On the street, the coming of darkness had driven the porch sitters inside. The blinds were down. On a lamplit corner, a punk did jive-and-slap with a couple of his road dogs. I felt better when we were in the car.

The Peugeot would not start. Jerry cranked it several times, then punched it, then got out and checked under the hood. After a minute's wait, Cuckold climbed out after him. Martin and Lewis. I made it three.

Whole lot of *merde*.

"Boys," I said, "I recommend you lock it back up and we walk fast for that bridge down there. Don't worry about the car. These kids have their pride."

Cuckold looked at me pathetically. "But I have signed for this car. From the embassy."

CHAPTER 8

I PARKED MY RENTAL CLOSE TO THE HOUSE. ILLEGALLY. Aiming for speed. Scared. And feeling plenty stupid.

I had wanted to ask Cuckold what he had meant about us making fools of the French even before the bombing of their research lab. It had become a mental itch. Yet I had gone brain-dead when I had the chance to put the question.

I needed sleep. R&R. A way out of a problem I still could not define.

Corry sat on my front steps. You could do that on my block, when you were not mixed up with bombers, kidnappers, and murderers. She looked like a kid sitting there. Until she stood up.

"I was worried about you," she told me. She had her 900-number voice on.

"Let's take it inside." I undid the locks as quickly as I could.

"Is somebody after you again?"

163

I ignored the question and shut the door behind us, hoping there were no hidden surprises behind the refrigerator. I started up the stairs, then doubled back. I went into the kitchen and opened the towel drawer.

"Here," I said, forcing the thirty-eight into her hand. "I must've been nuts to let you drop this on me. Where the hell did you come up with that thing, anyway? You borrow it from the mayor?"

She raised her eyes to mine. "It was Em's."

That stopped me. "Em wasn't a pistol-packer."

"He was scared. I told you. I didn't know what it was all about. I was afraid he was going to kill himself." She paused. "Or me." Inching closer. "Everything had gotten so bad between us. I hid it."

My eyebrows just about touched the ceiling. "You *hid* it? Right. And naturally, little Corry did such a good job that the demolition crew that took Em's place apart couldn't find it. Come on, Corry."

She squared her shoulders. "I didn't hide it in the apartment. I hid it at work."

"You hid it in a Senate office?"

"Wasn't that a good place?"

"You couldn't have gotten it past the guards."

"The X-ray machines are for the tourists. I have a pass."

I shook my head. "Corry . . . my dad warned me about girls who play with firearms."

"Oh, get off it, John. You don't know what it was like. You've got this fluffed-up romantic picture of Em. Well, he was a prick's prick. And he drank like a Russian. Half the time, he was bouncing off the walls. Or bouncing me off the walls. And I was a money slut for staying with him. Send me to the penitentiary.''

"I don't want to hear anything else about Em. You know, he was buried today.''

"How many sympathy bouquets did *you* send? You think I'm this black widow or something. Well, how about this scenario? I'm scared. I'm really scared, big Mr. Soldier. And I know more about Em's funeral than you do. He was buried at ten o'clock this morning. Whittier Cemetery. Old Massachusetts families only. The Right Reverend Francis Barlow presiding.'' She twisted up her small mouth. "They knew Em. They weren't about to be embarrassed by a low turnout. So they preempted it. Told the world to screw off. 'The Carrolls do not require the sympathy of the masses.' Ever met his family, John? They treated me like pond scum because my dad wasn't in the social register. They were *terrified* he was going to marry me.''

"Was he?''

"No.''

"Yeah?''

"He asked me. I told him no. I knew I couldn't take a whole lifetime of Em.'' Her face fell into bitterness. The real thing. "Try hanging with an alkie sometime. You can't even use the bathroom for half an hour after they've been in there.''

"Save it for your autobiography. I've got to go.'' I started up the stairs again.

She followed me. Gun in hand.

"Where are you going? What's going on?"

I charged into my bedroom. With Tish's panties and books still scattered on the floor. I got out a suitcase the cops had tossed around and began loading the necessities.

"Where are you going?"

"Careful with the gun, all right? I don't know where I'm going. I just need to get out of here. Too much traffic. I need to think. Sort some of this out."

"Let me come. I can help."

"Corry . . . military briefers always prepare three courses of action for the boss to choose from." I picked up a clump of socks from the floor. "First, the one you want the boss to pick. The second option is one you can live with, but that is clearly not as good as the first. The third one is so stupid, you know the boss wouldn't pick it in a thousand years." It was hard to tell brown socks from black in the crummy light. I threw them all in. "Taking you with me would be course-of-action number three."

"Please. You don't understand how afraid I am."

"You didn't look afraid sitting on my steps. You don't *smell* afraid, sister. And I don't see anybody after your ass. Except the usual suspects, of which there are thousands in this town. Tens of thousands." I settled for three crumpled pairs of jockey shorts. I did not know if I would be gone one night or weeks. I was due back in the office Monday morning. But I was not optimistic about the future. And I knew I would do whatever it took to find Tish. "Corry, I suspect that the only thing you have to be afraid of is proximity to me.''

"I'm afraid by myself."

"Call Senator Faust. Bet he'll put you up. And put that gun down. Guns are serious medicine.''

"I can't call him. I mean, I don't want to call him. I *can't* call him.''

I hit the bathroom, emptying shelves into an old canvas shaving kit. "I thought Faust was on the most-eligible list? Big ladies' man? It's your shot at the brass ring, baby.''

She sat down on the bed. Which had not been made in a very long time. She skated the gun across the mattress and lowered her face into her hands.

"I've been trying to explain. You never give me a chance.''

I stopped. "Okay. Last chance. What's this all about, Corry? I frankly don't see this as your preferred option for a Saturday night.''

She looked up. With the intensity of a woman in love. Maybe fear and love do the same thing to you.

"Somebody came to the office today. To see the senator. That never happens on Saturday. He doesn't permit it. Not even when they stay in session.''

"White House intern?''

"*Please*, John. I'm sorry about last night. I'm *glad* your girlfriend's still alive. But I'm not expendable, either. I'm a person, a human being. Just like you. And her.'' The color bloomed in those wet blues. "This guy. He was just . . . so out of place. Maybe Las Vegas. But definitely not Washington, D.C. He

and Faust were in there for, it must've been an hour.
It didn't make any sense to me. Faust is just so . . .
fastidious about people.'' She raised her face to the
light. ''The guy stopped by my desk and introduced
himself on the way out. Mr. Angstrom or something.
He said he knew you, John. He said it in a way that
meant he knew a lot of other things, too. It scared
me. I mean, it really scared me. I wanted to ask the
senator about him, but he took off like a rabbit. Right
after this Angstrom guy. He nearly knocked me down
on his way out the door.'' Her stare nailed me. ''Who
was the guy, John? What does he want from us?''

I looked down at her. And at her gun.

''Your suitcase still downstairs?'' I asked her.

We headed out 66 and stopped at a fast-food joint
in Manassas. The burgers of Bull Run. Corry talked
with food in her mouth. Something Tish had never
done. It was as if she had forgotten who she was for
a moment.

''So you think Senator Faust is mixed up in all
this?'' she asked. Touching away a fleck of mayo on
her upper lip. For a woman who looked like an aero-
bics instructor, Corry had a serious appetite for junk
food. ''I mean, that guy looked like *some*body's
problem. Your friend.''

''Why not? Everybody else seems to be wired in.
And Aley Aalstrom is not and never was my friend.''
I bit, chewed, swallowed, and asked, ''The senator's
been a big supporter of the NGFB, hasn't he? Mr.
We Need It Now?''

Corry almost finished her mouthful and said, "He's big on defense. Period. Faust never met a weapons system he didn't like." She licked her teeth and remembered. "He and Em were tight. Em used to put together these dinners for him at a gazillion dollars a plate. All corporate types. Faust would give them fifteen minutes on Mom, apple pie, and armaments. I used to have to go to all of them. Em liked to parade me. Feel me under the table. Then we'd go home and nothing would happen. Later on, I went to work for Faust. Em fixed it. I let him. I told you about that. I figured it was a big step in the right direction."

One thing I had noticed about Corry—you could ask her about chaos theory, and by the fifth or sixth sentence she would have the conversation back on herself.

"I'm not a Hill junkie," I said. "Don't even watch C-SPAN. So tell me. Is Faust for real? Or is a strong posture on defense just a moneymaker for the guy?"

She popped a last brown French fry into her mouth. "Oh, he's for real. Even has his own personal gun collection. He showed it to me at one of his parties. The guy's a barrel stroker. Real Freudian stuff. Asked me if I wanted to go shooting with him." She wiped her mouth. "He's a case. Loves to visit military bases. Kind of a hobby for him. If not an obsession. He doesn't have a lot of defense industry back home, so he prides himself on his impartial credentials. Defense industry loves it. They can't get enough. They could care less how he votes on Medicare or education. As long as he pushes the big-ticket acquisition stuff.'' She wiped her mouth a second time, although it was already clean. ''Em used to laugh about him. When he was drunk. He said that once Macon-Bolt got Faust up in an NGFB prototype, his committee would double the order. And it was more than that. Em and Bob Nechestny were betting on Faust as a potential number two man on the next ticket. Regional balance. Listening to it all made me feel like a member of the inner circle. It was exciting. I admit it. It still is.''

''Ever met Nechestny? Mr. Macon-Bolt?''

Corry looked surprised. As if I had asked a very dumb question. ''Sure. Em was his boy. All the parties. Do we have time for coffee?''

''Get one to go.''

I stood up. So did Corry.

''I've got to make a stop,'' she told me.

''I'll get the coffee. How do you take it?''

''Black.''

I got in line behind a scrawny guy in jeans and a worn T-shirt. He had a ratty ponytail, a rattier beard, and a trucking company cap. He talked country. Maybe never wore a tie in his adult years. Commuters wouldn't see him, except when he came by to cut their grass. But I knew guys like him from the Army. He was the kind of man whose great-great-grandpappy wore gray and clubbed the shit out of the Army of the Potomac until Grant came east and sat on him with the full weight of the Union. He counted out pennies to pay for his McNuggets. Born knowing Washington was out to fuck him. He fought our wars anyway.

I waited by the door for Corry and handed her the coffee. "More on Bob Nechestny, please."

The parking lot stank of truck exhaust. The car had an air-conditioner sourness. I had tuned the radio to a college jazz station before we stopped, and I let it continue playing low.

"Bob's a smoothie," Corry said. "Type who bought his manners when he joined his first country club. He knows the world jumps when he gives the order, so he doesn't feel like he has to make a lot of noise. Terrific suits. Knows how to work a crowd. Makes senators look like mannequins. God returns his calls. And probably worries Bob will be too busy to chat." She leaned into the seat belt to sip coffee without baptising herself. "I don't know what else to say. If he ever dies, they'll probably lay him in a temple instead of a grave. Nobody knows how rich he is."

"What did Em think of him?"

"Em admired him. Worshipped him."

"I never knew Em to worship anybody."

I turned off onto 29 South. With back roads in our future. Where I could register headlights following us in the dark.

Corry edged into her coffee again. "Maybe 'worshipped' was too strong. But Em was dazzled. The money . . . the access. The deal-making. He used to say, 'I don't know how the guy does it.' From Em, that was serious praise. And I think he was a little afraid of Nechestny, to tell you the truth.''

''Why?''

Invisible shrug in the darkness. ''Who isn't afraid of the boss? Nechestny was the ultimate boss.''

''You said Em was going to pieces over the last several months. That things were going downhill between the two of you. That he was drinking.''

''We didn't have much of a hill to go down.''

''Can you tie it to any events? The decline? Anything out of the ordinary happen?''

We bounced over rail tracks and Corry lifted the coffee high. A floodlit gas station flew a Confederate battle flag.

''Life with Em was never ordinary,'' she told me. ''I don't know. He was traveling a lot. We were best together when he was spending a lot of time on the road. You know how that is. I do remember one time. He'd been out at one of those hush-hush test ranges in Nevada or Utah or someplace. He came back from the airport already hammered. Absolutely stinking. That was the first time he ever hit me. It was so sudden. I never expected it.''

''Why didn't you leave him? When he hit you?''

She waited a moment to answer. I turned onto a rural route. Mazing our way to the west.

''Well . . . I told you. About the opportunity I thought he represented. I thought I needed him.'' She sipped at her coffee again. Then again. I had her white face in my peripheral vision. ''I guess this is going to sound sick,'' she said at last. ''But I think a part of me thought I deserved it.''

The jazz station was breaking up. We were well into the Piedmont. I turned up the volume and scanned through the channels. The Ford had a crappy radio.

I don't think either of us wanted silence. I settled on a DJ with a salesman's voice and a Nashville playlist. I did not listen to country very often, but I felt like I had heard all of the songs before. Then the hustler said we were going to get another news update from Atlanta.

It did not make the night any better. The Atlanta cops, the FBI, and the ATF had an Iranian immigrant holed up in a condominium. It sounded like a real siege. The reporter on the scene said the man was the prime suspect in the bombing of the aerospace research facility whose loss had been such a tragedy for area families and the nation.

I pictured a very frightened rug smuggler hugging the floor and wishing he had a flying carpet.

I did not believe an Iranian had done it. Unless he had been hired to mask the local talent. I still could not say who was behind the bombing. But I did not believe for a minute it was anybody with a turban and bushy eyebrows.

A number of nasty things had gathered for a jamboree in my stomach. I was beginning to sense how very small a chip I was in this game.

Small meant disposable.

*   *   *

I stopped at a motel in one of those Shenandoah Valley towns that live off agriculture and Civil War tourists. Corry came into the office with me. When I specified twin beds, the night clerk looked at me like I was king of the fools.

It was after midnight. Corry shut herself in the bathroom while I watched CNN. The condo siege in Atlanta was the big story. Corry came back out in a T-shirt, but she had panties on this time. She got into her bed and switched off the lamp on her night table. I lowered the volume but kept watching. With a sick feeling that I knew what was coming. Death live.

A little after one, the Feds and a local SWAT team stormed the Iranian's place. There was enough gunfire to make it seem like revenge for Desert One. They killed him. No officers down. I didn't wait for the commentators to start second-guessing. I turned off the TV and went in to brush my teeth.

I stumbled to my bed in darkness. Exhausted. But sleep was not on the program. Too much to think about. Too little clarity. And Corry's steady breathing.

After a while, she got up to go to the bathroom again. When she came back, she stood between the two beds. As if trying to make up her mind.

I closed my eyes like a kid afraid of the bogeyman. After maybe a minute, I heard her crawl under her sheet.

We were both worn down. Corry snored. No sleep for me, though. Jagged thoughts. Stabbing and re-treating. Answers that dissolved when I reached for them. Soldiers are trained to take the initiative. I was just a lab rat.

Then, in the darkness that's been haunting us since our cave years, revelation hit. The kind of thing beyond logic and reason. When you just know something.

Something bad.

I got up—very quietly—and felt in my travel bag for the pistol she had given back to me. Insisting we might need it.

John Reynolds, crouched down like the fool that he was. Champ Stupid. Bare feet on a gritty rug.

I drew the weapon out by the barrel, took it into the john, and shut the door.

The motel was not going to put the nearest Hyatt out of business. The fixtures were fifties white porcelain and the light was hard. I rolled the chamber. Then I opened the gun and dropped the bullets into my hand. I flicked it shut again and tried the action.

Click.

Okay. Whom did she expect me to shoot with it? I did not believe her story about how she had gotten her hands on the thing. I had not believed much of what she had told me. But I had not thought her through. Call Freud, Jung, and Adler to ask why, but she had become a blind spot. I wanted to cordon her off, to keep her at just the right distance. But there was no right distance. And there had to be more to her than a clinging case of nerves. Or even poor taste in men.

What was the gun all about?

I am not a weapons junkie. But I've been around enough of them. I went over the revolver thoroughly. Pretty simple piece of metal. Everything worked fine.

Then, as an early-morning afterthought, I checked out the bullets. At first glance, they looked normal. But something was off in the vegetable bin.

I put the pistol and the rest of the ammo down on the floor, then held one of the rounds up to the light. Squinting. Measuring with my eyes. Then I inspected each of the others. After that, I just sat for a long time.

Finally, I reloaded the thirty-eight, shut off the lights, and went back into the bedroom. My eyes needed to readjust to the dark and I went slowly. Quietly. I walked up to Corry's bed, bumping it a little, then stopped. Her snoring session was over, but she lay in the stillness of sleep. Her hair shone white.

I pointed the gun at her head. Holding it eight or ten inches back. And I pulled the trigger.

I pulled the trigger again and again, listening to six claps of the hammer and the following silences. Corry moaned once, but did not wake. She had given me a working weapon. But the bullets had been doctored. The first time I pulled it on somebody, I would have been dead.

My morning-after had come early.

When I could not bear looking at her anymore, I put the thirty-eight back where it had been sleeping in the luggage and slipped outside. I sat against the motel wall in my jockey shorts and T-shirt, watching the occasional car go by.

* * *

I went inside when the horizon began to crack and got a couple of hours of bad sleep. When I could not lie there any longer, Corry was still dreaming contentedly. She truly was a beautiful woman.

I showered and dressed. The noise lifted her eyelids a little.

"There's a diner down the road," I said. "I'll walk down and get us some breakfast."

"I don't eat breakfast." Voice husky with nightness. "Just coffee. Please. Black. And maybe some juice. Are you all right?"

I left. I wanted to keep on going. To leave Corry and all the rest of it in a cut-rate motel room.

The motel sat at the edge of town, where signs pointed off to the interstate. It was Sunday morning in a green world. Cars and pickups went by with families. Church-bound. Back in D.C., this was the hour to bagel-out and read the papers.

The diner was a bastion of contrariness. Old guys in suspenders, a couple of bikers. And a time-machine waitress. A family in their Sunday best sat in a corner booth. The smell of frying meat and coffee thickened the air.

I took a stool at the counter. Figuring I would eat first. I was in no hurry to go back to the motel. The waitress brought me coffee without the asking. The menu was not health-oriented.

It was hard to believe that entire civilizations had existed without coffee. The diner did it sharp and on the thin side. But hot.

Two old men laughed in their private world.

I ordered big. I was way beyond the chickenshit despair that steals your appetite. While the cook was doing the heavy lifting, I got change and bought a Sunday *Post* from a machine out on the sidewalk. The edition had closed too early to include the end of the Atlanta condo siege.

I drank more coffee. Amazed at the normalcy of the rest of the world. I was already dead to the news-papers, ancient history. Tish had been a blip. I ate fast, piggish, and even finished up the little packets of jam with the toast.

A burly guy sat down on the stool beside me. Arms cut off his T-shirt. Little Devil tattoo on a construction worker's bicep. He was as shaggy as a mountain man, beard and mustache dirty with gray. He looked just on the edge of unstable. Typical diner dweller on the American byways.

The waitress brought him coffee, topped me off, and went to pick up a plate of pancakes from under the warmer lights.

"Much in the paper?" Mr. Muscles asked me.

"You can have it."

"Thank you kindly." He reached for his wallet and dropped a twenty on the counter. "Breakfast is my treat. Now get the fuck up, walk out that door, and get in the white van."

I put down my mug. "And if I don't?"

He could take me. I had a soldier's muscles. He had real ones. And he did not look like he would succumb to elegance of form.

"Well, then," he said, smiling under his mustache, "I'll have to kill you right here." He looked at the big pink bow on the waitress's backside. "Have to kill her, too. And a bunch of these other good people. Just to make it look right." He took a quick sip of coffee. "Girl in the motel, too. And that redheaded wild woman of yours."

A big hand closed over my upper arm.

"Moment of truth," he told me. "All this shit has reached a point where we either achieve resolution . . . or clean house. Your call, Colonel."

CHAPTER 9

"SIT OVER THERE." MY ESCORT POINTED TO AN ARrangement of deck chairs by the pool. The big-buck surroundings made him look like an escaped jailbird. "He'll get to you when he's ready."

I sat. Under the shade of a blue-and-white-striped umbrella. In the pool, a man swam laps. Savagely. Doing a breast stroke, he thrust a tanned, shaved head up from the water. Followed by monstrous shoulders. I had seen plenty of swimmers with better form, but none with more ferocity. The guy was in a grudge fight with nature.

After a last heart-attack lap, he climbed out. Dripping. Hogging the North American oxygen supply. He stripped off his goggles, tossing them onto a table meant to hold long drinks. Coming toward me, he reminded me of a minotaur.

Scars webbed his body. Skin gouged and horned. He looked as if he had been taken apart and reassembled.

I stood up.

A big hand shot out.

"Roscoe Hunt. Call me Punchy. So you're the stud who's been pissing off everybody from the Buddha to Jesus Christ."

He wasn't a bully about the handshake. He didn't have to be. Firm, wet paw. Up and down and done. He turned half away and ripped an enormous towel from a stack on a bench. Rubbing his scalp, then fitting the towel over his head like a monk's hood. He crouched and stripped off his trunks. Grunting, he dried himself in the sunlight.

"Mind if I call you John?"

"Do I have a choice?"

He cocked an eyebrow. It rippled the bare skin above it. "Hell, everybody gets a choice, son. Life *is* choice. Free goddamned will. We just have to be prepared to pay for our wrong choices."

"Call me whatever you like."

He dropped the towel on the flagstones and pulled on a fine blue cotton robe. With the logo of the Oriental Hotel, Bangkok. A pitcher of water waited. The ice had faded to feathers. He picked up the pitcher and drank, ignoring the glass.

The back of his hand wiped brown lips. The skin around his mouth looked as if it had been charred.

"Truth be told, I wish I didn't have to call you anything," Hunt said. "Wish I'd never heard of you. You're a pain in the butt." He looked at me with green eyes hardened by intelligence. "But here we are."

I cocked my head toward the big house. "Not a bad place to be."

"I like it," he said. "Well, come on inside. We'll get us something to drink." He walked as though he really wanted to run. Too much energy for one body. "Magdalena," he called. "Magda*lena*."

You sensed immediately that Punchy Hunt was the real thing. He was what all the blustering Gabriellis wanted to be and could not bring off. He raised your fears, while the others just raised their voices.

My escort had brought me—after two changes of vehicle in wooded areas—to a horsey estate between Route 66 and Middleburg. The area was a theme park for millionaires. Nobody blindfolded me or played rough. It did not seem to matter that I saw where we were going. My escort and the succession of drivers seemed concerned only about being followed.

The estate was one of the serious ones you can't see from the highway. Just a turnoff with brick pillars and a "Private Road" sign. Arcades of trees. White fences as long as Third World frontiers. From a low hill I saw a small lake and a private airfield, wind sock dead in the heat. The house of white-painted brick looked like it had been built in the eighteenth century for a serious player. Every other generation had added a wing or a floor. It was big, gracefully imperfect, and unattainable. The kind of place that made a good citizen feel like a loser.

The back of the house had been redone with a lot of glass. A door slid open and a black Lab darted toward the general. Followed by a Hispanic in a maid's costume. She was plain enough not to cause trouble in the barracks.

"Let him out and he always wants to jump in the goddamned pool with me," Hunt said. I thought the dog would leap up on him. Just short, it stopped, sat, and showed its tongue.

"Good boy, Castro. All right. Come on." The general slapped his thigh and the dog closed on him. "Can't swim with a goddamned dog. Love the little mutt. But I don't want to go swimming with him. Magdalena?"

"*Sí, señor general.*"

"Get us up a pitcher of gin and tonic. Like gin and tonic, John? Only damned drink for this weather. Hungry?"

"I had a power breakfast."

Hunt grunted. "Just as well. Can't have a serious talk over food. That's Washington bullshit." He grunted again, with the dog heeling. "Fuckers never talk about anything serious anyway. You like that goddamned town?"

"It's an interesting place."

"No goddamned place for a soldier. Pick up all sorts of bad habits. Get sloppy. Worst thing that can happen to a man. Lose his discipline." He regarded me. "Looks like you keep yourself in pretty good shape."

"I do what I can."

"One of my boys do that to your eye?"

I shook my head. There had not been much swell-

ing or discoloration where Frenchy had nailed me.
But Hunt was accustomed to reading all the signs.

"A foreign relations seminar got out of hand."

He grunted and led the way inside the house,
showing me his back. A man who had forgotten how
to be afraid, Hunt was an exception among excep-
tions. If it had not been for Special Forces, I doubt
he would have survived in the military. There was
just too much of him. Probably wrestled the doctor
when his mother gave birth.

The air conditioning felt wet on my skin. I followed Hunt down a hallway lined with hunting prints
and the loot of an overseas career.

"Come on in," he said, opening a door. He held
it for me. When I passed by him, I realized how
much shorter he was. It was startling. He was shorter
than I was, but bigger in every way that mattered.
He could have ripped me apart.

He made the dog stay in the hallway and it flopped
dolefully. Hunt shut the door. "Sit down, sit down."
We were in the handsomest library I had ever seen
that did not come with a tour guide. I sat in a brown
leather chair of a quality I would never be able to
afford. Even if I survived long enough to make another major furniture purchase.

The maid knocked and the general told her to
come in. The dog whimpered for attention, but did
not cross the threshold. The maid laid down a silver
tray with a pitcher and the proper glasses. Then she
got out of Dodge. She had known exactly what Hunt
would ask for and had it ready.

"Good worker," the general told me. "Brought her up from El Sal. Whole damned family massacred. By our side. Roberto was scum. But he was our scum."

"That your way of telling me Aley Aalstrom's working for you?"

The general laughed. One big rush of noise.

"Hell," he said, "I knew you and I were going to get along, John. Yeah, well. 'This thing of darkness I acknowledge mine.' Can't run a foreign policy without folks like Aalstrom, and you can't run a business without them, either. When's the last time you bought a car off a Mormon elder?" He smiled, but did not laugh again. "You're smart enough to see the uses of somebody like Aley. Don't pretend otherwise."

The library was magnificent. Not huge. But big enough for a fine old desk with carved pedestals— dogs and stags chasing each other—and a quartet of gents' chairs. The expensive editions in the bookcases looked cherished and read. The shelves closest to me held several different sets of Shakespeare, none of them new. As in the hallway, the paintings were of hunting scenes, or of dogs or game.

I was just about to tell the general exactly what I thought about Aley and anybody who would employ him, when he stood up. He had followed my eyes.

"That's a Landseer," he told me. "Real thing. Hell, maybe it's not art the way Constable or Turner were art. But *I* like it. All those fag critics can bugger off."

"Landseer's respected."

"Hell he is," the general said. He poured two gin and tonics. "That Philly exhibition back in the eighties? Know why they did that? Bunch of Landseers were coming on the market. Drove the prices way up. It's business, John. The buck is the final arbiter of beauty. Follow art, do you? Most soldiers wouldn't know Landseer from a landmine."

I shrugged. "I've been to the big city. Didn't like everything I saw there."

He held out a glass and I accepted it. Figuring it couldn't hurt.

"I like the art trade. Better than Vegas. More substance. But take it from me, it's all about the money. And nothing but. Lay down enough auction-house money, the Metropolitan would stage a black-velvet painting retrospective. With a ten-pound catalog full of scholarly commentaries. 'Elvis as Allegory.' Ever read Marx?"

I nodded.

"Bugger didn't like to wash, know that? Same thing as goddamned Che Guevara. Wish I could've been there when we nailed his dirty ass. My personal theory is that Communism went down the tubes because the sonsofbitches had no sense of hygiene. Good hygiene is a hallmark of the disciplined man." He took a powerful drink. Able to inhabit fully whatever he was doing at the moment. "Cruelty isn't discipline, John. It's a manifestation of inadequacy, of failure—I've always seen it as a last resort, no more. When I go cruel, you know I'm serious. Frustrated. But let's stick to Marx. Now, that smelly-ass sonofabitch was no dummy. Understood greed. The way things really work. Just couldn't accept that greed wasn't a monopoly of the moneyed classes. Hated what he knew, romanticized what he didn't. Typical goddamned intellectual. But valuable, nonetheless. I find him instructive. Read Max Weber?"

I nodded again. I had been an excruciatingly dutiful student.

"Good for you. Weber's my boy. Greed isn't what brings us real wealth. It's the sense of duty. Of calling. The tirelessness of the true believer. The pursuit of a grail. Like being a soldier. Greed is for second-raters, John. Like that bitch with the hotels."

The gin and tonic was first-rate. And unreal.

Hunt gave a smaller laugh. "Now . . . I used to preach that the United States Army officer corps was the last surviving Calvinist institution in the Western world. Folks thought I was crazy. 'Old Punchy's had one too many grenades go off between his ears.' But you can turn that to advantage." He slapped a paw down on his thigh and the short sleeve revealed a crocodile-hide wrist. Burn scarring. "And the Air Force . . . they're nothing but goddamned Jesuits. Jesuits without God." He drank and waved his free hand. Sitting back down. "Now, I admire Calvinists, John. In their place. All that sense of duty. The discipline, the clarity of form. Conviction of being one of the elect. All twisted up with a terrible fear of failure. Makes a great officer." He looked at me with eyes that had seen more than I could imagine. "Trouble is, all that crap makes for a dumb shit of a civilian following retirement. I have personally seen my friends fail right and left when they took off their uniforms and tried to make a go of the business world. Reality breaks 'em like glass." He held up his own glass and I noticed he was missing two fingers on his left hand. "Me, I've really come around on the Air Force. Little shits are in touch with the spirit of the times. Do absolutely anything to get what they want. We need to study those boys."

He finished his drink and parked the glass. Leaning toward me. "Don't be a dumb fucking Calvinist, John. You don't have to go before your Maker in a robe of shining white. Minor transgressions are forgiven in the church of real life." He grinned. His teeth were too even. I wondered which enemy had claimed the originals. "Hell, look at the goddamned President."

"I believe in right and wrong."

"And so do I, John. So do I. But life's not as neat as we'd like it to be. How about a top-off?" He bounced out of his chair and poured another round. "Had I regarded the world as a domain of absolutes, I would have been dead before the end of my first combat tour. My career would have been short and not at all sweet. Goddamned failure to boot." We both drank. The Lab made a dog-dream sound beyond the door. "Well, I survived. And prospered." He shook his head over memories. "*Not* because I embraced that which was wrong. Hell, no. Because I recognized that sometimes it takes a sequence of small wrongs to get to a big right. I *do* believe that the end can justify the means. After all, that's why we have a military. Kill our fellow man so a greater justice will prevail. Right?''

''Where's Tish?''

''She's safe.''

''You have her here?''

''You know better than that, son.''

''What happens to her?''

He smiled. A rugged little smile. ''That's up to you. You have the fate of many people in your hands. You screwing the blonde, by the way?''

''No.''

''Didn't think so. Too much of a Calvinist. Now, if I were you, I'd fuck her brains out. Looks like a thoroughbred. And life does not give any of us an excess of chances. Fuck her. Enjoy it. You'll be forgiven.'' His smile broadened slightly, as if someone had twisted a screw at the back of his head. '' 'Down from the waist they are Centaurs,/Though women all above:/But to the girdle do the gods inherit,/Beneath is all the fiend's.' You one of those poor sonsofbitches who're afraid of women, John? Most men are.'' His smile quirked, marking private thoughts. ''Know why I love Shakespeare? Because the bugger had the balls to kill that self-righteous little bitch at the end of *Lear*. All she had to do was make her poor old daddy feel good. But she was just too much of a goddamned puritan, one of those little tin saints who have to turn out all the lights.'' He looked at me with forty-five-caliber eyes. ''Saints and puritans

fuck things up for all of us, John. Shakespeare understood how the world really works.''

''Who was in the car?''

He didn't get it.

''Who was in the car?'' I repeated. ''My car. The
body that was supposed to be Tish.''

His lips formed a burned and broken shell. A sort
of smile. ''That shouldn't bother the Calvinist in you.
Any more than it would a Marxist. She wasn't one
of the elect. Strictly *Lumpen-proletariat*. Homeless.
Mad. Worthless. Shopping-cart sweetheart. No one's
missed her. Calvin himself had no patience with
beggars.''

''Save the Wal-Mart theology.''

He made a kill-you-if-I-feel-like-it face. ''All right.
Let me put it to you straight. You don't give a shit
about that homeless woman. You're just glad it
wasn't your girlfriend in that car.'' He grinned with
the suddenness of an air strike. ''Occurs to me that
Miss O'Malley's a crackerjack Catholic. Understands
repentance. And forgiveness. The efficacy of works.
Charity. Faith, too. Great big buckets of it. But that's
just more—what did you call it? 'Wal-Mart theology'? I like that. You've got balls, son.''

''Even if I didn't care about the woman, I'd care
about the law.''

''God's law? Or man's? Can the bullshit.''

''What about Farnsworth? And Em Carroll?
They're missed. They weren't worthless. What about
all those people at the lab in Georgia?''

Hunt put down the glass he had emptied a second

time. "Avoid romanticism, John. It destroys your operational effectiveness." His face was serious, not mocking. Almost priestly. "That . . . those deaths were inexcusable. My people had nothing to do with them. *I* had nothing to do with them. I deplore them." His chin lowered, but his eyebrows climbed. He fixed me with those bayonet eyes. "I was called in because the whole business was getting out of hand. Run by amateurs. Clowns like Gabrielli." He caught my surprise and smiled again. "Oh, yes. Our friend the general. Horse's ass. Worse. Can't see past the dollar signs. To the damnation at the end. Not every man in Army green's a good Calvinist." Grunt. "Gabrielli's a fraud even unto himself. If he even has a goddamned self. Pretty typical these days."

"Why should I believe you? That you weren't behind the killings?"

Hunt made a face like a kid forced to eat broccoli. "You really think I'd be that sloppy? Hell, if Gabrielli and his blue-suiter buddies were still running this, you would've been dead days ago. And your girlfriend. And blondie. Whom you really should fuck. Cowardly not to. When you really want to." His smile returned. "Tell me you don't think about it."

His robe had slipped open. He stood and retied it. "Men don't *think*," he said, scanning his bookshelves. "They do not consider the ends of things. Or the sources, for that matter. We live our lives in a fog. Imagining lights just ahead of us. Hallucinating moral systems. For which there is no biological justification." He ran his fingers along a set of green books whose titles I could not see. "We believe in things that are perversions of logic. Even as we reject our most powerful desires. We reason away opportunity."

He turned to face me again. Cinching the blue robe tighter. "The truth is, we're cowards. Man is born afraid. Fear is his constant companion. Only fear is with him at the end." His lips turned up delicately. A rose opening. "When you grasp that fundamental truth, everything else makes sense. Religion. Civilization. Law. Government. You name it. Everything is a fortification erected against the fear that threatens to overwhelm us."

He took down a book and paged through it, but still spoke to me. "Fears come in two kinds, John. General and specific. The fears we all feel . . . and those peculiar to an individual or time and place." He snapped the book shut and replaced it on the shelf. "When you understand a man's specific fears, you have him." He looked at me again. "You know me. I mean, you know a little about me. The stories. Rumors. I'm sufficiently vain to assume you've brushed up against my reputation." He stood erect. The minotaur again. "Credit those stories, John. Believe in them. None of them captures the full reality. If driven by necessity, I could inflict so much pain on Miss O'Malley that she would truly go out of her mind. And I would have you there watching. Where she could see you. Don't lead us down that road, John. Exercise your free will for the good."

I looked down at my drink. Not a time for brave words. "What do you want?"

He stepped over to me and put his hand on my shoulder. "You know what I want. The disks. All of them. Every single one of them." He lifted his hand. Unaccountably, I felt the loss of the human connection. If Hunt was human. "Give back the disks . . . and I'll give you back Miss O'Malley. I won't hurt either one of you. Or anybody else involved."

He sat back down in his chair. A high judge on his bench. "And there's more. My employer—who is a genuinely great American—will pay you ten million dollars. Aalstrom was telling the truth about that."

I don't know if he caught my reaction. It wasn't much. But I distinctly recalled Aley offering five million. I began to understand my old non-friend's intense interest in the transaction.

". . . and here's what's going to happen," the general continued. "You're going to agree to take that money. And I'm going to be the middleman. I'm going to handle the deposits. You will actually receive two million, sufficient for your needs. I will retain eight. You will say nothing, because you will be grateful for your life and that of your beloved. As well as for your newfound wealth. Then you and I will have something on each other. A mutual guarantee of good behavior. In time, all will be forgiven."

"And if I don't have the disks?"

"That would be unfortunate."

"If I don't play? If I give them to somebody else?"

"You wouldn't make it across the street."

I was slower. But my second drink was empty now, too. I settled the glass on the carpet. "The disks . . . have the plans for the NGFB on them, right? Everything? The black stuff? All of it? Correct?"

The general nodded. "Is one of us surprised?"

"What if I turn out to have a martyr complex? What if I believe that airplane's a bad deal for my country? What if I *do* beat you out the door? And across the street. And put those disks in somebody else's hands?"

"Like most martyrs, you would die for a dying cause. For a *dead* cause. And you would effect no good whatsoever. You would destroy the lives of those around you. Out of vanity, not virtue. Your choice, John."

He walked across the room and laid his hand on an antique globe. Turning it a little. "I find romanticism the enemy of all that is good—and I do believe in good, my friend. We disagree only on the substance, not the concept. Washington is a city tragically prone to romanticism. No. That's wrong. 'Tragic' is too grand a word for the sordid nonsense on the banks of the Potomac. Washington is *pathetically* given to romanticism."

"You think it's romanticism to buy a three-hundred-billion-dollar airplane we don't need?"

Hunt was a master of his own reactions. He did not tweak a facial muscle. All he did was spin the globe under a big hand. Strategic roulette.

"No, John, it's not romanticism." Spoken in the

calmest of voices. "I believe buying the Next-Generation Fighter-Bomber is sheer realism. To oppose the purchase is romanticism."

"We don't need it. We can't afford it. And you know it."

He lifted his hand and shooed off a slow, invisible fly. "On the contrary. We *can* afford it. This is a very rich country, son. Richest in history. And we are spending a lesser proportion of our GNP on our national defense today than at any time since the Great Depression. And you might recall where that led." He patted the globe. As if it were a good dog. "There's plenty of money out there. Don't worry about it. Now . . . as for *need*ing that airplane . . . of course we don't. Not in the sense you mean it. We don't need it strategically." He looked down at the globe. Choosing a country to invade. "But we need our defense industry. That's our strategic ace in the hole." He spun the globe again. "Defense industry beat the Russians. Not our armed forces. Defense industry beat those sorry-ass Iraqis. Not twits like Gabrielli who move tanks at the speed of tricycles and worry about scratching the paint jobs." Huge shoulders rolled under the tree-bark skin of his neck. "Our defense industry is the most feared institution on earth. I would starve people to keep it going. I would starve infants to death, John. Defense industry is what keeps America on top. And I am determined that America should stay on top." He crossed his arms and pointed his full attention toward me. A minotaur with the eyes of a snake.

Suddenly, he grinned. "You're a hardhead. Aren't you? Here I am offering you salvation, and you just refuse to have faith." The grin decomposed. "Like weapons, John? Guns? Fine ones?"

"They have their place."

"Exactly right. Come on. Let me show you something." He retied his robe with a snug knot this time and led the way back out into the corridor. The dog rose and followed us. We entered a lower-ceilinged area. Probably part of the original structure. Hunt opened another door.

Stairs. Going down. I wondered if this was the trip to the torture chamber. Anxious to stay close to its master, the dog nearly knocked me down the steps. Hunt pushed on along a passageway to a vault door. He bent to an electronic combination lock and worked it quickly.

The room was twice the size of the library. It was full of guns. And edged weapons. This was no nutcase arsenal. It was a museum. Hundreds of muskets and rifles—and some automatic weapons—waited in long cherry racks. Some behind glass, others ready to hand. Swords, from Bronze Age fragments to modern ceremonial sabers, hung below the crown molding and gleamed in a fan on the far wall. There were crossbows, longbows, pikes, and axes. Helmets and breastplates. Carved clubs. Oriental weapons in the shape of animals.

Hunt took down a double-barreled shotgun that looked as though it had been worked by silversmiths. He cracked it open and held it high. Squinting into the barrel. Then he took two shells from a drawer, loaded the weapon, and laid it on a glass display case full of old military revolvers.

For a few seconds, he just admired the weapon. "Holland and Holland," he said. "A thing of beauty." Then he turned back to me.

"John . . . we are privileged to live in the greatest country in history at the greatest time in history. There is not an enemy who can threaten us at present. None on the horizon." He looked down the gleaming rows of wood and steel. "No, my friend, we're on top of the heap. And it is our mission—yours and mine—to make sure we stay there. To defend the new American empire that none of the politicians will even admit we possess. *With* the indispensable support of our defense industry." He laughed his longest laugh of the day. "We're the next best thing to gods."

"Senator Faust ever see your collection?"

Hunt grimaced. "Hell, it was all I could do to keep him from jerking off in front of me." He picked out a rapier and prodded the air, testing the weapon's balance. Then he hung it back on its pegs. "But let's stay on-message here. Those disks. They matter so much because of two things. First, for the short term, we don't want our secrets lying around so the bad guys can figure out where our vulnerabilities are. Longer term, it's about industrial superiority. Tens of billions of black dollars already went into that aircraft. And even we can't afford to give the technology away for free. Even if those who stole it could not build it, they could model beyond it. In fact, that would be the smarter strategy by far. Don't imitate, counter. We're in a constant state of virtual war with our former allies, everybody trying to outmodel everybody else. Looking for the big breakthrough. Our allies are envious creatures, John, small men and evil. They hate our superiority, our success. And they hate us. More deeply than do our nominal enemies. The Europeans would ruin themselves to spite us. The Japanese remain the monsters they have always been.'' He ran his fingers over a samurai sword displayed in a wooden cradle. ''There are capabilities built into the NGFB's technology you can't imagine. Paradigm-shattering capabilities. Even now, I can't share them with you. And we don't want to share them with anybody else.''

''What you're trying to sell me . . . is that defense industry is more important than the military.''

He lifted a hand to his chin and more reptile skin emerged from his sleeve. ''Yes. You don't have to like it. But it's the truth. Companies like Macon-Bolt protect us today. G.I. Joe's an anachronism.''

''You say that? After all you've been through?''

The general smiled indulgently. ''I enjoyed what I did. God knows what would have become of me had I not found the military. I would likely have come to a bad end young. But I loved my work in our country's service. I had an aptitude for it, a calling. I thrived in conditions that broke other men. I loved that which was forbidden to those of lesser strength.'' He shook his head. ''But I will not pretend my career was more important than it was. We lost most of the fights I was in. Truth is, we didn't need to be in them in the first place. The age of the warrior is over. Done. And it isn't coming back. I'm a dinosaur.''

"Christ," I said. "Look at the papers. It's all machetes and rusty machine guns out there. With the odd cell phone thrown in. It's Cain and Abel warfare. It's nothing *but* warrior stuff. How does the NGFB fit into that?''

He blew those considerations away like dust. "Do any of those fights threaten our country? Come on, son. That's all busybody stuff. Pimples on the ass of the world. We get involved because we're bored. If it ever got serious, we could wipe them out. We're just beating our meat.''

He picked up the shotgun he had loaded.

"John," he said, "I really thought you'd be more mature than this. I've tried to reason with you. But you're beginning to wear on me.''

He pointed the gun toward his Labrador and pulled one of the triggers. The sound punched through my skull.

The dog exploded across the carpet. Its head bounced off the far wall. Blood splashed my jeans.

The shot echoed. My ears ached. Hunt stared at me with such force that it drew my eyes away from the animal's death.

"I just want you to understand how serious I am," he said. "You have forty-eight hours to produce the disks.''

CHAPTER 10

I DROVE BACK TOWARD D.C. WITH THE END-OF-THE-weekend crowd. The woman who had set me up to die with a gun full of useless rounds sat beside me. She didn't speak, but I sensed her brain going like a hard little computer. What did she know? What did she want? When they delivered me back to the motel, she had been sitting on her bed. Watched by two gunmen. I guess her charm was wearing thin, because it did not look like they had established much of a rapport.

The desk clerk made me pay for an extra day since we had overstayed checkout time. He had no idea what was going on, probably did not want to know.

I knew more than I wanted to. But not enough to make anything good happen. I felt like roadkill. With a deadline to meet and no idea where to start. People I did not know were watching me and I had no idea how to hide. I did not know if I was being followed at the moment, or if they had wired my rental car with a locator, or both. For all I knew, the bastards were tracking me with satellites.

The green hills lowered into the outer burbs.

"Listen to me," I said to Corry, breaking the silence. "And don't interrupt until I'm done." I watched the road ahead and kept my voice low. "I don't know what you're all about. I still can't figure your angle. But I know you've got to be working for somebody. So let me give it to you straight. And you can report back to God Almighty or the Chinese or whoever pays your laundry bill."

A four-wheel-drive crammed with Sierra Club wannabes cut me off, but I had no anger to spare. "I don't have those goddamned disks. I don't even know what's on them. Oh, I'm just barely smart enough to realize there's some deep, dark secret swirling around the NGFB, but I don't know what that secret is. And I don't care. A week ago, I might have cared. Now I just want Tish back. Alive."

I let a mile pass. It was hard to speak to her, hard to know what to say. Maybe silence would have been better. But we're talking animals.

"And just for the record, don't say another goddamned thing about Em and what a shit you think he was. I've about got it figured out that he was a hero. Him and Farnsworth. The two of them. *Her*oes, baby. Whatever's on those disks, they thought it was rotten enough to risk their lives over. I don't care if Em drank. I don't care if he pulled the wings off flies and kicked your little gold ass—although I suspect that was a two-way street. All I know is that he was trying to do the right thing. To say nothing of Mickey Farnsworth. Those guys carried the flag up the hill, right into the machine guns. And I can't do it. And won't do it. All I want is Tish. And my own life. I'm as selfish as they come, lady. Maybe even more selfish than you. I'm scared shitless, and I want to live, and I don't know what to do. So pass it on to whoever you're working for. If you think it'll help.''

Route 66 had entered the cash canyon, with malls on one side, office buildings on the other. The exits led to Volvo country.

"You're wrong," Corry said.

"About what?"

"About me, for one thing."

"I don't think so, sister."

"I really am attracted to you, John."

"Just how stupid do you think I am?"

"You don't know *any*thing. You just refuse to understand. The first time we met, I had a feeling about you. You were so . . . solid."

"The word is 'thick.' ''

"Stop it. You don't understand how much I need somebody I can count on. Somebody . . . I don't know, just somebody who isn't out to use me." She laughed minutely. "If you want me to put it bluntly, somebody who doesn't just want to fuck me on the cheap.''

"You're overestimating both of us."

We passed the headquarters of the National Rifle Association and I thought of Punchy Hunt's arsenal.

"You don't know how attractive honesty can be."

I howled. "And you do?"

"You're crueler than Em. You're just slower about it."

"Definitely slower."

"And you're wrong about me 'working for somebody.' I'm not working for anybody."

That was the lie that pushed me over the edge. I shouted at her.

"*Fuck* you, Corry. Just fuck you. I'd shove you out the goddamned door, but I'm not going fast enough to make it worthwhile." I glanced at her. Briefly. Just long enough to hate that ineradicable beauty. "I know about the gun. I know about the goddamned *gun*, Corry."

She had great timing. She gave me just enough space to collapse back into a muddle of anger and helplessness.

"What . . . are you talking about?" she asked. With a very different tone in her voice.

"Go to hell."

"Please. Just tell me what you're talking about. I don't know what you're talking about."

I was blasting past BMWs. "The bullets. The *bullets*, Corry. Don't give me that shit about how I'm your love supreme. You know goddamned well the first time I pull that gun on somebody I'm dead."

"No."

"Yes."

"*No*. Please . . ." The girl was Meryl Streep going for her hundred-and-first Oscar. She was good. Even now, her voice was believable. As if she really had not known. "What do you mean, you would've—"

"The bullets are no good. They won't fire. Don't pretend you don't know."

I don't know what I expected. But it wasn't what I got. Corry sank into an arctic quiet just long enough for me to pass a semi. Then she began to scream. Kicking the dashboard, the floor. The hard life of a rental car. It was a stunning performance. Had I not known her better, I might have bought it.

Just before the turnoff for the Vienna metro stop, she found her way back to language.

"You're lying," she muttered. "You're lying to me. You don't know what you're talking about."

I ripped across the lanes and hit the exit ramp like a teenager with Dad's Corvette. Fishtailing through the maze of metro parking lots. Sunday-empty now, toll gates open. I pulled into a satellite lot behind a wall of shrubs and aimed for the far corner. Slamming on the brakes just in time to stay out of the trees.

"Get out," I said. But I didn't give her time. I jumped out of the car and ran to her door. Yanking at her. Forgetting the seat belt. I dragged her out as far as I could, then went back in for the buckle. Feeling her. Smelling her. Hating her. I pushed and yanked at her until she was on her knees on the macadam. Crying.

I went into the trunk, into the bags. The bully boys had not taken away Corry's artillery. I drew it out and walked back to her.

She cringed. Looking up at me.

I pointed the gun at her. With the late heat rising from the blacktop.

"Don't," she said. "Don't."

I pulled the trigger. Again and again and again. Listening to those chickenshit little clicks. Then I tossed the gun at her. And followed up by throwing her suitcase out of the trunk. I flung her purse against her shoulders.

When I looked in the rearview mirror, she was still lying on the ground.

Weekend repairs had shut down the in-bound lanes of 66 short of the river. The detour shunted into Rosslyn and I crossed over to Georgetown, which was a big mistake. The traffic was a mess even on Sunday evening and the sidewalks were dense as Calcutta with people who looked as though they figured the next person's life had to be better than their own. The crosswalks streamed.

I waited out the light at Wisconsin and M behind three muscle boys in a jeep with a roll bar. A medieval beggar-woman meandered between the lanes, holding up a sign warning us all against hormones in meat and world government. The light changed and one of the jeep boys grabbed the sign out of her hands and laughed as they pulled away. I almost hit her and caught a blast of curses.

A cop cruiser—one of those Crown Vics D.C. could not afford—flashed me before I got to George Washington University. I did not know if it was about nearly whacking the witch back in Georgetown or playing with guns in public places or the bigger stuff in my life. I pulled into the most expensive gas station in the universe and killed the engine.

"Out of the car," the cop told me. Inevitable sunglasses. Marks on his forearm that could have been scars. Or a gangland tattoo from the days before he switched sides.

"What's wrong, Officer?"

"You got an expired registration."

"This is a rental."

"Get out of the car. Now."

I got out of the car. His partner took my place behind the steering wheel.

"Get in the cruiser," Cop Number One told me. "Unless you want me to put you in it." He opened the door. There did not seem to be any real malice in him. Just a guy doing a shit job at the end of a hot day.

He drove me up to paleface Northwest, to one of those pockets a little too close to the danger zone for the lobbyists and SES types. No lights, no siren. No information. He worked the radio briefly, but I don't know the cop codes. He stopped the cruiser behind a school with a parking lot full of family vans and mothers with dark circles under their eyes. The cop let me out and pointed toward a sports field where grade-schoolers played soccer by the herd.

"Lieutenant Dickey's over there somewheres." The light was fading, but he still wore those sunglasses. "Don't come up on him from behind. He don't like that."

Dickey was halfway up a stand of bleachers. One of the few males making the scene. On the field, kids ran and collided while their mothers shrieked like Romans at a Christian-eating contest. Dickey held a portfolio open on his knees. Pen in hand.

I did not come up on him from behind. I climbed the bleachers, apologizing to mothers with bloodlust in their eyes. Dickey saw me, but went back to his work. I stood just below him. Finally, he shut the portfolio and zipped it. Gesturing to me to have a seat beside him.

"Fucking fag sport," he told me. "American kids ought to be playing football."

"Your son?"

He looked at me. "My daughter. But just look at those wimpy little boys out there, would you? She chews 'em up and spits 'em out. I mean, this coed shit has gone way too far. I worry about the future of this country."

He looked heavy and worn in the bleeding light. Almost human.

"So tell me about the blonde," he said abruptly.

I looked around. "Here?"

He waved a paw at a mother's back two rows down. "They're not interested in us. Listen. I fucking hate this. But I'm beginning to get this deep-down fear that there might be a remote chance I owe you an apology."

We both watched the kids. I tried to figure out

which one had sprung from Dickey's loins, but it was hopeless. They all looked too normal. "So what's the apology for?"

"I'm not apologizing yet. But I want to talk like gentlemen. And see what happens." He half rose from his seat. Yelling. "You see that? You see her? Go get 'em, Kath. Give it to 'em, you hear me?"

I had her now. A lanky girl with brown hair. On the hormone express to being a teenage knockout. She looked briefly in her father's direction, then trotted down the field with a smile on her face.

Dickey settled back down. And his voice hardened. "Tell me about the blonde."

I told him. Everything I could remember about her. I might as well have been some old Italian mama in the confessional. I surprised myself with my need to talk. Wondering all the while if Dickey might not be a much better judge of animals than I had given him credit for.

I was just a beaten old dog. Responding pathetically to the slightest sign of decency. Not good for much.

The field lights came on. His daughter ran over little boys who would run over her heart in a couple of years. While Dickey heard me out. I was ready to tell him all the rest, too. But I made myself stick to the subject of Corry Nevers. One sin at a time. I told him about the gun. And even about the metro parking lot scene.

When I was done, we sat for a while.

"You know," he said at last, "I worry about my

kid. I mean, how can I not worry? Her growing up in a world like this. I mean, I'm a goddamned cop. And I know I can't protect her from the crap that really matters.'' He looked almost as lonesome as I felt. ''I just hope I can keep her off the goddamned drugs, you know? Kids got no sense.''

''She looks like she's going to be a very pretty girl.''

Dickey snorted. ''That worries me, too. Anyhow. We're both dumb fucks. You and me both. Must be goddamned genetic.'' He began unzipping his portfolio again. ''I checked you out. Really good this time. And your redhead. You're clean.'' He grunted. ''Both of you. Looks like she took a shitty fall. Poor judge of roomies. And you're too goddamned dumb to make a drug dealer. And don't give me any I-told-you-so crap.'' He opened the portfolio on his lap and carefully moved his paperwork to one side. The heavy bureaucracy of copdom. He dug his big fingers into an interior pocket. ''I play fair,'' he said. ''As fair as I can, anyway. Here. Have a look at these.'' He handed me half a dozen photos.

'' 'Corry Nevers,' my ass,'' he said. ''Try 'Karen Aalstrom.' ''

The first picture was a mug shot of Corry. With a slammer number. Not looking her best. And, yeah. It read ''Karen Aalstrom.'' The second picture was of Corry and Aley holding hands on a beach. Flowered shirt over his gut. Corry in a bikini. Matching sunglasses. It had an FBI stamp.

I handed the photos back to him without looking at the rest. And laid my face in my palms.

"Born Karen Hinkel," he said. "Sacramento, California. December fifteenth, sixty-seven. A little older than she looks. Teenage runaway. Off to Hollywood. Nailed for very ambitious shoplifting. Tearful homecoming. And back to L.A. Calls herself an actress when she does paperwork. Had a couple of parts in movies a generous person might call art films or something. Busted for raiding the petty cash at a Mercedes dealership where she worked the desk. Cruising for Mr. Right, I guess. Charges dropped. And I wonder why."

I looked up at the high-summer sunset.

"Remember that big hooker ring out there?" Dickey asked. "Couple years back? Gal with the kraut name? And those movie stars? Our girl was the pride of the stable. Eleven charges, and she walked. Then the Malibu cops pop her for reckless driving in somebody else's car. Cocaine in her purse. Way above the 'personal use' level. And a cute little automatic, thank you. Sweetheart walks again. Oh, and this is all *after* the marriage to Mr. Aalstrom, who is another fucking story. I mean, can you imagine it? Letting your wife work as a hooker? Must be some kind of California thing."

He looked at a photograph. I looked, too. "I guess maybe she's a pretty good actress, after all," Dickey said. "Just never got her big break. Until now, at least. The 'Corry Nevers' trail was the best I've ever seen. Great papers. All the way back to birth. Blond-ie's working for real pros this time.''

He shifted his butt on the hard bench. ''Husband's trouble. Fraud charges. Extortion. Multiple counts of assault, and not all against men. Resisting arrest. Jails are crowded out there, so he only did fifteen months total. Got some very unappealing friends down in Mexico. And suddenly he's a straight arrow for the last couple of years. Jimmy fucking Stewart. And don't that make you wonder?''

The game was over. The kids muddled about as though the last thing they wanted to do was hook back up with their moms.

''I bet you're trying to figure out a guy like that and a looker like her,'' Dickey said. ''Me, too. But believe me, it really does take all kinds. Try my job for a couple of days.'' His daughter punched a little boy on the upper arm, then strolled toward the bleachers. ''Must be a hell of a marriage, though. They beat the L.A. stats for longevity. Maybe the guy's a sausage king. Anyhow, they got plenty of history between them. And an ocean view in Re-dondo Beach they can't afford. Two-year-old Jag just a car length from the repo man. California living. But the Feds put the tax man on him, and damn if the bugger didn't come up clean. And people think clean don't smell.'' He grunted and stood up. ''I figure you'll excuse me at this point. I don't want my daughter any closer to this. Cruiser'll take you home. We'll talk tomorrow.''

''We *need* to talk,'' I said.

"I been telling you that for days, soldier boy."

"Please. Just a minute." A little girl with huge gypsy eyes was closing on us. Feminine now. Skinned knees and all. "I need your help."

He looked at me. With his overcooked eyes. "I been telling you that, too. Now get out of here. And try not to turn up dead."

I was starting to feel at home with the dead. You're not supposed to be in Arlington Cemetery after hours, but I did not care anymore. All my life I had played by the rules, and all it got me was this. A home away from home in a boneyard. My girl grabbed by a Shakespeare-shitting goon with billions of dollars and the arsenal of democracy behind him. Dead friends. I sat by Farnsworth's grave with my back against a tree wide enough to swallow my shadow.

"So what's on the disks, sir?" I asked the headstone. "What's the big secret? What was worth dying for?"

I had imagined that I possessed a redeeming degree of self-knowledge, a perspective on my limitations. I had never realized what a hopeless case I was until Dickey showed me the photos of Corry. Or Karen Aalstrom. The one of her and Aley holding hands on the beach was beyond pornography.

Everybody was lying. And I actually had been on the verge of believing Punchy Hunt when he told me he had been brought in on the case just days before to clean up the mess.

Bullshit.

Bullshit, bullshit, *bullshit.*

If Corry was hooked up to Aley, and Aley was hooked up to Hunt, even I could figure out that Hunt had been in on all this at least since Corry hooked up with Em. This was a setup of long standing.

Poor old Em must have looked like a security risk to the black hats a long time back. Lonely old Em. With his life gone to shit and a bottle on the next pillow. Corry would have seemed like an angel. In a very literal sense. He had not suspected a thing. She had played him so beautifully that his big worry was that she was about to leave him.

Corry had killed him. I would have bet my life that she led him out of that restaurant after his last supper and guided him down the street to where fate was waiting. She had known exactly what was coming. Maybe it was even Aley who pulled the trigger. And Hunt had blessed it. That was certain. And Bob Nechestny was Em's boss. He would have been in on it, too. Em had grabbed the disks. He was about to hand them over. To somebody who could John Law the big boys. With Farnsworth working as a go-between. But Corry had blown the whistle. Then walked arm in arm with Em until the bullets hit him. She had treated me kindly in comparison.

An ant wandered up my wrist.

There was still so much I could not understand. Corry and her husband were working for Hunt, who had to be working for Bob Nechestny, Mr. Macon-Bolt Industries. And Corry had to know I did not have the disks. Yet Aley figured I had them. And Punchy Hunt thought I either had them or knew where I could get my hands on them. There was money on the table, and everybody wanted his share.

I thought I had Corry's pistol figured out now. I was supposed to carry it as protection when I turned over the disks. The bad guys would set things up to make me nervous, and I'd reach for the gun like a country boy on the streets of Laredo. My share of the money would lessen considerably.

Hunt was going to rip off Nechestny and Macon-Bolt for eight million. Or ten, if he killed me. Which seemed likely. Aley didn't realize that Hunt was working the same scam on a higher level and he was ready to settle for five. So he and Corry could live happily ever after in Mondo Redondo.

So why didn't Corry tell him I didn't have the disks?

The frogs were another story. Day late and a dollar short. Talking a hundred k when the kitty had run up to ten mil. But they had been right about a few things. Among them, that our own people had laid down the bomb at the lab in Georgia. I was convinced that The Hunt Club had done the deed. It gave a new twist to the old Groucho Marx joke about not wanting to be associated with any club that would have you as a member. But I did not know *why* Hunt's boys had hit the lab. I could not make the key connections. And I still wanted to know why Robespierre and Danton thought our side had played them for fools. I should have asked, but didn't.

A jetliner's position lights floated down toward National. The boneyard crickets were so loud they covered the sounds of the aircraft and the city. I kept very still, watching for the least change in the shadows. I had sneaked out of the roof hatch of my own house, working down the block like an amateur burglar. Any place but D.C. and I would have been busted. Then I worked the alleys over to Pennsylvania Avenue Southeast. Took a cab to Dupont Circle. Where I surfed the crowds. I strolled in the door of a late-night bookstore and hustled out the cafe entrance at its rear. I took another cab. Across the river to the Marine Corps Memorial. Cabbie thought I was nuts. And he was right. I climbed over the wall into the cemetery. And worked my way through a hundred and forty years of dead soldiers to Farnsworth's grave. Still worried that somebody had tailed me all the way.

The night held still. The nearest movement I could see came from the headlights bridging the Potomac.

I could have slept. Maybe should have. But there was more to do. I just wished I could make my brain work. My body was a lost cause.

If Hunt was a stickler for timetables, I had about thirty-six hours left. And not a single clue to the location of the disks.

I wanted Tish back. Doing the right thing would have been nice, but I was ready to settle for considerably less. They could have their NGFB, if that was the price of Tish's life. I could swallow it. Em and

Farnsworth were dead, and dumb heroics were not going to bring them back.

The thought was bitter.

Dickey was the only one of us who really gave a shit about justice. At least the only one still alive.

I needed allies. Any I could get.

Publicity was out. I had no doubt that a public move on my part would kill Tish immediately. She was prime evidence, and Hunt would make sure she went away. But I had decided to work with Dickey, if I could do so quietly. It was a forlorn hope, considering that the D.C. cops could not even crack the gang that was chopping the heads off all the city's parking meters. And, against every shred of patriotic pride I had left, I was even going to take a chance on the French.

I said goodbye to Farnsworth and left the cemetery by a different route. I walked up to a little row of Third World feed troughs between Henderson Hall and Route 395. And I called the French embassy from a hooded pay phone. An earlier user had conjugated the Spanish verb *chingar* on the nearby wall.

The weekend duty officer was a typical junior dick afraid to bother his superiors. He did not want to give me Colonel de La Vere's home number. Until I told him I knew who bombed their research lab.

De La Vere was sleeping. For the first thirty seconds, he was stupid. For the next thirty, he played dumb. Finally, I said:

"Listen, fuckhead. Just tell your sorry-ass buddies Lieutenant Colonel John Reynolds is going to be waiting for them at the far end of Pentagon North Parking in half an hour. If they don't know where it is, explain it to them. Tell them I'll wait thirty minutes, then the deal's off. Screw this up, and you'll spend the rest of your career in Djibouti.''

I hung up. And started walking.

Cuckold showed up in one of those big Citroëns shaped like the stuff that crawls out of drains at 3 A.M. I got in the passenger side. We drove.

''Where's Frère Jacques?'' I asked him.

Bandage pale on his snout. He kept both hands on the wheel. As if the car might have a mind of its own.

''Working. Your friend. This Aalstrom. We are watching him.''

''Turn right,'' I said. ''You found him?''

''There is always a way. He has an arrangement with a waitress. In Arlington. But we have seen no movement, no activity.''

''He'll move. Just wait. He thinks he's playing for big stakes.''

I guided him to the mud flats behind Crystal City. Scummy, infested. When they built the Pentagon, they dumped all the waste there. Now weeds would not grow. We parked at the edge of a construction site. There was a partial view of the city. Blocked by highway bridges.

''So,'' Cuckold said, ''what is so important? What is it that cannot wait?''

"Plenty. But first I want you to tell me something."

He shrugged. The French have a way of shrugging that makes you want to crush their little shoulders.

"On our first date," I began, "you said something about the Americans making fools of you. I was under a little stress, and my recollection may not be perfect. But I think you said something to the effect that we didn't have to bomb your lab because we'd already made fools out of you. What was that all about?"

"It's true. You did not have to make the bombing. This was a terrorist action. Of great viciousness. For nothing."

"How do you know it was for nothing? You shits stole the plans for the NGFB. Tens of billions of dollars' worth of research. Now, maybe my fellow Americans tend to be creatures of excess, but I think I can see why they might have gotten angry that you ripped off Uncle Sam's most expensive secret."

Cuckold laughed. Everything about him made me want to smack him. My new ally.

"I don't know," he said. "Maybe you are a fool. Or maybe a liar. Or both things. But if I must say it out loud, I will say it. Yes, you have made fools of us. Terrible fools. This was our most important program, to find out the secrets of this airplane. And you . . . give me the English words . . . you 'set us up.' You made us go through all of the steps, spend all of the money, so much time. But you cheated us. You gave us false plans. Then you watched us build the program to copy your technology, and you laughed. You knew all along that what you gave us would not work. So we were already the big fools. There was no need to kill so many people. There was no need . . .''

I felt sick. I got out of the car because I thought I was going to vomit.

I understood now. I had it. And it was worse than I thought.

I didn't throw up. I just stood. Dizzy. Staring up at the bug-ugly high-rises of northern Virginia.

''Oh, Jesus Christ,'' I said. A plane roared overhead. We were just a gunshot from the runway at National. ''Oh, Jesus.''

Now I knew why they wanted the disks back. Now I knew why it was worth so many lives. Now I knew why Em and Farnsworth had risked everything.

Cuckold came up beside me. Tough little sucker. Good on his feet in the dark.

''Fuck off,'' I said. There were tears in my eyes, but I did not think he could see them in the bad light.

''And you can go to fuck yourself as well,'' Cuckold said. ''Are you all right?''

''No.'' I did not think I would ever be all right again.

''You know something. Tell me what it is that you know.''

I fingered the corners of my eyes and waved my head. ''You already know it. We're all dumb shits. I should've figured it out on day one.''

''What is it that I already know?''

I turned and looked back across the river. Broken view. Some light, lot of darkness. I thought briefly about Corry. Because even that was easier than thinking about what I had just learned. I looked at my city and realized that Em had not gotten Corry her job on the Hill. He just thought he did. Faust was wired in with Nechestny and Hunt. My think-tank bud, Rob Burns, had it exactly reversed. The senator had been working Em. Faust and Corry were sharing the same hymnal. And God only knew how many scumbags in uniform like Gabrielli were involved. Plenty of them had to know. How many Air Force generals were involved? Had to be a bunch. If it spilled over to touch the Army. This was enormous. And where did it all end?

Tish and I were bread crumbs.

"What is it that I must know?" Cuckold said.

I looked at him. "You're all shits. I'm pissing pink lemonade because of you."

"And I must wear these supporting things for my kidneys. And my nose is very bad. The nose is very distinct in my family, and now it is ruined. I think we are even."

"There's no such thing as even."

"What do you want to tell me?"

I toed the ground, dawdling like a kid. I was about to tell him one of my nation's greatest secrets. Something I had not known myself five minutes before.

"Don't you get it?" I finally asked him. "Don't you *see*, for Christ's sake? They *had* to blow up your lab. *Because* the plans didn't work. We didn't slip you fake plans or doctored ones or anything else. You had the real thing. And we had to destroy every last trace of it, all the evidence.'' I could not look at him. "The goddamned airplane doesn't work.''

"That . . . makes no sense.''

"Hey. I thought the French were supposed to be so cynical.'' I laughed. It was the sound of an animal dying. "All of this . . . it's all because the Next-Generation Fighter-Bomber's nothing but a great big fraud. It's all lies. It's a fake.''

"That's not possible.''

"The hell it isn't. We've got B1 bombers we couldn't use in the Gulf war. We've got B2s that have to live in intensive-care wards. This isn't a first. It's just bigger this time.''

"I think you are lying. You are trying to fool us again.''

I wanted to grab him. Almost did. "Okay. Your turn again. Tell me. What was wrong with the model you were copying? What made you so sure the plans were bogus? How did you know it wouldn't work?''

Cuckold made a puffy little sound. Like a kid pretending to smoke a cigar. "For one thing, the matter of stealth was questionable. Our computer models indicated that such an airplane would be detected by the latest-model radars.'' He thought for a moment. I wondered if he was censoring himself. "And the composite materials. This is your big secret, I think? The thing you most want to hide? Well, our scientists did not believe the materials to be stable. That is why they believe you have made fools of us. The compound would begin decomposing in . . . I think they have said five years. A few more years, and the aircraft would be worthless. Melting. Like the ball of wax, you know? We thought you were trying to bankrupt us, then leave us defenseless. So we would need to turn to America for everything.''

I stood with my head bowed and my hands stuffed into my pockets. ''That's it, pal. Capitalism at its finest. Just think about it. We build that goddamned airplane. And by the time the production run's ending, the fleet's already rotting away.'' I looked at him. With my whole face twisted. ''And then what do we have to do?''

''You would need all new airplanes.''

''And it won't matter that Macon-Bolt took us for three hundred billion. It'll be the only contractor left standing. The NGFB contract's going to put all the other defense aerospace players out of business. Macon-Bolt will buy them up for ten cents on the dollar. Or less. And the patriots at Macon-Bolt will say they're sorry about the NGFB and they don't know how it could have happened. And we'll give them a contract for six hundred billion to try again. It's fucking beautiful. From a business point of view, it's a hell of a lot better than building something that works and lasts.''

''This cannot be true.''

I held out my hands, palms up. ''Believe what you want. I'd bet my life on it.''

Cuckold leaned back against the car. ''I think you

are already betting your life. You cannot put the same chips on different numbers.''

''Skip the Cartesian shit. You know what I mean.''

''If you are right . . . this is a terrible thing.''

''I'm right, pal. And your scientists were right. You did everything right. You grabbed the secrets. Your boys cracked the code. And now you've got me standing here at zero dark thirty spilling the beans.''

''If this is all a true thing . . . tell me why they have made the bombing of your own laboratory.''

I looked down at the chemical mud. I was shivering. Not from cold. But from the sort of fear that hits you when you are truly weary and lost.

''I don't know. Not yet. Could be any number of reasons. Maybe a whistle-blower. Maybe parallel research that came up with the wrong answers. I'm going to find out.''

''If you live. I think now they will want to kill you very much. When they look in your eyes and see that you know.''

''I'm going to live. And I'm going to beat these shits. And you're going to help me.''

CHAPTER 11

I CAME TO MY SENSES IN THAT POISONED LOT IN VIR-ginia. When I realized that the NGFB was the biggest scam in history.

I am a creature of doctrine and training. But the two had come apart on me. My doctrine held that those in uniform could be trusted all of the time and that our government could be trusted most of the time. I held a fundamentalist's conviction as to the virtue of those I served. I *need* to believe in something. I think belief is the most basic human need, even more irreducible than the impulse toward sex. Like most of the faithful, I rejected evidence that threatened my beliefs. Luther had the psychology of my kind down cold when he wrote the hymn ''A Mighty Fortress Is Our God.'' I need big, thick walls. My training, on the other hand, had conditioned me to attack: You could not decide an issue in your favor without going on the offensive. Throughout my ca-

reer I had attacked—mentally, at least—those who
slighted that which I revered. The collapse of my
beliefs left me on the defensive, stunned, and reacting
to enemies I could not identify with certainty.

Now I knew my enemies. The fallen angels. And
I was going to attack.

Like most military people, I am also a creature of
fear. I lived for two decades in the safety and comfort
of regulations that divided good from evil with tran-
scendent clarity. Yet all the while, fear shaped my
life: the fear of failure, of not measuring up, of losing
the regard of my comrades, of taking the incautious
step that leads outward from the garden, of revealing
the imperfections I recognized in myself. A thousand
years ago, I would have been one of those dull-witted
Crusaders who kept plodding eastward while the
smart guys had fallen out to loot Byzantium.

Now I decided to throw away the regulations, to
break the rules, and to shift the fear into the lives of
others. It was time to stop worrying about losing and
start trying to win. The first step, according to my
hundreds of thousands of dollars of taxpayer-funded
training, was to identify the weak spot in the enemy's defenses.

That part was easy.

We stopped to pick up Cuckold's sidekick. He was
on stakeout. Keeping tabs on Aley Aalstrom. Cuckold rapped the window of the rat-bite Peugeot with
his knuckles. Hands flew up in a martial-arts defense,
striking the steering wheel. Sidekick had been snor-

ing. He was embarrassed as only a Frenchman can
be.

We left the Peugeot and lumped into the Citroën.
With me in the backseat like Grandma. Heading
north to the city.

"Listen," I said, "if we're going to work together,
you need to tell me your names. Or make some up."

Voltaire and Rousseau glanced at each other.

Dummy quiet.

Then Cuckold said, "I am Henri. He is Gerard."

"Delighted to make your acquaintance. Here's the
deal. I know which street he lives on. And I have a
fair idea as to the block. But—"

"There is no problem. We know where he lives."
Henri the Cuckold wiped a finger below his nose.
Cleaning an invisible mustache. I wondered if he had
shaved one off for this job. "This is a long affair.
All of these people who are involved. Perhaps not
all. Many. When we first became interested in the
airplane, we watched them. Only we made a mistake
with this one. We saw only the women. Always the
women. We decided he was not a serious man. We
have not watched him for some time. We had
stopped even before you bombed our laboratory."

"*I* didn't bomb your lab."

"Before your people bombed it."

"They weren't my people, either."

"Your countrymen, then."

Yes. My countrymen.

"I find it strange," Henri went on, "that in the
great land of democracy, where all men are created

equal, such men live in ways no longer permitted to the aristocrats in France."

"It's just money," I said. "His family owns an entire state."

We crested Arlington ridge. Washington lay before us. City of stars fallen to earth.

"We need to talk terms," I told him.

"Tell me your terms," Henri said. Wary.

"You do everything you can to help me rescue Tish O'Malley. Anything happens to her, it's a deal breaker."

"But you do not know where she is."

"I'll find her."

Henri thought about that. Maybe he did not believe me. "This is agreeable. We will do everything to help that is not foolish."

"The foolish stuff, too."

"Maybe not so foolish. No absurdities. But I think we will agree. More?"

We pulled onto the bridge. Bright banks of lights. Nighttime construction work. Traffic lifelined down to one lane.

"You get the disks. If and when I locate them. But you promise me that the government of France . . . or somebody . . . will publicize the fraud. Tell everybody that the goddamned airplane doesn't work as advertised. Knock Macon-Bolt in the mud."

Henri and Gerard spoke French to one another. Gerard shrugged muscular shoulders, then lit a cigarette. I opened a rear window.

"I think this will be all right," Henri told me.

Turning his head to talk. Glancing back at the freeway between phrases. "France will be glad to embarrass these people. I would say 'to shame them,' but
I think they have no shame. So there will be an
embarrassment in public. I believe it will be so, but
I cannot promise, of course. I must refer it."

"Then refer it. Next point. I'm not going to be
popular around here when this is over. You get Tish
and me out of the line of fire. You set us up someplace where we can rebuild our lives." I knew I was
at their mercy on this one. Maybe they would just
give me a bullet when they had what they wanted.
There would not be a diplomatic protest.

More French. Big, smoky gestures from Gerard.
Younger and dumber, he still seemed to be the
final authority.

Henri ran his hand back over his close-cut hair.
"This is not such a problem. You have my word. If
you help France, France will help you."

"Last point. You offered me a hundred thousand.
That's bullshit, and you know it."

"How much do you want?"

"Five hundred thousand. Dollars, not francs. And
this is not a payoff. I'm not selling you the disks.
That's separate. But I'll need money to set up a new
life with Tish. If she wants to hang around. And I'm
not going to have a lot of handy credit references."

Another conversation between Ravel and Debussy.
Gerard turned, gave me a suspicious look, and muttered something I could not hear.

"I think this will be approved," Henri said. "But I must refer this, too. It is a great deal of money."

"It's fucking peanuts."

Henri canted his head. I could imagine the expression I could not see. One eyebrow lifting higher than the other. A slight pucker of the lips. The eyes counting ghost bills.

"I will ask," Henri told me.

"Ask hard."

"I will try. It is not so easy today. In the old days, there was always extra money for such purposes. But now . . . you see how things are."

We crossed the Mall on Fourteenth Street and hit the downtown government ghetto. Monumental buildings, lit up for nobody. After midnight, the streets were as dead as an archaeological site.

"All right. Do what you can," I said. "Now let's review. You're committed to help me get Tish back. Alive and kicking. If necessary, you'll get us out of here and help us make a fresh start. You'll ask about the money, and you'll confirm the business about publicizing the flaws in the NGFB. In return, I hand you the disks. If and when I get them."

"And . . . if you do not find the disks?"

"You still help me get Tish back."

"I think I am not making such a good bargain."

"Bullshit. If you do get those disks, you've got your arms around the world's biggest secret. Real comeback for *La Belle France*. And revenge for the lab bombing. I get crumbs."

Suddenly, Gerard spoke. In French. That spitting

tone. He flicked an empty hand toward me. Then he tossed his cigarette butt out of the window and dropped back into his sulk.

"What's the matter with Maurice Chevalier?" I asked Henri.

That Gallic shrug. "Oh, he just thinks you make plentiful demands. For someone who has so many enemies and no friends at all."

We stopped at a stucco-front mansion in Kalorama. No brass plate, but I figured it had some connection to the French embassy. Gerard went inside while Henri and I stayed in the car and crafted the questions he would ask our target.

"We need something concrete on the Nechestny connection," I told him. For the third time. "Not logic, not insinuation."

" 'The smoky gun,' " Henri said.

"Yeah. A smoking gun. Details. And why did they hit the lab down in Georgia? That's big. We need a chain of evidence we can tip to the media. After we get Tish back."

"No media," Henri told me. "Not this kind of publicity. Not yet."

"Okay. We'll defer a decision on that. But we need the story on that lab."

"I think you need this more than us."

I shook my head. "It all fits together. You can't separate it." I rubbed my eyes. Exhausted. Moving, I was okay. But I could not take much more waiting.

A police cruiser rolled by. More bored than curious. I really was anxious to talk to Dickey. I intended to play multiple hands. To do whatever it took.

Gerard came back out lugging a small rucksack in his left hand, fresh cigarette in his right. Tools of the trade, I figured. I had expected to see the metal suitcase with the little pain machine they had used on me.

In the car, Gerard handed Henri a 9mm-sized pistol, then cleared his own and rammed in a fresh clip. He did not offer me any artillery. But he did toss me a dark rag. It took me a couple of feels to puzzle it out. Commando mask. Made out of a synthetic fabric. Holes for the eyes and mouth. Lot better than hacking the leg off a pair of panty hose. As we pulled out, he threw me a pair of gloves, too. Material thin as a condom. And even more sensitive. No fingerprints.

Short run over the buffalo bridge into Georgetown. Even in the bottom hours of the night, parking was a problem. We cruised, with Henri and Gerard cursing in turn. My ear had tuned sufficiently to understand Gerard's complaint that this was worse than Paris.

We parked six blocks away. There was nothing closer that was also legal. The Citroën did not have diplomatic plates and it was not the time to get towed.

Three bad customers prowling residential streets. No dogs and no leashes. Well past the Wilson Pickett hour. Nobody would have mistaken the guns shoved under Cézanne's and Monet's alligator shirts for colostomy bags. Plus Henri's bandaged nose. A good cop would have sniffed us a ward away and busted us on smell alone. The best we could hope for was that an observer would read us as three gays still sorting out the dating game and look the other way.

"It is on the next block," Henri told me. "Come. There is an alley. We must be quiet now."

I'm good at quiet. I've done the night patrols and the bedroom exits. But I was clumsy compared to these boys. Serious training behind them, and *beaucoup* experience. They moved with vacuum silence. The tension of their bodies had changed magically. As if the bones and muscles had downshifted. I watched their backs intently. They seemed on the edge of evaporating into the darkness. We eased past a row of garbage containers and the smell had more weight than my companions. The frogs were so good it jarred me. Like finding out the Sunday-school teacher is also an exotic dancer.

The city sounds came back to me. Sirens. Snake-pit hiss of traffic in the distance. Music, mostly drums, from a bad neighbor. And the insect prickling that haunts our world.

One high lamp in the alley. Taking the lead, Gerard shied around it. But I saw the shadow of his forearm dip into his pack, emerging with the hand disfigured and extended. They really had worked the site before. He moved directly for a metal box mounted on a pole, snipped it open, and went to work with a mini-light clasped between his teeth.

Henri closed his wire fingers around my bicep.

With his free hand, he pointed toward the back of a pale house built to imitate the townhomes in his part of the world. Freestanding, though, with little rat-catcher alleys on each side. From the back, the house was four stories. Up on the street side, it would be three.

He lifted his chin, as if his hand did not provide direction enough. "There," he whispered. "You see?"

I looked. Trained to be observant. Yet I had not noticed until cued that there was a soft glow behind a pair of blinds on the top floor.

"Listen," I said. "This guy's got an artillery collection. Serious firepower."

"Be quiet. Do not worry. His guns are locked in a room with an alarm. He is afraid of them."

"You hope."

"When we go inside," he said, "there will be stairs. Always the stairs. You must walk with a spreading of the legs. The feet must touch only the sides. Lightly." He judged me in the darkness. "Perhaps you are thinking too much."

I was. This was the point of no return. The beginning of the counterattack.

"I'm crossing a line," I told him.

Henri stood so close to me that I could smell the long day on his breath. "I think you have crossed this line sometime before," he said. "But now you are aware. Put on your mask. And the gloves." His voice was almost fatherly. He understood people, too.

I aped him as he prepped for action. His face, the pale bandage, disappeared.

Gerard came up. A spook. Mask on, head like a chunk of dark metal. There was no wet, no light, where his eyes lurked. We followed him over a slat fence, one at a time. Maybe I had thumped him around, but Henri went over like a young cat. I did not hear either one of them land on the far side. I did my best, but I was bigger and less trained. And a lot stiffer. I came down with a paratrooper thump.

Gerard was already across the garden. A tiny light traced a section of basement wall, then stopped at another utility panel. Bell Atlantic was going to have a serious repair job on its hands. Security systems only stop amateurs. Of course, in D.C., where breaking and entering is just another teen sport, that's usually enough.

While Gerard handled the comms and sensors, Henri climbed the steps to a screened-in porch and let himself inside. The boys were quick. I let Gerard follow him, then brought up the rear. Keeping enough distance to allow reaction time.

I wondered whether, if the night went bad, one of the 9mm rounds might not turn out to be for me.

We entered the house. A heavier darkness. The sound of three men breathing in a hallway. And music, downbeat jazz, from an upper floor. I sensed Gerard smiling. The music made everything easier. Although it also meant the target was probably awake.

Our eyes tuned, enriching the surroundings. The

silhouettes of my new partners. The vertical pool of a mirror on the wall. Beyond an archway, the night-time blue of kitchen appliances.

We began to move.

I followed them up the stairs. Moving as I had been told. When I put my hand on the banister for steadiness, the wood was wet. Then I realized that the wet came from my own palm. Sweating in the glove.

The music grew louder. On the second-floor landing, I heard other sounds streaming from above.

Senator Faust was living up to his reputation.

Maybe monks are never surprised by burglars. But some trade-offs are not worth making. As soon as he picked up on the level of activity upstairs—the moans and the guy grunts—Gerard galloped up the remaining flight of stairs. Followed by Henri. I waited a few seconds and reached the bedroom door just in time to catch the senator's delayed reaction to the intrusion.

He was fat. Not just hefty the way he looked in his well-cut suits in the photos or video bites. His belly and thighs and cow tits covered so much of the bed that at first I could not see the girl under him. Then I saw a foot and a calf. And another foot, a slender arm. The woman was lying belly-down.

Faust lifted himself, fell back clumsily, then finally succeeded in separating himself from his lover. He plopped on his rump beside her, eyes huge, mouth chewing fear. He made no attempt to protect the girl. Instead, he struggled up off the bed and stood with his back to a window blind. As if jumping were a consideration.

It takes far longer to describe this than it took it to happen. Action goes fast. Gerard leapt behind the senator like a panther and got a paw over the man's mouth. His other paw stabbed a pistol in Faust's ear.

For the first time, the woman on the bed moved. She had a fine, glistening body. Even flattened and splayed, it possessed an elementary clarity that you might see once or twice in your lifetime. If you're lucky. She pulled a muss of sheet and pillow toward her. Covering herself. But instead of covering her nakedness, she tried to shield her face.

She was too slow. I saw her.

It was Corry Nevers.

I watched. Useless. Henri slapped Corry—or Karen—out of the bed. Plenty hard enough to earn respect for his seriousness. She did not bother with the sheet at all now. Maybe she thought nakedness was her best armor. Or maybe she wasn't thinking at all, caught off balance for once. She probably was not accustomed to being the one on the receiving end of bad surprises. I wondered, stupidly, why she did not look at me or ask for my help. Forgetting that I wore a mask.

Henri got a fistful of the hair at the back of her head and steered her from one door to another, opening each. A bathroom. A shallow linen closet. The last door before the one by which we had entered was exactly what he was looking for. A walk-in closet. Without windows. In a masterfully coordinated gesture, he let go of her hair and gave her a knee between her ass cheeks. She stumbled into the darkness.

"Do not make a noise," he told her. "If you wish to live."

I could have told him she was too smart to scream. Except when a man wanted her to.

He shut the closet door.

Faust was not wearing much senatorial dignity. He stood naked and shaking with fear, dick shriveled, paunch trembling. Astonishing, what money can do. He had been linked with actresses and anchorwomen, and he had the reputation of being the town's most eligible and irresistible bachelor. Nothing but an overripe pear on stumps. A skinned pear. His flesh had the whiteness, almost the translucence, of the great slabs of lard the butcher sold to poor people when I was growing up. Lard, with curls of matted, colorless hair. Where his thighs and belly came together, his body creviced softly. It almost had the look of a maw, of something that devoured the small and vulnerable.

His eyes were the worst, though. The eyes of a true coward. You could see that Corry had disappeared from his mental horizon. He would have helped pitch her out the window if it would have saved him a pinch on the cheek. His eyes were self-concerned without intelligence, vicious without strength. When Gerard dropped his hand from the senator's lips, a strand of drool trailed like a skein of spiderweb. The mouth showed a big emptiness of the kind you see when people remove false teeth. But I kept going back to his eyes. Colorless chips. Shifting from one of us to the other. And back again. I wondered what he saw.

Henri and Gerard tied the senator's hands with a necktie that had been tossed over the back of a chair. Then they sat him down in the chair, on top of his discarded clothes. His love handles contoured to the wooden arms.

"Please don't hurt me," he said. In the voice of a ten-year-old. Then he began to cry. "You can have anything you want. Money. You can have the girl. She's—"

Henri struck him across the mouth. Very, very hard. Blood burst from Faust's lower lip. The words stopped.

When they grabbed me that first night, they had not touched my face.

Henri bent close to the man's snout. Grabbing fistfuls of the man's cheeks, distending his face. It looked as though the meat would rip away from the senator's gums.

"You think . . . how is it you think I would touch a woman . . . who is dirty with your filth? You think we are thieves? You are the no-good fucking thief. You are a filthy thief, a pig. And you will be the dead pig if you do not help me."

He let go of the senator's face. Red-and-white flesh showed where the gloved fingertips had been.

"Please," Faust said. "Anything. What do you want?"

"Is it true that this airplane, the Next-Generation Fighter-Bomber, does not work?"

I saw the first glint of intelligence return to the senator's eyes. "Oh, now . . . it's a damned fine . . . it's . . . there's only a few little problems . . . see, it's—"

When you punch a man, you don't wind off one of those Hollywood haymakers that fill up a screen. Unless you want to be the first one on the deck. You get in and jab short and direct with a recoil finish that reloads your arm like an automatic weapon. But slapping somebody is a different art. A slap can go for the long arc, the buildup of force.

Henri reached over his left shoulder as if to scratch his spine, then brought the backs of his knuckles down at the back of Faust's jaw. Jumping teeth. I could feel the crack in the man's ear. Faust must have weighed two-fifty, but he nearly spilled out of the chair.

Before the senator could recover, Henri thrust his hand in between the man's legs. Grabbing balls. Not a job I would have wanted. Faust began to scream, but Gerard slapped a hand over his mouth again. The senator wriggled and jumped, clamped his eyes shut, and nodded his head in short jerks. Sweat exploded from his skin.

Henri let go of the guy's glories and wiped his glove clean on the bedsheet. "*Cochon,*" he muttered.

Gerard let the pain calm just enough, then he removed his hand from Faust's mouth. Wiping the blood from his glove on the drapes. He stood ready to clamp back down.

Henri returned to the discussion. "Listen. You are a man with alternatives. You can make a stop to the pain now. Or I can finish so that there is no more lovemaking for you." He smiled harshly, lips closed. Then added, "No fucking the little girls, huh? Would you like such a life, you mountain of shit?"

"Please," Faust said. Sweating. Panting. Still unable to fully open his eyes. *"Please."*

"Tell me about the airplane. Tell me how it does not work."

"I don't *know*. I'm not a scientist. I don't understand—"

Henri sent a fist straight into the man's nose. It was a beautiful jab. Better than anything the guy had used on me. Bone crunched. The instant the fist withdrew, blood streamed downward, joining the slower flow from Faust's lip.

"I am not a scientist, either," Henri said calmly. "So you will not need the technical langauge. I think you should talk to me."

"I'm a United States senator," Faust cried.

Henri laughed. Then Gerard laughed, too. Gerard gave the man's ears playful little tugs. Then he closed his fist around the left ear and tore it away from the senator's skull. As if doing a magic trick. He closed a glove over the man's mouth again.

I had never seen such a thing done. My stomach twinged. I was not remotely capable of playing in

the same league as these boys. And I did not want
to play against them.

I do not know if Faust fully realized what had
been done to him. He got the pain, though. He bent
forward hugely. Rocking. In agony. Face all tears
and blood. Gerard bent over the chair, following the
senator's misery, hand clamped firmly over his
mouth. He tossed Henri the ear.

Henri dangled it in front of Faust's eyes. And the
eyes changed. Several times.

This is something you do not want to see.

Faust finally understood that things were going
mortal. United States senator or not. Gerard tenta-
tively freed the man's mouth. And Faust got away
from him. He collapsed onto the carpet, blood drain-
ing onto pale blue pile.

The ear thing spooked me. I did not know how
you could ever make such a thing right. We had
crossed another border.

Henri tossed the ear onto the bed. He knelt beside
the senator.

"You pig," he began. "Do you know how many
French citizens have died in your explosion? How
many lives are ruined? So many families? Children
without the father? You have done this to us . . .
and all we ask is that you talk to us in return. That
you tell us about this airplane. And why you have
made the bombing." Slowly, as if the world had
ground down, Henri looked up at me. "And about
this bombing in Georgia. This killing of your own

people.'' He turned back to Faust. "You must talk to me now. It is my last offer.''

"I can't hear,'' Faust moaned. "I can't hear."

Somehow we all knew that he could hear. He was not lying, though. He just did not understand what had happened to his body. The stump of his ear must have hurt ferociously. Maybe there were big sounds in there that were hidden from us. He kept reacting to Henri's words, believing all the while that his hearing was gone. I worried that he was beyond the possibility of sensible thought or speech.

"I will take the other ear,'' Henri said. "Then your eggs. Maybe your eyes. I will take you apart into pieces.''

Faust cuddled himself. Going fetal. Weeping. But he began to talk at last.

"I never wanted . . . to do it. Nechestny. He did it. He paid. Gabrielli. And Hunt. Hunt's a madman. Crazy man. He loves to kill things. Kill anything. The airplane's too soft. Melts like a popsicle. But they can treat it . . . make it last long enough . . . the full production run. Other things. Systems. The electronics. Nothing really works. Not the way they say. But the stealth. That's the worst. The skin.'' He cried harder, pawing his skull with bloated hands. Then he gathered himself to speak again. "French stole it. You stole it. You're French. I know it. You knew everything. Whole deal could have collapsed. So much money. Macon-Bolt . . . everything riding . . . once-in-a-lifetime deal . . .'' He sobbed himself down to a level no man should ever reach.

Maybe people get there in concentration camps. "Had to kill the French. Kill them all. All the French. Kill everybody who knew. Hunt wanted to kill more . . ."

"And the other bomb? In your own laboratory?"

Faust began to shiver. Going into shock, I figured. Henri smacked him across the face. An awkward blow, the angle bad. But it was enough to bring the senator back to the realm of the living.

"Tell me about the other bomb."

"GAO. Fuckers. Fucking goddamned bastards. Goddamned shits. Running their own . . . their own goddamned tests. Using our labs. Our people. Behind our backs. They were on the trail. General Accounting Office. Bastards every one. Think they're God's gift . . . had a team in the lab. Had to get them. Get everybody who might have known. Could have spoiled everything. Hunt said we had to kill them all."

Henri had begun to pant. "And where are the disks?" he asked Faust.

"Don't know." His voice rose. "Oh, God. I don't know, I don't *know*. Everybody wants them. Kill for them. Hunt's going to find them. But I don't know anything . . . nothing else . . . please . . . "

"Where are the disks?"

"Please don't hurt me anymore . . ."

Henri rose and planted a shoe at the bottom of the senator's belly. Flattening him on the carpet. Blood and lard. Ruination of the divine gift. The Frenchman moved his shoe down to the senator's crotch.

Faust screamed. The shoe jumped to his face. The great body went into convulsions. Until Henri kicked it back to stability.

Faust's eyes stared through the ceiling.

"There is nothing . . ." Henri said, allowing the first genuine emotion into his voice, ". . . not a thing I could do to you . . . no thing of adequate horror . . . to punish what you have done." He shook his head. "I wonder if it is real to you even now. All that you have killed and destroyed. In your filth."

He drew a switchblade from behind a trouser pleat and landed like a hawk.

"Forgive me," the senator begged. In a shrunken voice. Eyes unseeing. Time all fractured. "Oh, God. Please forgive me. I'm sorry. So sorry. Don't hurt me anymore."

Henri began at the pulp where an ear had been and traced the knife into the fold between Faust's double chins. The blade must have been extremely sharp. It cut smoothly. I had heard that a man could not feel his own throat being cut, but I still do not know if it's true. Faust did not reveal what he felt. He closed his eyes and his bloody lips trembled.

I had not expected this. But I did not move to stop it, either.

We stood and watched him die. It was hyper-real, yet fantastic. I could not accept this as a scene in my life.

Blood slopped into the carpet.

I came back to life when Gerard moved toward

the closet door. I knew what was coming. And I spoke for the first time.

"No."

Gerard stopped. Both Frenchmen looked at me. It crossed my mind that maybe I would be left lying here, too. But I was not afraid now.

"No," I repeated.

Maybe there was something new in my voice. Or maybe Gerard had just been showing an excess of initiative and was unsure. He made no further move toward the closet. We stood suspended in time and that room. Waiting for God to make a decision. I needed Henri to back me up. Even if Gerard was somehow in charge, I hoped that the two of us could stop this.

I feared their training and their rules, their habits and desires. Even now, I could not let Corry die. Just like that. She was too real to me.

"Leave the girl," Henri told his comrade finally. "She has no importance."

He was wrong about that, of course. But I was not going to tell him. Maybe I should have.

"That wasn't part of the deal," I said. "Killing him."

The Citroën bugged from traffic light to traffic light on Massachusetts. Gerard snoozed. As though the business behind us mattered less than a pizza delivery. Henri drove. And thought about what I had said.

Caught in the web of signals by the Convention Center, he turned his face back over the seat.

"You're right," he said. "This is not part of the deal. It is not included and not excluded. But I think he does not matter to you."

"Killing matters."

The light changed. We hopped to the next signal. On the corner, a creature in a smeared track suit bent into a waste container. Puking or searching.

"That is naive," Henri told me. "But you are not naive. You lie to yourself. You do not break free of the things you are supposed to believe. Sometimes I think you are like a slave. A slave to the pleasant beliefs. In Africa, I have seen so much death it became boring. I walked through corpses the way a child wades in the sea. Without a thought. Rice is worth more than the lives of men and women, John. Water is worth more." He stopped, but began again before I could respond. "I have seen the bodies . . . slaughtered like the cow. The beefsteaks cut from them. Men eating men. And in Paris, they lie. Like they lie in London, in New York. They will not put this in their newspapers. Because it does not match their philosophies, their educations. Think of it. Men who will discuss with you the merits of the flesh of a child, why it is better than that of a grown man. Men who laugh with their great white teeth. While they roast a woman's buttocks. You think killing matters? Then you are a child. Humans are thrown away like the toilet paper." He flung an arm at the windshield. "Look at this city around us."

"Killing matters."

The Frenchman shook the back of his head at me. Driving again. I imagined a hard little smile on his face. "Oh, yes. It matters. But not in this way that you mean. It matters because such a man deserves to die. He has earned his death. There is always a price to pay in life. But his life . . . the life itself . . . that is unimportant."

"No."

We drove past a ruin where the rear wall had been lopped off an old tenement. Behind Chinatown. On the left, the National Public Radio building slept, dreaming of the good causes of its youth.

"And what should we do?" Henri asked. Anger denting his accent. "Should we collect the evidence? Chase this man with the law? Ask your government to judge him?" He laughed. As though laughing hurt. "I think there would be no justice. Only great lies. Deals, perhaps. But there would be no justice."

It was my turn to think. As we rounded Union Station with its spotlit facade, I said, "Your government . . . was his murder authorized? Did you actually have permission to do that? Or were you just inspired?"

He shrugged. "What does it matter?"

"You didn't have permission. Did you? It was just your call."

"There is no justice. There is no justice any-where." He made a right turn. "Men must make their own justice. Men of courage. Otherwise . . ."

He lifted a hand from the wheel and snapped his fingers. *"Le déluge."*

Gerard roused briefly, then lolled again.

"And the law?" I asked. "It doesn't matter at all?"

We came up beside the Capitol. The dome glowed through the trees.

"I believe in the law," Henri said. His voice had calmed again. "Until it interferes with justice. I believe in the law for the minor concerns. Does your law protect the small against the great? Can you say this with honesty? Would this man have come to justice?" He turned up East Cap. "Suffering is for the small people. For people such as us. For the people in these laboratories. For their families. But for the great, there is only scandal. Then there is a book and a new wife. A fresh start. *Merde.*"

He understood America.

"Stop here," I told him. "I'll walk the rest of the way." We were in front of the Folger Library. White marble glowing in the hot night. As good as civilization got.

Henri curbsided. "So now we are done. Until tomorrow. Be careful. You have the pager number, the telephone."

"The whole world's watching," I told him.

"What?"

"A mantra. From an age of belief."

He grunted. "I think you are a stupid fucking dreamer. But we must work together now."

"You're wrong, you know. I do care that he's

dead. Not for the sake of his personality. I believe the law is all we have, in the end. Even now, I believe that."

"The law will shit on you."

I shrugged and cracked the car door. "Probably. And I'll still believe."

Gerard stirred again. Henri looked at me with the eyes of a revolutionary on the barricades. "You must be ready to fight."

"I'm ready to fight. But murder takes getting used to."

"Listen, John. There will be more death. Expect it. Only hope it is not your death." His tone of voice carried no threat. I believed him. There would be more death. I was ready to participate in it. But I did not have to like it.

"We'll see," I said, moving to get out.

"No," Henri told me. "*You'll* see."

I walked up East Capitol toward home. Broken brick sidewalks. You had to pay attention even by daylight.

I reminded myself of a woman who has made up her mind to have sex but still feels obliged to protest her innocence. I knew Henri was more in the right than I had admitted. But I hated it. Faust had it coming. If anybody did. A great trust betrayed. But I still would not have done it myself. Not like that. Maybe it meant I was a coward. Maybe it meant I was the weak link.

The truth is that I was meant for a middle-class life

and church on Sunday. June, Wally, and the Beav. I believed in God—especially when I wasn't thinking about it—and critical thought did not come naturally to me. I would have made a lousy Frenchman.

In the interval between two streetlights, a figure stepped out in front of me. A figure with a gun.

"Give it up, motherfucker. Come on. Give it the fuck up." Soft voice filled with hatred.

He was a veteran, not just a kid out to finance a new pair of sneakers. He kept enough distance between us to prevent any countermoves. And he stood with his legs set apart and staggered, like a fighter. Ready for any crap life might throw back at him.

"Okay," I said. "All right, now. My wallet's in my back pocket. I'm going to reach into my back pocket."

"You just shut up and give it the fuck up, motherfucker. You just toss that thing right the fuck over here."

I lobbed the wallet at his feet.

"Now get the fuck down," he told me. "Get down on you fucking belly."

I got down on my belly. I did not believe he would shoot. He seemed too organized, too smart. But life is full of surprises. It struck me that it would be one hell of a twist if, in the middle of all that was going down, I got waxed by a mugger.

"Shit, motherfucker," he said. "This all you got?"

"That's everything."

"You ain't even got no fucking phone cards."

I did not answer. Let him roll.

"You be one sorry-ass poor motherfucker," he said. "Ought to cap you and put you out of you misery like a goddamned dog."

"There are two credit cards in the pocket."

"Shit. You think I'm that dumb? I don't want you damn credit cards." A flying wallet hit me on the top of the head. "You stay there, hear me? You stay right the fuck there, you sorry motherfucker."

I stayed right there. I listened to his footsteps pick up speed until he was fading at a sprinter's pace.

When the sound died, I rose and picked up my wallet. Wearily, I gathered the papers and cards he had scattered. It was the least exciting thing that had happened to me in a week.

CHAPTER 12

▲
▼

BLOOD PAINTED MY DREAMS. UNTIL THE PHONE WOKE
me.

I jerked up. Caught in a twist of sheets. The bed-
ding was soaked with nightmare sweat. Daylight
scoured the room.

I had a hangover head. Without the pleasure of
drink.

The phone cord had twisted. I dragged the cradle
onto the floor, firing needles of noise into my ear.

"Hello?"

"You awake, soldier boy? I wake you up?" Dickey's voice.

"Yeah. I'm awake."

"That's a good thing. 'Cause we got serious business to discuss."

"My phone isn't secure, we shouldn't—"

"Shut up and listen," Dickey said. "You just listen to me a minute. I got a dead senator. Throat cut

like a poor little lambie. And that ain't the half of it. Looks like the guy was tortured by serious sickos. Unless he was maybe impersonating that artist fuck with the ear cut off.''

''Shouldn't we wait and talk—''

''*You* wait. I'm not done. So I got this dead senator, right? And me and my new Army buddy just happen to have a mutual acquaintance who has been working for this senator. As a staffer, they tell me. Working her little tail off, I bet. Ain't life in this town rich? And here's where it gets really interesting. Me and my bud happen to know that she is one naughty girl. With a hit-and-run sheet that goes back to her training-wheel days. And what, you are about to ask me, does this have to do with saving the taxpayer the cost of a senator's pension? Well, just coincidentally, there are blond hairs on this dead senator's pillow. And elsewhere. And if a cop with a basic understanding of human biology can trust all those nasty stains on the bed, there was a totally different sort of activity going on before the senator's reelection bid got canceled. Yet there is no blond body, living or dead, at the scene of the crime. And this fuck did not commit suicide, let me tell you.'' Dickey let off one of his don't-this-world-stink? whinnies. ''Me, I got FBI snots fresh out of college crawling all over the place because it's a goddamned senator, and they're so smart they know everything. Except they don't know what me and my Army buddy know. Now let me ask you something, your hero-ship. Are you awake enough to put these simple

facts together and guess who those blond hairs might
belong to?''

"We need to talk."

"You keep telling me that."

I was afraid. Shocked awake. Afraid with layer
upon layer of fear. I was an accomplice to a murder.
Among other things. And Dickey had just told the
big, bad world that he and I had a meaningful
relationship.

My thoughts rushed, but my thinking was glacial.
Dickey knew exactly what he was doing. And I failed
to get it.

"Just tell me when and where," I said. "Name
the place."

Dickey gave me another nose honk. "I'll get back
to you. Right now, I'm up to my ass in self-righteous
J. Edgars and meat-eating reporters. But don't take
off for Mexico, all right? And you might want to
steer clear of Miss California. Don't you go aiding
and abetting a felon on me."

He hung up. I flopped back down on the bed. I
just wanted to think for a minute, to reconstruct
something that resembled a viable future. I had, at
best, a day left until the deadline Hunt had given me.
And everything was coming apart instead of coming
together. The disks were as far away as ever. I was
in serious trouble, no matter what happened. And the
woman I loved was a lot worse off than I was. Had
she been lying beside me, I would have held her so
tight it would have taken God and an army of angels
to pry us apart.

But even Tish and dead senators and Dickey and blond hairs on a pillow could not hold me in the land of the living. My body foreclosed on the sleep debt. Which was massive.

I blew it again.

The next time I woke, it was twilight. Corry sat by the bed. With a gun in her hand.

"Wake up, sleepyhead," she told me.

"What?"

Corry smiling. But not making nice. "I was hoping you'd talk in your sleep. That you'd call my name. It would have meant a lot to me."

"What do you want?" The sheets were brinier than ever. Despite the air-conditioning. I sat up against the back of the bed, drawing the sheet with me. Shy. Or just scared.

"Maybe I want to thank you. I owe you my life." She wagged the gun slightly. "By the way, I changed the bullets."

"I don't know what you're talking about."

She smiled. A girl born to win. At any cost. "Don't treat me like a fool. I know it was you. I knew it was you the instant I turned around. The way you move. The cut of the shoulders—you know you have nice shoulders, by the way? I've seen a lot of shoulders. I know it was you, John. I'll always know you."

"Want to fill me in?"

Corry still smiling. "And your voice. I know you so well. You don't realize. I heard you say, 'No.'

Then you said it again. I knew what was happening. I know that you saved my life."

I just wanted to go to the bathroom and piss. "I would've hated to see a great marriage come to a premature end, Mrs. Aalstrom."

It took her a moment to absorb that. But she managed it. "I knew you'd find out sooner or later," she said. "It was inevitable. But that doesn't mean you understand."

"Can I just go to the bathroom for a minute?"

"No." She lifted the gun a little. She did not hold it like a girl. Corry was loaded down with medals from the battle of the sexes. "I want you to have a sense of urgency."

"I thought you came to thank me."

"Among other things." She filled her chest and gave a soap-opera sigh. "I suppose I need to clear the air. About Aley. And all that."

" 'And all that.' "

She looked at me with Actors Studio tenderness. "I suppose I'll never be able to make you understand completely. You want me to be Salomé. The ultimate bad girl. Damned forever. Beyond redemption. And you think you're John the Baptist. You want it all to be so clear. Good and evil. Wicked or wonderful." She smirked. "You're just such a *guy* sometimes. But it's not that easy. Sure, I've done things I'm not proud of. But I'm not necessarily ashamed of them, either. Those things were about survival. Sur*vi*val, John. And getting ahead. *Try*ing to get ahead. I hustled. You don't know what work is until you've lived that life. Rich kids are the lowest life form in the universe. Yeah, and I stole. From other people who stole. And Aley . . .''

She smiled. But her voice turned as bitter as a mouthful of aspirin. ''I was young. He seemed . . . he seemed like a guy who had everything. Everything I wanted.'' She allowed herself a different kind of laugh, a very small one. ''Yeah, he had it. He just didn't know how to pay for it. Neither of us did.'' She was good at meeting my eyes. But this time she looked away.

The gun held steady, though.

''You live and learn,'' she said. ''It took me a long time to learn. You keep thinking, This time it'll be different. This time I'm really going to make it. And you do foolish things. There was a time in my life when Aley and I deserved each other. We were perfect . . .''

I shifted my back. More sweat. ''And?''

''And now,'' she said, ''there's you.''

''Corry—or do you prefer Karen?''

''Corry, please. I've begun a new life.''

''All right, Corry. Just how stupid do you think I am?''

Cat smile. ''Oh, your stupidity may be immeasurable. It's one of your many attractive qualities, John. I've had plenty of men who thought they were smart.''

''You know I'll never believe another word you say.''

She lost her smile. And leaned toward me. ''That

would be sad. Even tragic. Because we were made for each other, John. You're everything I always wanted. Only I didn't know it. You're a white knight. An honest guy. Loyal.''

''I just happen to be loyal to somebody else.''

She waved it away. A queen dismissing a fool whose wit was slower than hers. ''That won't last. She won't hold your interest. There's too much of you and too little of her. You're baby-sitting.''

''I'm going to marry her. When we get through this.''

''*If* you get through this. If *we* get through this. And . . . maybe you should ask her first. I don't think she'd go for it. She'd say yes, then she'd freeze up. She'll fade on you. Disappear. She's fluff. And deep down inside, she knows it. She's afraid of you.''

The light was dying. Tish was dying. I had no time.

''So . . . I should just forget about Tish? And marry you?''

''You could do worse. I'd make you happy. Once you got your devils under control, I'd know how to make you happy. I'm strong enough for you. And it wouldn't have to be marriage.''

''Of course, there is the matter of the living, breathing husband.''

''The one who gave me a gun to protect myself? With dummy bullets? Who's so fucking greedy he wants all the money for himself? The husband who wants me dead?''

"Every marriage has bad patches."

"John, this is serious. You and I . . . we could make it. We could bring this off. We could beat them all."

I shook my head in wonder.

"*Lis*ten to me," she pleaded. "We're talking ten million dollars. *Ten*. Tax-free. Do you have any idea how much money that is? How much did Aley offer you?"

"He said it was five."

"See? Everybody's lying. Except me. John, even if you don't want to be with me . . . do this with me. Help me. Even if you don't want to be with me at first, I'll give you six million. No, seven. That's fair, isn't it? Seven million dollars? All you have to do is help me a little bit. You won't regret it." A woman pleading, with a gun in her hand. Another new experience. "I have what you want, John. I have what you need."

I lost it. You just hit a point and you snap. We are not rational creatures. I barked something and jumped out of bed and stood there in my birthday suit. Too angry and frustrated to give a damn anymore.

"I'm going to the bathroom. Shoot me, if you want. But let me tell you once and for all, sister. You do not have one goddamned thing I want or need."

Her eyes held me for a moment. Those great eyes. The kind of eyes that ruin men's lives with false candor. As I was turning away, she said:

"How about the disks?"

*   *   *

"There's not much time," she told me. "You have to really listen."

I was listening.

"Aley's going to call you. This is it. The big one. It's his last chance. He's desperate. He knows Hunt will cut him out if he doesn't produce this time. We can turn that against him."

"Where's Tish? Where are they keeping her?"

Economical shake of a blond head. "I don't know. And that's the truth. Hunt keeps everything in separate compartments. Aley doesn't know, either."

"Why should I believe that?"

"I swear to God," she said.

I lifted a corner of my mouth. "You don't strike me as the religious type."

"Please listen. He's going to call soon. You have to get it right. Agree to meet him. But you say where. And set a tight deadline. Cut down his reaction time. And don't go to meet him, or Hunt, or anybody, on their turf. Once they know you have the disks, they'll do anything it takes to make you tell them where they are. Then they'll kill you."

"How will I prove I've got the disks? Or that you've got them?"

She reached into her purse. Without shifting her eyes from me. She tossed a disk onto the bed. It landed halfway out of its jacket.

"Give Aley that one. It's the real thing. Then talk money."

"And Tish."

"He'll lay out how they'll do the funds transfer for you. In return for the disks. He'll give you the number of an account in the Caymans and the matching codes. So you can verify the payout." She switched the pistol to her left hand and stretched the fingers of her right. "Aley's got a triple cross set up. He's going to tell Hunt you're the one insisting on using the Caymans account, that you've been working a scam all along. Hunt won't like it, but he'll release the funds. It's small change to his crowd. Although he is one stingy sonofabitch." I wondered if she had enjoyed a close relationship with Hunt as well. "Then Aley cues the account so that your confirmation query triggers another transfer. To Panama this time. Into an account even Hunt won't be able to track. And it'll look like you did it. Hunt kills you in revenge. Aley keeps the money."

"Wasn't it supposed to be Aley and you?"

"That's why he gave me this." She lofted the gun. "With the sandbox bullets."

"And?"

"The money?" She smiled. It was an ugly, sincere smile. "Fuck Aley. That shit. I know more about offshore banking than he ever will. The instant the money hits Panama, it's out of there. Straight to Luxembourg. Straight to us, John." She leaned toward me in the early dusk of the bedroom. "He'll think Hunt screwed him after all. But he won't be able to do anything about it."

I looked at her. Looking for holes. "Except Aley's

bound to wonder why his dream girl is suddenly gone. Don't you think he's going to suspect you?''

She prodded the air lazily with the gun. ''I'll be too disappointed. No, I think I can make his life sufficiently unhappy that he won't suspect a thing. I figure if I stay with him . . . say six months . . . then file for divorce over one of the countless other reasons he's given me . . .'' She straightened her Sunday-school posture. Little Miss Prim. ''Besides, that'll give you time to wrap up the thing with your girl. More than enough time.''

''You're a confident woman.''

''I know you, John. I know her. There aren't more than a dozen different types of people.''

''And how do I know you won't do a job on me? Or kill me, for that matter? Maybe pay somebody a couple of bucks to do the dirty work. How do I even know that disk is real? You've got so many angles, this could be a setup within a setup within a setup.''

''Have an alternative?''

''I could wait.''

''Until your redhead strolls down memory lane? For keeps?''

''Listen . . . I don't give a damn about the money, Corry.''

''Everybody cares about money.''

''I don't.''

''Yes, you do. You will.''

''Six months pass . . . and you're ringing my doorbell, ready to hand me seven million bucks? And give me a kiss besides? I'm supposed to believe that?''

"I'll give you a lot of kisses. I'll kiss you like you've never been kissed.''

"I'm going to do what you want. In the short term. You know that. But don't imagine that I trust you. In any respect. Don't confuse necessity with volition.''

"You'll learn to trust me, John. I'm trusting you with that disk. With my life. They'd kill me. Aley would kill me. He'd make it ugly.''

"What about the disks? Where are the rest of them?''

"I have them.''

"But you don't trust me? Not enough to tell me where?''

"It's better if you don't know. In case anything goes wrong tonight.''

"That's reassuring.''

"It's practical.''

"Okay. At least tell me how you got them. When everybody else has been digging tunnels to China trying to find them.''

She canted her head. Posing for a magazine cover. Hair wandering across her cheek. She probably would not have made it as a model, though. Successful models all have some little flaw.

"All right. I don't mind telling you that. I got them from Em. He had them.''

I hung my head. Hit from the front, back, and sides. I should have seen it on day one.

"Em was going to go public. Wasn't he?'' I asked

her. I wanted to hear it from that perfect little mouth.
"Or turn them over to the GAO? Or to somebody
else?"

"Em was stupid," she said.

"That makes two of us."

"Em was stupid in a different way."

"A better way."

"A useless way," Corry said. "Don't romanticize
him. Em was a shit. He was a fucking drunk with
so much on his conscience he was afraid of dying."

"Was he dying?"

"Yeah."

"Cirrhosis?"

"Cancer. He hit the jackpot."

"You're cold."

"Try realistic."

"I never know what to believe."

"Try trusting me."

I laughed. "Like Em did?"

"I'd do anything for you."

"Then tell me something. When they killed
Em . . . you didn't come straight here from the police
station. Did you?"

"No."

"You went back to the apartment. And grabbed
the disks. That's why they tore it up. The disks were
supposed to be there. Only you saw the main chance.
And you had your own key. And you were quick."
I admired the tactician sitting in front of me. Wondering how she would turn out as a strategist. "So
who did it? Hunt's boys? His goddamned Hunt Club?

You grabbed the disks and stashed them and showed up sobbing on my doorstep. While your teammates went nuts hunting for the goods.''

"Yes. Now do you believe that you can trust me?"

"No. Where'd you stash the disks?"

"I won't tell you that."

"Who shot Em? And don't give me the big-bad-black-boys crap you gave the cops.''

"Aley did. Aley shot him. It was the first time he killed anybody. He panicked. He ran. That's when I knew I had to grab the disks myself. That I couldn't depend on him.''

"And you knew it was going to go down. You walked Em right into the ambush?"

"Em had it coming. He was a shit."

"Let's just agree to disagree on that. So . . . how'd you do it? Did you get him to bend over and kiss you? To distract him? Or was it just supposed to be a miracle meeting on the streets of Washington, Em and his old Army acquaintance Aley Aalstrom?"

Corry brushed stray hairs back over an ear and leaned toward me. "John, do you know that your girlfriend can't have babies?"

"Don't change the subject."

"Would you like to know why she can't have kids?"

"No."

"Then we both have to accept that some things are best left buried in the past."

"Leave Tish out of this."

"You're the one who's so intent on including her in our lives, John."

"Tish has had a hard-luck life, Corry."

Corry laughed. A human being should not be able to laugh like that when he or she is still young. "We make our luck. She doesn't understand that. Or anything else. I know the type. She probably did this big remorse number on you. All weepy. 'Oooh, I can't have little babies for you . . .' Get a grip, John. Her kind doesn't feel remorse. She's just sorry she got caught."

"Go to hell."

"You believe in the image you've created of her. She's just a slut on temporary good behavior. Because she thinks she won the lottery. And she wants to make sure she gets the payout. If you did marry her, it wouldn't be six months until she was down on her knees giving a blow job to some agent or promoter. Or maybe just the paperboy."

"You're poison."

"I'm honest."

"No. You're not. You're the devil."

"John, do you know what happens to romantics? Their kids come out looking like some other guy."

The phone rang. And we both stopped. As it rang for the second time, Corry told me:

"Tell him you have what he wants. Tell him you'll meet him. On your turf. This is our chance, John."

*   *   *

It was a woman who introduced herself as Melissa. She offered me a special low introductory rate on a new MasterCard.

I hung up. "Telemarketer."

Corry had a way of sharpening her eyes that made me think she was getting a sight picture on an invisible rifle. "It was that policeman. Wasn't it?"

"No. It was a credit card offer. Really."

"John, we need to discuss this. What have you told the police?"

"Next to nothing. Just what I had to tell them to get them to put me back on the street."

"Was the cop the one who told you? About me and Aley?"

"Yes."

"What else does he know about me?"

"He thinks you're trouble. He warned me to stay away from you."

"Is he watching me?"

"I suspect he'd like to. But this is D.C., sister. The cops are in a round-the-clock sewer diving competition. We're small stuff."

"Has he made any connections?"

"No. Not really." I had, though. Corry was too good for Hollywood, but for once, I had more information than she did. That told me she was not plugged in all that tightly with Hunt and company. Who had been tapping my phone. Hunt wasn't sharing the power information with Corry. Or, I suspected, with Aley. I liked it like that. But I also believed that Hunt would see Corry as one hundred percent disposable. Thanks to Dickey's phone call, Hunt knew the cops had connected her to the Faust murder. Which was not a Hunt-approved action. Hunt might just be anxious to talk to Corry about that.

The stakes were going up and up.

"Don't tell the police anything you don't have to," Corry said. Voice earnest. "It won't help."

"Corry, I'm at the point where I'm afraid to talk to myself."

"And that other one. The French guy who was here. The one you fought with. Has he tried to get in touch with you again?"

I wondered if this was a test question. If it was, I was ready to fail.

"No. I think the cops scared him off. The frogs are still hot about the lab bombing. But even the French are smart enough to figure out that I'm not connected."

"Stay away from them," Corry said. "Don't talk to the French. Don't talk to anybody. I'm the only one you can trust, John. Believe me."

The phone rang again. We both jumped.

It was Aley.

"John. Hey, Johnny boy. The clock has been fucking ticking. Ticktock. So you got good news for me, or what? Moment of truth."

"Maybe."

"What the fuck is that? 'Maybe.' *Talk* to me."

"Not over the phone."

"Don't waste my time, Johnny boy."

"Fuck you, Aley. I've done enough of an analysis

of the situation to figure out that you need me a lot more than I need you. You're a flunky. So can the bad-boy act.''

''John, you remember all that shit about snuff films? You know, where they gang-fuck some babe and torture her? Kind of cut her up piece by piece? Then kill her? Right on camera? Well, I am here to tell you that cinema verité is not just a legend of our time. They make 'em right across the border. Little ranch down the highway from TJ. Your redhead's got star quality.''

''Doesn't work, Aley. Try sugar.''

''Try getting real. The curtain comes down in the morning, Johnny boy.''

''Here's the deal, Aley. I've got something you want. And I'm prepared to give you a taste. If you say, 'Please.' ''

''Tell me you got them, John. Say it.''

''Meet me at Monsieur Paul's. Pennsylvania Avenue. Southeast. I'll be at the bar. In half an hour. If you're late, I'm going straight to General Hunt. And you can go make Mexican movies for a living.''

I thought I had it all sorted out at last. And I had already begun to shape a plan. I walked out of the house. Into the concentrated end-of-the-day heat. Leaving Corry upstairs in her web. I turned the corner fast. Heading for Monsieur Paul's, where Capitol Hill gets strange.

A kick-ass energy surge powered me. I imagined myself taking charge of the whole mess at last. For the first time, I had cards *and* chips. And I was ready to cheat like a Congressman in a tight reelection campaign.

Then I recognized Mary Farnsworth. Bent over. Locking the Cadillac Seville that had been the general's pride and joy.

She saw me. And barely kept her excitement within the bounds of decorum. Queen Mary. The last person I wanted to see mixed up with desperados. I wondered if anything would ever really go right for me again.

"I don't know *how* you live here," she told me. "Parking is just an impossi*bil*ity."

"Mary, you promised me you'd—"

She hushed me with a fine, small gesture of the hand. "Oh, I did every last thing you said. But . . . do you understand what Louisiana is *like* this time of year? Besides, I could not stop thinking about Mickey. And I began to feel like the most shameless coward. Just running away. *Flee*ing. Just like that. Without even knowing what I was fleeing from."

"Mary, this is serious."

Her bearing changed. She reared like a drill sergeant confronted with a cruddy pair of boots on parade.

"My husband's dead, John. I think I can appreciate the seriousness in that."

"You shouldn't be here. It's dangerous."

"And what about *you?* I kept thinking about you, John. I thought you might need a friend. To stand by you."

"You can't help me now. You have to leave."

Her eyes surprised me. Reserve melted into yearning. An ache to do something, anything, in the face of immeasurable loss. "I don't want to burden you," she told me. "That would be the last thing. It's only that . . . given all that's happened . . . I didn't know if it would be safe to telephone you. You see, I found them."

"Mary, you need to get out of here. Now. Please."

"But I found them. Those disks. I thought you might need them."

I hurried Mary into an alley. Not a crack dealer in sight. Or anybody else. Gray birds pecked garbage.

"Stay in the shadows. Away from the light."

"I just thought you'd want to know . . ." She was confused now.

"You bet. Tell me about the disks. How many? Where were they?"

Mary shook her head. As if looking around for answers that had slipped from her mind. "I was . . . John, you have to understand. With Mickey . . . I mean, I was so terribly upset. *Dev*astated. I wasn't thinking at all. But when I came back, I had to go to the bank. To our safe-deposit box. For our personal papers, records." She wrinkled her fine mouth. A shadow twisting within a shadow. "It should have been obvious. I should have thought about it immediately." She touched at the sweat that covered every forehead in the city. "I was just such a fool. You see, we always kept a big safe-deposit box. I had to keep all my jewelry in it. Mickey insisted. He had that dread of crime soldiers seem to acquire. Well, wasn't it just the most obvious place in the world for him to keep those disks?''

''How many of them are there? Is there any writing on them? Where are they now?''

She shrugged. ''Oh, there must be dozens. I don't know. I didn't count them. I was so excited. Perhaps . . . oh, would sixty or so sound right? That's just a guess, now. But you can come over and count them. I brought them home. They all have Macon-Bolt stamps on them. With a lot of numbering. And they're marked 'Top Secret.' Was Mickey supposed to keep anything like that in our private box?''

''Mickey—I mean, General Farnsworth—was a hero. He knew exactly what he was doing.''

She regarded me with a sorrow the new darkness could not mask. ''Then why is he dead? I miss him so, John.''

CHAPTER 13

THE CUSTOMER NEXT TO ME AT THE BAR LOOKED LIKE Gertrude Stein in a biker's jacket. Monsieur Paul's had a core gay clientele, but it was open to other human variations. Tish and I had gone there a few times to hear friends of hers play jazz. Of all the establishments I could have picked for the meet with Aley, I figured Monsieur Paul's was the likeliest to surprise him and keep him off balance. Besides, the kitchen did a good club sandwich.

I had the third triangle in my mouth when Aley came in. Funny to watch him. L.A. boy or not, the atmosphere hit him hard. He saw the crowd, not me.

Management kept the bar dark. During the day, the sunnies ate at the sidewalk tables and drank bottles of beer. At nightfall the vampires came out. And plenty of victims drifted in. The joint provided good people watching at all hours. I enjoyed watching Aley.

I left the last quarter of the sandwich and worked

toward him through the performance-art boys. He finally saw me. A what-the-fuck-is-this? expression split his lips.

We did not shake hands.

"You hitting from both sides of the plate now?" he asked me.

"Your problem," I told him, "is that you never met Mr. Right."

"Up yours, Johnny boy."

"You're going to fit right in. Have a seat. Over in the corner. It's more romantic."

I let him lead the way. Shirt too shiny. Jacket expensive but loser-snug in the armpits. Padded shoulders. With organic padding at the butt of his trousers. A heavyweight in the heat. No weaponeering, as far as I could tell.

"So what's with the circus?"

A splendid human specimen with a West Indian accent loomed. "What going to be your pleasure?"

"Two drafts," I said. "Whatever."

"You're deep in the shit," Aley told me. "Right down to the wire. So talk to me. You got the goodies or not?"

It was strange as hell sitting there. Wondering how much he knew. Thanks to Mary Farnsworth, I knew Corry was out to beat me. But were she and Aley playing as a team, after all? Or was she out to beat him, too? The disk she had given me had some alpha-numerics printed on its label. It looked convincing if you did not know what you were looking for. But it did not look like the disks Mary had described.

Who knew what the real disks looked like? Hunt had to know. Did Corry and Aley really believe they could bluff the big boys? I did not rule out the possibility. The scent of money makes folks stupider than the prospect of cost-free sex.

I had the aces. Or I would have them as soon as I got across the river to Mary's house. But no matter which way I turned, I was sitting with my back to a door or a window.

If I was going down, I was not going alone. It was going to be a fight. Keeping Tish alive constituted a clear and worthy mission. Maybe we had a chance. But I could not expect to outmaneuver everybody else—I had to let them outmaneuver themselves.

I tossed the disk onto the table and watched Aley. I expected him to grab it. But he only stared at the thing.

"How do I know it's real?" he asked me. "That could be something you picked up at Computerland."

"You don't want it, I'll go." I reached for the disk.

He flattened a swollen hand over it. "Just fucking wait. You listen to me. If it turns out you're blowing smoke, I'm going to introduce you to misery like you never imagined. To say nothing of your trash mick bitch."

"Aley, you're more impressive when you keep your mouth shut. And that's just what I want you to do. Until I tell you to open it again."

The waiter brought the beers. I suspected the guy was one of the bar's key attractions. He floated away, muscles and air, twirling his tray on an index finger.

"The disk is good," I said. "And you know it. Now let me tell you how we're going to work the battle handoff. You are going to give me a phone number. And you are going to be standing by that phone at a quarter to five tomorrow afternoon. Sixteen-forty-five, pal. At that time, I will designate a location within the city of Washington. You will be there at six P.M. Eighteen hundred on the dot. I will name a very public location, with more witnesses than even Hunt could take down. Tish O'Malley will be there. And she will look as healthy as Tarzan. General Hunt will also be there. Make it happen. Accept no substitutes."

Aley opened his mouth and raised both hands.

"Save it," I told him. "My deal, or no deal. And I've got it fail-safed. Any of the Hunt Club boys try to move on me between now and tomorrow afternoon, the disks will be in French hands before the HOV lanes open up. And one more attendee. General Gabrielli will be there. In uniform. Tell Hunt to make it happen."

"What's that monkey Gabrielli got to do with the great apes?"

I sipped my beer. Acting calmer than I felt and hoping it came off. "Insurance. If Gabrielli's there with all those stars and his nameplate, he won't want any rough stuff that might get him dirty in the public eye. We'll keep the swap clean that way. No double crosses. And I'll have backup.''

Aley snickered. "My ass. You're so deep in the shit you couldn't find backup to sing harmony at your funeral. Get real.''

"Know why I invited you here, Aley? Because you never were anything but a pussy with hormonal confusion. So let's talk money. Ten million. Not five. Hunt told me. Yeah, you're master of your emotions, all right. I wish I had a mirror so you could see your face. So smart. So tough. Well, let me offer you the break of your life. It's a deal. I'll settle for the five. You take the other five. And I won't feed you to Hunt.'' He really was small-time. Corry was a thousand times more accomplished as a hustler. "Your turn to talk. Tell me about the money. How it's going to work.''

He shook his head in disgust. "Just fuck you. It'll go to the Caymans. It's all set. Here's how it happens . . .''

Aley laid it out. Exactly the way Corry said he would. I could not get a constant fix on how much anybody really knew, but Corry seemed to know more of whatever there was to know than Aley did. Maybe they were still in it together. But I was starting to buy Corry as a triple-crosser. Maybe going for a quadruple.

There were so many layers of lies, a Southern belle could not have kept them straight. I let Aley talk. Then I let him pay for the beers. And I made him add to the tip. He started to stand up, but I got a foot behind one of his chair legs and yanked it in behind his knees.

"One more thing," I said. "You killed Farnsworth. Didn't you?"

"What the fuck? You wired or something? You're talking shit."

"Truth or consequences. I just want to know. Let's see some eyes. Talk to me, Aley."

"What does it matter who killed him? Fucking nigger busybody. They in short supply this week?"

"I'm just sentimental. Tell me you killed him."

"John, we are talking ten million dollars. And that's just the trickle-down effect for the little people like you and me. The old shit was on the heart-attack express. Old and in the way."

"Just say you killed him. I don't even need the details."

"You wearing a wire? What is this?"

"No wire. But here's the deal. You try to beat me out of my five million, and I'll put the Farnsworth murder on you. Fair's fair."

Aley smiled in recognition. "Shit. We all have our price. Don't we, John?"

Mary Farnsworth's kitchen. With the blinds closed. The disks lay on the table between us. They looked real. Felt real. I was going to bet my life that they were real.

"Mary, you're sitting in front of three hundred billion dollars. Give or take a few billion." It was the kind of thing she did not need to know. But it was also the kind of thing you can't resist saying. "If you let me take them, neither one of us will ever see a penny of it."

"I don't want money."

"I know. I'm just talking. It's a human disease."

Mary smiled. But the valiant attempt at warmth faded. "More coffee, John?"

"Please." I had driven the most convoluted, back-assward route imaginable to get to Mary's place. Then I parked several blocks away. I gave the neighborhood's sensor lights a workout. Slipping through backyards. Thanks to the leash laws, there were no dog problems. When I arrived at her back door and gave the triple-secret club knock, she had coffee waiting. On Judgment Day, Mary would be out there serving iced tea to the damned.

She poured me another cup of her New Orleans roast. Blended with chicory. She refilled her own cup, parked the pot with her customary grace, and sat back down like a woman with something to say.

"John . . . are you a Christian? Forgive me for being so awkward. I mean, do you con*sid*er yourself a Christian? I suppose it's a terribly personal thing to ask . . ."

I reached for words. "My church attendance has been pretty spotty."

"But do you be*lieve?*"

I looked down at the disks. This was not something about which I was comfortable talking. Nor had I expected to talk about it. Death, disks, and theology. I suppose it all matched up.

"Mary . . . I'm not sure I'm the kind of person who really knows what he believes. I'm a trial-and-error kind of guy." I smiled, a real lemon-biter, thinking of a long sequence of errors. "I just may be the sloppiest believer on earth. But . . . at the end of the day . . . I guess it's there."

"We all need faith, John. I wish you faith. *Strong* faith."

"Don't worry about me."

She gave me those wonderful brown eyes. "Oh, I don't. Not really. Not that way. You strike me as a natural believer. The sort who has the faith but not the habits. And that's what's important. Not the rituals, comforting though they may be. God is . . . ultimately unknowable. We're too small for God. I have always seen you as a worshipper, though. In your way. Sometimes plain human decency is a form of worship. Perhaps a very high form." She scrubbed her hands together. Not a very Mary-like gesture. "This is *so* awkward."

"Is there something you need me to do?" I drank the piercing coffee.

She placed her hands flat on the tabletop. As though she had suddenly regained control of them. The nails shone unpainted. "John, you know Mickey and I were always active in our church."

I nodded. And drank.

"I have always considered myself a good Christian," Mary said. "I have been blessed with faith." She rolled that beautiful face slightly to the side. "I have counted many blessings. I know I am an imperfect being. A *very* imperfect being . . . and I have certainly been guilty of the sin of pride . . ."

"What is it, Mary?"

In the thin light, her eyes looked like long, dark hallways.

"I always assumed," she continued, "that I adhered adequately to the tenets of my faith. It was vanity. I see that now. A lack of self-evaluation, of the critical faculty applied where it is most needed. I *believed* that I believed in the Christian virtues."

I tried a smile. "Mary, you're probably the most saintly person I've ever met. If sheer kindness counts for anything . . ."

She shook her head. "No. No, that's not true. My soul . . ." She leaned toward me and her voice dwindled to a whisper of bones. "My soul is filled with sin. And I can't help it." Her eyes held me. Their grip was just short of physical. "John, do you know who hurt Mickey? Who killed him?"

"I think I do."

She gentled a hand toward the disks. "Can you use these to hurt whoever it was?"

"Yes. I can do that."

I would never have believed her face could change so. Or that any face could change so. Those precise, drawing-room features took on the bone-thunder look of a vengeful prophet.

"I want them to suffer," she cried. "I want them to pay. I don't care if I'm damned for it." The granite began to crack, to melt. Tears burst through, water from the rocks. "I want them to hurt the way I hurt.

I want them to hurt the way Mickey hurt. And I don't care about anything else in the world.''

To my amazement, Dickey had a listed home number. I had been prepared to work my way through layers of police bureaucracy to reach him, but the recorded voice read me his number and would have dialed it for me if I had not been calling from a convenience-store pay phone in suburbia.

I called, he answered.

"It's John Reynolds," I said. "I need your help."

"You bet you do. What're you doing calling me at home at this hour? Wake up my daughter and all."

"Please. This is important."

"And it just can't wait till morning, right?"

"It can't wait until morning."

"You got rocks, I'll say that for you. What's your major malfunction this time?"

"I need a phone number. It's unlisted. For a Roscoe Hunt. Retired general. A.k.a. Punchy Hunt. Ever heard of him?"

"We move in different circles."

"He's got a big spread ten or twelve miles out of Middleburg."

"So that's where our defense dollars go."

"Some of them."

"All right. Jesus. I'm going soft, I swear. Give me the name again."

"Hunt. First name Roscoe. Nickname's Punchy. Horse farm about—"

"Yeah, yeah. Got it. Call me back in . . . give me twenty minutes. The whole world's asleep."

"Thanks. I owe you."

"You got debts Bill Gates couldn't pay." He hung up.

I figured Dickey would come through. Anticipating, I got back in the car and headed west. Thinking about an Elvis Costello song. A favorite of Tish's. With the line "I can give you anything but time."

I knew where I was going. I simply did not want to be shot when I arrived. I was going in clean. No real wampum to trade. Mary and I had hidden the disks inside the empty PC casing in her husband's library, the one that had been looted of its hard drive. I figured it was the safest place in her house. The disks sure as hell would not have been safe with me.

File me under "Unprepared for the Twenty-first Century." I never had a car phone or a cellular to call my own. Now I saw the value. I had a bad time finding a pay phone in the yuppie belt off 66. I had to push on to a gas station where Route 50 hits 15 and the big rigs backroad down from Maryland and parts north.

When I called, Dickey had the number for me.

"I'll phone you in the morning," I told him. "I pay my debts. At six o'clock tomorrow evening, you'll have all the murderers you can handle in one place. But they're not going to go gently into that good night."

*   *   *

Hunt did not answer his own phone. A guard-dog voice just said, "Hello," and waited.

"This is Lieutenant Colonel John Reynolds. I need to talk to General Hunt."

Fido did not respond immediately. I began to wonder if he had hung up. But the phone noise did not change. Finally, he said:

"You're not on the list. Call back during business hours."

"I need to talk to him now. Tell him it's John Reynolds."

"You're not on the list, buddy." I could feel the phone pull away from his ear.

"Wait," I said. Or yelled. "Three hundred billion dollars. Computer disks. Tell him."

"What is this shit?"

"Hunt's going to lose a lot of money if you don't get him on the phone. And I guarantee you he'll lose his temper, too. You know what happened to that Labrador of his?"

"Stay on the line."

I stood in the almost-cool of the night. Watching a big gal with a time-warp Charlie's Angels hairdo pump gas into a pickup. The truck had a bumper sticker that said, "Impeach the President—and her husband, too."

Hunt's voice came on like a storm.

"Watcha got? What is it? That you, Reynolds? Start talking."

"It's me. I want to see you."

"You have my disks?"

"No."

He blew the rhythm. After the pause, he said, "Aalstrom just told me you did."

"I need to see you. You're being scammed. I'm on Route 50, fifteen minutes from Middleburg. Headed your way. I'd like to make it inside the gates alive."

Hunt laughed. Then chopped off the sound with an invisible axe. "Reynolds, you got more balls on you than a fifteen-foot Christmas tree, you know that? You tell me you don't have my disks, but you want to drive right on into the belly of the beast. You trying to run some kind of scam yourself, boy? Or are you just crazy?"

"Try me."

"Damned if I won't. Come on out here. Let's have us a talk. If you're fucking with me, I'll kill you with my bare hands."

CHAPTER 14

THE GATES TO HUNT'S ESTATE STOOD OPEN. I DID NOT see any guards. But I was certain Hunt's boys saw me. I followed the country road that served as a driveway for about a mile, with a gauntlet of trees black on the flanks of my headlights. The road was flat but gave the illusion of a descent into an ever-thicker darkness.

Suddenly, the landscape opened and climbed. The car crested a low ridge. Across a field I picked out two silhouettes carrying those jagged, chopped automatic rifles that look like pieces of modern sculpture.

In the background, a pair of red lights floated up above the trees. I cranked down the window. Engine noise confirmed it: A plane had taken off from Hunt's private airstrip. I wondered if it had to do with my problem or with some other grand scheme to take over the world with guns and money.

Another defensive line of trees. Slight movement,

perhaps imagined. Good soldiers waiting for an enemy to attack. I half expected to see the outline of dug-in tanks.

Bright windows marked the big house. I braked hard at the last minute and stopped just short of a steel swing gate. I didn't remember it. But there had been a lot on my mind during my last visit.

Three boys in black emerged from the shrubs. One stood behind the gate. Directly in my headlights. Pointing a weapon as angular as a swastika at my windshield. The other two spooked along the side of the road. A big voice said, "Get out of the vehicle. Clasp your hands behind your head." No malice in it. The tone was as routine as the kid at the Burger King drive-through.

One of the boys patted me down, intimately enough to make a positive impression back at Monsieur Paul's. Real high-security prison frisk. Then they went through the car. And under it. With flashlights.

Out in the big-bucks peace of Middleburg, Hunt had a little army of commandos. In black uniforms. Faces mottled dark with camouflage. These were not weekend warriors. When the reception committee was done with me and my rent-a-Ford, one of them just called out, "Clean." The guy with the mini-malist automatic pulled the gate open.

I drove up the rise to the house and parked next to a pair of four-wheelers. More security around the parking apron. By the time I got to the front door,

Hunt filled the opening, a minotaur black against the lights of the entryway.

"Wondered if you'd pussy out at the last minute," Hunt said. "Then I figured, Naw, this boy's gone to too much trouble. He's going to play out his hand. Come on in."

He turned and marched down the hallway. A red dragon reared across his back. Hunt went barefoot, with massive, scarred legs pumping under khaki desert shorts. The black hairs had been burned off the muscle of one of his calves. Those legs were an encoded history of the man's life. But my eyes pulled back to the dragon. Emblazoned on seductive blue silk, writhing over Chinese characters I could not read. The wrap was cut like an old-fashioned smoking jacket and tailored to fit. Above the collar, a purple scar meandered down the back of Hunt's skull. But every line of his body seemed to converge on the dragon.

I got the same impression as the first time I saw him: a man who had been blown apart and reassembled.

"Hell, let's just use the library," he told me. "Still haven't got the goddamned armory cleaned up to academy standards." He pushed open a door. The lights were on over the bookcases. He had known exactly which room he would use. He was the kind of guy who knew exactly how much ammo to hump and who never forgot the spare battery for the radio. A two-canteener. "Sit down, sit down. Want a drink?"

"I'm driving."

He smiled at that. "Maybe. And maybe the boys'll have to bury you out back before sunup. Sure about that drink?"

I shook my head. "I'm not much of a drinker."

That got a snort. "Hell, son, a couple of days ago I would've said you weren't much of anything." He looked at me with eyes of pure jade. "Now I'm not so sure. You don't mind if I have one, I take it?"

He bent to a cabinet. Hidden mini-fridge. A bottle of Stoli bobbed up in his right paw. His left drew out a can of V8 Juice. "Nothing but goddamned vitamins," he said. "Take care of your body, your body takes care of you. Make me happy and tell me you were yanking my chain on the phone. Tell me you have my disks."

"I don't have the disks."

"Aalstrom told me you did. What happened to them?"

"I never had them. Aley's a liar."

"Why'd you tell him you had them? He says you even gave him a taste." He dropped into one of the leather chairs that fit you like a lover. It looked like he was drinking blood.

"He's got a disk," I said. "It's bogus. At least, I think it is."

"You don't fucking know?"

"His wife gave it to me. To give to him."

One of Hunt's eyebrows lifted a notch. Like the range slide on a rifle.

"I think they're out to screw each other," I told

him. "But I'm one hundred percent positive they're both out to screw you."

Hunt dimpled his chin and looked down into his glass. "You know, that woman has the makings of a great courtesan. Just lacks patience. Haven't been fucked like that since I left Thailand." He smiled with half his mouth. "Figured I ought to test-drive it. And I guess you still haven't?"

"Not my type."

"Hell, boy, she's everybody's type. You're dumber than dogshit, passing that up. So she gave you a disk? To give to Aley? To tease me with? Now how about explaining that to an old soldier who's been hit upside the head a couple of times too many?"

I leaned back in the big chair. Half expecting iron clamps to leap across my chest and lash around my legs. But I only got that glorious softness.

"Here's my take on it," I began. "You be the judge. Either she's out to beat everybody, including Aley. Or she and Aley are working together on the double cross. No matter which way I cut it, though, they're both out to use me to blindside you. For the money. I'm here to bet my life that the disk Corry gave me is a fake. They're setting up a hand-off scenario in which you have to transfer the money. Temporarily, as far as you know. So I can confirm it and feel secure. So I can imagine I'm in the driver's seat. For a millisecond. Only the instant I make the call, another electronic transfer occurs. International borders pop up like fire walls. The ten million disappears. And we're both cut out. Thanks to the wonders of information-age banking.''

Hunt's face locked up.

"You wouldn't realize what happened," I went on. "Not immediately. You'd have other things on your mind. Fires to put out, dragons to slay. Accounts to settle. By the time you exit the battlefield and get those disks into a computer for a look at the contents, they'll be high in the sky and over water. And you won't have the code to follow the money. They only need a couple of hours. Maybe less.''

"I'd find them," Hunt said. Voice of stone.

"Sure. But they don't believe it. They think they can bring it off. She's sure of it. I suspect she's even ready to toss you Aley. Not much of a sacrifice. And so what if you do find them? The damage is done. You've blown your shot at crisis management. And you look like a horse's ass. Scammed by a drunk-tank hustler and a slut for all seasons.''

I concentrated on keeping my voice sober and firm. Although I probably sounded like a prisoner begging his executioner for five more minutes.

"They've spotted your one weakness." I avoided his eyes when I said that. Looking just to the side. At the blue silk on his shoulder. The way you avoid locking eyes with a really mean dog. "You're over-confident. And they are not as dumb as they seem. What Aley lacks in table manners, he makes up for in his knowledge of international banking. And she knows more than he does. A lot more. She could pick the devil's pocket and make the poor bugger smile in the process.''

I tested his eyes again. And found them opaque. He might as well have been an idol carved into the wall of a cave. "They've got it figured. An excuse for every move. Cover stories for their cover stories. The deal goes down. They fade on you. As if they're just plain scared. After all the carnage. You're supposed to blame me for the bad disks and the missing money. I'm dead, you're out ten million, your credibility's in the sewer, and Macon-Bolt goes shopping for a new security messiah.''

Our faces were two masks—mine a crude wooden thing meant to hide fear.

Hunt rubbed his thumb back and forth across the side of his glass. A look of amusement had grown on his face. It was the kind of look that was just a hair-trigger short of fury.

"Well, fuck me,'' he said. "Now . . . just what's to stop me from killing you and that redhead of yours and tidying up the sandbox? Before I look into the Aalstroms' family values?''

I leaned forward. "Two things. First, I expect you to live up to your reputation. The O-Club stories claim that, in addition to being the meanest sonofabitch in the gutter, you were also a guy who paid his debts. Who never left a comrade behind. A young SFer lieutenant who got shot to shit in the Laotian highlands carrying out the corpse of a CO he personally hated.''

His eyes had changed again. He could have stared down lions.

"Maybe I'm a chump," I said. "But I figure you owe me. For the preemptive info. I'm saving you ten million bucks and a major embarrassment. And all I want is my girl back." I wished I sounded more confident, more convincing. "She won't say a word. She'll do what I tell her. You set the rules. Just let her go."

Hunt drained his glass and pawed his lips dry. "Reynolds . . . that gal of yours must be one hell of a screw. Or else she's the possessor of talents as yet undivined by old Punchy Hunt. You know, she asked my boys for pen and paper. Wanted to write you a little old letter. Just in case she didn't make it back to your loving arms. God Almighty, I feel like I'm in the presence of true love. Now, I still might kill you. After all, you are one hell of a security risk. But I'm thinking. You said there were two reasons why I shouldn't cut your throat and throw you in the cookpot. Try number two."

I wished I had taken him up on the drink offer. I had been trying to appear rigorous, macho, clean, confident. Now I was ready to drink straight from the bottle.

"You need me to play through the scenario. To give you the walking, talking proof. I told Aley—"

"I know what you told Aalstrom. Just talk to me."

"All right. Tomorrow evening, at eighteen hundred hours, Corry—or Karen, or whatever her name is—she and I will link up with Aley in Union Station.

Then we'll meet you in the main hall for the handoff. She and Aley don't know the location or the specifics yet. I've been holding it back. As if I'm afraid and clinging to my only card.''

I looked into the mask of his face. Maybe it was a trick of the lighting, but his cheekbones seemed to have climbed. To barricade his eyes. He looked like a devil in an Oriental pantomime.

''One of us will be packing the bogus disks,'' I went on. ''Probably Aley, by the time we meet you. He'll grab them from whoever has them. Sheer nerves. I'm not going to call him till sixteen-thirty or so. So he'll be sweating. And pissed. After I call, he'll spend a couple of minutes wondering just how close he can cut it with you. Afraid you'll try to set up your own double cross. Then he'll panic. Afraid he's going to blow the whole deal. And he'll call you. Say just before five. To pass you the location for the transfer. And to make sure you've transferred the funds. When we're all on-scene at Union Station, he'll be nervous as a whore in church. And she'll have her eye on him, not on you. He's the one she doesn't trust. But you have the intel in advance. You can set it all up, preempt the bank transfers, grab Ozzie and Harriet on the way out. Or follow them. However you want to do it. You'll have them red-handed.''

Hunt rubbed his jaw. Heavy beard. Unshaven since the previous morning. I could hear the whiskers crisp under his fingers.

''What if you're wrong, boy? What if Aley already

put that disk in my hands and it's sound as the Federal Reserve?"

"He didn't."

Hunt grinned. Showing those replacement teeth. The originals would have been brown with coffee stains and tropical medicine. "No. He didn't. But what if he does?"

"He won't. Not if he's in on the scam with Corry. And I think he thinks he is. Although she's probably angling to triple-cross the double-crosser."

"Gets kind of fuzzy, doesn't it? Kind of like applied morality."

"Ask him to deliver the disk I passed him. He'll make every excuse in the world to delay handing it over."

"But . . . if you're right . . . and I press him . . . he'll run for the jungle."

"Which is why you need me. To walk the line. At eighteen hundred."

Hunt stood up. And calmly set his glass on a table loaded with photographs of a young soldier with lost colleagues. I noticed one photo in particular. I was glad Hunt's back was turned. So he could not see the stunned look on my face. The last linkage had just fallen into place.

Hunt walked over to the Landseer doggie painting and stared at it. Back still to me. Feet planted apart, roots embedded in the floor. The dragon fidgeted on his back. As though his muscles were wrestling under the fabric.

" 'His captain's heart,' " he said, " 'which in the

scuffles of great fights hath burst the buckles on his breast, reneges all temper . . . and is become the bellows and the fan to cool a gypsy's lust.' '' He groaned. A speared beast. ''That bitch.''

With slow arms, he lifted the painting from the wall. He tossed the frame into the air.

I never saw anything like the performance that followed. Not outside of a Jackie Chan preview. As the painting fell, Hunt punched through it and caught it. His hands and arms moved so quickly my eyes could not tune. He chopped and hacked at the frame, keeping it up in the air. Juggling. Smaller and smaller pieces. He screamed. And smashed the splinters ever smaller. Flipping them high. Double-cutting them with the edges of both hands. Howling.

After maybe ten seconds, he stopped cold. Leaving a mess of wood chips and shredded canvas on the floor. He had a new career waiting as an art critic.

He flopped back down in his chair. Gasping. For the first time, he looked old.

''The bitch,'' he repeated. ''That little bitch.''

Suddenly, he mastered himself again. But his face remained pink. He had done the unforgivable. He had lost control. And it embarrassed him. As every man will, he tried to make a joke of it. In his sandpaper fashion.

''My theory of art valuation,'' he said softly, still searching for oxygen, ''is that there is a finite supply of the salable. Each time a piece of value is destroyed, the relative value of the surviving pieces climbs. Followed, if erratically, by their selling price." His face shone rose, with spots and lines of darkness. "Think of it as creative destruction."

He looked down at his hands. One bled along a finger. He watched the blood bead and streak. "Aging teaches us the laws of entropy. On a very personal level. Still, the notion of killing a piece of womanflesh as fine as that little blond bitch does not appeal to me. I have . . . I've had to do many things in life that do not appeal to me. My survival was conditional upon it. Can you understand that?"

Yes. I could understand that. Still I said:

"You wouldn't have to kill her."

His eyes gave me two seconds of pure disdain. Then he shook his head slowly and said, "I'm tired. This should have been a small job. Nothing at all. I want to end it." The jade eyes were flawed now. "You really don't have any idea where those disks are? The real ones? I could make you a rich man."

"Sorry."

He grimaced. "Nechestny's a horse's ass, of course. Greedy. Could've made an airplane that worked. More real potential. Could have sold the services a pretty good one now and a better one later on. But no. Old Bob had to go for the big kill. It's all a game to him." The martial arts display had been dazzling. But now Hunt's lips were purple and black. There were unexpected spaces between his words. "I don't expect you'll credit this, John . . . but I have always believed honesty is the best policy. This world's so goddamned crooked . . . honesty is like a suit of shining armor. Oh, you might move a little slower. But you're more apt to get there . . . alive.'' He stopped to glut his lungs. A dying minotaur. "I am a violent man. It has been my trade. But I don't like to think I'm truly a dishonest one. There are roles . . . to be played. Jobs to be done. Certainly, you might conceive of honesty differently than I do. But . . .''

He snapped back to being old Punchy Hunt. "Hell, boy, it's all crap. Every bit of it. I'm tired and talking trash. So you just listen to me. You hit the goddamned lottery. I don't know if it's brains or balls. But I'm going to see to it that you walk. Redhead, too. *Af*ter you deliver my two little scumbag shit traitors into Daddy's loving arms.'' He pawed his cheek. Streaking it with blood. "Union Station, huh?"

"Safest for me. The crowd. Witnesses.''

Hunt laughed. His lungs had come back on line. An act of will. He smacked a big bare knee with his palm. "Damn, you're not as dumb as you look. Now . . . what's all this bull Aley was laying down about how you want Gabrielli there? In uniform?''

"More security. Gabrielli's scared. If he's there in his greens, the center of attention with all those stars on his shoulders . . . I figure he won't want you doing the damn-damn on anybody. Where it might turn into the ultimate photo op.''

He smiled. A pondering smile. "Why not? Good experience for old Gabe. Lay some fear on him. Goddamned therapeutic. Don't know how we ever let a craven shit like him pin on all that rank. Goddamned peacetime Army.''

"And Tish."

He nodded. "Yep. And the instant those disks change hands, I want you to un-ass the area of operations. ASAP. Tow your girlfriend right on out of there. Don't wait for permission. Leave that building at warp speed. I'm going to have things to discuss with our friends from California."

"And call off Gabrielli. I want to go back to work."

"Don't worry about Gabe. He's fully booked. Now . . . tell me one more thing. Are you happy in the Army, John?"

I shrugged. "It's been good. Tastes a little sour at the moment."

Hunt puckered his lips. A thinking gesture. "Tell you what. You decide you want to pack it in . . . retire . . . you call me up. This wild bunch I got working for me could use an injection of sanity. You've got balance. And balls. I'd have plenty of work for you. Good work. Not like this Nechestny crap. Christ, I'm sorry I ever hooked up with the guy." He stretched out a paw. Handing me an invisible gift. "Don't jump to conclusions. I know you're sitting there thinking, Screw this ape. I wouldn't work for him in a million years. But think about it. Let it simmer. Till all the present danger passes into the cavalcade of memories. I'd take care of you. And the work's not all covered in slime like this one. Our country needs good men who can work in the shadows."

"I'll remember the offer."

He smiled. More fake white teeth. "Diplomatically put. But let me just lift the blinds one little bit for you. The world is not as it seems. At least, not as it seems to the common man. We're reconstructing this country. Streamlining it. Key people . . . from industry, government . . . the military . . . we want to ensure that talent continues to be rewarded, that America not only remains the world's leader, but widens that lead."

He gave a dismissive wave. "Now, I'm not talking right-wing political crap. Or left-wing, either. Politics is for people who lack power and don't really understand how to get it. Politicians don't run anything. The people who run the politicians call the shots. Like it or not, that's the truth of it. No, what I'm talking about is a core—an expanding core—of people who understand what needs to be done, people who have the money, the power, the vision . . . the talent. The guts. People who understand that the Constitution, while a beautiful document—and I'm the first to admire it—folks who realize that the law does not always extend far enough. People . . . who would do anything for this country."

I did not know what to say. But he did not expect me to say anything.

"And don't waste another minute trying to stop the Next-Generation Fighter-Bomber. It's going to happen."

"I hate that airplane," I said.

"Well, channel your hatred more constructively. I understand you, John. We're not as different as you think. I know you're thinking about your dead friends.'' He opened his arms like a priest giving the blessing. With the blood drying on his face and hand. ''Well, they're dead. Can't bring 'em back. We all have dead friends in this business. You have to move on.''

He put his paws on his knees and levered himself out of his chair. ''Now get out of here, son. Before my mood changes.''

I got out of there. But with the gate closed behind me, I made the mistake of thinking about what he had said. About his crowd of insiders running things. Even if it were true, I did not want to believe it. Self-delusion has its place. Anyway, I had more urgent things on which to expend my dwindling brainpower. Or so I tried to convince myself.

New possibilities haunted me.

Middleburg looked expensive even at two in the morning. The fox-hunt crowd. They wanted to be English in the worst way. And they were English in the worst way. Riding britches and Range Rovers. Overcooked food. Acres of pastel hats at the Gold Cup. Overdressed women with time on their hands. And pet polo teams. Now and then an heiress shot an Argentine horseman. It made Karl Marx seem pretty sympathetic.

On the other hand, I was not in condition to render an impartial judgment on anything.

I thought of Tish. I had no guarantee that Hunt would turn her over to me, or even that she was still alive. I decided I should have demanded proof. Then turned on myself for even thinking something so stupid. I had pushed Hunt as far as I could. And I had gotten off easy.

So far.

I tried as hard as I could to believe he would bring Tish to Union Station. And that she would break into a great big smile when she saw me. Tearing away from her captors, running toward me—I could see it as though it were already a memory.

I just wanted her alive. I no longer cared about her past. Anyway, mine was nothing to lay on a snow-white altar cloth. What mattered was that I loved her. We could improvise from there.

I stopped at the gas station where I had used the phone on the drive out. I tanked up, bought a Diet Coke and a pack of cupcakes, got a couple dollars' worth of extra quarters, and ate supper on the hood of my car. With my hands shaking. My body had stood by me when it counted. But the pent-up fear was spilling out now.

I had one more call to make before I went home. A couple to make after sunup. And a friend to betray. As he had betrayed me.

I dialed an emergency number the frogs had given me. Henri the Cuckold answered.

"It's John Reynolds. Tell me when you're awake."

"I am awake."

"You don't sound awake."

"I am listening."

I pictured him rubbing his hatchet face. Blinking his eyes away from a bedside lamp.

"This one's for Lafayette," I said. "You need to be standing by this phone at four-thirty in the afternoon. At that time, I will give you a location in the city of Washington. If you are there promptly at six, you will see me or one of my companions hand over a bag to a couple of military-looking men. The computer disks you want will be in that bag. The men receiving them will be the people who blew up your research lab."

"You have the disks?" He was awake now. "Why not—"

"No. I don't have them. But I *will* have them. It's complicated. And no, I can't pass them to you ahead of time. First, I won't have them until the last minute. Second, this is the only way I can get my girl back. You promised you'd help me rescue her."

After a little too much hesitation, he said, "We will keep the promise."

CHAPTER 15

I KNEW CORRY WOULD BE WAITING FOR ME WHEN I GOT back. To hear my take on how it had gone with Aley. And she would damned well want to know where I had been since I left him.

That was fine. I wanted her on edge, worried about losing control of the whole scam. Corry with a clear head was an enemy of mankind.

At first, I thought she had fooled me and gone. Dead quiet on the home front. I found her upstairs, racked out on my bunk. She did not react when I switched on the overhead light. So far gone she was mouth-breathing.

We were all worn down. That was good, too. Unless it made somebody jumpy on a trigger.

Corry lay curled up like a child. Pistol loose in her hand. I could have snatched it and thumped the crap out of her. But I'm a sucker for the social rules.

"Get up," I told her. In my best drill-sergeant imitation. "My bed isn't part of the deal."

At last I found a weakness in Corry Nevers, alias Corrine Nevrosky, a.k.a. Mrs. Karen Aalstrom, nee Karen Hinkel. She could not find her way back to sensible life. Too damned tired. She flapped and half rose, dropping the pistol, then reaching frantically to recapture it, eyes flashing open and quitting again. I gave her my reading light full-face. It turned her into Dracula's favorite bride.

For one bad instant I worried about the gun. She gripped it fiercely in that small hand. Fingers so stressed I thought she might start shooting blindly. Instead, she shook her head and shoulders, determined to conquer herself, and forced those blue eyes open.

"Where were you?" she demanded. On brain delay, she looked at her wristwatch. That made it worse. "Where the hell have you been?"

"Walkin' after midnight."

She raised the pistol. This girl clearly needed time to put on her cosmic makeup.

"Pull the trigger, Corry. And you'll be back in L.A. screwing deadbeats for dinner. If you're lucky."

She closed a second hand over the gun. Steadying the aim. I suppose Corry had been thin in the self-control department for a while. The tantrum in the car should have tipped me. What conned you was her ability to carry herself with royal confidence when she had a grip. You figured her for the world's strongest human being outside of the steroid set.

"I want to know where you've been. And don't lie to me."

I flopped down in the chair she had occupied the evening before. "Arlington Cemetery. Thinking. I'm not as quick as you. Or as confident. I had to consult a friend."

That wild streak of panic in her eyes again. "*Who was it?*"

"A dead man."

"*Who did you meet?* You're so goddamned stupid, I should never—"

"Your social skills are deteriorating. I didn't meet anybody. Except your loving hubby."

"What were you doing? Don't fuck with me, John."

Remarkable that a face so full of hatred and mottled by sleep and pillow lines could remain so beautiful. After you banged up against Corry Nevers, you would always read history with a different eye. Understanding the follies of great men. And the siege of Troy.

"Kill me and we're both going to have a bad day. I did exactly what we agreed. And Aley said exactly what you said he'd say. Then I went to Arlington and sat on my ass in the dark. Talking to my ghosts. We all have our little quirks."

"Did Aley believe you? Was he—"

"He took the disk. He'll be standing by the phone."

She dropped the gun to her side. "Don't try to do

me, John. I'll come through on everything I promised you. Don't blow it for both of us.''

"It's up to you now, sister. You'd better be able to produce the rest of the disks. Or there is going to be a serious tide of unhappiness.''

"Don't let me down, John.''

That earned a smile. "Just honor your part of the deal. And I don't mean the money bullshit. That's all yours. I just want to walk away with Tish self-propelling next to me.''

"She'll stumble on you. She'll always stumble.''

"Then I'll pick her up and carry her.''

Corry left. Stroking the thirty-eight in her purse. Any muggers working the graveyard shift were going to get more than they had bargained for.

I was beginning to feel good and warned myself not to get overconfident. It seemed like I had it wired at last. I had even known she would leave. Because she needed to link up with Aley, to lay out a different set of lies. Maybe she had to report in to Hunt, too. And she would need to refine her airline reservations, now that the timeline was set for the deal. She would have to fetch the rest of the phony disks that were supposed to make her rich and leave me dead. All before meeting me in the bar at the Dubliner at five-thirty in the afternoon.

I had not told her any more than that. Just, "Meet me at the Dubliner. It's a yuppie boozer on Massachusetts. Bring the disks.'' That enraged her. But she had tried not to show it. I was performing according to her script. More or less. And she did not want to blow it now.

I went to bed. Allotting myself four hours' sleep. I dreamed in basic black. When the alarm went off, I was homicidal. I hit the john, then pulled on my running gear. Not exactly my preferred activity after a short, bad sleep, a week of deprivation, and a couple of beatings. But this was a special run.

I jinked through traffic and down alleys. With the heat raising its fist. I was sure somebody would try to follow me. Probably in a car. But I knew the one-way streets, the vacant lots that cut across blocks, the old tradesmen's passageways. I did a pair of underpasses, doubling back both times so a trail car could not follow. It was the wildest dash in D.C. history that did not involve street crime.

At the end of it, I walked into the shabby fortress where Dickey hung his hat. The desk sergeant judged me sufficiently strange to merit a handoff instead of a brushoff. He called Dickey, who came out of a hallway looking even more swollen than usual.

"What the fuck?" he said. That translated as "Good morning."

"Time to talk," I said. "For real."

He looked me up and down. And snorted. "Nice legs. I hear you were back in fag country last night."

"I'll tell you all about it," I said. And this time I meant it.

We sat in his office. Drinking lukewarm brown vinegar that only cops and old NCOs would call coffee. I told him everything I knew. All of it. As clearly as I could. He turned out to be a good listener once he got what he wanted. I wondered again how much of his spiel was the real Dickey and how much of it was the persona a smart cop had crafted over the decades. Looking like a fool has its advantages. If anybody knew that, I did. Of course, the difference between Dickey and me was that I had been the real thing.

"Christ," he said at the end of it, "it's enough to make me wish I was on the mayor's bodyguard detail."

"I couldn't lay it out earlier. I didn't have all the pieces. And I didn't know who I could trust."

He treated me to a smile. "Now you figure you can trust me?"

"If you were on anybody's payroll, you'd wear better suits."

He let the remark go by and sat back. "I should bring the FBI in on this. By all rights."

That scared me. I should have seen it coming. But my thinking had been so blurred, I had imagined Dickey would want to handle anything going down on his own turf.

I did not want any other players in on this game. Especially not *federales*. The field was already too crowded, the score too close. And I had committed too many fouls myself. The FBI was not going to award me a trophy as Most Valuable Player.

Before I could come up with a counterargument, Dickey said, "Thing is, they'd just bitch it all up.

At this point. Come stomping in like elephants. The fucks.'' He chewed into his cheek. "I got to tell them. But I don't see why I got to tell them just yet.''

Dickey sipped cold coffee. The taste made his double chin quiver. "So I got one question. And it's serious. Why Union Station? Sounds to me like Mr. and Mrs. Commuter could find themselves in the middle of the O.K. Corral. There's a serious public-safety issue.''

I nodded as though I had thought it all through. But I had not. For all my training in plans and operations, I had been as sloppy as a second lieutenant. And my selfishness embarrassed me. I had chosen Union Station because of the crowd, ignoring the fact that the crowd was made up of real people. The truth was that I had forgotten that Tish and I were not the only people on the planet. Maybe I was becoming a real Washingtonian.

I could not change the swap site. It was too late and the tolerances were already too close.

"This town's got enough of a problem with headlines,'' Dickey said. "I don't go for this Union Station business one bit.''

"I had to pick a public place. If I tried to do it in private, they'd kill me for sure. And Tish. And everybody else.''

"Sounds to me like these bad boys might do it anyway.''

"I don't think so. Not unless it all goes to shit. The common denominator of all the players left standing is their desire to avoid more publicity. The bombings . . . the killings . . . it all got way out of hand. There's no rug big enough to sweep any more trouble under. The industry pricks, Hunt and his boys . . . the French . . . to say nothing of Frankie and Johnny from L.A. . . . nobody wants to end up in the spotlight.''

''But they're shooters.''

I pulled at my running shorts. They were almost dry. And sticky as a spilled margarita. ''I figured you could handle that. Anyway, they're not sloppy. They hit what they want to hit with the first shot. No debris.''

Dickey looked at me. Face scrubbed of any expression. ''Listen, partner. You're overestimating me and my department. I only know two officers who hit on the first shot, and they're both certifiable. A setup like this takes skill. And planning. Rehearsals, if you want to do it right.'' He looked at his watch. ''And you come in here giving me less than eight hours to stage the invasion of Normandy. It's going to be a miracle if nobody gets killed.''

I hung my head like a beaten prizefighter. In a cop's shabby office, in the slam-dunk morning light, my plan looked a lot shakier than it had the night before. I ached to believe it still could deliver success. But faith slips.

Dickey's eyes were different, though. There was life in them now. Detective Lieutenant Dickey, the original pissed-on cop. His thoughts had moved beyond me. Maybe he was dreaming of one last great bust to cap his career.

The best I can say of the two of us is that we believed, in our different ways, that things might just work out. Against all odds. People don't understand how idealistic cops and soldiers can be. All the public sees is the uniform and the face you learn to wear above it. Dickey seemed to me to be fighting the good fight in a city committing suicide. I felt like I was duking it out with the whole world. I figured we both wanted to do what was right. It was a lousy combination.

He let me out the back door of the station and I made my way between squad cars down for lack of spare parts. He signaled to the patrolman on motorpool duty to let me pass. I faded into the heat of the side streets.

I went home. Showered. Dressed for success in khakis and a polo shirt. And treated myself to a crabcake sandwich at Eastern Market. The Last Lunch, since there might not be a Last Supper. For good luck, I put a big tip in the plastic bucket. Then I lingered over my plastic tray. Struggling to war-game everything that could go wrong. The truth is, I was thinking like a punk. Short-horizon stuff. I could not get beyond my reunion with Tish. It's a good thing I could not foresee all that was coming. I would not have been able to go through with it.

Panhandlers on the sidewalk, then metro limbo. I headed downtown underground. Riding with the gentlemen of leisure who had figured out the secret of summer afternoons in the city. A guy with a deep scar down his cheek wore a T-shirt that read, "Just because I'm black doesn't mean I'm a criminal."

I had one more loose line to reel in. And I had to do it in person. The bastard would not have taken a phone call from me. Not now. So he was going to get the living, breathing, unhappy John Reynolds. I was playing the politics of inclusion. No deserving party was going to be left out of the game.

A sax player blew old Broadway hits by the metro exit and a Central American pushed flowers in the heat. Office studs moved fast along the sidewalks, hurrying through the exhaust haze in shirtsleeves and ties, too young to be so soft around the middle. A few old-schoolers dehydrated in their suit jackets. Women in pearls wore a wet shine on their foreheads and a hatred of panty hose in their eyes. The whole K Street hustle.

The lobby was so cold it startled you when you came in. But I stayed hot. I came out of the elevator like a fighter coming out of his corner at the beginning of a round.

"May I help you?" the receptionist asked.

"Check with Burns before you call the cops," I told her and the flock of secretaries.

I banged through the door to his office.

All those handshake, shoulder-hug photos. Couple of Presidents. And the ex-cabinet members who re-write history and take consulting fees from dictators. Shortage of females, but the town had been late to change. Corry Nevers would have brightened up the walls. Shame he had missed her.

My friend and betrayer, Robert Mayhew Burns, opened his mouth wide enough to swallow a cannonball.

"Yeah, fuckhead. It's me."

It is a wonderful thing to see fear in a man born of fine lineage. It's a very democratic event.

Rob Burns was a fitness-club type. Just like his sister, who had dated, drained, and dumped me. But I was bigger, stronger, and a lot meaner than Mr. Think Tank. He did not have time to get all the way out of his chair. I helped him up with one hand on his throat and the other blasting into his gut. When he hit the wall, books tumbled.

His secretary was in the doorway. I did not have to see her. I could hear her, feel her. I knew precisely the look of rupture she would have on her face.

"Tell her if you want her to call the cops. *Fucking tell her.*" I loosened my grip on his neck.

He gasped. Talking in separate words. "It's . . . all . . . right . . . nothing . . . friends . . . shut . . . the . . . door, Joanne . . . all right . . ."

"Mr. Burns—"

"Shut the door."

"Don't shout at the help, Rob. What would Granddad say?"

The door closed. And I was alone with the last traitor in the pack. A guy I had really liked. Who had sold me out to Punchy Hunt on one side, and to the French on the other. He was going to make a brilliant cabinet member someday.

I wondered how thick those office windows were,

whether I could send him flying down to the street if he played it wrong.

I threw him back into his chair. Then I sat on his desk and put my foot on his chest. Rolling him back against a credenza where family photos stood isolated from the upstart trash.

"I'm one dumb sonofabitch," I told him. "It's really unbelievable. I was so dumb. But you were stupid beyond belief, pal." I shook my head. "Jesus Christ, it couldn't have been money. Or is the family silver in hock?"

The punch just above the belt buckle had been one of the few perfect things I had accomplished in my life. He still could not breathe properly. And he was terrified of this sudden contact with reality.

"Don't . . . be a fool. Power, John. Only thing this . . . town understands. Got to be connected. Never meant to harm—"

I was never a bully, except emotionally, and my fights tended to be eruptions, not sadistic choreography. This was a new experience. I had time to plan exactly where and how I would hit him. Time to shape the fist so I would not sprain a finger or my wrist. Time to come down off the desk at an angle that gave me maximum leverage. I aimed where his left canine would be hidden at the corner of his mouth.

Bonus play. I got two of his teeth. He spit them into his hand, dropped one, and began to cry.

I had never realized it could feel so good to hurt another human being.

"Yeah," I said, "that's me. The dumb fucking soldier. First your sister fucked me, then you did. I bet your family reuses toilet paper." I was as angry at myself as I was at him. I had really believed this human being was my friend. If only in a Washington kind of way. "De la Vere almost screwed it all up on you. Showed up unexpectedly. Right? Looking for results. Christ, you must have panicked. Just couldn't get him out of your office fast enough. And then I showed up too soon. But I was soaking wet and blind and thick as day-old cement. You danced circles around me. You'd make a great con, you know that?"

He looked at me. Bleeding. Thinking too much. I realized I was being stupid again.

"Hell, Rob. What am I talking about? You *are* a great con. In a city of master criminals. You were the information clearinghouse, tipping the frogs to Hunt and selling out Hunt to the frogs. And giving me up to everybody after I strolled by asking the wrong questions. You're the man who can't lose." I had thought of myself as cynical before all this began. Now I was amazed at how naive I had been. "So tell me. Who do you think is going to be more anxious to kill you? De la Vere and his boys? Or Punchy Hunt?"

Do not believe the saints and sociologists. Fear can be a beautiful thing. When you see it in the right pair of eyes.

"Don't . . . you can't . . ."

"The hell I can't."

"Please."

"Man . . . does it hurt when you say that word? Say it again."

"Please."

I folded my arms. I was not worried about Rob striking back. He was a worm caught on the sidewalk after the rain.

"Great riff," I told him. "I admire it. All that Anglophile crap. Family history as a cover story. Brilliant stuff."

"Please, John. We can work this out. Please. General Hunt doesn't need to—"

I gave him a little openhanded tap on the side of the mouth where I had punched him. He shied.

"That's my decision. Who to tell and what to tell them. It's my turn now. Although, as a military man, I have a soft spot for people who obey orders."

Anxious eyes. "What do you want me to do?"

I wasn't ready to tell him yet. I wanted him to hurt a while longer. "Why the French? I've figured out the Hunt connection. But why sell everybody out to the frogs? Tell the truth now, Robbie."

He looked down. Probably wondering if a chump like me could understand the calculations of policy at the strategic level, the nuances of the international order. He spoke to me in a lecturing tone, a professor with blood on his chin and shirt. I let him yap. The poor bugger did not know how to talk any other way.

"The Brits . . . are backing off on European integration. The single-currency thing. France is going to lead. All of Europe. Germans are rich. But they're afraid. Afraid to lead. France . . . is the key. We've got to play the French card. If we want leverage in the new Europe. Trade. The military thing. The Mideast connection . . ."

I snorted. "You are a no-go at this station."

"What?"

"That is the dumbest political analysis I've ever heard. You sleeping with a French girl or something?"

"France is going to—"

"Can it. That's enough. The answer is that you wired yourself in with the French because you're stupid. Now let's talk about Em." I tossed him the box of tissues from his desk. "Not a bleeder, are you?"

"I don't know a thing about Em."

I would have liked to hit him again. It felt so good. But I did not want his face to look any worse. He had a public appearance coming up.

"Bullshit. Ever been in Punchy Hunt's library?"

Rob shook his head. Patting his hurt little mouth.

"Didn't think so," I told him. "Hunt has his own kind of social standards. So let me tell you about his library. Lousy art that costs a bundle. Leather-bound sets I think he actually reads. And memorabilia aplenty. Photos. He's got this round mahogany table right by a big leather chair. Table's covered with framed photographs. Some of the frames are works of art in themselves." I glanced around Rob's office, at his photo display. "He's more selective than you. But then, he generally knows who's going to come through his door. Anyway, there's a photo of Hunt as a lieutenant colonel. Wearing a big shit-eating grin. Standing beside your old man. Back when Daddy was doing the OSD ticket punch. I didn't notice it the first time. Hunt's so damned impressive. Riveting. But last night I saw it. And everything fell into place. Brother, you should have stayed on Hunt's side. Exclusively." I smiled. With all of my own teeth. "Got a spare shirt in a drawer? Maybe in a closet? You seem like that kind of guy."

Rob nodded.

"Good. Because you're going to need it. But we'll get to that." I leaned down toward him. "I couldn't figure out how the bad guys made me as a connection so quickly. They seemed too good, too aware, too fast. They were waiting for me every time I went to the john, ready to hand me the soap." I looked at the frightened little man in the chair before me. He was not that small physically, but he was miniature in spirit. "I should have figured out the French connection. But Hunt . . . that was another matter. I'm not a genealogy expert. Then I saw that photo. And I got it. The real Hunt Club isn't those thugs with war toys he's got patrolling his spread. It's a blueblood thing. Hell, your families probably really did hunt together, back before genetic decay set in. I'd forgotten, you see. One key part of the Punchy Hunt legend. Kid from rich family goes to West Point. Volunteers for Vietnam. Folks in my line of work worshipped Hunt for that. For the self-sacrifice. The guy did great things for his country. Back then."

"He's still doing good things, he—"

I lifted his face in both my hands. As if about to kiss him. Instead of a smooch, I worked my thumb through the skin into the brand-new gap between his teeth. "Save it. I have a deep-seated need to communicate. So there it is. Hunt. You. And Em. God knows who else. Old money getting a plus-up. And yeah. Power. Does Bob Nechestny really run Macon-Bolt? Or is he sort of a puppet? Your little pet risen from the lower classes." I let go of his snout.

"Nechestny's naive. He doesn't know what it really takes in this town."

"Thank you. Now back to my little story. Money and power and old families. The stuff that made America great. But Em got an attack of conscience. He did the unforgivable. He broke ranks. Tell me— did it bother you more that Em was trying to expose your three-hundred-billion-dollar rip-off, or that he was doing it with a black general? I don't expect you to answer that. I'm allergic to platitudes."

"What do you want?"

I raised my eyebrows as theatrically as I could. "What do I want? Maybe good government? Integrity? Peace in our time? An honest return on the defense dollar? You're bleeding again. Hey, I'm a simple guy. All I really want at this point is my girl back."

"There's nothing I can—"

"Wrong. You're going to help. You're going to do exactly what I tell you. Or I'm going to let the frogs know you've been playing a double game on them with Punchy Hunt and Company. Then I'm going to let Hunt know you've been triple-crossing him. They'll kill you, Rob. And they'll make it hurt on the way.''

The man was so frightened he could not speak. His lip bubbled pink spit. And he began to shake. With the spirit upon him.

''All you have is a walk-on role. At six o'clock, you are going to be standing by the Center Cafe in the main entrance hall of Union Station. When I'm gone, go down to the john and run cold water over your mouth. It won't hurt much. Then put on your clean shirt. If you don't have a clean tie in the office, go around the corner to Brooks Brothers. I'm sure you've got a charge account that goes back a century.''

''What's going to—''

''Shut up. Or I'll break your nose for shits and grins. I am not a happy man today.''

''What if I don't—''

''I'll make two phone calls. And the race will be on to kill you. Six o'clock. Make that five of. If you're late, the deal's off.''

''What do I have to do?''

''Look important. Make your family proud of you.''

I really did want to hurt him some more. I liked myself less with each passing hour. But getting past decency and mercy also has a wonderful lightening effect. You can loathe your behavior and feel really good about what you're doing at the same time.

At the door, I turned around one last time and looked at the coward in the desk chair.

"Aren't you even a little bit ashamed?" I asked him. "Your kind used to sacrifice for this country. First to volunteer in war. Dollar-a-year men in peace. Obligation. Responsibility. *Noblesse oblige*. You were the best we had."

"Don't kid yourself," he said.

I had two hours to kill before my bar date with Corry. So I went to the National Gallery. To see my second-best girl.

I figured the National Gallery was safe and close to Union Station. It did not attract many killers. It had pay phones. And I needed a dose of civilization. With all its discontents. I needed to believe that something of worth might be salvaged in the end. That it wasn't all ugly.

The girl was my secret. It was possible that I had shared her with only one other man. In over a hundred years. High-schoolers on class trips yawned past her, and women in glasses with graying hair pinned up admired her for all the wrong reasons. While my number two redhead just stood there with her American Mona Lisa smile, waving her goodies. Winslow Homer had painted her. The picture was formally titled "Autumn." The real name had to be "Fuck me."

Maybe Homer shared the joke with a couple of pals. Or maybe he kept it to himself. The armies of art historians never realized what he had done. Despite a recent retrospective that analyzed the guy to a second death.

We see what we expect to see. That flaw had damaged my ability to compete with Corry and company. One old girlfriend told me I had rose-colored contact lenses glued to my eyeballs. But she had a doctorate, and thought about what she was going to say a day in advance, and could never sustain relationships. I seemed to have better luck with redheads.

I stood in front of that painting, trying to zen out my jitters, with the air-conditioning not quite working and tourists slumping by like plague victims. In the winter, when the all-in-black crowd came out to pose, I had seen the tragically hip blow off my sweetheart as Homer at his weakest, sunk in his Norman Rockwell mode. My second-best girl wore the laced-up, exclusionary clothing of 1877, a black hat and snug black velvet jacket, with a heavy oyster-gray skirt. She stood on a damp forest path, surrounded by leaves the color of Tish's hair. A white-gloved hand held the ruffle of her skirt up to her waist. If you did not crack the code, you just figured she was holding the cloth up out of the mud. But if you knew how women looked—if you knew how they felt and smelled and a little bit about how they thought—you saw that Homer had played the greatest erotic joke in the history of painting.

The damp, fleshy folds of cloth and their shadows form an image as explicit as a rotten-hearted porno mag. Only Homer did it with style. The model must have been a hoot. I bet Homer never got over her.

When you finally figured out her smile, she made Corry Nevers look like a schoolgirl at a pajama party.

I never told anybody about my gallery girl. Not even Tish. I was afraid word would get around and some Bible-beater from the Hill would have my alternative darling imprisoned in the National Gallery basement, where I would never be able to see her again.

I broke my communion to make my calls from a pay phone by the men's room. Tipping the players to the Union Station meeting place and the six o'clock be-there-or-be-square linkup time. I staggered the calls and trolled the galleries in between. Giving everybody just the right amount of time to fight the traffic, park, and rush to the grand hall. Now and then I got an attack of the shakes.

I even called Colonel Maurey, my boss at the Pentagon. I left a message on his answering machine. Promising I would be in for work at the usual time in the morning. I did not qualify it by adding, "If I'm still alive." None of us can really imagine his own death. And I had gotten my fill of theatrics.

Everybody was anxious. Everybody wanted to play. Homer had his joke. Now I was going to have mine.

The best call was the one to Aley. He was squirming. Dying to get the deal done. His response to the Union Station location was, "What is this shit you are laying on me?" Followed by a suspicion as natural to him as weakness to the flesh. "So what is it,

Johnny boy? You planning to get on a train and ride or something?''

His macho spiel sounded about as tough as cellophane now. He could not wait to dump the financial data on me.

"So, Johnny boy? You prepared to copy? You got a call to make. Confirm that you're a rich man. Make sure nobody tried to screw you at the last minute. You got to look out for number one.''

I pretended I had a pen and paper. Watching dads lead their anxious sons into the men's room. Aley read off a list of numbers. A phone code for the Caymans. The bank access number. An account access number. More codes to unlock the deposit information. Financial numerology.

"You need me to repeat any of that?'' he asked me.

"I've got it.''

He repeated it all anyway.

"Call in, Johnny boy. This is the ultimate Dialing for Dollars. Do it now. And don't trust anybody. Confirm that deposit.''

The moment of truth was coming. Everything Aley had longed for. The pressure put him in competition for the title of Jumpiest Man on Earth.

I was another contender. Scared as hell. As the time ran down, my palms started getting damp. The hairs prickled on my forearms. And my feet were sweating. I worried about Tish. And about myself. Dickey had me concerned now about a slaughter of the innocents during rush hour. I had made some remarkably dumb decisions. I could only hope they had been less dumb than the decisions made by everybody else.

That was just possible. Soldiering teaches you a few basic things. For example, battles are not won by the most competent army, but by the least incompetent. Murphy the Lawgiver is the patron saint of mankind. And there is no bomb as unstable and volatile as the human heart.

Just before it was time to link up with Corry, I went in to look at the Renoirs. I hate Renoir. In a couple of minutes I was in a sufficiently brutal mood to face what was coming.

The Dubliner is one of those bars that fake history. Dark wood and dark beer. The windows are small and the rooms are deep. It's always twilight inside. The food is bad, in keeping with Irish tradition, but they know how to draw a Guinness or a Harp. In the evenings, different Irishmen take turns singing the same songs. Kids who work on the Hill come by after work to romanticize a heritage their ancestors were only too glad to leave behind. But a drinker could do a lot worse. In this town.

Corry sat at the backmost table under a print of the Easter Rising. She was drinking a whiskey sour. In an Irish pub. The girl really had no shame. She saw me and froze for a moment. As if she had not really expected me. When I sat down beside her, I smelled the earlier drinks on her.

"How many of those have you had?" I asked her.

Corry shifted a big soft purse that could have served as a weekend bag. The kind of thing women who can't make choices lug around. She moved it from my side of her chair to the other. Letting me know how protective she felt about the disks.

"You don't understand," she said. With drink in her voice. Almost enough to make the emotion real.

"Buck up, girl. You need to be ready for action."

She laughed. "Look who's talking. When were you ever ready for action? I could've given you the best action of your life."

I moved the whiskey sour across the table. She moved it back.

I wanted her edgy. Not falling-down drunk.

"Corry . . . these people don't fuck around. You don't want to—"

She threw the drink in my face.

"You think you're too good for me," she said. "Fuck you, John."

There were only half a dozen other people in the bar. But we suddenly attracted far more attention than I wanted.

I wiped my face with a paper napkin. Wishing the sting of the alcohol out of my eyes. Just walking from the National Gallery to the bar—allowing for a few side-street doglegs—had soaked me in sweat. The drink added sugar. Like glue. On my shirt. In my hair.

I kept my voice down. Although I would have been glad to punch her. "Corry, you can straighten your ass out right now. Or I'm walking."

But her emotions were ahead of me. She barely listened. Wetness in her eyes. And fear. Confusion. A sinner on Judgment Day.

"It's time to go now," I told her. "Get straight. We're going over to Union Station. It's the last stop."

"I have to go to the ladies' room," she said. And she stood up. With reasonable competence. Scraping her chair back.

She knew where she was going, so it was not her first trip to the can. I wondered how long she had been sitting and drinking.

She swayed a little. In handsome linen slacks. Baby-blue blouse precise at her shoulders, with a slight drape at the waist. Good clothes for traveling.

Just before she turned the corner, she wheeled and looked at me. With a smile you never want to see on your wife. Or even on a transient girlfriend. Not a ghost of trust in the girl. She walked back toward our table. With the steadiness that comes of great concentration. She grabbed the purse. With her genuine, authentic, fake computer disks.

It was a nice touch.

I watched her walk away again. Even now, I did not know her. Had she planned to throw a drink at me all along? To complete the effect? Was she that good? Was she far less drunk than she was acting? If so, the girl was wearing a whiskey-based perfume. Was there even a sliver of real emotion in that woman?

The one thing I believed about her was her fear.

I guess I never learned to recognize love. But I knew fear when I saw it.

She had gotten the world just where she wanted it. And now she was afraid of what she had done.

A waitress brought me ice water and a stack of paper napkins. Unbidden. Maybe there is understanding and kindness in the world.

"How many drinks has she had?" I asked.

The waitress thought for a moment. She was largish and blond in a way that drives Arabs nuts. With dropout's eyes.

"I could check at my station. I think five or six."

Lot of afternoon booze for a small woman like Corry.

"It's all right. I'll get her out of here as soon as she comes back. What's the tariff?"

"Let me get the bill."

I dipped and wiped and wished away the whole past week. The boys along the bar had lost interest when Corry disappeared, but the barkeep had a nose for trouble and kept his eyes on me. I would have liked a drink myself. But there was no time now.

I paid and tipped big. Just before Corry came back. She marched in like a mean little soldier.

"Time to go," I said again.

She looked at me with those deadly blues. "Couldn't we just sit for one more minute?"

I checked my watch to make her happy, but I already knew we were out of time.

"Got to go," I told her.

"But it's right across the street."

"We're not going in the front door."

"I need a minute."

"This is it, Corry. Now or never."

"I need a minute with you."

"Thanks for the drink."

Her eyes did not waver.

"I love you, John. Can't you see that?"

"You'll get over it."

CHAPTER 16

AT THE BACK OF UNION STATION THERE IS A MULTI-level parking garage built to bankrupt tourists. You can slip in from the H Street bridge over the rail yards. We did just that. Avoiding the regular entrances.

Getting there was a minor trial. Corry still had her walking skills. But barely. And she would not trust me to carry the bag with the disks. I wanted to move fast across those prairie-wide avenues. Corry was good for only a funeral march.

The heat smelled. So did I. Corry had whiskey on her breath. I had it caked into me. Along with a sugary lime smell. We passed a squatter dressed for January. His resident flies deserted him for me. That's how I went to Armageddon. Leading a drunken beauty who thought lying was mankind's basic mission. Waving flies away from my face.

The gasoline air in the big garage sat a few degrees

331

cooler than the day outside, but Corry found the up ramp hard going. She still would not trust me with the bag full of disks.

I let her struggle. Pissed. I maneuvered through the level where they held the rental cars for the Amtrak crowd. Figuring that was the approach my fans would least expect me to take. I looked hard for the bad boys. Hunt would have scouts out. Dickey, too, I hoped. Maybe even the French. But nobody in the garage had that trouble look.

I had the pulse. The rush. Any fly that sucked up my sweat was going into an adrenaline frenzy. I had been here before. A few times. Bad times. In that moment, Union Station blurred with half a dozen shitholes scattered around the world. Where the U.S. Army does the quiet things that let our fellow citizens live the sweet life back in the Land of the Big PX.

Corry came up beside me. Lopsided with the bag weight. Sweating jewels.

"Something the matter?" she asked.

I shook my head. "Just stay up with me."

"I can't go so fast."

"Just stay up with me. Keep it together, girl."

I knew she would listen now. Frightened people are easier to steer than a kiddie car. If they think you are unafraid.

A carillon chimed. Six. We were late. But the gang would hang. I had no idea what their various plans would be. But every last hustling shitbird would have one.

Hunt. The frogs. Dickey. And Aley. Maybe even

Mr. Think Tank. And Corry all whiskey, fear, and greed. Planners. Schemers. Dreamers.

Our lateness bothered me. It was one more part of my plan going off track. Like Corry's unexpected appetite for booze. I had tried to do everything with Command and Staff College precision. Forgetting that all that Leavenworth junk works only with other Leavenworth types. When it works at all.

"Wake up," I said. "Get alert, girl."

"I meant it," she told me. "What I said. About the money. Your cut."

"Save it for your marriage."

"I'm coming back. In six months. I mean it."

"Worry about the next six minutes."

We made it inside the rear entrance, mezzanine level. No shooters or grabbers by the automatic doors. There were rows of boutiques, left and right, shopped by travelers too early for their trains. I had told Aley to meet me in the store that sold the Disney paraphernalia. It was my private joke. On a Mickey Mouse kind of guy.

I stopped just short of Uncle Walt's capitalist legacy.

"Wait here."

"What?" Corry asked me.

"Just stand here. I'm going in to get your beloved."

"Don't leave me alone."

"Do what I say. Stand right there against that wall. Keep away from the windows."

"We should stay together."

"No. I don't want you trapped inside. If it all goes to hell. I'll be right back."

What I really meant was that I wanted her available. If Hunt and his boys had decided to screw me and do a premature grab. I was not going down for this damsel if I could help it.

Aley stood behind a rack of cartoon-figure ties, watching for me. He had positioned himself against a camouflage of colors and wore a windbreaker three months ahead of the weather. The jacket was zipped halfway up. I had no doubt that he had a gun under it.

"You make that call?" he asked me.

I nodded. "We're good to go."

He sighed. Then he registered my empty hands.

Panic burned his eyes. "Where's the merchandise, Johnny boy?"

"Your wife's holding it."

He looked at me. Calculating. And twisted up his face. "I wouldn't trust her with a dump I took last week. Let's go."

"Where's Hunt?"

"Downstairs. You'll see."

"Tish?"

"Too much fucking talk, all right? Everything's like little Johnny wanted. Your birthday party, okay?"

He was shaking. Trying not to show it. But he was shaking like a prisoner under an icy shower.

We were all afraid.

"Let's just fucking move," he said.

I led the way.

"Bitch better be there. If she—" Then he saw her. Where I had parked her. And he laughed. "Ain't she just a package?"

"She's a package."

He bumped against me and sniffed. "Hey, you fucking stink. You been hitting the sauce or something? That fear thing nibbling at you?"

"Your wife shared her drink with me."

We came up to Corry. Aley got a really good whiff. "Fuck, Karen. One hell of a time to fall off the wagon."

"Yeah? Show me your veins, you goddamned junkie." She turned to me. "You know he's a needle boy?"

"Could we postpone the domestic bliss? Let's just do this. All right?"

Aley gripped me by the upper arm. There was real strength in his hand, meanness. If he was into syringes, it was meth, not heroin. I let him hold on to me. Fighting the instinct to put him down on the marble floor. I wanted him certain that he was in charge.

He spoke to Corry. Or Karen. Surprising me one last time. With what he did not know.

"He really had them, huh?"

She nodded.

"You checked them out?" he asked her.

"Like I have a fucking computer."

"I mean, they look all right? Our boy hasn't been playing swaps or anything?"

"They look all right."

The rest of the world cruised by. I guess we just looked like three happy shoppers. I could not spot any of Hunt's hired guns. Which I took as a very good sign. He was keeping the operation small. Tight.

I did not see any of Dickey's boys, either. That was not a particularly good sign. I was short of friends.

Aley turned his full attention to me. "I'm going to tell you one time and up front. Your role in all this is to keep your mouth shut. You are going to walk between me and Karen. Karen, give me the disks."

"I have them."

"Give them to me, all right? You're fucking drunk."

Corry let him take the bag. He hefted it.

"Okay. Feels righteous. We're going to take that big walk now, John boy. Down those stairs over there." He nodded toward the spiral staircases that led down to the center arcade on the ground floor. "Tourists get in the way, screw 'em. Three abreast. All the way. At the foot of the stairs, we turn out into the main hall. Hunt will be just where you wanted. With General Bootlick, in full regalia. And your drop-down redhead slut."

"Get your hand off my arm."

He let go of me. And laughed. For an instant. "Yeah? Now listen. Final instructions. Your mouth stays shut. You are decoration. Do anything funny, and the war's on. Redhead gets the first bullet."

"Fuck you, Aley. You're shaking so bad you couldn't get that pistol out of your jacket without shooting yourself."

We began to walk. Down the streets of Tombstone. To my surprise, Corry gave my hand a quick squeeze. With her eyes on the horizon. I wish she had not done that. There was a little too much humanity in it. I did not want her real.

"Nice and slow," Aley muttered.

Almost to the stairs. I glanced from side to side. Trying hard to spot anybody or anything that looked out of place. Anything that felt off. Any pair of eyes flashing an excess of interest.

I just wanted the plan to work. This one time in my life. Just let me trade the joker disks and Hunt's delinquent hired help for Tish. And let us go. The rest of them could fight it out over the fool's gold and who had done the most cheating. Just let Tish and me get out through those big front doors.

I had warned the frogs that they might be recognized and needed to hug the edges. They seemed to have taken the warning seriously. It was a good sign that they stayed out of sight. Let them make their move after Tish and I had gotten offstage.

Hunt was supposed to be waiting by the Center Cafe in the main hall. With my think-tank buddy as the surprise game-show guest.

I wanted Hunt to react to the unexpected presence of Robert Mayhew Burns. To say just one public word to the bastard. And let the French make the connection. Then let Mr. Old Washington Blood strategize his way out of that. Or invoke his family's contribution to American history.

I would have felt a lot better if I had caught a glimpse of Dickey's whipped-hound-dog face.

At the top of the stairs, I took one last, hard look at the world around me. Aley knew street-punk tricks. But he did not possess the whole tactical framework for staying alive. Stairs, escalators, and elevators were fatal choke points. The curved staircase had marble flooring one flight down on the left, a two-story drop to a food court on the right. Once we stepped onto those stairs, we were trapped until we walked away from them at the bottom.

"What's the matter with you?" Aley said.

"Nothing."

Corry stumbled and I caught her. Feeling the brief push of her breast against my forearm. I got her straight and she looked at me. With those Hollywood eyes.

She shook her head. And said plaintively, "You just don't know."

"For Christ's sake," Aley said. "Is there a love story I'm missing here? Get a move on, huh?"

We started down the stairs. Corry's flats tapped on the marble. I could feel Aley's nerves blowing holes in his skin. I felt sick to my stomach.

I saw it coming. I think I had known it before I really knew it. Call it a premonition. I had shied like a snaked horse at the top of those stairs. If Corry had not stumbled and hit my reflex button, I might have hung there until somebody dragged me down.

Two men dressed like kids. L.L. Beaners in baggy jeans. Sports logos and earrings. They had the effect down. If you did not look too closely at their faces, you would have figured them for sixteen going on six years in Lorton. But the faces had years of grown-up trouble behind them.

Joking and jiving at the bottom of the stairs. They waited until we were almost to the middle. Then the taller one caught me looking. And made his move. Partner following.

Guns materialized from under the layers of hip. Pistols the size of howitzers. The hit men lunged up the steps toward us.

I tried to shrink myself. Crunching down like a kid who sees a whipping coming. It was a stupid, useless, and natural thing to do.

Shots. Thunder in the marble temple. Lightning flashing an arm's length away. They had automatics. Blasting fast and out of rhythm with each other.

Even professionals get the monster in their eyes when they do the job. The act pumps them. They breathe like winded dogs and they'd sweat at the North Pole. I saw only one hit man's face after the shooting began. For a strip ripped off a second. Killing was his drug. And he was superhigh on it.

I thought it would be the last face I saw.

Beside me, Corry did a dance. Still on her feet. But jerking. A sixties go-go dancer. A wild hand slapped my arm.

Gushes tore out of her back. Flames of blood. Sprays of it. Followed by shreds of dark red meat.

I saw her face for an instant before she fell: a perfectly beautiful woman. It was a waste beyond calculation.

Aley said, "Fuck," one last time and crumpled against me. He knocked me onto my rump, hard against the lip of a stair.

At my feet, Corry twitched like a snake with its back broken. There was more of her spread over the stairs than there was left in her body.

A moment of iron silence stopped the world.

One of the gunmen grabbed the bag with the disks. They took off like Olympic hurdlers. Brilliant at their work. The job had been done with speed, shock, and just enough overkill not to mark them as professional assassins.

I had not mattered to them.

Screaming all around me. Running. I heard a whistle and torn bits of language.

I got to my feet. Rising from the dead. Running after the killers. A creature of faulty instincts and the wrong kind of training for real life.

I must have looked like the craziest man in the world. Smeared with blood not my own. Barehanded. Chasing killers.

The pros did not have to worry about me, though. Not on any count. By the time I reached the bottom of the stairs, the gunmen were deep in the slaughterpen crowd and I had regained my true focus. My life had not flashed before my eyes when the guns came out. But Tish had. The gunmen went for the side entrance. I cut left. Toward the main hall.

Wondering if Tish would be there. Wondering where the hell Dickey's boys were. Too dumb to realize a security guard might take a shot at any bloodstained, running male.

I crashed between two dazzled grandmoms. Eyes white, shopping bags heavy. They did not know what was happening around them. I sent one of them spinning. The other shrieked, "Lucille!"

I made it through the portal by the Godiva Chocolates stand. With the gunshots still echoing, the rush-hour crowd looked like a cockroach convention after the lights came on.

That grand hall. Great space. Under the guardianship of stone legionnaires perched up on the balconies. This time I would have preferred living cops.

Hunt was there. As promised. Standing tall. With Gabrielli beside him. Hunt looked cool. Just waiting for an invisible light to change. But Gabrielli had the jumps.

Rob, my think-tank buddy, stood a few feet behind them. Mug swollen. Body cowering.

Or so I imagined.

Tish was not with them.

And Dickey had let me down worse than I knew.

I stopped maybe ten feet away from Hunt. As if it was time to go for our six-guns. But the only gun that mattered now was the one I felt in the small of my back.

"Don't raise your hands, soldier boy," Dickey's voice commanded. "Just walk. Straight ahead."

I started moving. Immediately.

In a bitter, satisfied voice, Dickey said, "Maybe I'll start wearing better suits now. What do you think about that, smart-ass?"

I had been around enough violence to know that it blinds those unaccustomed to it. When anyone insists they can describe all the details of a crime scene, that person is either a combat veteran with a lot of survivor's scars or a liar. The little drama Dickey and I were acting out did not even register on the human cattle around us.

I was more furious than scared. At that moment. I wanted to fight back. But I did not know how. A gun in the small of my back impressed me. Enough to keep my anger just short of any further stupidity.

I wanted to land fists, and walked on like a sheep.

As we approached, Hunt looked me up and down. Then turned away and strode toward the doors. Gabrielli looked me over, too. But his eyes had the cartoon jitters. Rob Burns glanced from side to side in wonder. Amazed that this play could go on without interference. He still had no sense of the reality of this world.

"Keep moving," Dickey said.

No steel in my back now. But I sensed him right behind me.

A voice so calm it sounded mechanical came over a public-address system: *"There is a disturbance in the center hall. Please use the side corridors. There is a disturbance in the center hall . . ."*

We left the building. Through the automatic doors. A Lincoln Town Car, the serious bureaucrat's vehicle of choice in D.C., waited curbside. Upscale anonymity. Surrounded by guys in sunglasses and suits. They looked like Federal Marshals, the ultimate D.C. cover.

I watched Hunt direct Rob Burns to the front seat beside the driver. Uniform brass flashing in the sun, Gabrielli got in the left rear. Hunt waited for me. Face as bland as paperwork. He had seen a lot worse. Before breakfast.

"Nice try," Hunt said. "Get in the goddamned car."

I did. But first I turned and gave Dickey the eyes. Aching for him to feel just one tiny sliver of guilt.

"Some cop," I told him.

Hunt climbed in behind me. Pressing me against Gabrielli. A Lincoln will hold three wonks in the backseat. It's a tight fit for three soldiers.

No police escort. We just pulled into traffic behind a Red Top cab. Driving down streets I knew. From jogging, walking, driving. D.C. had become my city. Without any meaningful realization on my part. Now it was my last city. And it looked different. Familiar and foreign at the same time. I felt a tourist's hunger to see everything. One more time. Each monument and statue, every color and sign of life. My advantage over the death-row boys was that I got to go out by the scenic route.

I was scared now.

Gabrielli smelled like the rest room in a truck stop. Hunt was ice. Rob Burns looked straight ahead in the front seat. He and Hunt were still playing on the same side of the game after all. The French had let me down. But Rob did look nervous. Like a petty thief who had just blundered into a cop bar. I had done a serious number on his face back in the office.

I figured the least I could do was screw him on the way out.

The car entered the Eighth Street tunnel. Heading onto 395. The driver was good. In the heavy slop of rush hour.

I said, "So where are Rob's friends? The frogs, I mean. Didn't he tell de La Vere—"

"Shut your goddamned mouth," Rob yelled. He sounded like a girl.

"Rosencrantz and Guildenstern are dead," Hunt said calmly. "They had a traffic accident. On the way to Union Station." After a few car lengths, he added, "I think you should confine your concerns to the fate of young Prince Hamlet, John. This is the final act."

The car popped out of the tunnel. Back into the killer sunlight. And bounced over a pothole. The prospect of my death reached a new level of reality.

But you can't just fold. The rule is never give in. Never give up. If your captors think you have already accepted your death, it just makes it that much easier for them.

"And Tish?" I asked Hunt. "Is she still alive?"

That got a little smile. "You have a nineteeth-century sensibility," he told me. "It's rare these days. But I think you should be quiet now." He liked his I'm-an-educated-culturally-astute-soldier riff, though. And he knew I got his jokes. So he said, "Ophelia is irrelevant. This graveyard scene plays differently." I felt his tree-trunk leg against mine. In an air-conditioned hearse. "Know why you remind me of Hamlet, John? Because you and he are both troublesome, meddling motherfuckers who turn everything in the neighborhood to shit. You can't leave well enough alone. You spoil things. The king should have taken care of him in the first act. For the good of the state. Now shut the fuck up."

We crossed the river. Slowing as cars crowded onto the bridges from one access ramp after another. Even the best driver could not do much.

Struggling to keep his voice calm, Rob turned his puffy lips toward Hunt. "He's . . . got rather a fantastic imagination, you know. I mean, you understand what I was doing, right, Punchy? How I had to work it? The way I explained the French thing?"

"I understand," Hunt said.

We ramped down onto the George Washington Memorial Parkway. Heading north. A pickup loaded with lawn mowers almost hit us as we merged. It could have been good news for me. Maybe a chance to run. Even a hospital bed would have been better than what I was facing.

Hunt's driver hugged the right lane. I watched the river. And the city beyond. It seemed impossible that I might never see it again. That I might never see anything again. The monuments looked white and beautiful.

"Tish didn't do anything," I said. My voice shook. There was no hiding the fear now.

"Guilt," Hunt said, "is an abstract concept I find useless. I told you to be quiet."

All of this was nothing but an annoyance to him in the end. My death was a minor chore.

The Rosslyn high-rises loomed and Gabrielli spoke for the first time. "You know, Punchy, I really have a lot on my plate. If you've got everything under control . . . you could just drop me along here and I could hoof it over to the metro stop. Get back to work."

"Later," Hunt said. With finality.

A guy in a sports car who looked like he had never had a date in his life cut in ahead of us. Hunt's driver hit the brakes, said nothing, gave gas again.

Beyond the fringe of trees, the river and the far bluffs looked beautiful. Beautiful, beautiful, beautiful. I was so scared. Paralyzed by the beauty of the evening traffic. I fought my emotions, wanting to preserve a shred of dignity. As if it mattered. I felt my eyes wet and I looked away from the landscape. I forced myself to remember every charge I had outstanding on my credit card. To keep from breaking down. I wanted to cherish every minute of life. But I could not face it.

I felt pulverized by the thought of dying. It was real and unreal. I figured it was going to be a long ride to Middleburg and Hunt's private killing ground.

I was wrong. It wasn't long at all. A few miles up the parkway, the driver snapped the car out of the stream of traffic. Onto a ribbon of blacktop that led back into the trees.

Fort Marcy. The remnants of Civil War earthworks. I had stopped once to see what the place had to offer. Nothing except a few big mounds of dirt. And trees. Two Park Service signs and an orphaned cannon pointing nowhere.

Fort Marcy was a spot where disillusioned pols shot themselves. Everybody else just drove on by.

The driver had been given his instructions in advance. He parked at the far end of the empty lot. Out of sight of the surrounding roads.

Everybody was amazingly calm about this. Rob Burns had his nerves almost under control. Gabrielli had accepted his part in things. The driver was cut from ice. Hunt was Hunt.

There was none of that small-time haste, none of the confusion that is supposed to go along with murders. The driver turned off the engine and got out. In his element now. The executioner. He walked up into the brush.

We all followed. My legs unwilling.

I should have heard birds singing. Leaves rustling. Something poetic. But the big rasp of the traffic drowned out every other sound. As it would swallow the sound of the shots. Not two hundred yards away, commuters were heading for their homes in the burbs. Listening to NPR. Or some soft-rock station running giveaways. It was a drab way to go.

Still, a part of me did not really believe I would go. I could not possibly die.

Someone had tossed a Big Mac wrapper in the weeds. When I lifted my eyes, I could just see a roofline toward the river.

My voice arrived before I had the words fully shaped.

"You . . . okay . . . you can do whatever you're going to do to me . . . but you don't have to hurt Tish." I lost it. At least partway. "*Please*. I'm *begging* you. Just let her go. If she's alive."

Hunt snorted. "You must have read Walter Scott as an adolescent."

The driver stopped walking just short of an earthen parapet that a hundred and thirty years of rain had not been able to melt. The fort had guarded the city against Lee and Jackson. Maybe soldiers other than me had died here. There had been no battle on the site, but maybe there had been one of those little skirmishes that are briefly reported, then lost to history. As I would be.

"Here," the driver told Hunt. "This is good." It was a professional assessment. A spot well hidden from casual observers. You could hear the world of men, but not see it. A Park Ranger would find me when he stepped into the brush to take a piss.

Rob stopped beside the driver. He would not look at me now.

I balked at going forward. A born bully, Gabrielli gave me a push.

My heart beat so fast it was almost a constant.

I wanted a chance. Any chance. But I had Gabrielli

behind me on one side, Punchy Hunt on the other. With the driver and Rob just ahead.

We all stopped.

I tried to plan a run. They would shoot me down. But I would not die passively. And there might be a miracle. I might escape somehow. I believed there were miracles on this earth. I had never seen one. But I believed in them at that moment.

Then I knew I would not run. I did not want to be shot in the back. That suddenly seemed terribly important. Ridiculously important. Besides, running would have taken a form of energy I did not have now.

I decided I would at least throw a punch at the end, to show them I was a fighter.

I wondered if my limbs would obey me.

I made up my mind. I would hit Hunt. Even if he wasn't the guy with the gun. Nobody else really mattered.

They had me penned. The driver stepped closer to Rob Burns. Gabrielli gave me another punch between the shoulder blades. Driving me into the circle.

I went mulish. Gabrielli pushed ahead and tugged me by the arm. I jerked free. But I was surrounded now. I could see each pencil-point whisker on Gabrielli's jaw, smell medicine on his breath.

Rob backed away. As if I were contagious. He stood on the driver's flank. Blinking.

Hunt's presence swelled behind me.

A horn complained from the highway. I closed my eyes, then immediately opened them again. In panic.

Afraid someone would pull the trigger before I had a last chance to look at the world. To smell it. Feel it.

I saw the blue sky through the trees.

The action of a semiautomatic clicked back and came forward again. The driver. Then a second weapon snapped. Hunt.

I began to pray. Like a terrified child. Wordless.

I could not move. I wanted to resist. Ached to fight. But I could not see a course. My arms would not do anything but twitch.

To his credit, Hunt did not expect somebody else to do his dirty work. Maybe he enjoyed killing. Some men love it.

He stepped in between me and Rob Burns and lifted his pistol. He had slipped on a pair of black gloves.

He shot Rob in the bridge of the nose.

So different than Corry's dying. So much simpler. Rob's head snapped back. Lumps of crap blew out the rear of his skull. The head jerked forward again. He fell dead.

Nothing but a car backfiring.

The driver shifted, smooth as Fred Astaire, and fixed his pistol to the back of Gabrielli's skull.

Hunt reversed the pistol in his hand. Extending it to Gabrielli. Who gave him the most confused look in history.

"Take the gun," Hunt said matter-of-factly.

Gabrielli obeyed. For an instant, his eyes strayed to me. But Hunt's force pulled his attention back. Gabrielli held the pistol as if he had no idea what it might be. An odd piece of machinery. Drooping below waist level.

"Put the gun to your temple," Hunt told him. "I'm going to give you thirty seconds to make the most important decision of your life."

Gabrielli raised the gun a few inches. Conditioned to take orders. But he did not lift it all the way.

"Put the fucking gun to your head," Hunt barked.

Gabrielli lifted the pistol until the barrel touched the skin between his ear and his ghost of a sideburn. Then he jerked it away. Hot.

But the weapon stayed close to his head.

"Punchy, I . . . what—"

"Shut up. You don't have time to talk." Hunt lifted his wrist so he could read the time. Big gold Rolex. "Here's the deal, Gabe. Thirty seconds from now . . . or sooner . . . you'll pull that trigger." He did not even look at the man with the loaded gun. "Otherwise, I'll kill your wife, the son she's watching at soccer practice, your daughter in college, and the mother you dumped in a fucking rest home. As well as you. Twenty seconds left."

"Punchy, I—"

"Shut your mouth." Hunt rammed his face up against Gabrielli's. The ultimate drill instructor. *"You scum fuck. I'll kill every fucking one of them. I'll do it slow."*

Just as abruptly, he turned his back on the man. And looked at his watch again.

"Eight seconds. Save your family, man."

I watched Gabrielli's face. There was nothing else

in the world worth watching. Nothing else it was possible to watch.

He was crying. Big, sudden tears. Like raindrops on his face. A clown mask of a face. So much of everything, of every possible thought and emotion, passed over his features in those seconds. Fear. Anger. A lot of hatred. The terror beyond fear. A flicker of sentimental recollection. Time is not a constant. But it is unforgiving.

"Three seconds," Hunt said. "Two."

I don't think Gabrielli ever considered turning the gun on Hunt. The barrel did not move even an inch in that direction. It shook in the air.

"One."

I knew he was going to do as ordered. And it looked like he would botch it, miss the aim. Just bust up his skull. Or blind himself. But not end it.

At the last instant, Gabrielli pressed the pistol firmly against his ear and pulled the trigger.

I closed my eyes.

The shot hung in the air. My ears ached. Dead meat thumped dirt.

Hunt closed a big hand around my bicep. I opened my eyes. Gabrielli's last expression was one of embarrassment. An irrelevant response of the facial muscles. His head had a lopsided shape. The day had turned into the worst anatomy lesson in the world.

"Places to go," Hunt told me. "And things to see."

The driver knelt to test neck pulses. There were

brains all over the bushes. But Hunt's boys did things by the book.

Before we left, Hunt took a last look at the bodies. And snorted. "Your pal Burns," he said. "You know he was a big player in the Washington gay scene? Not that I give a good goddamn. The bravest human being I ever knew was queer as a three-dollar bill."

No. I had not known. D.C. is the last closet.

"Serves that sonofabitch Gabrielli right, though," Hunt went on. "He was a disgrace to the goddamned uniform. Two-bit thug. *He* was the asshole behind the Mickey Farnsworth killing. Totally unnecessary. And I liked Mickey. Shit-for-brains idealist that he was." Hunt nudged the black stripes on Gabrielli's trouser leg with the toe of his shoe. "Gabe and that bastard Faust were in it together. Trying to steal my operation. Frogs did us all a favor when they took out that inflated sonofabitch. Saved me the trouble."

He glanced at Rob's body. "They look like a couple to you? Folks are going to figure it was just another love affair gone wrong. Gabe shot him, then shot himself. 'Don't ask, don't tell,' right?" He gave me a playful punch that hurt. "You see, John? There really is justice in this world. Sometimes."

"Is Tish all right?"

He thumped me on the shoulder. Happy. He had enjoyed his theater piece. Suspense to the end. For everyone except the director.

"Our white knight," he said. "Didn't think they made 'em like you anymore." Then the humor faded.

He came close and I noticed he was sweating. He gave off the rich smell of the killer. "Just get back in the car. And ponder mortality. We're going to go watch some television."

CHAPTER 17

HE WAS SERIOUS. ABOUT THE TV BUSINESS. HIS DRIVER
hustled us back toward Hunt's estate. The suburbs
ran out. Small towns with Confederate hangovers
huddled along the highway. The horse farms began.
Middleburg drowsed in the hot evening. I did as I
had been told. I pondered mortality.

Violent death shifts your cosmic house off its
foundations. The pipes come loose. Plaster falls
in on you. And there had been a lot of death.
Death on a personal level. Ugly as a public toilet.
Yet I still hoped to survive. I told myself that if
Hunt meant to kill me, he would have done it back
at Fort Marcy. And made it look like a love
triangle.

Hope is the opium of the people. Religion is just
a format. Like philosophy. At the moment, my religion was battered and my philosophy was gone. But
I hoped beyond reason. That I would live. That Tish

355

was alive. I *believed* she was still alive. With all the
fervency of a snake-shaking Pentecostalist.

Hunt was right. I was yesterday's man. With a
flawed sensibility. It was not just that I believed in
the wrong things. It was that I believed, period. Hunt
was the man of the future.

But even his confidence had limits. As soon as the
gates to his property opened, I spotted the first ele-
ments of his private army. Out in force. They were
real pros and a civilian would have missed them. I
picked them out in the treeline. Camouflage not quite
the right shade. And the inevitable movement. If you
expected them, you saw them.

At least fifty armed men. Maybe more. Little teams
in one position after another. In an open swale hidden
from the road, I even saw a guy crouched under
a manpack antiaircraft missile. Hunt had not taken
any chances.

It had all looked so smooth. But maybe the day's
outcome had been a near-run thing. Maybe the
French had been a real threat. Maybe there were ele-
ments involved that I had not managed to trip over.
Maybe Tish and I were nothing but a footnote in
this history.

Hunt caught me looking.

"I need to call them off," he said. "Show's over.
'Our revels now have ended.' Almost." He gave one
of his snorts that heralded a change of tone. This
time he went lighter. "You'll pardon me if I don't
consider you a serious threat, John."

We parked and went in that commanding house.

The Hispanic maid waited at the door like a nineteen-fifties housewife.

"Bring those drinks, Magdalena," Hunt told her. "We'll be in the library."

For a moment, I hoped that his flair for the theatrical had positioned Tish in his library. With her mouth anxious under that wonderful hair. I imagined an explosive smile and the way she would rise from her seat.

She was not there.

"Sit down," Hunt told me. "Over there this time." He glanced at his watch and opened a cabinet. Revealing a television screen. He picked up the remote. Smiling. And dropped his butt into one of those magnificent leather chairs.

"I think this is going to impress even you," he told me. "Hell, it impresses me. Bob Nechestny's the only businessman in America who could get a spot on CNN whenever he wanted it."

A familiar face warmed into focus. One of Ted Turner's gals, carefully selected to be presentable but not threateningly pretty. The drinks arrived. I accepted mine with an unsteady hand. The anchorwoman bracketed clips of a confrontation over a broadcasting tower in Bosnia. Where U.S. troops were set to remain for the next hundred years.

Then she said: "Remaining with security issues, there was a remarkable development in the defense industrial sector today. For that story, we go to Kurt Lustkrieger in Washington."

The screen filled with an earnest face positioned

in front of a corporate-looking complex. "Yes, Barbie, it was a startling day that shook up the traditional way of doing business here. Robert Nechestny, CEO of Macon-Bolt Industries, made what defense analysts are calling a revolutionary announcement that will set new standards of accountability in America's major weapons purchases."

Cut to a common-looking man in a perfect suit and crimson tie. Standing behind a podium. The corporate god himself. Reading. His voice was assured, but not emotional. There was just enough warmth in the tone to suggest honesty. He wore glasses you sensed came out only for a text.

"Ladies and gentlemen, I come before you as a man accountable for a major failure. Our scientists, in the course of rigorous testing, have discovered flaws in the design of the Next-Generation Fighter-Bomber, set to be America's premier combat aircraft in the new century. These flaws are fully the responsibility of our company, and our company will fix them at no cost to the taxpayer. Further, in view of the inevitable delays to the deployment of this essential system, Macon-Bolt Industries will discount the cost of the program to the Department of Defense by nearly twelve billion dollars over the next five years. We at Macon-Bolt pride ourselves on serving our country and its brave men and women in uniform, and those interests will always come first."

The correspondent came back on-screen. "Barbie, it was truly a day of revelation and change. Mr. Nechestny went on to announce that our French allies will be given a major role in the further development and production of the Next-Generation Fighter-Bomber, which will then become not only America's but NATO's dominant combat aircraft over the next decade. Analysts were startled, since the French aerospace industry had been regarded as Macon-Bolt's last remaining competition. We're looking at a new era in international cooperation in the arms trade here. Returning to the main theme—that twelve-billion-dollar refund to the taxpayer—shortly after Macon-Bolt's *mea culpa* announcement, the White House issued a press release praising the company's integrity and its contribution to the national defense. Back to you, Barbie."

The anchorwoman returned and told us, "More on the Macon-Bolt announcement and the volatile afternoon on Wall Street coming up on Business News."

Hunt laughed out loud. And clicked off the television. He laughed again.

"A thing of goddamned beauty," he said. "And a thing of beauty is a joy forever." He drank and the hospital smell of gin sanitized the room. "Nechestny's a goddamned genius. Frogs won't know what hit 'em. He'll own the Eiffel Tower, screw their wives and daughters, and they'll give *him* nylons and chocolate bars." Hunt granted me an intimate smile. "And I'll save you any concern on his behalf. Bob isn't going to the poorhouse any time soon. Macon-Bolt's stock dropped twelve bucks a share after that announcement. Nechestny grabbed the opportunity for a major buyback. Stock closed two and a half points higher than the opening price. Made a nice pile myself, if my broker didn't dick it up. Refill, John?''

No. One drink had a lot of hitting power today. I craved water. With about six separate layers of dried sweat on my skin. And one layer of whiskey sour. The air-conditioning felt lush and poisonous.

''And don't you worry about that little discount to the country,'' Hunt went on. ''Old Bob'll just wrap it into program costs. Macon-Bolt won't lose a nickel. And the NATO deal's going to be big.'' He put a hand on his knee and leaned forward. ''Get my point yet, John?''

Yes. I got his point.

''You know,'' Hunt said, ''I look at you and I just see a permanent hardhead. You're just an incurable dumb-ass idealist. You remind me of old Mickey Farnsworth.''

''I take that as a compliment.''

''You would. And I suppose it is one. In a useless sort of way. But let's remember that poor old Mickey's dead.'' He looked into his glass and rattled the ice. ''The age of idealists is over, son. If there ever was one. The only thing idealists do is crap on the sidewalk and call it art. And it is a terrible goddamned waste. At least in your case. You have potential.''

''Thanks.''

Hunt waved a paw at me. ''Now, don't go getting goddamned smug. When all the dust settles, I want you to try to think clearly. Step back and look at the big picture. I'm telling you, John, the alliance between our defense industry, our military, and Congress is going to keep this nation on top for another fifty years, maybe a hundred. Maybe forever." He swept an arm across the room, across the world. "Everything that happened this past week . . . it was all nickel-and-dime monkey business. Small-time. Sideshow of a sideshow. Now the winners keep an eye on the sideshows. But they concentrate on what's going on in the big tent."

I knew he was right. But I *still* believed in something better. Even if I could not see it, describe it, or begin to shape it.

"Tell you what," Hunt said. "We're done now. At least, I'm done with you. 'The rest is silence.' I want you to just go on home. And don't waste time and energy on those disks Mary Farnsworth has hidden away in that old PC box." He read my face. "Oh, they're the real thing, all right. But it doesn't matter now. Hell, you keep 'em. As a souvenir. And don't worry. Nobody's going to touch Mary. I promise you that."

He got to his feet. Minotaur rising.

"What about Tish?" I asked.

Hunt made the wrong face. "John . . . you came to me—so you claimed—because I'm a man who pays his debts. Well, I'm paying my debt to you. You're walking out of here alive. George is going to drive you home. But you do not have a further line of credit." He folded his arms. "It's time for you to go now."

So that was it. Tish was dead. Gone. If I had really been an idealist, or just a man worth a damn, I would have punched him. Fought him. Even if it killed me. Instead, I walked out of that library door and down the hall with an emptiness inside me that was as broad as all the prairies on the continent.

At first, Hunt just followed. But out in the twilight he took over the lead. We came around the corner of the house and funneled between a brace of body-guards. Hunt's Lincoln waited on the spotlit parking apron.

There was a shadow in the backseat.

It was Tish.

"Next time," Hunt told me, "let's be on the same side from the beginning."

But I did not care about old generals anymore. I did not care about anything except crossing twenty feet of parking apron and getting that car door open.

We made a clumsy mess of it. Tish trying to get out, me trying to get in. She looked startled and weary. And as beautiful as heaven. We collided and she kissed me all over the face and cried. Her guitar case and a big gym bag had been stuffed in the back-seat with her, making our reunion crowded and won-derful. She worried over the blood on my clothes— Corry's blood—and I told her it was nothing. I don't really remember the car starting or driving back down to the public road. I only remember holding

my woman so tightly she had to ask me to let her
breathe.

Our mouths were dry and we stank like two apes.
But as soon as we got in the door, we headed upstairs. And almost made it. The action started on the
landing. Several dynamic iterations of calisthenics
later, we were on the bed. I never had changed the
sheets, and it was just as well.

We had not talked. And did not talk. There was
too much to say, and I guess we were both afraid of
some of it. Anyway, nothing that could be put into
words was important now.

We were noisy, though.

Toward midnight, in a gorge of quiet, the doorbell
rang. I let it ring a second time. And a third. Before
an alarm went off in my back brain.

If it was trouble, I did not want it coming up here
where Tish lay. I jumped out of bed, trying to remember where my khakis might have landed.

"Don't go," Tish said.

"Just for a minute," I told her. Not sure if I would
ever be coming back. It had all seemed too good to
be true.

A fist began pounding the door. I jumped down
the stairs.

It was Dickey. Alone in the porch light. Holding
a couple of folders.

He looked at my bare chest and feet.

"Sorry about the timing."

"What do you want?"

"Can I come in for a minute?"

"Do I have a choice?"

He considered me with cop eyes.

"Yeah," he told me. "This time you get a choice."

I looked down. His suit had not improved yet. And his shoes had carried him down a lot of sidewalks.

"Come on in," I said.

He dragged the last of the day's heat in with him. I shut the door against the city night and we stood in the hallway. Letting the central air put things right.

"I don't owe you any apologies," he said.

"I didn't ask for any."

He lifted his hand. "I'm not here to screw with you, okay? And I don't owe you any goddamn apologies. Or explanations. But I just want you to try to see my side. Between two guys who maybe want the same thing but go at it in different ways." His face showed loss. Years of it. Decades. "A guy wants to be a good cop. The academy lesson plan and all that. The sacred rule of law. But it all just gets so big and fast. And bad. I mean, look at this city." He pointed through the wall. "Just look at it. We're so far from the goddamned rule of law that it's all a cop can do to try to hold back the rule of evil. And not every cop in the department wants to do that much."

He looked at me with a face sanded raw by his work. "You think we would've ever gotten a single case to court on this one? To say nothing of your dip-passport French pals who killed a United States senator. No, buddy, you just look at what we did get.

We came out okay. Maybe we didn't get all the bad guys. But . . . by my working standards . . . we got a pretty good score.''

"I just want to put it all behind me," I told him.

He twisted up one side of his mouth as if a hook had caught it. "Yeah. But you're going to think about it. I know your type. You'll think about it till the day you die, soldier boy." He shifted his potato-sack posture. Energizing himself to go back out of my door and face his streets. "Anyway, I don't want your stomach to get upset every time you think about me."

He thrust out his hand. Offering the folders he had brought with him.

"Here. They're a gift. City Hall won't miss them."

The entryway light was weak. I had to lift the folders to read the titles on the cardboard lips. They were police records. One for Tish, one for me. Hers was a good bit thicker.

"I'm going to marry her," I told him.

He shrugged. "You could do worse. It's all a crapshoot."

And he left.

I double-locked the door behind him. I stood dully for a moment, looking at the folders but not really seeing them. Lot of weariness to sleep away. It was no time for serious thinking. I started upstairs. Then I noticed Tish's guitar case and the King Kong gym bag she had picked up somewhere along the way. I went back down the steps stone-legged, dropped the files on the stereo stand, and picked up her baggage. I wanted to see her buck naked playing that guitar before I went to sleep.

When I entered the bedroom—our room, our fortress—Tish half rose from the sheets. That would have been a painting.

"Is everything all right?"

"Better," I said, "than I ever thought it could be. Hey, I brought your stuff up. Would you do me—"

"Oh," she said. "John. I forgot. That bag. He said it was for you. That scarred-up guy who looks like a bull."

The bag suddenly felt heavier in my hand.

Body parts? A bomb? I was weary and incautious. Anxious for closure. I put down the guitar case. And yanked open the bag's zipper. Blow us to kingdom come. At least the timing was good. Go out on a cloud of ecstasy.

The bag was full of money. More money than even bankers see in cash.

Tish gasped.

"My God," she said. "He told me . . . I mean, he said it was something he owed you. I didn't . . ."

I held up two fistfuls of banded hundred-dollar bills. Baffled. Then, slowly, I grew one of those little smiles you get when you realize the joke really is on you.

"The guy's crazy," I said. "He's got one of those warped nineteenth-century sensibilities."

Tish did not hear me. She was never a greedy girl. Except in lovemaking. But a mountain of cash like that would turn the head of a saint. She got out of bed and stood naked in front of the money.

"So," Tish asked finally, "do you, like, have to report this on your taxes?"

I took the disks from Mary Farnsworth and mailed them to the General Accounting Office with an anonymous letter. Nothing ever came of it.

The money amounted to exactly five hundred thousand dollars. It was my commission from the pile Hunt ripped off Nechestny to pay himself for the phony disks. He probably took Macon-Bolt for twenty or thirty million, not ten. Plus expenses. In their different ways, the French, Aley and Corry, and Faust and Gabrielli and Rob Burns had been set to blow the deal. Hunt had used me as bait to draw them out of their holes. I had not saved the country or the defense budget. But I had done a mighty good turn for old Punchy. Law of unintended consequences.

I was smart enough to realize the money was a reward and not a bribe. I was not important enough to bribe.

If I really had been an idealist, I suppose I would have sent the money back to Hunt. I didn't. I used my connections—the kind you build up over the years in the intelligence world—to launder it. I knew Mary Farnsworth would not have accepted a nickel, so I arranged an anonymous quarter-of-a-mil donation, in General Farnsworth's honor, to a scholarship fund for minorities. It pleased Mary—she wept with pride when she told me about it. The other half is parked offshore in Tish's name. We have an agreement. As long as we stay together, she is not allowed to touch a dollar of it. But if she ever gets restless and puts on her traveling shoes, it's hers. No matter what happens, she'll never have to count pennies in a one-room apartment again.

We're getting married next June. Mary Farnsworth is hosting the reception. She's become the mother Tish never really had.

I went back to work. Nobody wanted to pry into what happened. People made little jokes and let it go. They had no idea. And didn't want one.

As soon as I could, I took another week of leave. And flew up to Massachusetts. Habit of the tribe. I laid my flowers on Emerson Carroll's grave and saluted. In the end, he had been a good soldier. But not a lucky one.

And I went back to General Farnsworth's grave. Regularly. I talked to his headstone like an old widow. He remains my hero. But there is vanity in all of us, and it takes eccentric forms. I had to find the workman with whom I had spoken the afternoon of Farnsworth's funeral. I had to prove to him that he had been wrong. That there is still loyalty in the world. That some of us do come back.

I was certain I would run into him eventually. But I never did. Finally, I went to the cemetery's admin offices and inquired. I even remembered his name. Rickie York. Richard York, probably.

After searching the records, the personnel clerk told me that no such man had ever been employed at Arlington.

AUTHOR'S NOTE

THIS IS A WORK OF FICTION, SO IT IS LESS INTERESTING than life. It is, however, more succinct and manageable. When it works, fiction gives the illusion of immediacy, born of compression and exaggeration. We see that which lies before us with unnatural clarity. *If* the author has luck.

The writer of fiction is the adult counterpart to the child who comes home full of tall tales. Fiction is lying, born of an old compulsion. Yet when masters write, it brings us to a greater truth. In lesser hands such as mine, this form of entertainment still may serve good ends—or so I have convinced myself.

The novel you have just finished has two purposes. The first is to be sufficiently engaging to finish in the black and keep my publisher happy. The second is to shine a storyteller's lamp on a problem of national importance.

Traitor's characters are fictional (in the case of Tish, inspired by listening to Aimee Mann's brilliant disc, *Whatever*, while driving in the rain). But the problem of massive corruption in the defense industry is real. As a serving soldier, I was appalled by it; as a citizen, I am enraged. The fact that this corruption is, in most cases, technically legal disgusts me. It should disgust you, too.

Each year, we spend tens of billions of dollars on weapons that do not work as promised and that are inappropriate to our needs. It is impossible to kill these programs. Too much is at stake. While contractors speak piously about giving our men and women in uniform "the best," and about jobs for the American worker, defense acquisition is really about fantastic profits torn from a system that lacks serious accountability. In Washington, those in power know the system is corrupt—morally, ethically, and practically. But there is no constituency for change in our capital. Defense contractors are big campaign and PAC contributors; they are a major source of advertising revenue for the media; and they hire retiring generals and admirals at generous salaries, ensuring that these officers will not speak out for reform while on active duty. My beliefs are generally the same as those of John Reynolds in this book—the plot is fabricated, but the spirit is true.

I do not imagine that a one-man crusade disguised as a thriller can change much. But it is the best I can do. I hope that readers will carry a sense of this problem with them after they have finished the book and put it away on a back shelf. One man can do little, but informed Americans pulling together can accomplish a great deal over a span of years. Defense procurement reform is an idea whose time *will* come—hopefully before a military crisis.

The current system does not serve either our soldiers or our citizens well. While we, the people, constitute the wealthiest nation in history, we cannot afford waste on this scale. We *need* a strong defense—but we are getting the wrong defense. Anyway, our national defense begins in our classrooms—not in the boardrooms of contractors. Given the deep pockets of defense industry and the genius of its lawyers, it will take time to clean up this vicious and lucrative system. But I believe it can be done. Honest men and women still can win in this country, if they do not fall victim to the cynicism that is corruption's great enabler.

There is a lighter side to this book, of course. Since my childhood in the Pennsylvania coalfields, where the world came to us through paperbacks and three black-and-white television channels, I have loved the *noir* masters of print and film. They described a great, smoky, seductive world in which the women cocked their eyebrows like Lauren Bacall and the men toughed it out to the final showdown. The dialogue was the way people *should* have spoken; the stock characters were endlessly renewable; and the same old plot was eternally fresh.

The creators always gave good value, and you sensed that their morality—it was ferocious behind the murk—was closer to the real texture of life than were the entertainments for which junior-high-school students were supposed to settle in those days. Hammett, Chandler, Cain, and all the Hollywood people right down to a boozed-up screenwriter named Faulkner, policed the fog of my adolescence. This novel is a grateful, inadequate tribute to them.

I wish more books could be this much fun to write. It was a labor of conviction and love. Even my editor's suggestions were as seductive as Veronica Lake. If the masters of the genre were alive, the incredible scandal of our defense industry would inspire them to new masterpieces—but those giants are dead. The reader will have to settle for this three-hundred-page fan letter.

I hope you found it a good read.

—Ralph Peters